Shadows of Shields

by

David L. Thompson

Copyright © 2020 David L. Thompson
This edition 2024

All rights reserved, including the right to reproduce this book, or portions thereof in any form. No part of this text may be reproduced, transmitted, downloaded, decompiled, reverse engineered, or stored, in any form or introduced into any information storage and retrieval system, in any form or by any means, whether electronic or mechanical without the express written permission of the author.

This is a work of fiction. Names and characters are the product of the author's imagination and any resemblance to actual persons, living or dead, is entirely coincidental.

ISBN: 9798341009141

Edited by Stephen Thompson
www.essteemedia.com

www.publishnation.co.uk

Other books by David L. Thompson

forever feeding ducks
Two Different Worlds
The Lovelace Paradox

January 1963

1

Tuesday 1st January 1963

The first person Sebastian Crawley kissed in the new year of 1963 was a sixty-year-old widow with pickle onion breath. She was wearing a paisley pattern green dress that was desperately trying to ride up over a backside that contained half her body weight. The tight-lipped peck occurred three seconds into the festivities and was followed by a hearty embrace that all but squeezed the air out of him. Thankfully, she moved on to crush someone else after regaling them with the remnants of her last meal of 1962.

The second person Sebastian kissed was a red-headed girl slightly older than himself. She looked to be around twenty-five, and he found out later that she was the first female graduate he'd ever met and, by definition, the most intelligent woman he'd ever kissed.

Unfortunately for Sebastian, she also moved on to someone else, but not before whispering, "Hi. I'm Alice."

Her voice was soft and husky. It wasn't local. It sounded as if she'd come straight from the BBC. The fresh smell of warm, minty breath lingered briefly but the taste of her lips remained with him until it was spoilt, a minute or two later, by another mature woman whose vacuum cleaner of a mouth tried to suck the life out of him; she left him with a red smudge covering a large area under his nose.

After he released himself from her clutches and wiped his face with a napkin he'd found on the edge of a nearby table, he sought a quiet corner of the room from where he surveyed the party.

There were about a hundred people present, representing all age groups, all of them clamouring to welcome the new year and take advantage of whatever opportunities were presented to them. Neighbours old and new struggled to capture the moment and sought comfort or titillation, depending on their circumstances. Petty domestic squabbles were suspended, and new allegiances forged. Everyone knew that the truce would end as soon as someone drank too much or said something that pushed the boundaries too far. The new day would reveal that their world hadn't changed at all; not in the slightest.

Spotty teenagers openly quaffed beer, smoked cigarettes and talked about music and sex – mirror images of their parents. They pretended to be wise and experienced in such matters – just like their parents. Their grandmothers sipped the bubbly, sickly sweet yellowness of *advocaat* and tapped their feet to the strident chords of Hank Marvin of The Shadows. Children skipped between drunken adults in a never-ending chase, glorifying in staying up beyond midnight while remaining confused as to why the coming of the new year was so hallowed by grown-ups.

The remnants of last week's Christmas decorations still hung in festoons around the ageing beige coloured walls of the community centre, waiting for Twelfth Night. Ruffled paper Santa's pinned to the walls laughed cheerfully at the crowd while competing for space with notices for lost cats, Christmas Fayres and forthcoming council events that promised to succour the needy – or at least the electorate.

Sebastian's eye wandered around the room trying to pick out the woman who'd told him her name was Alice. He found her near the temporary bar, surrounded by a bunch of men eager to show her what a real man could do. He smiled to himself. He watched as she kissed them all lightly with a Happy-New-Year superficiality. None of them received even a hint of the tenderness that he felt she'd bestowed upon him. This woman was interesting. He decided to watch, and wait, and see what happened.

That was his nature. Caution was his strength, and his weakness. Many times in the past he'd stood back and observed a situation before deciding to intervene, or to walk away. He'd managed to preserve his youthful good looks by avoiding confrontations and fights. On the other hand, he'd lost out to bolder, more confident or belligerent men when it came to wooing the ladies, although he'd had his fair share of success. Finding women who were willing to 'go all the way' were few and far between. He wasn't prepared to get engaged or married just to get regular sex.

Sebastian turned towards the window and watched the woman's progress around the room in its reflection. After a few moments, his gaze went beyond the dirty glass and took in the flurries of falling snow. He sighed. It had started falling a week ago and hadn't stopped since. The initial euphoria of a white Christmas had changed to frustration since the deep and crisp and even covering of Christmas Day had turned into a frozen, salt-pitted, slush splattered nuisance that had been covered by layer after layer after never-ending layer of freshly fallen snow. Sebastian wasn't a fan of snow. It was OK on postcards and Christmas cards, but the magic ended there. The reality was that snow was cold and wet and very inconvenient. It was also bad for business.

He felt a slap on his back that almost rattled his teeth. He turned to see a ruddy-faced drunk who lived in the same street grinning amiably at him. He'd lost control of his eyes.

"Happy New Year, young fellow-me-lad," he said as he pumped Sebastian's hand maniacally. "Happy New Year. Let's hope the Russians let us live to enjoy another one."

His comment about the Russians was perfectly relevant. The past few months had seen the world waiting with bated breath over the Cuban missile threat. Kennedy's facedown with the Russian premier, Nikita Khrushchev, had made the world realise that global hostilities and nuclear annihilation was still just around the corner. The fact that two different countries thousands of miles away could threaten and posture and, at a whim, draw the rest of the world into an Armageddon scenario made Sebastian shudder. His own experience as a National Service soldier in the Yemen had demonstrated to him that local squabbles could quickly escalate into tribal conflict and armed intervention.

Sebastian smiled as he recalled a photograph he had in a box in his bedroom. It showed him, Ivan, Preston Pete, George the Brummie and Gyles from Buckinghamshire with Mohammed, Asif and Iqbal on top of a tank just outside Aden. Little did he know at the time but it had been the start of his business relationship with the area.

Sebastian returned his felicitations, and the man, Mr. Brown or Mr. Green or something like that, moved on to spread his own cheery *bonhomie* amongst his friends and neighbours.

"A penny for them." His grandfather's voice sliced through his thoughts.

"What?" said Sebastian, who hadn't realised he'd been daydreaming.

"You're standing there looking out the window with a cheesy grin on your face," his grandfather said. He raised his eyebrows. "Some woman you were thinking about?"

Sebastian snatched a glance at Alice then shook his head. "No. As a matter of fact I was thinking about Aden."

"Aaah, National Service and life in a middle eastern shithole, eh?"

Sebastian dismissed the comment with another shake of his head. "Good times, good friends."

"That's where it all started for you, wasn't it?"

Sebastian shot him a sideways look, wondering whether his grandfather was mocking him. He decided he wasn't. "It was certainly the beginning for me."

His grandfather handed him a glass of rum. "Here you are son. Happy New Year."

"Thanks, grandad. Here's to your continued good health." He downed the drink in one gulp and gave out a low 'aaaaaaaaah' to relieve the pressure in his chest and dissipate the alcohol.

"Thanks, son." He gave a little cough to demonstrate that he wasn't completely out of the woods yet. "You know, I'll never completely recover from this war wound." He coughed again. "Anyway, I'd best spread myself around the room. I've got a few drinks waiting to be necked. See you later, son." Tommy Heath gave a wave and moved off.

Just then, a crash of empty glasses smashing on the floor brought the whole room to a sudden stop. A gangling young man collecting glasses had been pole-axed by Sebastian's pickle-onion-breathed widow demonstrating The Twist to anyone who cared to watch. As the tempo of her gyrations increased, so had her instability; the shoulder charge on the young man was inevitable. She now sat on the floor with her stockinged legs either side of the glass collector in a sea of broken glass. Chubby

Checker sang on as the room collectively froze for two seconds. Once the world assessed that no-one was injured, assistance was rendered to the embarrassed youth and the brazen widow, who covered the areas of flesh above her stocking tops and quickly recovered her dignity.

Sebastian reached for his drink and cast his eyes around the room again, looking for Alice. He saw her finish a conversation with an old man sitting in the corner and move to the end of the bar. He watched as she sucked on a straw poking through ice in a half pint glass of what appeared to be orange cordial. Out of the corner of his eye he saw a couple of men straightening their ties and deciding who would be first to demonstrate their prowess to the mystery girl from the south. Sebastian walked quickly over to the bar and beat one of the men to Alice by a yard. He stood between him and Alice. Alice glanced over his shoulder and coyly expressed her sympathy to the defeated potential suitor with a raised eyebrow and tilt of the head. The man adjusted his tie once more and returned to his mate.

Sebastian gazed into Alice's deep, amber eyes and sipped his drink. A quizzical look drifted across her face. Nothing was said for nearly a minute. Curiosity made Alice the first speaker.

"And?"

Sebastian sipped his drink again and ran his tongue over his lips before replying. "And? Nothing."

The eyebrow lifted again. "Oh! I thought you had something to say."

Sebastian shrugged. "I'm still deciding what my devastating opening line should be. You see, you're not like all the rest. You're interesting."

Alice smiled. "And by accident you say the right thing."

"Huh? Look, sorry, I've a confession to make. I don't do this very often and I've not rehearsed anything. I haven't got a standard line. I just go with the flow, if you see what I mean."

Her eyes twinkled. "You don't know you are doing it, do you?"

"Doing what?" Sebastian didn't want to appear to be some sort of womaniser or modern-day Lothario. He just wanted to talk. "Let's start again. My name is Sebastian and I know you're Alice. I've never seen you before and I think you're interesting.

Just look around the room." His arm swept from left to right. "There's nobody else like you here. You're unusual, and that intrigues me."

"Like an iguana," she said softly.

"A what?"

"An iguana. It's a large tropical lizard."

Sebastian's brow creased. Perhaps he should walk away. This woman was complicated. Or was she just sophisticated?

Before he could decide she said, "I'm teasing you. You're not used to it, are you?"

Sebastian relaxed a little, although his brow remained creased. "I don't know what to say," he confessed. "I'm not used to girls taking the piss out of …"

She interrupted him.

"Is that because I'm unusual? And interesting? Or is it because you've never had a proper relationship with a woman?"

Sebastian put his drink down on the counter and prepared to walk away. This woman was more trouble than she was worth. He didn't need the hassle. Yes, she was interesting but any relationship with her would be dynamite. He could live without the volatility she would bring.

Alice spoke again. "I didn't have you down as a quitter."

Sebastian didn't hide his simmering anger. "I'm not a quitter. I just decide whether or not something is worth the effort."

"Am I worth the effort?"

"I haven't made up my mind yet. Maybe today isn't the day to make that decision. Maybe our paths will cross some other time."

"Or maybe they won't," she said airily while looking over Sebastian's shoulder as if she was scouting for his replacement.

His rival still lurked nearby, still adjusting his tie. A few awkward seconds of silence passed between them as Elvis sang prophetically, his greatest hit of last year, *It's now or never*.

"I'm going to ask you a question. I want you to answer it truthfully, without wisecracks." He cleared his throat. "Are you … umm … worth the effort?"

The question hung on the air alongside Elvis. Then she smiled and leaned towards him. Her lips brushed against his. Her arms encircled his neck. She pulled him towards her and whispered, "Only you can decide that."

Sebastian's rival gave up adjusting his tie. From across the room, Sebastian's grandfather raised his glass and winked in his direction.

It was a Bank Holiday. That meant the whole world could lie in bed if it wanted to. Sore heads and 'dickie tummies' no doubt abounded in the streets and houses across the nation. The exception was in Thomas Heath's house in Catherine Street, South Shields. He knew when to stop drinking. He never suffered the effects of a hangover, unlike his daughter Billie, Sebastian's mother, who he frequently had to carry to bed.

Tommy threw open the curtains and rubbed the heel of his hand against the window to melt and remove the frost from the inside of the window. A brave black cat wandered down the street on its way home from a night on the tiles. Its owner was probably festering under three blankets and an eiderdown somewhere nearby. Tommy turned away and breathed into his hands. Time to make the fire.

He cleared yesterday's debris from the fireplace and reclaimed some of the unburnt coal. He placed balled up newspapers and sticks on the grate and covered them in small pieces of coal. He scraped a match along the poker and when it sparked into life, he lit the heap in several places and watched the flames spread. Splinters of burning wood started to crackle as he went into the kitchen to fill the kettle and place it on the gas stove, lighting the ring with another carefully placed match. He reached into the stone pantry and picked out the packet of tea. Three heaped teaspoons disappeared into the teapot warming itself in a knitted cosy. As he waited for the kettle to boil, he wandered back into the sitting room to check the fire. There was still a fair bit of smoke about, but it was being sucked up the chimney in a very satisfactory way. The kettle whistled for Tommy's attention. He poured the boiling water onto the leaves in the pot and cloaked an extra layer of tea cosy over the top, then gently turned the teapot in a clockwise direction three times.

When he'd finished his breakfast, he piled more coal onto the fire and placed the dishes in the sink for later. He returned to his comfy chair by the fire and thumbed through the Radio Times. He knew there would be nothing on TV but maybe there'd be a good radio show, a play maybe. He scanned the listings, but nothing grabbed his attention. He put the magazine back in the rack and settled back once more.

"Happy Birthday, Tommy," he muttered to himself.

Billie Crawley's eyes shot open as she felt a firmness throbbing against her buttocks and a hand enclose her left breast. The air was heavy with stale alcohol and the aftereffects of eating ham and pease pudding sandwiches. Another throbbing, of greater magnitude, pulsed inside her head. She rolled her tongue around her mouth to induce some moisture

"And you can stop that now, Jack Tozer," she said, her voice tired and husky and clammy.

Jack Tozer grunted and turned over, almost bouncing Billie out of the bed, snorted twice, then settled into a baritone rumble.

Billie thought about getting some aspirin from her bag, but that would mean getting out of bed in the freezing cold and going to the kitchen for a cup of water. At least it was warm where she lay. She picked up her watch, a present from Jack for Christmas. It was almost eight o'clock.

She lay on her back and contemplated the events of last night's New Year's Eve party. It hadn't been one of the best gatherings, but it was OK. There had been a lot of Jack's police pals there, and a few councillors from the Watch Committee, the board who decided who got promoted and who didn't.

It was her first event with Jack. They'd been courting for about eight months – ever since her birthday in April. Jack was a Police Sergeant and carried some authority. He'd been a police officer since coming back from the war. He told everyone who cared to listen that he'd seen action in Greece and Italy, and his service record corroborated that. What he didn't say was that he'd never fired a rifle in anger and spent most of the time driving a lorry.

Jack was fortunate to live in what had been his parents' house, although both were now dead. This meant that he was a man of means, and Billie thought she'd scooped the jackpot on Littlewoods Pools when Jack asked her out. She was relatively happy, but the constant bouts of heavy drinking were taking their toll on both of them.

Billie's thoughts turned to her father. It was his birthday. He'd been born on the first day of 1896. Today he was sixty-seven. She pictured him having breakfast in his chair in front of the fire. He would have a newspaper in his hand or the radio would be blaring out. Her father was well read and took an active interest in current affairs. People would ask him about things they'd read in papers or seen on the telly, and Tommy Heath would always have an opinion ready. He read three newspapers every day – The Times, the Daily Mirror and the Shields Gazette. He listened to the news broadcasts on the BBC's Home channel and was often found tuning into other English speaking channels in foreign countries. He considered his opinions to be informed and balanced because of it.

Billie squirmed into a new position and Jack spluttered in mid-snore.

She'd be forty soon. and she wondered what her prospects would be for the future. Her thoughts were cut short as Jack rolled over and commandeered most of the bedclothes. Her decision was made for her. She made a break for the bathroom and left Jack to ferment in his own version of paradise.

2

Sebastian put his key in the lock and turned the handle of the ancient front door of his grandfather's house in Catherine Street. He looked forward to walking into the living room to be welcomed by a roaring fire and a steaming cup of tea. This was one of the things he loved in life – a fireside chat with his grandfather.

There would just be the two of them. His mother would probably be with Jack Tozer in his house in Harton.

The living room door opened, and Tommy stuck his head into the passage. "I thought I heard someone. I knew it wouldn't be your mother. Have a good night?"

Sebastian smiled. "Yes and no," he said while hanging his coat and scarf on the clothes pegs in the passage. "Yes, from the point of view that I've met a very interesting woman – intriguing even. No, with regards to having a passionate night."

He followed his grandfather into the living room.

Tommy said, "That's a pity. She looked like a bonny lass to me. A cut above the normal tart you knock around with."

Sebastian laughed. For an intelligent man, his grandfather sometimes used the language of the streets, which was not surprising given his service in the war and many years on the factory floor.

"Most of the girls I meet just don't interest me." He went to the sideboard and opened the top drawer. He took out a present and handed it to Tommy. "Happy Birthday, grandad."

"Well thanks, son. That's very nice of you."

Tommy tore away the shiny wrapping paper to reveal a brand new bakelite pipe and a pack of coarse Virginia tobacco. He beamed a smile back to Sebastian, who acknowledged his thanks with a chuckle.

"Something else to kill yourself with, grandad."

"This won't kill me. It brings up all the gunge off my chest. If anything, it does me the world of good. I always feel better after I've had me pipe. Now then, tell me all about it. You know, about this woman of yours."

"There's not much to tell, grandad. She's been to university and got a degree. If fact she's got two degrees – an ordinary degree and a Masters degree."

"In what?"

"Politics and Economics."

"Bloody hell!" said Tommy, "There's nothing worse than a woman who thinks she knows how to run the country never mind actually being in charge of the purse strings as well."

"She's a socialist."

"Bloody hell!" he retorted again, "As if we haven't got enough of them around here." Tommy was a lifelong Tory and he'd taken a lot of stick over the years from his workmates. He'd often said he'd never voted for anyone who'd won. "This woman's getting less attractive to me every time you open your mouth."

"She went to Oxford University and then did her Masters in some Ivy League university in America." After a moment he added, "What's an Ivy League university?"

Tommy sucked on his pipe – as yet unlit. "They're the top universities in America – like Oxford and Cambridge are over here. I think it's safe to say that she's a highly intelligent woman. So," he raised an inquisitive eyebrow, "what's she doing with you?"

Sebastian had already thought of that himself. What *was* she doing with him? If the truth be told – nothing; at least nothing yet. A little bit of him was genuinely interested in her. At the same time, a little bit of him wanted to take her to a hotel and 'shag her 'til she screamed for mercy' as his friend Mick was fond of saying.

His mind went back to the early hours of the morning. Sebastian and Alice had left the community centre about one o'clock and sat in her Wolseley 1500 MkIII parked in a side street, talking. The engine rumbled effortlessly. The heater blasted out a satisfying heat. They'd stayed all through the night talking and laughing. Their conversation occasionally interrupted by the antics of drunken revellers and warring couples. They'd talked about how the New Year did that to people, how it polarised their feelings and emotions, and sometimes that spilled out into the public domain.

The talk had been light and fluffy at first, but that soon developed into discussions about world affairs. Alice had taken centre stage, her eyes flashing anger and passion as she spoke about injustice and how it could be put right. She described how she'd cried with relief when the Cuban missile crisis had ended. She extolled the virtues of President Kennedy, though was circumspect and mysterious when Marylin Monroe was mentioned. Alice had denounced Harold Macmillan's Tories and forecast that a future labour government under Hugh Gaitskell would solve everyone's problems by giving the country back to the people.

Sebastian had looked around the Wolseley and wondered how she had a car like this? And what kind of socialism allowed someone to go to university, travel to America and study there?

They'd kissed twice when parting; the first because it seemed the best way of saying goodbye and the second because he couldn't contain himself and she hadn't objected. There'd been no embrace, no embarrassing fumbles, no awkwardness, no feigned ardour. Just two seconds of soft, inviting pleasure and a hint of promise.

"You seem to be doing quite a bit of that lately," said Tommy, bringing Sebastian right back to the present.

"What?"

"You, standing about with your mind in neutral."

"I was thinking, that's all."

"Oh yes? About Little Miss Marx?"

"As a matter of fact, I was."

"Thought you said you didn't have any 'slap and tickle'?"

"We didn't. We talked the whole time. Well, at least she talked. I did a lot of listening. She knows what she's talking about."

Tommy shook his head in despair and pointed his new pipe at Sebastian, using it to stab home his points. "You mean she's been spouting a whole load of shit – trying to turn your head. That's what socialists do. They keep spouting all that claptrap about the Labour Party being for the working man and the Conservatives being posh toffs trying to screw them. Look at this country since the war. Like the Prime Minister said, 'we've never had it so good'. And the socialist's think they can do better. Bloody hell.

Bloody hell." Tommy shook his head and replaced the pipe between his teeth and stared into the fire.

"No need to get your knickers in a twist, grandad," said Sebastian as he settled into an armchair on the other side of the hearth. "I've heard all the arguments before. Never heard them from a woman, though. It's interesting to get a female perspective now and then."

"And she's the next Ellen Wilkinson, then, is she?" said Tommy.

Sebastian shrugged. "Who's that?"

"A Jarrow MP. Died in office in 1947 ..."

As Tommy started into a eulogy for the politician, Sebastian drifted back to ...

"It's my uncle's car."

"It's nice."

"He likes nice things."

"So where is he tonight?"

"He's staying with friends down south. I'm staying in his house and I've got use of his car."

"That's nice."

There was a brief silence while both of them considered their options.

"What does your uncle do?" Sebastian asked.

"He's not really my uncle. Not in the biological sense. My father and he were great friends. His sister, Constance, taught dad to play the violin. I grew up in Surrey. That's where my uncle comes from."

"You didn't answer my question."

Alice gazed out of the window and thought for a moment before replying. "He's in politics."

"Well there's a surprise," said Sebastian in mock horror.

Alice smiled. "Now who's taking the piss?"

They both laughed.

"So, who is this uncle of yours?"

"Uncle Jim is a Member of Parliament."

"Wow! I'm impressed. Where is he the MP for?"

Alice said, "I call him Uncle Jim. It's my pet name for him. That's what his first name is – but you know him by his other name."

"Which is?"

"Chuter."

"Chuter? Chuter?" The penny dropped. "You mean Chuter Ede, our local MP?"

Tommy coughed. "So, you didn't say, what is she doing with you?

Sebastian shook his head innocently. "I don't know, grandad. I really don't know. Who knows, maybe she'll be gone by the weekend and I'll never see her again."

Tommy noticed the flash of sadness that accompanied his grandson's words. He got up and threw some more coal on the fire and watched the sparks and puff of smoke. He coughed again. "Any idea where your mother is?"

"Probably with PC Plod in Harton."

"He's a sergeant."

"He's a prick."

Tommy laughed. "That's as maybe but he's your mother's boyfriend."

"My mother's current boyfriend, you mean."

"Now, now, son. Just because your mother's been unlucky in love doesn't mean that you shouldn't show her boyfriend some respect. He might be your step-father one day."

Sebastian shuddered. The prospect wasn't an appealing one. He'd never known his father. Many years ago, when he'd asked his mother about him, she'd started crying and appealed to her father for help. Together they had taken Sebastian to Minchella's Ice Cream parlour and given him an ice cream. Then they had told him the story.

Reginald Algernon Crawley hailed from the nearby village of Cleadon. He was a farm hand on a local farm. He'd met Billie Heath at a pub in South Shields and fallen in love. She was sixteen. Billie became pregnant and Reg offered to marry her, and in August 1939 they were married at the Registry Office in Barrington Street.

Within a month, war was declared on Germany and Reg was drafted into the army. Six months later he was dead. Billie received her telegram as she cradled her son on the doorstep of her father's house.

Sebastian drained his cup and placed it on the table. "My mother is a big girl. She decides what she does, not me. I don't try to influence anything she does or says."

"But she always has your interests at heart," said Tommy.

"I suppose so. I just wish she'd settle down."

"Isn't that what she's trying to do?"

Sebastian shrugged. "It's just that she's had umpteen blokes over the years and sooner or later they dump her."

Billie's quest for love became well known in her neighbourhood, and she was never short of a date. Tommy had proved a wonderful baby sitter, and Sebastian had more 'uncles' than any man could wish for. As a result, Sebastian was on nodding terms with quite a few people. It was these people who bought stuff from his market stall.

"And she keeps bouncing back." Tommy shifted his weight in the armchair, which creaked in protest. "Your mother falls in love easily. It's as simple as that. When your father died, she was left to bring you up by herself."

"With a bit of help from you."

"It was a difficult time for both of us. She was sixteen, with a baby, and I was a grandfather at forty-three, without a wife."

Vivien Heath had died giving birth to Billie in 1923.

Difficult births seemed to plague the Heaths. When Sebastian had been born after a tortuous labour, Billie had been informed that she was unlikely to become pregnant again. A hysterectomy five years later removed the possibility entirely.

Sebastian got up and went to the kitchen after picking up his cup. He put it in the sink and walked back into the living room, stretching his tired limbs.

"Are you off to bed then?" asked Tommy.

"No. I'd better get around to Blanche's. I promised her I would be her first foot." He glanced at his watch. "I'm only about eight hours late. She'll understand."

Tommy nodded. "She's a nice woman. She's been your mother's friend ever since she left school. That's another one who's been unlucky in love."

"I don't think she's looking," said Sebastian.

"Probably not. But she's not as young as she used to be. She'll miss the boat if she's not careful."

Blanche Fada lived just around the corner in Broderick Street. It took Sebastian four minutes to walk there even with tricky conditions underfoot. A flurry of snow had started and stopped during the time he'd made the journey.

He rapped on the shiny, black door and waited for a few seconds. The door cracked open a few inches and a swarthy face peered around it.

"Happy New Year, Blanche," said Sebastian as he puckered up for a kiss.

She opened the door and allowed him in. "Come on in, you silly bugger. It's bloody perishing out there."

"Well that's not the best new year's greeting I've ever had."

She playfully cuffed him across the ear and then put her arms around his neck. "Happy New Year" she whispered before kissing him on the lips.

He apologised for his lateness and she dismissed it with a shrug of her shoulders. He refused the traditional alcoholic drink and opted for a cup of tea. He made himself comfortable and watched her prepare the brew, smiling at her fluffy slippers – a gift to herself at Christmas.

Blanche was the product of a Middle-Eastern father and an English mother. She was his mother's best friend, although she was five years older than her. Through the years, she had taken a special interest in Sebastian and he now counted her as being one of his own friends. During his teenage years he'd even fantasised about making love to her, and he thought that she had probably fantasised about him. Nothing had taken place between them and nothing probably ever would. Their friendship was too important to include sex. Whenever Sebastian had a problem in his life, the two people he talked to were his grandad and Blanche. Both were gifted with knowledge and insight, but in matters of the heart he leaned towards Blanche more often than not.

"What did you do last night?" he said as she brought in the tea tray.

"I stayed up until I heard Big Ben on the radio and the klaxons from the ships. Had myself a glass of rum and went to bed."

"But you knew I would be calling."

She blinked playfully at him. "I knew that Sebastian would be Sebastian and get himself fixed up with a woman somewhere and I wouldn't see him until this afternoon if I was lucky."

"You know me too well."

"So, who was the lucky girl, then?"

Sebastian gave her a quick résumé of the evening's events and his meeting with Alice, omitting her relationship to Chuter Ede.

"She sounds nice."

"She is. I'd like to see her again."

"Good. I hope you do. It's about time you got someone permanent. You don't want to end up like me now do you?"

There were a few moments of silence before Sebastian spoke again.

"Do you ever get lonely?"

"All the time, but I never let it get me down. I've got a few friends."

Her friends were usually male, and they often stayed the night. Blanche never worked but always had money. He had once asked if she was a prostitute and she'd replied that all women were prostitutes to some degree. Later, she denied selling her body but agreed that friendly bedfellows usually left something behind when they left. She said that she'd known most of these friends for several years and that their relationship was based on mutual respect, comfort and, of course, sex. He could see why. Blanche was comfortable to be with. She was relaxed and discreet. She was attractive. Her brown hair was parted on the left and cascaded freely onto coffee coloured shoulders. She was slim, had full lips and good bone structure. Her nails were long and tapered. Today she wore a brown blouse and slacks that covered long, slim legs.

Her friends were men of substance, men of influence and affluence. Most of them had something to do with the sea and were away a long time. Some of them knew each other and accepted the arrangement. Blanche was not only warm and friendly but was also a picture of discretion. She shared the lives of her men. She remembered the names of their wives and kids and their birthdays and anniversaries. She'd never met any of their families but knew their interests and foibles. It was a job she loved.

"No friends last night, then?"

She smiled wryly. "My friends are never available at New Year, or Christmas, or Easter, or any Bank Holidays. They have other places to be on those days. I've got no doubt that I'll have a visitor or two by the weekend, though, if they can get through the bloody snow and ice. I hear some of the roads are closed. This weather makes you want to try those two-week trips to Spain. 35 quid all in."

Sebastian said, "You didn't see mam last night, then?"

Blanche shook her head. She offered him a top up for his tea, which he declined. "She was out with Jack Tozer. I think they were going to the policeman's ball, or something like that. She wasn't looking forward to it but Jack insisted."

Sebastian frowned.

"I know you don't like him much, love. He likes a drink and he's full of his own self-importance. I don't think he particularly likes me. Probably because I once told him to keep his hands to himself, and the fact I'm not white."

"Mam seems to like him. Do you think it'll last?"

"Who knows, love. He's a policeman. He'll be here for a few years yet. He might even get promoted again. He's got his own house and he's not short of a bob or two." Blanche shifted her position on the settee and looked him straight in the eye. "Your mother has never told any of her boyfriends that she wanted to break off the relationship. It's always been the fella who's ended it. I don't know why that should happen other than I know that your mother can be a bit of a doormat at times. She hasn't got your grandfather's, or your, sharpness of mind. What she does have is the capacity to love anybody and everybody. If they treat her OK, then she's OK with that. Have any of her boyfriends really loved her? I couldn't say. But eventually they've all dumped her."

Sebastian nodded. Perhaps she had struck it lucky with Jack Tozer and he should be more amenable to the man.

Sebastian left shortly afterwards and returned home to grab a few hours' sleep. His grandad was out somewhere, probably The Fletchers Inn along the street, and his mother was with her boyfriend. The old damp house whistled a morbid winter tune. He wondered what Alice was doing. He imagined her wrapped in silk in Uncle Jim's mansion.

The world beyond his bedroom was freezing but at the moment he fell asleep, Sebastian was enjoying a relatively warm glow. 1963 was going to be an interesting year.

3

It was cold and frosty. Billie Crawley stumbled and slid her way past the Town Hall as it tolled one o'clock. She gathered her clothes closer to her body and tied the belt of her camel coloured coat tighter to keep out the chill. Small clouds of breath pulsed out of her lungs at each precarious step. Snow still covered some of the pavements, although there were long stretches that had been cleared by shopkeepers the day before, only to be replaced by the glistening patterns of a hard frost. She wore flat shoes with a good grip on the heels, and soles that minimised the slip and slide. She carried her white party stilettos in a bag. No-one during the two mile walk from Jack Tozer's bed had managed to conjure up a new year's greeting.

The downhill stretch of Fowler Street presented little difficulty to Billie's sturdy shoes. Near the bottom of the street she turned right into Catherine Street and crossed the road to her father's house. Ordinarily, she wouldn't have dreamed of leaving Jack in bed, but he was on duty soon, it was a Bank Holiday, and that meant double pay. When you were earning as much as twelve hundred pounds a year, Billie figured that that was a good bit of extra cash.

Jack was still suffering from the effects of the beer when she'd left and couldn't drive her home, but he'd have recovered enough to drive to work later.

As she pushed her key into the lock she wondered where she'd put her father's birthday present. He'd been hinting for a new pipe since Christmas Day when he'd opened his presents and been disappointed that a pipe wasn't there. She'd bought one the day after Boxing Day. He'd love it.

She walked into the living room and found a dying fire. She shovelled a pile of coal onto the grate from the scuttle nearby and watched as the flames flickered to life and plumes of smoke wandered up the chimney. Dad wasn't there and Sebastian's bedroom door was closed, a gentle snore resonating from his room. Billie put the kettle on and made herself a spam sandwich.

She smiled ruefully. That was her life in a nutshell. A life in a cold room. She missed her mother. A mother who she had never met. A woman who never had the opportunity to teach her daughter how to 'go on' in the world.

Not having had that special bond with her mother that her school friends had talked about was the low point of her childhood. On reflection, she'd endured a lifetime of lukewarm tea and spam sandwiches. Where was the prawn cocktail and fillet steak? It was the main reason why she called her son Sebastian. It was a posh sounding name and it would earn him a better life.

She chewed slowly without relish or savouring the taste of the meat.

School hadn't been much fun. She'd found it difficult to make friends and she'd never really been interested in classes. It was only after leaving school that she found someone to love, and it had been thrilling. It had ended so suddenly. The only people in her life who hadn't dumped her were her father, Sebastian and her friend Blanche. At least they hadn't dumped her, yet.

She made tea when the sandwich was finished, and then settled into her father's armchair, absorbing the heat from the crackling fire whilst she stared into the flames. Soon her drowsy memory drifted to a time when she had sat around this same fire with her father after she'd asked him for the umpteenth time about her mother.

"Dad, I know Mam died when she had me. Will you tell me again how it happened?"

"Okay. pet, what do you want to know?"

"Everything. I know you've told me before but I'm older now. I know some things go wrong when you have a baby."

Her father had sighed and gazed into the past to recover painful memories.

He told her that her mother had been a wonderful woman. Not gifted with brains but she'd been the most warm-hearted human being her father had ever met. Her eyes had sparkled from the day he'd first met her. And even as she lay dying the sparkle remained undiminished until it was replaced by a terrible look of pure fear when she realised her daughter would never know her.

She'd cradled Billie until she lost consciousness and drifted into another place.

Billie had listened to the story with tears in her eyes. She imagined her mother as a sleeping beauty and wished that her father could have been a Prince Charming to wake her up with a kiss.

"Why am I called Billie? It's a boy's name."

"That one's easy. You know how much I love football." She'd wiggled her head in mock frustration. "Your mother was rushed to hospital on 28th April 1923, which was a few weeks before her time and the same day of the cup final between Bolton Wanderers and West Ham. More than two hundred thousand people turned out to watch the match at Wembley Stadium; it was brand new then. Of course, it couldn't cope with that many people and before the match started, people spilled over on to the pitch. The referee delayed the start to allow the police to control the crowd. The story goes that the police called in their mounted section and a white horse helped push the crowd back off the pitch so the match could go ahead. That cup final is now known as the White Horse Cup Final. It was a miracle the game got finished. The white horse was called Billie, and you were my little miracle. I'd lost my Vivien, but God spared you, for which I'm grateful." He reached across and stroked her cheek. "You've got your mother's eyes."

She liked having her mother's eyes. She wanted everything that her mother had.

Billie returned to the present and caught herself before the mug slipped from her grip onto the floor. She yawned as she wandered into the kitchen debating whether she should go to bed or curl up on the settee for forty winks. She decided the latter. It would be another hour or so before dad came home from the pub. Then he would no doubt go to bed himself for a nap. Shortly after that, Sebastian would get up and she could prepare their evening meal. Today was going to be mince and dumplings. There were some parsnips and carrots in the pantry, despite the cost of vegetables rocketing through the bad weather, and she had a tin of peas. Some Yorkshire Puddings would crown the meal. She curled up and slept.

Sebastian stretched and yawned. He reached for his watch and noted that it was just after three o'clock. The pointers and numerals of the watch glowed green in the dark. He listened for signs of life as he gathered the bedclothes around him to stave off the cold, damp air that filled his room. He heard his grandfather trying to sing along with Roy Orbison, although he had the sense to leave the highest notes to the singer himself.

Sebastian braced himself and flung back the blankets and shivered into his clothes. The house was freezing. He would have to talk to his grandad about moving to a better place. There was talk of demolishing the street to make way for new houses. However, in the past, grandad had shaken his head at the mere mention of moving and had muttered "this house is special".

Sebastian walked downstairs and into the living room. The smell of cooking wafted from the kitchen. His mother sang brightly to Helen Shapiro. Grandad sat in his chair, eyes opening and shutting as he fought off the onset of sleep. Roy Orbison had gone home.

"Happy New Year, mam."

Billie put down the potato peeler and embraced her son. "Happy New Year, pet. Did you have a good time?"

"OK. You?"

Billie grimaced and shrugged her shoulders. "Same as you, I suppose. OK. There was a lot of toffee-nosed people there. Jack spent a lot of time drinking with his mates, but we had a couple of dances. I'm happy if he's happy."

She returned to the kitchen. Sebastian glanced at his grandad and saw him shaking his head.

"What have you got planned for tonight?" Tommy asked Sebastian.

"I'm seeing the lads. We're meeting at Sammy's place."

"Not meeting the new girlfriend?"

"She's not my girlfriend. She's just a woman I've met who I like."

Billie appeared in the doorway. "What new girlfriend?"

Tommy laughed mischievously and picked up the *Radio Times*.

Sebastian sighed then spent the next ten minutes giving his mother a condensed version of his meeting Alice.

"When am I going to meet her?" asked Billie.

"Hang on, mam. I've just met her. Why would she want to come here?

Tommy dropped the Radio Times on the floor. "And what's wrong with this place? Are you embarrassed about where you live? Or is it us that you're ashamed of?"

Sebastian spluttered, "I'm not ashamed of who I am, where I live or who my relatives are. It's just that…" his voice tailed off as he saw his grandad's face widen with his mischievous grin again. "Bastard," he said, and walked out of the room followed by his grandad's laughter and the sound of his mother berating her father because she hadn't got all the information she could from Sebastian.

Later, after one of his mother's mince dinners, Sebastian arrived at his friend Sammy's house in Holborn. His belly was full, but he accepted some treats from Sammy's parents after declining another meal. Samir al-Aziz was unemployed and earned a living from other people's goods. He stole things.

Sebastian recalled the first time Sammy had told him of his lifestyle. A couple of years ago an article had appeared in the Shields Gazette about a series of burglaries that had happened in the business area of central South Shields. Sebastian had passed a light-hearted comment to Sammy about the article and Sammy had admitted that he was the burglar the police were looking for. At first Sebastian refused to believe him but Sammy had described the burglaries in great detail. He'd even chanced his arm at shop breaking. He described how he would identify premises without an alarm and attack them during the night. He'd also perfected the art of causing an alarm to activate at an office or shop that drew the attention of the police. The police would attend and call out the keyholder to reset the alarm. Sammy would wait until they left and cause the alarm to be activated again, usually by using a stick through the letterbox to slightly disturb something inside. The alarm would activate and the process with the police and keyholder would start again. Eventually the keyholder would leave the alarm off for the rest of the night, and then Sammy would break in and steal whatever was available.

Sammy had never been caught, although there had been a few close shaves. Sebastian had also heard little bits of information from Jack Tozer when he was the worse for wear from drink and passed on information to his friend. Sometimes Sebastian had received one or two larger items from Sammy and passed them on to a contact in Newcastle. It was risky, but he was wary. Sebastian knew it was only a matter of time before Sammy was caught. And Sammy knew it as well. As far as he was concerned, it was an acceptable risk.

Sebastian and Sammy were joined by the rest of the 'gang', Mick Monroe and Steven 'Bull' Cowell. They were all the same age, having met at school. Mick worked down the pit at Westoe and Bull worked in the shipyard at Readheads, just down the road from where they were now. Mick was a Protestant of Irish descent and Bull didn't know his heritage or religion, nor did he care. Mick was quick-witted but Bull was 'slow'. Mick was slim and small-framed. Bull was large and powerful, hence his nickname.

Sammy stretched out on his bed. Sebastian took the only chair. Bull leaned against a chest of drawers. Mick slid down the wall and sat on the floor and started telling the lads what he had done. Which wasn't much.

He'd used his subtle charms to persuade a girl to let him have a grope. Spurred on by Bull, Mick gave a blow by blow account of his very brief liaison. They hung on every word, except Sebastian, who grinned, knowing Mick would be embellishing the story.

Bull shuffled to his feet. He wasn't a storyteller. He had simply got pissed and gave his story a full stop by letting out a loud and protracted fart.

Sammy leaped up and opened the window despite the freezing cold outside. It was the lesser of two evils – freeze or be poisoned. Bull was banned from farting again and after a few moments Sebastian closed the window again.

Snow was falling outside.

Sammy remarked that he had attended a family event – a cultural thing, he explained – and hadn't started celebrating until after his parents had gone to bed. Even then it had been a few drinks with some cousins.

Sebastian told his story again but left out Alice.

"Looks like we've all had a bloody good time, then," said Mick sarcastically. "I'm not a great lover of New Year, except sometimes you can get your end away without having to go through all the shit of courtship."

The group nodded in unison.

Sammy said, "Did anybody make any New Year's resolutions?"

They swapped self-conscious glances before Sammy added. "I've made one. It's the same as last years. I promise that I'll never be caught."

The group smiled as one.

"The life of a thief," Mick teased. "Some of us have proper jobs."

"I didn't hear you complain last year when I got you that watch."

"I was frightened to wear it for months in case someone recognised it."

Sammy grinned. "It was a bargain."

"Breaking into a Solicitor's office was a bit risky."

Sammy's grin widened. "Nothing ventured, nothing gained."

Sebastian turned to Bull and said, "Have you got a New Year's resolution?"

Bull grimaced. "That means something I've got to promise to do for a year doesn't it?"

"Sort of."

"I'm going to get a girlfriend."

The other three turned to each other in surprise.

"I met a girl last month and she's nice. Got lovely tits as well. Although I haven't felt them yet. I think I'll ask her out on Saturday.

"Wow," said Mick. "Make sure you get a haircut. When the barber asks you if you need something for the weekend, say yes."

Bull blushed a little.

"What about you, Mick? What's your ambitions for the next year?" Sebastian asked.

"Me? Well, all I'm hoping for is a decent pay rise and maybe a holiday in Butlin's. They reckon a lot of spare women go there. I fancy having a go at some posh tart in a chalet. After that, who knows? I could do with a bit more excitement and a few extra quid. I need to buy a car."

Sammy said. "You'd make a great burglar. Light, quick, nimble. You'd get over walls no problem at all."

Mick laughed, "Me? A burglar? Can't see it. What resolutions did you make, Sebastian?"

Sebastian raised an eyebrow and steepled his fingers as he raised them to his lips. "I honestly don't know. I'm making decent money and there's lots of opportunity out there, but I feel as though I'm in a bit of a rut as well. I need to do something else."

His friends waited for clarification.

"I'm not sure what it is, but I feel like I need to move on. I can feel the frustration building and I haven't a clue what to do next."

"You need a woman," said Mick. It was Mick's solution for everything.

"If it's excitement you want," said Sammy, "you can come and work the nightshift with me."

"It's not that kind of excitement I need. I want something I can get my teeth into. Something I can grasp with both hands and do something with".

"Like a woman," laboured Mick.

Sebastian ignored him.

The conversation had reached a dead end and turned to football and the effect the snow was having on fixtures – most of which were postponed. As usual the debate was heated and disjointed, with Sunderland's chances of promotion to Division One being the key topic. It took an announcement from Sammy's mother that she was preparing for bed to bring an end to the evening. They bade each other farewell and made their separate ways home.

At the Market Place, Sebastian stepped into a telephone box. He lifted the telephone from its cradle and fed some pennies into the slot at the top. He dialled a short number and heard a female voice. He pressed button A.

"Hello?"

There was a brief silence on the other end.

"Hello?" said the female voice. "Who is it?"

"Sebastian."

"Oh! I never expected to hear from you so soon."

"I was checking that you'd given me the right number." He could sense her smiling.

"I'm not in the habit of making mistakes like that."

"Maybe not. But I like to be certain of things."

"Certain of what? That it was the right number, or certain that I'd be waiting for a phone call from you?"

"Were you?"

"Was I what?"

"Waiting for a phone call from me."

"I was hoping, but I didn't expect it today. I thought that maybe you would ring later in the week."

"I can if you want me to."

He heard her laugh.

"Why don't we just make arrangements now?"

"OK. What do you fancy doing?"

"Hmmm. I don't know yet. Why don't I pick you up from your house on Friday and we'll decide then?"

"OK."

He gave her his address.

"Around seven?"

"OK."

"See you then. Bye."

"Bye."

Sebastian replaced the telephone in the cradle and pushed button B. The unused coins tumbled back into the tray like a jackpot.

The few hundred yards walk home passed without registering in his mind.

4

Friday 4th January 1963

"Anything in the papers, grandad?" asked Sebastian as he settled down onto the settee with a cup of tea in one hand and a bacon sandwich in the other.

Tommy Heath set down *The Times* on the floor beside his chair "Dick Powell died. Cancer."

Sebastian nodded, unconcerned.

"The government's considering extra aid to the shipbuilding industry. Fifth year of recession. Bottom's falling out of shipping. Lots of surplus seamen. High unemployment."

Sebastian stifled a yawn. "Anything else?"

"South Shields is getting a new general hospital. Hugh Gaitskell was coming to Shields on the 19th but can't now because he's ill. George Brown is coming in his place."

"Is that it?"

Tommy didn't answer. If there had been more he would've said so. Instead, he said, "You seeing Little Miss Marx tonight?"

Sebastian sighed and shook his head. Was this just a normal enquiry or was he being ultra-sensitive about it?

"Alice is coming for me at seven."

"I'd better go and put a clean shirt and tie on and have a shave." He rubbed his hand across his stubble.

"She's not coming in."

"Oh?"

It was an 'oh' that carried plenty of judgement. It was an admonishment, and a query. It carried all the hallmarks of 'are we not good enough for her?'

"I was thinking of going to the pictures. She won't have time to come in before it starts. There's a Norman Wisdom picture on."

"God forbid," said Tommy. "He's too stupid for words, that man. Not like Tony Hancock. He's a class act."

"But he's not in a picture at the Savoy."

"Point taken."

Sebastian drained his tea and put the cup in the kitchen. "Right, I'm off to get ready."

"Plenty of hot water in the boiler," said Tommy as he picked up the newspaper again.

Alice arrived twenty minutes late and didn't want to see Norman Wisdom falling about. She drove to The Britannia pub in Cleadon through the freezing rain that didn't seem to make much impact on the piles of snow at the roadside. They ordered a pint of beer and a port and lemon before settling down in the lounge. The place filled up quickly, and before long the usual fog of cigarette, cigar and pipe smoke permeated the room. Every now and then the door opened and closed, causing the smoke to curl and eddy around the room. A fire crackled in the grate nearby.

The people were a bit more affluent than the people Sebastian normally associated with. He spotted one or two familiar faces but knew no-one very well. In his usual haunts people were always coming across to exchange a few words.

Alice asked, "So, what's been happening in your life so far this year?" A smile danced beneath her eyes.

Sebastian gave her the short version – meeting the lads on New Year's Day and conversations with his mam and grandad and Blanche. He briefly mentioned a business call to a supplier in Newcastle. He then asked her the same question.

"Not much. I spoke to mum and dad and Uncle Jim. He's staying away for a week or two. He's got to be back for Gaitskell's visit on the nineteenth. They're opening the new Labour Party Headquarters in Westoe Road. They're calling it Ede House after Uncle Jim."

"Gaitskell's ill. George Black is coming instead."

"Brown," Alice corrected. "George Brown." But she was impressed by his knowledge all the same. "I do hope Gaitskell gets better soon. I'd like to meet him. He's a bit of a hero of mine."

Sebastian wondered if she was taking the piss again because he'd got the name wrong. It didn't seem so. Quite the opposite. Her smile had brightened – if such a thing were possible – and she looked genuinely concerned.

"Tell me, Alice, what's the real reason you're up here in the north east?" The question was something that had been on his mind since their first meeting. "I mean apart from what you said on New Year's Eve."

"The real reason?"

"Why do you stay here?"

She took a sip of her drink before answering. "I like the people," she said with a sparkle." Then added, "I'm what you might call unemployed."

Sebastian reacted instinctively. "You don't know what being unemployed is. A man on the dole gets £2 17s 6d a week. With all due respect – someone like you doesn't know what they're talking about when they talk about life on the dole. I know people who are probably lying in bed fully clothed to keep warm because there's no coal for the fire. They've probably shared a big bowl of broth made from pig's trotters and frozen vegetables, with a chunk of stale bread. Take a look in the mirror. What you're wearing would feed their family for a month."

Alice sat back. "Wow. Where did that come from?"

Sebastian shrugged. He might not be politically savvy, but some things upset him, and this was one of them.

There was a brief moment of silence before Alice touched his hand on the table. "I'm sorry, I didn't mean to imply …. I am unemployed simply because I haven't got a job. I'm not going to register as unemployed down at the labour exchange." She withdrew her hand. "I admire your passion," she said with a smile. "I've had a privileged upbringing. I'm the first to admit that. But that upbringing taught me there are many, many people out there who are, like you say, living in poverty. And it's the responsibility of people like me to make sure that the future for those people is better than their past. That's what Uncle Jim is trying to do here in South Shields. Yes, I know that sounds patronising, but it's true."

Sebastian forced a smile. This was their first date. The way it was shaping up, it may be the last as well. He took a swig of beer and left a little in the bottom of his glass. He wondered if he should have another.

Alice said, "They say you should never talk about politics and religion in a social setting." She glanced around the room.

"Although I'm sure that there are a few people in here putting the world to rights, right now."

"Do you want another drink?"

She shook her head.

Sebastian went to the bar and stood for a few seconds trying to catch the eye of the barmaid. It gave him some thinking time. He ordered and waited.

"Can I get you that?" said a man who appeared at his side.

Sebastian didn't recognise him.

"Thanks, but no thanks." His brow creased as he looked him up and down. "Anyway, why would you want to?"

"Just trying to buy a man a pint." His dark brown eyes sparkled as though they held a secret. He had a crooked grin and a pencil thin moustache. "We have mutual friends."

Sebastian was intrigued. "Mutual friends? Who might that be, then?"

The man gave a mysterious grin. "Oh, you probably don't appreciate them yet."

The barmaid delivered Sebastian's pint and he handed over a half crown and waited for his change.

"You're talking in riddles, mate."

"We'll talk again sometime soon, Mister Crawley." The man's grin widened, if that was possible. He nodded farewell and unrolled a cigar as he wandered to the other side of the bar.

Sebastian took his change and returned to where Alice sat pensively.

"Who was your friend?" she asked.

"He's no friend of mine. I've never clapped eyes on him before."

"He seems to know you."

He shrugged. "I have no idea who he is and I'm not in the least interested in what he's got to say." Under cover of supping his pint he gave the bar a quick glance to see if the stranger was still there. He was smoking and watching Sebastian. Sebastian wiped a frothy moustache from his top lip and said, "I'm sorry. I shouldn't have snapped at you like that."

"You gave me a bit of a start. But to tell the truth I was beginning to wonder if I had misjudged you, if there was any fight in you. You have feelings, political feelings, I mean. You care, and that's important to me." She leaned across and kissed him lightly on the cheek.

He smiled sheepishly. "Politics is not my strong point, but sometimes ..."

"I know. Sometimes you have to stand up for what's right." She took hold of his hand and they enjoyed a moment of solidarity until she said, "I've been invited to a preview opening of the new Grosvenor Grill next Friday lunchtime. Would you be interested in going?"

Sebastian knew that the Grosvenor Grill was being promoted as a brand-new luxury restaurant at the South Shields Sports Stadium. He'd seen the lunch menus in the Gazette: three set lunches at 3s 6d, 5s, and 6s 6d. 6s 6d seemed an awful lot of money for a midday meal. You could buy a record at Savilles for that and still have thruppence change. It sounded a little bit posh to him, but if Alice was there ... "OK," he said.

Saturday 5th January 1963

The knock on the front door was loud, strong and authoritative. Sebastian glanced at his watch as he made his way down the corridor. It was nine a.m. precisely. He gently eased the door open, trying to prevent cold air from coming in and warmish air escaping. The clean-shaven face of Jack Tozer beamed back at him under a trilby hat, thick blue scarf, blue tie and blue herringbone overcoat. Even the welts on his polished black boots shone.

"Come on, Seb. Stand aside and let me in. It's brass monkey weather out here."

He strode down the corridor into the sitting room without invitation. He took off his hat, coat and scarf and handed them to Sebastian with a 'thank you'. It was those things that irritated Sebastian about Jack Tozer, but he let it pass without comment and played the servant.

Jack said, "I thought you would've been on the stall today, lad. There's money to be made."

"I've made arrangements for..."

"A cuppa tea would be nice, Seb. That's a good lad. Now, then, Tommy, how's you?"

Tommy sat in his usual chair by the fire. "Champion, Jack. Thanks for asking. Still feeling a bit …"

"Well, never mind, Tommy, I'm sure you'll be as right as rain shortly. Now where's that tea, Seb?"

Sebastian boiled inside and Tommy's face reflected flames.

Tommy said, "So how's the world of crime these days? Are the criminals still getting away with it?"

Jack missed the sarcasm. "Detection rates are up on last year, but the numbers of crimes are about the same." The next point was accentuated by his right forefinger being waved around, then stabbing himself in the chest. "No criminals are messing around in my back yard without answering to me."

"Detection rates up? That's good. Now only eighty per cent of criminals are unpunished."

This time Jack saw the barbed comment and arrowed his gaze at Tommy. "We do our best, Tommy. Things like somebody pinching a bottle of milk from your doorstep are almost undetectable and don't warrant observations being kept for weeks on end to see if it's a regular occurrence. But serious crimes get the resources allocated to them, and we're good at detecting them. What would you prefer?"

Tommy shrugged. "If I was the victim of crime, whatever it was, I wouldn't be happy if the police chalked it off as a minor crime. It isn't minor to me. I'm unlikely to fall into the serious crime category."

"Unless you're murdered, or assaulted, or burgled."

"I've got nowt to pinch."

"Maybe not, but there are other people out there that have." He shook his head as he pondered what to say next. "We *are* having a lot of trouble with burglaries," he confessed. "It's been going on for some time. Nothing spectacular you understand, just the usual small offices and shops. Whoever is doing it, and we think it's one person, is getting away with a lot of stuff." Jack shook his head again, then nodded. "We'll get him soon. We've got a plan."

Sebastian came in with a tray complete with teapot, cup and saucer, and thoughts of Sammy in his mind. He went back into the kitchen to fetch the milk bottle, spoon and bowl of sugar. Jack prepared his tea and carefully poured some onto his saucer, then sipped it noisily. That was another thing about Jack that annoyed Sebastian.

Just then Billie walked into the room. "Morning everyone." She was dressed to go out.

"Morning," they all chorused.

"And what are you doing today, Sebastian?" Billie asked.

"Stall," he said.

"In this weather?"

"I've stuff to sell."

Sebastian had a small business buying and selling coffee and tea from Aden. He also sold ethnic bric-a-brac. His customers were mainly the Yemeni population in the Laygate area of South Shields, but his stall in the Market Place gave an outlet to the wider population of the town.

The tea was from the Khat plant. In the Yemen, the locals chewed the leaves of the plant until it generated enough moisture to swallow. It had a stimulant effect that lasted a long time. Users talked long and hard and made personal and community decisions when using it. It was a cultural thing, and usually a man thing. Sebastian had tried it a couple of times but couldn't get used to the sour tasting leaves. He'd learnt that the leaves lost most of their effectiveness in a relatively short time after picking, and barely stood the journey from the Yemen to the UK. However, some of the stimulant properties remained if the leaves were dried and made into tea. It was this process that allowed him to transport the tea back home and sell it at the market. Even then Sebastian had to consume it with either lemon or honey to make it palatable. Usually he gave it a miss. He had recognised a business opportunity when he saw the Yemenis chewing and drinking the stuff. It was consumed with the same passion used by his family and friends when they drank alcohol.

Samir and his family had helped him build his contacts. When they heard that Sebastian was going to Aden for his National Service, they had given him a letter of introduction to their relatives in the area. Sebastian had carried soft gifts and photos to them, and they had treated him like you would a member of the family. Contacts and promises had been made and kept, and, as a result, after he had completed his tour of duty, Sebastian returned to the Yemen and arranged to import local goods to

England. It wasn't a million-dollar business, but it kept him fairly well-off compared to his friends, who were pushing for fifteen quid a week after grafting for forty-two hours in a factory or the local shipyards.

The stalls were set out in parallel lines around the ancient Town Hall. A few hundred people milled around seeking a bargain. Sebastian nodded at a few folk and he acknowledged waves and greetings from fellow stall holders. Jackie, the man who he paid to open the stall and staff it, was sitting on a stool and wearing a donkey jacket, a thick grey muffler and a flat hat, and thick soled boots. His craggy face was sucking the end of a Capstan for all its worth. Sebastian asked the right questions about business traffic and received the wrong answers. Business was poor. He sent Jackie away for an hour to get himself a cup of tea and some breakfast, and, more importantly, to thaw out. It was bitterly cold, even though some watery sunshine tried to make itself known. It was failing miserably to compete with the snow, but it was enough to raise spirits a degree or two.

Sebastian stamped his feet and flapped his arms while assessing the mood of the crowd. It was the first Saturday of the New Year and people were eager to return their lives to somewhere resembling normality. However, he knew the public were fickle creatures and many would be put off by the weather.

A couple of people came to his stall and browsed. Sebastian knew this type of customer. They came, they browsed, and they handled the merchandise; they replaced it and moved on. They were never going to buy anything, so he didn't use his silver tongue to try and convince them that they needed it.

A man in a herring-bone overcoat and a brown trilby approached the stall. He smoked a thick cigar with a sweet, pungent aroma. He paused and nodded at Sebastian who noticed the man's moustache curled up at the edges when his toothy grin appeared and spread over his face. Sebastian recognised him as the man from the pub last night.

The man raised his hat and said, "Good morning, Mr. Crawley. It's a lovely day considering."

"Who are you? said Sebastian.

"My name is unimportant, Mr. Crawley. I'm just a man who likes to have a drink in a pub on a Friday night and a stroll through a historic thoroughfare on a crisp Saturday morning. It is nice to see the sun, is it not?

"Are you following me?"

"Why would I do that, Mr. Crawley? Why would I need to follow someone when I already know who they are and where they will be?"

For the first time, Sebastian noted he spoke with a foreign accent, although he couldn't pinpoint a country of origin.

"So you say this is just a coincidence, then?"

"What kind of coincidence is it that allows two people who live in the same town to cross paths? Is that coincidence or fate? Only God knows, Mr. Crawley."

Sebastian said, "Then I'll wish you good day, and goodbye, mate."

The man nodded and almost doffed his hat towards Sebastian. "Good day, Mr. Crawley. God may wish our paths to cross again."

Sebastian watched the man until he was swallowed by the crowd. By the time Jackie returned to resume his post, the incident had slipped from his mind.

5

Wednesday 9th January 1963

Tommy Heath was in his usual spot when Sebastian entered the living room for breakfast. Tommy had completed a nightshift at Tyne Dock. He was having a bacon sandwich and a cup of tea before going to bed.

"I don't know how you do it, grandad. You put in a ten-hour nightshift four days a week and you still manage to be awake when I am."

"Then you should get your arse out of bed more often. If you had a proper job like your mates, you'd be at work right now instead of lying about the house."

They'd had this argument many times in the past. His grandad insisted that the only way to earn a proper living was by working regular hours at a recognised place of work. You knew you'd earned your wages when you got that little, brown, windowed envelope and felt the thickness of pound notes. Sebastian declined to work the argument over again so asked for his latest news bulletin instead.

"Macmillan and Edward Heath have held talks over how we're going to join the Common Market. There's hell on about the new diesel trains from Newcastle to Shields. Apparently, they're full up after five o'clock when they get to Hebburn and hundreds of people have been left waiting on the platform."

"Is that it?"

"No. You can emigrate to Australia for ten pounds if you apply to their office in Manchester."

"No thanks."

"They're bringing in parking meters in Newcastle. It'll cost you sixpence to park now."

"I haven't got a car."

"The Mona Lisa's on display in Washington. That's the American Washington, not the one in County Durham."

Sebastian nodded.

"That's about it, really, unless you need to know that the biggest box office draw in the US is now Doris Day and not Liz Taylor."

"Good. I like Doris Day. What's the weather forecast like?"

"Bloody freezing and more snow. Where are you off to today? Seeing Little Miss Marx?"

Sebastian sighed. "No. I've got some business to see to, then I'm calling in on Blanche. I'm not seeing Alice until Friday."

Tommy heaved himself out of his chair and drained the dregs of his tea with his last mouthful of sandwich. "Bedtime," he said.

Sebastian completed his business by noon and made his way to Blanche's house in Broderick Street. She appeared to Sebastian to be very tired, maybe slightly unwell, when he saw her at the door. She wasn't her usual, bright self, and she seemed distant. It didn't suit her.

They ate a corned beef sandwich and drank a cup of coffee. They shared a packet of Tudor crisps. Sebastian thought it best to let Blanche lead the conversation and waited for her to say what was on her mind, but for a long while they only made small talk.

The grandfather clock ticked away the gaps in the conversation. The fire in the grate spluttered, in danger of dying.

"Have you ever heard nothing?" she said at last.

"How do you mean?"

"Have you ever heard silence?"

"You can't hear silence."

Her eyes drifted to the shadows that lurked where Sebastian couldn't see.

"Last Sunday I was sitting here reading the papers when I felt compelled to look at the clock." She nodded at it. Sebastian looked. It was nearly half past twelve. It loudly ticked away the moments of life.

"I stared at it for a few seconds and it just stopped … just like that…" She snapped her fingers to demonstrate the suddenness of the moment. "It was spooky. I waited for something to happen, but nothing did. I don't really know what I was expecting …" her voice trailed off.

Sebastian said nothing. He gazed at the clock almost expecting a repeat performance. It ticked on.

Blanche continued. "I could hear it; then I couldn't. That's when you find out that silence can be deafening." She stared into the dimming coals in the grate. "When you've had a life changing experience you become a different person. You actually see things in a different way. You react differently." She knitted her brow as if wrestling with some internal conflict, her fingers tightly entwined, her voice quiet. "I cry a lot now. I never used to. My mother used to call me a hard-faced bitch, but I wasn't, you know; I just didn't cry. Nothing seemed to connect with me, that's all. Now I cry at the drop of a hat; at a film, or if I see a baby cry.

She conjured up a recent memory and described it. "I saw an old lady the other day, with a bag full of shopping. She could hardly carry it. Every few yards she stopped to switch hands. Her head-square was frayed and pulled over her forehead. There were specks of rain on her glasses and the wind was blowing her coat open. I felt sorry for her. She just got on with it. Yet I cried. I cried for her, and I cried for me. I cried for every old woman that's ever lived. I cried for her poverty, her life and her future; whatever future she has left. And I cried for the future of her family." Fresh tears formed in her eyes and began rolling down her cheeks. "And I didn't even know who she was."

Sebastian shifted in his chair. Are you alright, Blanche?

Sebastian immediately regretted his words and searched for a more appropriate response. Blanche's life had been full of broken promises and her cupboards were full of skeletons. The attic was full of shields and lances from passing knights-in-shining-armour, yet the horse trough was still outside her front door and she kept a tin of *Brasso* handy in case any other knights came to stay. What could he say? He didn't even know what the problem was.

"It doesn't matter," he said eventually, and again wondered at the emptiness of his sentiment.

"I'm having a bad day, Sebastian. It happens occasionally, especially this time of year. I get a bit down. I look back at my life and think to myself that I ... I ... I need to know that if I went missing someone would know that I wasn't there anymore."

Sebastian reached over and grabbed her hand. He didn't know if it was the right thing to do or not. He just felt that he should.

She responded. Her hand grasped his. She sobbed.

Sebastian moved closer and held her closely, saying nothing, waiting for the tears to subside. Eventually she freed herself and picked up a handkerchief she had on a magazine rack beside her chair. She blew her nose. Another edge was daubed against her eyes. She settled back.

"I'm sorry," she said simply, her pallor returning to normal and her eyes regaining their steel and depth.

Sebastian shrugged. There was nothing to apologise for. A bad day was a bad day. Everybody had them. He'd known Blanche for years and every now and then she had a complete change of personality lasting from a few hours to a few days. It was strange. It was Blanche.

He changed the subject and told her about his own strange experience – of the two 'coincidental' meetings with the same man last Friday and Saturday.

Blanche regained her focus and asked questions including 'Did he have a tattoo on the back of his left hand?'

"Do you know something?" Sebastian asked.

Blanche hesitated. "No. No, I don't. But whoever he is, I don't think it's good news."

"I'll wait and see. He seems pleasant enough, but I have this feeling that he's not what he appears to be."

Blanche agreed, and said she needed to get some more coal for the fire.

Friday 11*th* January 1963

Tommy walked in the door bringing with him a cloud of freezing air from the street outside. The fire was roaring. Usually he was back from work before everyone got up and the job of getting the fire started, or sometimes managing to revive it from the embers of the previous night, was his. On the table next to his chair sat a tray laden with a pot of tea, covered by a knitted tea cosy, a mug, milk and sugar.

"I'll get you some toast, grandad. Shouldn't take a minute."

Tommy was too surprised to answer. He took off his jacket and boots and put on his slippers. He settled himself into his chair and waited for a few moments until Sebastian arrived with three slices of buttered toast.

"What's the occasion?"

Sebastian shrugged. "I was awake and I thought of you tramping your way from work in the cold and ice and thought that it would be good for you to walk into a nicely heated house and have your breakfast made for you. You do it for us most of the time."

Tommy sipped some tea. "It's well appreciated, son. There was a big snowfall last night. About three inches."

Sebastian rushed to the window and cleared some frost to see for himself. The world was white. One set of footsteps led from Fowler Street to the front door of the house. "Bloody Hell! I'm supposed to be going to the Grosvenor Grill today, with Alice."

Tommy munched the last of his toast and settled back into his chair. "Well, that's indoors so I wouldn't think the weather would be a problem. It's only a mile or two away."

"Alice is picking me up."

"There you are, then. No need to worry, unless she crashes the car in the snow and kills everyone. If this weather keeps up the Prince of Wales will have to ski back to the Palace from the airport."

Sebastian looked at him blankly.

"Prince Charles. He's just had his first skiing lesson in Switzerland. He must be preparing ... Never mind."

Alice pulled up outside the house in the Wolseley, its heater working overtime. Sebastian stepped carefully from the door of the house to the door of the car in shiny black brogues that complimented his dark suit. He quickly slid onto the leather seat and slammed the door behind him. The chill of the leather drained the heat from his backside.

"It's bloody freezing."

"And it's hello, lovely to see you, from me." She proffered a cheek.

"Sorry," said Sebastian. "Hello, lovely to see you." He kissed her on the cheek.

Alice drove off and turned into Anderson Street then left again into Ocean Road, where the snow had been eaten away by traffic and the Council gritting lorries. The journey to the Sports Stadium was relatively trouble free.

The Grosvenor Grill was part of the South Shields Sports Stadium. It had been refurbished and rebranded as a 'posh' restaurant. There were several local dignitaries and local men of note, with their wives. They all appeared to know each other. Alice knew several people. Sebastian was on nodding terms with one or two.

They sat at a table for two and ordered their food. Tomato soup for both of them, followed by steak and onions for her and steak and kidney pie with vegetables for him. Her sweet was jam sponge with custard, and his was fruit salad and cream. She drank lemonade and he had a pint of Exhibition beer.

Throughout the meal Alice talked little about her past and even less about her future. She had plans for sure, but they weren't quite decided. Her ambition was to go back to America and work in politics, hopefully on Kennedy's democrat platform. She hailed him as a charismatic visionary. But for her to do that she would need some doors to be opened for her, and that fell to her Uncle Jim to put in a good word for her.

"A woman should be able to make it on her own, but men still control the future," she said somewhat bitterly.

Sebastian eased back in his chair and watched her as she talked, wondering if she'd have been the same woman with the same drive and ambition if she'd been born in this town? He was brought back to earth when she asked him a question.

"What?"

"You weren't listening, were you?"

"What was the question?"

"I was asking you about the bomb."

"What bomb?"

"About banning it."

Sebastian shrugged his shoulders. Bombs were necessary, weren't they? He'd seen several explode when he was in the army. We needed them to make sure the enemy were kept in their place. And that's what he told her.

"It's a much bigger question than that." She leaned forward for emphasis. If we allow the proliferation of arms to continue, we'll end up annihilating ourselves and the world we live in."

"Everyone's got nuclear weapons. That doesn't mean they're going to use them."

"Everyone has them," she said, exasperated. "That's the point. The history of government's is that the state will use whatever weapons it has to gain the upper hand. We could all end up in a nuclear holocaust that'll end civilisation as we know it."

Sebastian frowned.

She lowered her voice, but it held an edge of anger in it. "In actual fact, everyone doesn't have them, but the one's that do are rattling their sabres and seeing who's got the biggest balls.

Sebastian smirked internally.

"When the Americans dropped bombs on Hiroshima and Nagasaki, the world changed. Science became a tool for producing bigger and better bombs instead of finding the cure to disease and pollution. Where's the humanity in that?" She didn't wait for an answer. "The risks to world health and the damage being caused to the environment aren't even being considered. That's why I joined the CND."

Sebastian knew CND stood for Campaign for Nuclear Disarmament, although he knew nothing about it.

Alice continued. "I went to Aldermaston that Easter, '58, it was. It was great to be with people ... people of all ages, all walks of life, and from every part of the country ... standing as one against nuclear proliferation."

Sebastian worked hard to suppress a yawn. He was pleased he did it well enough for Alice not to notice.

"Look at Cuba. That was scary. Krushchev nearly caused another war. And people have no say in it," she said with more than a hint of incredulity. "It's unbelievable that the we are so helpless."

A waitress came to clear the table and Sebastian took the opportunity to suggest they move to the bar. A helpful hand in the small of Alice's back guided her. Without asking Alice, he ordered her another lemonade and himself a bottle of brown ale.

"It doesn't mean a lot to you, does it?" she said.

"There's a time and place for everything. I was once told that if you're not in control of something, why worry about it. We've got no control over Russia or America, so we might as well stop looking up into the sky expecting bombs to fall down on us and just get on with our lives."

Alice grimaced as if in pain. "That's too simplistic, Sebastian. We can't just sit and let it happen."

"We can't vote for Kennedy or Khrushchev."

Alice glared at him. "You're a political pygmy. You can't see things on a world stage, can you? You're too busy thinking about South Shields. There's a world beyond the borough boundary, you know."

Sebastian poured his drink before answering.

"Look around at the people in this place. Most of them are people who've lived and worked in this area all their lives. They care about the place. They've invested their future here, and the future of their families. Some were elected by people like you and me. We are shaping our future here together, because we live here. What these people do has no bearing on what happens outside South Shields. If they had concerns, they would mention them to the only person they know who has connections with the outside world. And that person is your Uncle Jim. He's been here umpteen years and done his best. But, in reality, what has he done that affects anything outside the borough? I can tell you. Nothing. Absolutely bugger all."

Alice seethed for a moment. "I don't think we have anything in common, Sebastian. You sit politely and listen to me and think about sex, and you stifle yawns when I talk about my hopes and dreams. I don't like being patronised. You need to work on your manners when talking to women." She turned away, grabbed her coat from the cloakroom and stormed out the door. She hadn't touched her lemonade.

Sebastian leaned against the bar and sighed. "So much for manners," he muttered to himself. Then he started out after her, made two steps, sighed again. Was it patronising to go after her? Did she need her own space? Would he be acting out the typical male chivalry role? How could he be sure what he was doing was right? He drained his beer and ordered another.

There was a fireplace at the far end of the room. Flames danced and waved like a Turkish belly dancer. He lifted up his glass of brown ale and held it so he could see the fire through it. The reds and yellows transformed into the mellow tones of amber and burnt orange. The warmth, the intensity and clarity of colour struck him. They were the same shades as Alice's eyes.

"Bollocks," he said, and wondered if it was too late to go after her.

He felt a presence standing by him. He glanced to his left and saw a familiar grin beneath a pencil moustache.

"Good afternoon, Mr. Crawley. Your lady friend is upset, no?"

"Piss off"

The man laughed. "She is not as interested in you as you are in her?"

Sebastian didn't answer.

"She is a beautiful lady. She has a fiery temperament, I see."

"What the hell are you doing here?" demanded Sebastian.

"I have been invited by the owners." He wafted his invitation card in front of Sebastian. "Although I know that you were not. You were invited by Miss Alice, and even she is here as a substitute for someone else who could not attend."

Sebastian had failed to read the name on the invitation card. But one thing he did notice was a mark on the back of his hand at the base of his thumb. It was a tattoo, about half an inch long. It reminded him of *The Saint*, a television series starring Roger Moore as Simon Templar, a Robin Hood type character who took on individuals and organisations that he saw to be abusing their power. He always left a calling card at the scene: a stick man with a halo.

This man's tattoo was also a stick man, but without the halo. It appeared to be jumping over some wavy lines. The significance of which failed to register with Sebastian.

"How do you know that?"

"I am a man who comes by information easily."

"Who are you?"

"My name is Shafiq, Mr. Crawley. Are you now any wiser?"

"Well listen here, Shafiq, I'm getting a little bit irritated by you appearing like a pantomime genie. Whatever you're selling, I don't want it."

"I am not in that line of business, Mr. Crawley, although my interest in you is truly professional. I do not think it is wise of you to make me ... disappear, like a genie, like Miss Alice. My employer is interested in you. It would be wise to show me some respect."

The grin never left his face; he remained relaxed and cultured.

Sebastian, on the other hand, was dealing with a morass of thoughts and feelings and anxieties. Alice. Blanche. Shafiq. Love. Tattoos. Bombs. Alice. He excused himself and went to the toilet. When he returned, Shafiq had gone. Outside, the mid-afternoon gloom had drained the world of colour. He grabbed his coat and stood at the door of the Grill buttoning it up. Alice. Blanche. Shafiq. Bombs ready to detonate.

His brogues took him home.

6

Saturday 12th January 1963

Billie Crawley stood in front of the mirror and teased her hair into shape, the same style as Marilyn Monroe had in her last picture. She'd read that Marilyn had problems with men and been prescribed medication, but she'd stood up and knocked the world for six. Billie could do worse than look up to her. It was such a pity her role model was dead.

She was standing in the front room of Jack Tozer's house in the Harton area of South Shields. Jack walked into the room wearing a dressing gown over his white vest and y-fronts, and plain slippers over black socks. He snuggled into Billie's back, grinding his groin into her buttocks and reaching around to squeeze her breasts.

"Give over, Jack. I'm just about ready to go out."

"I've got an hour to spare."

"Well, I could do something for you if you gave me a lift home?" She raised an eyebrow.

Jack's libido waned. He uncoupled from Billie. "I haven't got time to do that. I'm at work shortly. We're implementing a new plan to catch the burglars we've been having trouble with. They've put me in charge because it was me who suggested it. I might get another promotion out of this."

"If you catch them."

"Yes, we'll have to catch them."

"Do you have any ideas?"

He patted the side of his nose with a forefinger. "Secret."

Billie nodded. After a few beers Jack would tell her anyway. She moved on.

"I went to the shop yesterday and do you know that tomatoes are fetching sixpence a pound! A tanner for tomatoes! It's the same for apples. Tatties are seven pence, and eggs are four and six a dozen."

Jack reached into his jacket, which was hung over a chair, and took out his wallet. He extracted a ten shilling note and handed it to Billie.

"Can you get me some supplies, love. You know what we eat. You won't need any more than that. Buy yourself a cake or something."

Billie snatched the money from him as she said, "I'm not your skivvy, Jack Tozer. I'm more like a part-time wife."

Jack's gaze hardened. "You're free to go any time you like. Nobody's keeping you. There's the door." He didn't even bother pointing to it. "If you're not happy here, then go."

Billie immediately apologised and pecked him on the neck. She slid her hands underneath his dressing gown and felt for the opening in his underpants. Jack's reaction was immediate. He sat down and pulled Billie between his legs. She felt his right hand reach up and clasp the back of her head. He began pushing her face towards his groin.

She'd fix her hair again when he was finished, and she'd get the bus home.

Alice lay indolently on a *chaise longue* in her uncle's house with a cup of Brazilian coffee in her hand. The other hand idly twirled her hair and pulled it down over her eyes to her lips. She licked the ends and made them curly, a habit carried over from childhood and commented upon by her room mates at university on both sides of the Atlantic.

She'd replayed the conversation with Sebastian several times and had asked herself if she'd over-reacted. Her answer was 'probably'. It bothered her. Her passion for politics sometimes intruded into her personal life and she just couldn't get the right balance.

She had only known him for less than two weeks, but she knew she was attracted to him – and him to her. There was a huge gulf between them socially and politically; but something between them managed to bridge the gap. It wasn't just physical attraction. There was a spark of something she couldn't quite put her finger on. She'd asked herself if it was love, but she'd rejected that out of hand. The idea was preposterous. Who the hell believed in something that suggested love at first sight?

Alice sighed. It was over now anyway, wasn't it? She doubted that he would hang around and wait for her. And she didn't know how to contact him anyway. She could ask around but what would be the point? She had to ask herself was it worth the effort? The thought made her smile. He'd said that when they first met. *She* had posed the question then, and he'd obviously decided that she was. If that was what he'd decided, then that was good enough for her. Was Sebastian worth the effort? She didn't need much time to think about it. He was. She'd give it another try.

The telephone rang.

Alice smiled. A genuine feeling of elation swept through her body.

7

Saturday 19th January 1963

Sebastian sat on the settee in his grandad's house in Catherine Street waiting to be picked up by Alice. She was due at the opening of Ede House in Westoe Road, and she had invited him as her escort. The 'misunderstanding', her word, that had blighted their last rendezvous disappeared during the telephone call.

"Hello?" she'd said.
"Hello" he'd said.
"Who is it?"
"A political pygmy." The fact that *he'd* rang *her* seemed to have been enough of an apology to warrant the 'misunderstanding' comment from Alice. It wasn't a big enough issue to fall out over, as far as they were both concerned.

Ede House was the new headquarters of the local Labour Party, named in honour of Alice's 'uncle', Chuter Ede, the local Member of Parliament. Mr. Ede was due to attend, and so was George Brown, the Deputy Leader of the Labour Party. The news that the Leader of the Party, Hugh Gaitskell, had died the day before overshadowed the euphoria of the local Labour members.

Sebastian's grandad had dismissed Brown as the next leader of the party, saying that he was "taciturn, argumentative and a drunk." He had reluctantly paid Gaitskill a compliment by saying he was "a committed and honest socialist."

A car horn honked outside in the street. Sebastian rose and looked through the curtains. Alice was in the Wolseley. Obviously, Uncle Jim's return to the borough had not stopped Alice from using his car.

It was still cold when Sebastian slid onto the seat next to Alice. She proffered her cheek, which he dutifully kissed. She then drove off.

"Pity about Gaitskell," was his opening remark.
"Don't talk about it," she said.

Her eyes were damp. Sebastian knew she thought that Gaitskell was going to be the shining beacon of the Labour party and surely the next Prime Minister.

Disobeying her own instruction, she said, "I knew that things were taking a turn for the worst when they issued a statement on Wednesday saying that he wasn't responding to treatment."

Sebastian said nothing. He was playing by the rules. A gust of wind rocked the normally robust Wolseley. Instead, he said, "There's a storm coming."

He saw her quick look at him. He wondered whether or not she was debating if he was talking about the weather or that he had conjured up some political metaphor for the impending Party leadership election that was now inevitable. But no, she might be thinking he wasn't bright enough for insightful political innuendo and decide that he was indeed talking about the weather. Another freezing gust of wind seemed to endorse the latter point of view.

The journey to Ede House was a short one and it took just a few minutes. Sebastian gazed at the people in the street as their car sailed past them. Most of them would be unconcerned about the changes in the Labour Party leadership. They might be aware of their MP having the local party headquarters named after him as they took over their new offices, but most of them were trying to make their way home or to the pub for a night of beer and fags. A few would go to social clubs to be entertained by the local Cliff Richard or Adam Faith. Some would 'batten down the hatches' to protect themselves from the weather and try to keep the cold from seeping into their bones.

Alice parked the car and quickly ushered Sebastian through the main doors and into an office. Several people stopped talking and turned to see who had invaded their domain. Sebastian smiled at them and nodded to one or two people, who courteously nodded back before resuming their conversations.

"Uncle Jim won't be here for a few minutes yet," Alice said in a quiet voice. "I won't introduce you if that's OK. The atmosphere is a bit fragile because of the circumstances. Just let it wash over you."

That was good advice, thought Sebastian. He hadn't planned to do anything anyway. He would just wait and watch and see if he could read what was happening. He enjoyed watching people and how they reacted to each other. He grabbed himself a drink and stood in the corner while Alice circulated and shook a few hands. One or two people, councillors he thought, kissed her on the cheek.

The door opened and a senior policeman entered the room, followed by a uniformed police sergeant.

It was Jack Tozer.

Jack greeted several people in the precise tone he usually saved for official functions. Not so long ago, Jack had been sinking pints of beer with these people and calling them by their first names. Now, he was calling them Mister or Councillor or just plain Sir. Jack spotted Sebastian in the corner and made his way across the room.

"What the bloody hell are you doing here?" he snarled through a fixed smile.

"Good evening to you, Jack," said Sebastian. "I thought I'd pop in and welcome Mr Brown to the north east. I also thought that Mr Ede might want some of my advice on local matters." He sipped his beer.

"Don't take the piss, son. We don't need comedians here. This is serious business."

"I thought you were out catching burglars?"

"A policeman can be called upon to do many things at the drop of a hat. Policing isn't all about locking up drunks or taking reports of stolen bikes or seeing old ladies across the road. Some of it is deadly serious." He emphasised the fact by raising an eyebrow.

"I'll be careful not to drop my hat, then."

Jack's stare became a glower as he blew out his cheeks to keep control of his temper.

Sebastian said, "Calm down, Jack, we don't want you to blow your next promotion by giving me a slap now do we?"

Jack was about to reply when they were joined by Alice.

"Alice, this is Sergeant Jack Tozer. Jack, can I introduce you to Alice."

Alice smiled and held out her hand. Jack took it and returned a sickly smile. Sebastian wondered why women didn't see right through the fake charm.

"I'm extremely pleased to meet you, Alice. I noticed you as soon as I came into the room and wondered why such a lovely lady was standing in a room full of old duffers like these. Unfortunately, I haven't got time to chat." He looked over her shoulder towards his Superintendent, who was summoning him by waving his hand. "Duty calls. Perhaps we'll meet again." He turned to Sebastian and said "Have a good evening, Mr Crawley. It's been nice talking to you."

"Smarmy git," said Alice after Jack had gone.

Sebastian gave a little laugh. Obviously not all women fell for Tozer's fakery. "Yes, he is. He's my mother's boyfriend."

"Oh dear,' she said. 'Condolences to your mam."

Sebastian laughed again, this time at the way she said 'mam'.

Sunday 20*th* January 1963

By default, there was no place to go other than a car park near the sea front. Uncle Jim would be home, so they couldn't go to Alice's. Sebastian lived in his grandad's house, so they couldn't go there either. The car park at the little beach near the north foreshore was as good as anywhere else.

The wind howled and rocked the car backwards and forwards. The inside gradually steamed up. Sebastian was aware that any passing policeman would check them out, but they weren't doing anything unlawful.

Their conversation was a little more relaxed than last week's efforts. Whether by accident or design, the subject of politics was absent. They talked of their pasts, music, likes and dislikes, and hopes for the future. The weather worsened outside, in stark contrast to the warmth that grew inside. Alice told him about a job offer she'd had at Ede House and the possibility of a secondment in America by the end of the year.

Sebastian heard the words and was about to comment but a maroon flash drew his attention. "What the hell was that!" He opened the door to get a better look and was blasted by icy wind. Visibility was poor but he scanned the horizon between the piers.

Alice climbed out of the car. She pointed.

Sebastian followed the line of her finger and saw a ship swaying like a punch-drunk boxer. The roaring winds lashed and battered the bruised hulk as it listed to and fro.

"It's hit the Black Middens," shouted Sebastian through the tumult.

"What?"

"The Black Middens. They're rocks just below the surface of the river on the north side. The ship's out of control. It's drifting towards the sands."

"We'll have to call the coastguard, or the police, or someone," shouted Alice.

"They'll already know by now." He pointed to another red maroon lazily falling through the skies despite the weather. "There's nothing we can do."

They both stood for several minutes wrapping their coats tightly around themselves and scanning the water for signs of movement.

Shortly, a police car arrived and then Volunteer Life Brigade came with some equipment. Sebastian heaved a huge sigh of relief. There were people here who knew what they were doing, and they set about the task with professional ease.

The keel of the ship scraped across some small rocks and stuck firmly in the sands. The easterly gale pounded the hull and gave rise to concerns that it might overturn. There were signs of activity on board.

Alice slipped an arm through Sebastian's and rested her head on his shoulder. "Thank God they're alive," she said.

They watched as a rocket type of machine was assembled on the beach.

"What are they doing?" asked Alice.

"I think they're going to shoot a rope over to the ship. There mustn't be any other way of getting them off safely."

By now there were dozens of people milling around shouting instructions and mouthing advice. Most of them wore white caps, oilskins and wellington boots.

The first attempt at getting a rope to the ship failed. To Sebastian, it seemed like an age since sighting the first maroon. He realised that it wouldn't be long before dawn broke.

A second attempt at securing a line to the ship was successful and an 'A' frame contraption was mounted on the beach. By this time, Alice was watching the proceedings from the gentle comfort of Uncle Jim's Wolseley.

A Breeches Buoy was loaded onto the taught rope. The Buoy, a flotation device with a fitted harness, was hauled towards the ship, and soon the first seaman endured the perilous journey from the ship, over the foaming frenzy of the water, to the arms of his rescuers. The Buoy was sent back for the next seaman, and then the next. Several of the stranded mariners were whisked away to the Ingham Infirmary to be checked out. By now, the rescuers were cold and damp and drained of energy and Alice had joined a group of women providing hot tea and soup for them. Sebastian had also stepped forward to offer any assistance he could give.

"Grab hold of this rope, lad, and heave when I shout," said a short, stocky man with a thick white beard.

Sebastian did as he was told and readied himself.

"Stand with your feet apart and lean back," instructed the man. "Let your bodyweight take the strain. If you pull with your arms, you'll be spent after the first man lands."

Sebastian nodded and waited for his orders.

"Heave," shouted the man, and everyone in line strained every sinew. The line went taut and Sebastian saw the Breeches Buoy sway and dip as another seaman was brought foot by foot along the rope. The seaman braced himself against the wind and spray and uttered a silent prayer as brute strength and the elements fought against each other.

Sebastian's feet were losing their grip in the sand, so he dug a little hollow with his heels and used it to gain more leverage. His knees and calves were suffering and, despite the warning from the man with the beard, his arms were also showing signs of strain.

"C'mon, lads, he's nearly there," shouted the man, just as a wave engulfed the seaman's legs up to his waist. "Keep that line taut."

Sebastian leaned into his task and grunted and cursed along with his fellow volunteers. Eventually the sailor was beached and was quickly surrounded by policemen and rescuers, who wrapped him in a blanket and led him away. Despite the freezing wind and the icy spray, Sebastian found himself sweating, but he gathered his mettle and gritted his teeth and pulled with all his might with his fellow man to see the next seaman safe to the beach.

A few more of the seaman dangling from the Buoy became immersed in the water and had to be rescued from the briny by the exhausted volunteers, who would never let up as long as there were sailors to be rescued. To Sebastian's surprise and to the great merriment of all around, one crew member was brought ashore cradling a small dog.

Sebastian tried to ease his tired muscles by stretching and rubbing them. He stood panting as he watched the Captain of the vessel leave the bridge for the last time. He saw him salute his ship and straddle the Breeches Buoy. Sebastian and his fellow rescuers hauled him to the safety of the beach, glad that their toil was over at last and relishing the prospect of a mug of steaming hot tea.

The whole crew, wet, weary and dispirited, were taken to be checked out at the hospital while the *Adelfotis II*, the ship, battered and bruised, wallowed and waived her farewell in time to the overture caused by the incessant slap of the waves against her empty husk.

A windswept and stained Alice sidled up to Sebastian.

"All over?" she enquired.

He nodded. "Bar the shouting. Everyone's safe."

They surveyed the beach together. The clear up operation was in full swing. The crowd that had been there through the night had, in the main, slipped away and been replaced by others. Fresh observers had taken the place of itinerant bystanders and, no doubt, the wreck would lie on the rocks for ages until its fate was decided by Lloyds of London or some other similar body.

Sebastian looked at his hands. They were red and sore. Blisters had formed and burst during his exertions.

"I'll take you home," Alice said.

It was nearly high noon.

Sammy lay on his bed. The radio was on, but he wasn't listening to the boring commentators that were having a conversation about the weather. His mother was downstairs making lunch. Tradition had been anglicised over the years in their Yemeni household, to the extent that a Sunday lunch was roast beef and Yorkshire pudding. The familiar smells permeated the house the same as in any northern home.

Times were tough. The weather had curtailed Sammy's nocturnal activities. It was simply too cold and too wild for him to be scaling the walls and roofs of offices and shops. He'd often lain here and scolded himself for putting himself through the anxiety and risks involved in burglary and then selling the proceeds for a pittance. He took the risks and other people profited from reselling. He had always focused on small businesses and corner shops. He knew their profit margins were small and he regretted that, but they were the easy targets. They either couldn't afford robust security systems or were too complacent about protecting their businesses. He had ambitions of pulling off a decent haul that netted him a few hundred pounds, but the bigger jobs meant greater risk. The police recorded all crime but hardly ever investigated the type of crime Sammy was involved in. However, one day his luck would desert him and he would get nicked.

After speaking to Sebastian, Mick and Bull a couple of weeks ago about their new year's resolutions he'd been visited by Bull, who said he was interested in making some extra money. It wasn't that much of a surprise. Bull was a gambler and often lost money on the horses, and he also played cards – badly. And with the prospect of a relationship with the girl with the 'lovely tits' Bull needed to make some spare cash. He didn't think Bull would do it as he was a bit on the slow side, and thickset. However, being big had its advantages. He could carry more for a start.

Bull's insistence swayed him. Usually Sammy preferred to work alone. You worked by yourself, for yourself, and you didn't need to discuss things in advance. You made your decision and went with it. If your plan backfired or was interrupted in some way, you made another decision and followed it through. That method had stood him in good stead for a couple of years now, but, he supposed, working with Bull wouldn't take much planning. Bull did as he was told. He accepted that anyone he worked with was more intelligent than himself and if someone was successful in what they did, then they were good at their job.

He would think that because Sammy had never been caught, he must be brilliant at breaking into shops and offices. Bull saw it as easy money.

Sammy had warned him not to tell anyone about what they planned, least of all Mick and Sebastian. They would counsel against his involvement and point to his decent job at the shipyards as a reason for playing it safe, so Sammy decided he would only involve his friend at the weekend. The trouble was, the freezing cold weather hadn't broken since Christmas and the forecast was for seven degrees of frost in the next week. It certainly wasn't burgling weather.

He reached under his bed and retrieved the book he had with all his successes and the tiny proportion of his failures where doors or windows had defeated him or the risks had been too great. He totted up the approximate values of stolen property and measured it against what he'd made. He used his schoolboy maths to work out the percentage. It was less than ten per cent. Although he had made hundreds of pounds over the years, he had stolen thousands of pounds worth of property. The police must be stupid not to have found out about him. But how would they know who he was? He was like the wind – unseen and random. Even the coppers from *Dixon of Dock Green* or *Z cars* couldn't stop Samir al-Aziz in his pomp.

8

Friday 25th January 1963

"It's bloody freezing in here!" said Tommy Heath to himself when he entered the house after his nightshift on the docks. Back to usual, he thought, after Sebastian's lovely effort the other day. The week had been absolutely freezing all around the country, down to 19°F. There'd been reports of the Thames freezing over in some places. On top of that there was a coal shortage in the South East. The weather was playing havoc with everything, from public services to football fixtures. No-one was untouched by the weather.

The news that there was something like 815,000 people unemployed was grim. Just after Christmas wasn't a good time to be without a job and the weather made seasonal workers redundant. Tommy shook his head as he constructed another fire while waiting for the kettle to boil. Its soft whistle sounded just as he held the match to the paper and kindling. It would take a while for the heat to permeate the room but the tea did the job from the inside. He picked up the *Gazette* from the previous evening and browsed through it.

The *Adelfotis II* had been the mainstay of the local headlines since Sunday. The ship was still stuck on the sands. Sebastian's version of events had been graphic but a coherent narrative from the paper was more illuminating and they added some background to the Black Middens, and even some geology, which put the whole thing into perspective. The rest of the news didn't add much to the stories he'd heard on the radio through the night this week. The strangest story was that which featured two East German police officers jumping from a building at the border into West Berlin. They had broken their heels when landing. Tommy shook his head and wondered what was going on in Berlin for them to do that. Surely life in the east of the city wasn't that bad.

He heaved himself out of his chair and put the fireguard on the hearth. He couldn't allow a spark from the fire to escape and burn the house down. He knew the law said that only coke should be burnt for 'clean air', but coal was traditional and much more satisfying. He had been in favour of the Council rejecting The Clean Air Act three years ago even though South Shields had become a 'black spot' for air pollution since.

He decided he would sleep for a few hours and then take a walk to the *Old Highlander* in King Street to pay his respects on its last day before closing. It held part of his youth and its passing deserved to be commemorated in his memory. He'd come home and make something to eat and settle down in front of the telly. He'd missed *Steptoe and Son* and *Bootsie and Snudge* yesterday, but there would be other stuff worth a look tonight. The *Radio Times* lay beside his chair. He'd look later.

Sergeant Jack Tozer stood at the main junction of town. The Bank was behind him. The other three corners of the intersection were occupied by pubs. The town's main thoroughfare, King Street, was to his left and that led up to the Market Place. King Street properties held the highest rateable value for commercial premises in the Borough. Rates were at a premium and the owners expected robust police protection during the hours of darkness, which was most of the time in winter. Jack Tozer and his team had done that last night, and right now the team were freezing cold and sitting in the station drinking a cup of tea. He surveyed the area with a clean sweep from right to left. Nothing had happened. At least nothing had been reported yet. He would leave after nine o'clock. By then everyone should be at work. Any premises would have rung 62222 to report a burglary to the local nick by then.

He was disappointed. The cold had kept everyone in. Those people that had been seen in the area were obviously workers. Those who were not, were checked out on the Burgess Roll and found to be OK. One car had been stopped. The owner wasn't listed on the Roll but had recently renewed his Road Fund Licence. A nocturnal visit to the Local Taxation Office confirmed who he was. The Police had keys to the Taxation Office for just this purpose. Cars taxed outside the Borough were more complicated. A check could take days or weeks.

"Are you not going home?"

Jack turned to see Detective Sergeant Smith standing to his right. His pipe billowed out clouds of the distinctive *Balkan Sobranie* tobacco, which conjured up the dark, aromatic lustre of the Middle East. Jack coughed. Detective Sergeant Smith waited for an answer.

"I'm waiting to see if anything's reported," said Jack.

Smith nodded sagely. Jack saw that it was a strategy he agreed with. A strategy he would have employed himself. A pretty office worker walked past them into King Street. Both policemen's eyes followed her shapely form until she was lost from sight.

"You've got to get an arrest, Jack."

"I know that, Smithy. I'm not a fool. I know my neck's on the line here."

Smith nodded again. Jack had been told that Smith wanted everyone to understand that this was a CID job and not one for coppers who didn't appreciate the finer points of the criminal mind.

Jack continued. "I can't arrest anyone if no crimes are being committed, can I?"

Smith raised an eyebrow and sucked on his pipe. "There's plenty already in the crime book." There was a pause before he added. "You know that the chances of you catching someone in the act are remote. It'll be down to a stroke of pure luck. There's no substitute for intelligence gathering. When you start shaking trees, who knows what'll fall out."

"Well your lot haven't found anything."

Smith bristled but checked his response. "Enquiries are continuing," he said.

"They must be bloody long enquiries, then," said Jack. "What's happening to all these informants your detectives are getting paid for. Not one of them has a clue who's responsible for this crime wave. Not one."

"No need to raise your voice, Jack. I'll bet you that your little charade of crime investigation gets nowhere. I'll tell you this. If this burglar continues the way he is, it'll be one of my men that catches him and not one of yours."

Detective Sergeant Smith turned on his heels and strode away. Jack snorted contemptuously and turned the other way into

King Street. A revolving blue light coming from the police box in the Market Place, at the top of King Street, caught his eye and he went to investigate, walking the regulation pace of two and half miles an hour, hoping that a burglary hadn't been reported. At the police box, PC Pattinson was taking details of a call. He replaced the handset and said to Jack, "There's been a burglary in Coronation Street."

Jack's heart dropped. He could picture Detective Sergeant Smith's grin already.

Two hours later, Jack sat in the police station canteen with a bacon sandwich dripping in fat and a mug of steaming hot, strong, sweet tea. His team had ended their tour of duty and headed home. He remained. He was tired and cold but things needed to be done. This was his scheme. It was his plan. And he intended to keep a close watch on everything that could scupper it.

The scene of the burglary had been visited and Jack satisfied himself that it hadn't been committed by his 'target.' The scene was too messy. The solicitor's office had been vandalised to some extent, and files had been emptied on the floor. An attempt had been made to carry a typewriter away, before being abandoned, probably because it was too heavy. Stationary had been taken, as had a petty cash box. No. This wasn't the man he was after. His target was more subtle than that.

The best thing about the incident was that he came into contact with the receptionist at the solicitor's office. Jack thought that she was well stacked and curvy, and she was about forty years old, and owned her own house. Her husband had died two years ago. She was bright and intelligent, and Jack got the impression that she was getting over her grief and just about ready to start casting the net into the sea of courtship. He made sure she understood that he was free and unattached, and she admitted that she liked strong, authoritative men. Jack had promised himself to make follow up enquiries when he was next on dayshift.

He felt empowered, engorged. He adjusted his pants to give himself room to grow. He needed to see Billie.

Sebastian sat on the settee in Catherine Street. His mother sat opposite him. Grandad was at the *Old Highlander* pub in King Street saying his farewells.

Sebastian stretched and yawned. He hadn't been sleeping well since the shipwreck. He didn't know if it was the trauma of the event, or a combination of being cold and wet.

"Blanche says you haven't been around lately."

Billie raised her eyebrows but said nothing.

"I've only seen her a couple of times myself recently. She's a busy woman."

Billie shot him a suspicious glance. Was Sebastian trying to say something other than the obvious?

"How long have you known Blanche?"

Billie sighed. "Since we were at school together. She was older than me. Your grandad didn't like me knocking about with Blanche because of the age difference. She was very mature and some of that rubbed off on me." She paused briefly. "I was going to pubs at fourteen, and clubs not much after that."

"Blanche said that you got on like a house on fire."

"Blanche was a good friend."

"Was?"

"I meant *is* a good friend. It's just now that I've got Jack, and Blanche has her ... friends. We don't seem able to arrange a chinwag."

"She's a busy woman." There was a brief silence before he added, "Did she know my dad?"

This was a conversation Billie didn't want to have.

Sebastian watched as his mother gathered pieces of information and edited them in her mind. Eventually she spoke.

"Yes. Blanche knew your father, although they didn't particularly like each other. She was a bit too wild for him."

Billie disappeared into her own thoughts. Her husband had been a nice man; a man with dignity and compassion. He cared deeply about her, but their union was all too brief. His death was another blemish in Billie's past. Since then she'd sought happiness in others, but no-one had come close.

She'd decided long ago that there was no point in going for looks in a man because that meant she was doomed to failure. It was the same with money, or sex. A combination of all three usually meant that the man was famous, married, or committed to someone else. They were heartbreakers. The only man any woman needed was someone who made her smile. If you were smiling, life wasn't as shitty as you first thought when you got up that day. Of course, all this became compromised when you were having a bad day. And with her fortieth birthday just around the corner, today was a bad day.

"Mother?"

Her thoughts returned to Sebastian. "Blanche and I were free spirits in 1939. At sixteen I thought men wanted me. But all along they only ever wanted sex."

Sebastian squirmed. Maybe he shouldn't have asked the question.

"The war was coming, and men were leaving in their droves. I got pregnant and your father offered to marry me. Blanche tried to persuade me not to. If I had known that I would be a widow in six months I would have listened to her."

"What did grandad have to say?"

"Dad was magnificent. The worst thing he did was shake his head when I told him I was pregnant. He sat in that chair." She pointed at Tommy's chair next to the fire. "And all he said was 'I love you, Billie. I'm sorry I couldn't be more of a mother as well as a father to you.'"

The tears began to roll down Billie's cheeks. She dabbed them with a tiny pink frilled hankie that she withdrew from her handbag.

Sebastian choked back his emotions. He was getting something from his mother that he never expected. A silence lengthened between them, neither choosing to break it, and both of them thinking their own thoughts.

Eventually she said, "I don't know what you think of me, Sebastian. I'm not the best mother in the world. I've made my mistakes – probably more than most – but I've always tried to do the right thing. Honest I have."

Sebastian reached across to his mother and raised her into his arms. "I love you, mam. We might not have had the best start in life but we're OK, aren't we? We've got each other. And grandad is always around to put us right."

She lifted her face and gazed lovingly into his eyes. "Yes, we have, son. We're a family. A slightly crazy family, yes, but we do have each other." She kissed him lightly on the lips and pushed him away as though she had become slightly conscious of what she'd disclosed. "Do you want a cup of tea?"

She didn't wait for a reply and vanished into the kitchen. The clatter of cups and saucers gave them both time to collect their thoughts. Then Billie's voice floated into the room. "Anyway, you asked about Blanche. There was one time I asked her about her friends and she said 'It's alright Elvis singing *Love Me Tender* but sex is just a functional act. In reality it's not very pleasant unless you're in the mood for it, or in love with the person you're with. What is it really? In truth it's a lot of embarrassing 'ooohs' and 'aaaahs' with plenty of pushing and shoving and unpleasant sights and smells. And when it's all over you have the problem of extracting yourself from the situation without hurting yourself or your partner. You say nice things and act as though you've had a brilliant time, but after all's said and done, you just want him to piss off and leave some money on the mantelpiece.'"

"Mother!"

Billie entered the room with a tray and teapot. She waved away the protestation from her son. "Not literally of course. But you have to realise it's like that for a woman. She's got to get something out of a relationship. If it's a ring that's fine; if it's not, then it's every woman for herself. Blanche always says that if you've got some blokes balls in your hand, you can either stroke them or squeeze them. Either way, you can make him do what you want."

Sebastian surprised himself. He was shocked. He'd never heard his mother say anything like this before. Luckily, before he was forced to comment, he heard the sound of the front door slamming against the cold and a few seconds later a ruddy faced Tommy Heath rolled into the room with his cap on, his pipe in his mouth and a *Shields Gazette* under his arm.

"Aaah just in time for tea."

Billie and Sebastian looked at each other and burst into laughter.

"What?" said Tommy.

The remnants of sausage, egg and chips were congealing on Tommy's plate as he sat and read the newspaper. He'd told Sebastian of his 'quick' farewell drink in the *Old Highlander* and how he'd met some like-minded people there. The quick drink led to three more pints and a hearty send-off for the place. The cold weather hadn't spoilt a good afternoon.

"Anything new in the paper, dad?" said Billie as she lounged across the settee. It was something of a ritual in the family to ask Tommy about the news.

"The Electric's going up in April. That's probably because we've used up most of it in the past month. Kennedy wants us to join the Common Market but that prat De Gaulle's not too keen on it. Bloody idiot, he is. He forgets who rescued him and his country during the war. Oh! And that dog that was taken off the shipwreck the other day has been sent back to Athens. It's been given to some other sailor to be taken home. Something to do with quarantine laws." He peered over the paper. "Are you not going out with Jack tonight?"

"He's working. He's out trying to catch that burglar that's been giving the police a hard time. I hope they catch him soon. Jack's really worked up about it. He hasn't got time for anything else these days."

Tommy glanced at Sebastian, who sat in an armchair with his eyes closed. He said, "I'm sure a man of his expertise and enterprise can manage to catch a little thief in the dead of night. After all, there can't be many people wandering the streets in the early hours of the morning, never mind a bloke with a hooped shirt, mask and a bag marked SWAG."

Despite having his eyes closed Sebastian smiled at that one. The stereotypical image of a burglar didn't fit at all with the image of Sammy. If the police were looking for a burglar dressed like that, then Sammy could quite cheerfully walk down King Street with a television under his arm and not be stopped by Jack Tozer and his team.

Sebastian stretched and stood up.

Tommy said, "And what about you? Are you going to see your flaming redhead?"

"No. I'm not. She's not *my* flaming redhead. She's her own woman."

"That's a nice thing to say, son." Billie said.

Tommy rolled his eyes. "What's she doing tonight? Curled up in bed reading the Communist Manifesto? Or is she trying to work out who will succeed Gaitskell?"

"I don't know. I'm not seeing her until next Friday. I think she's gone down south to see her mother. She's a bit poorly."

"Well that's OK. You have to look after your parents. Look at your mother, she's looking after me now." His gaze landed on Billie. "Another cup of tea, pet, if you wouldn't mind?" He held out his empty mug to her. She took it unquestioningly and went into the kitchen to put the kettle on.

"As a matter of fact," said Sebastian quietly. "I'm going to see Blanche."

Tommy shot him a suspicious look without saying anything.

Billie shouted from the kitchen, "Tell her I'll catch up soon."

He wrapped up against the cold and walked the short distance to Blanche's. As he reached the bottom of the street, he saw a man leave the house and duck into a car. Sebastian wasn't close enough to see who it was. He felt a bit uncomfortable going to see Blanche when one of her 'friends' had just left, but he was here now and might as well pay a call anyway.

He knocked on the door and waited a few moments. A straight-faced Blanche answered.

"Come in," she said a little too brusquely for Sebastian's liking.

"Is this a bad time?"

She shook her head. "No. Why do you ask?"

"It's just that I saw…"

"Oh, him. Oh no, no, no. He wasn't a friend in that way. He isn't a friend in any way at all. He's just someone who works for a friend from a long time ago. It's nothing."

Sebastian wasn't quite convinced. Her description of the man didn't make much sense, but whatever Blanche did, or whoever she saw, was of no concern to him.

She said, "Would you like a drink? A drop of rum?"

"Yes, please. That would be nice."

She poured two drinks and they settled down to chat in the easy way of a brother and much older sister, honest, open, caring, a shared past, not even a hint of sexual tension.

"I'm not a prostitute, Sebastian," Blanche said at one point. "But don't forget that even a prostitute has the right to choose who she shares a bed with. She has her own rules and criteria. If she makes a mistake, she suffers the consequences of losing money or exposing herself to violence. A prostitute has more scars than a hero from Greek mythology. Only the scars are not so visible." She laughed. "It's just the way I work. My friends leave me a few quid for their bed, breakfast and evening meal. I'm like a B&B, but I get to choose my clients and what I do with them."

"You're not worried what the neighbours think?"

"I couldn't give a toss. No-one has said anything. Everybody is too concerned about making their own way in the world to notice someone else trying to do the same thing. Trains, buses and cars are full of people with their own hang-ups and focus. They don't seem to realise that they are like wallpaper; a background to someone else's pattern. Some people try to stand out from the crowd, but others, like me, are happy to remain beige. Beige is the colour of blended lives."

Sebastian thought about that. Did he have a blended life? Was he content to be beige? Maybe so. He hadn't exactly stood out from the crowd, but then again, did he want to. His business needed customers and he had to promote it. That meant having some sort of profile that was easily recognisable. But at the same time, some of his business crossed the boundaries of legality. And then it wasn't wise to have a high profile. It was difficult to place himself. Did he value his work and life so far? That wasn't an easy question to answer also. Would he prefer someone else's lifestyle? He hadn't really thought about it. Was he happy with himself? The fact that he couldn't provide an answer indicated that he wasn't confident of his response. Alice was a long way from being beige. She was trying to be anything but.

He recognised that people tended to over value themselves, that they only had to live to be a good person. They believed their judgement to be infallible. They thought their opinions counted for something. Others measured themselves against their friends, usually in a positive light, but nobody wanted to swap lives with their friends, because their friend's lives were just as boring as their own. Of course, they may covet their bank balance or house or loved ones, but when push came to shove the lives they led were of their own making. It's what they were used to, it's what they were happy with.

Sebastian sipped his rum. The rich, warm liquid quickly gave him the inner comfort that only alcohol can give.

Blanche said, "Have you seen that strange man you mentioned to me last time you were here?"

"As a matter of fact, I have. I've seen him around a few times. Strange fella."

Blanche looked pained.

"Why? What's the matter?"

"Noth ... nothing," she stammered.

"It can't be nothing, Blanche. Your face says otherwise."

Blanche sighed. "Can you describe him to me?"

Sebastian shrugged. "OK. I'd say he is probably about five eight tall, thick black hair, swarthy complexion, bit of a moustache. He spoke as if he knew something I didn't, in an accent that was a little bit Geordie but a little bit foreign. I can't identify it."

"Anything else?"

"Not really. He was very well dressed. His clothes were of good quality. He didn't get those from *Weaver to Wearer*."

"What about his skin?"

"His skin?" Momentarily, Sebastian was nonplussed. Then he remembered their previous conversation. "He had a funny little tattoo on his hand. A little stick man, like *The Saint*."

Blanche closed her eyes and groaned something unintelligible.

"What is it?" Sebastian asked.

"You don't want to know, Sebastian."

"Yes, I do. What is it? Who is he? He's called Shafiq."

"Oh God!"

"Blanche. Who is he?"

"The tattoo. Is it like a little man dancing over some water?"

Sebastian nodded. The way Blanche slumped into her chair suggested that this wasn't going to be good news."

"It's a gang tattoo."

"And?"

"They've been running Shields for years."

"You mean running, as in ruling? I've heard about them, how can you live in the town and mix in the circles I work in without hearing them mentioned along the way, but I don't know anything about them. It never occurred to me to find out about them. I thought they were big time criminal types, like Al Capone. They've never been part of anything I've been involved in before."

She nodded.

"It all started with the Mill Dam riots just after the Great War in 1919. They say it was a riot that was racially motivated, but it was more about jobs. Some Yemenis were arrested, and some were deported. The same happened in 1930. This time a policeman was stabbed. The police seemed to favour the locals over the Yemenis. Those were bad times for foreigners. All they wanted was work, but the Shields folk resented it. They saw foreigners taking away their right to work, though some locals married and had babies that were obviously half-caste." She looked Sebastian firmly in the eyes. "I was one of those early babies."

Sebastian didn't realise he'd been holding his breath. He let it out in one whoosh before filling his lungs again.

"Some of the Yemeni community resented the fact that they were being considered as second-class citizens to the locals. They formed a group that worked to get around local customs and practices. Inevitably, they did some bad things, but they grew stronger and stronger. They managed to infiltrate local businesses and bribe a few councillors and policemen. They identified themselves through the tattoo of a man dancing on sand."

The news hit Sebastian like a gale force wind. Sand Dancers was the name that people in the North East gave to people from South Shields, much like the more generic Geordies that applied to everyone from Tyneside, or Wearsiders from Sunderland.

Blanche said, "You should never cross a member of the Sand Dancer gang."

Sebastian gulped the remainder of his rum and poured himself another.

"So Shafiq is part of the Sand Dancer gang?"

Blanche nodded slowly.

"What does he want with me?"

"I don't know. But there must be some sort of angle they're interested in. They like to take their time. They won't be in a hurry that's for sure."

"Blanche, how do you know this?"

"I ..." She bowed her head and become subdued. "... get to know things ... you know ... through my friends."

Sebastian's brow narrowed querying the remark.

She said, "I just listen. They talk about anything and everything. They speak about whatever comes into their head and I help them do it." She thought for a while then said, "It's such a boost to their ego. It means that they're interesting, or at least what they're saying is interesting." She smiled. "I keep a diary. I've done it for years. No-one knows about them. Well, no-one except you now."

"Do you have any friends who are Sand Dancers?"

Blanche shook her head.

Sebastian made a mental note to discuss the Sand Dancers with his grandad; he would know about them. He might even ask Jack Tozer.

Thursday 31st January 1963

Tommy Heath, as usual sat with a cup of tea in one hand and the local newspaper in the other. The smell of fried onions wafted in from the kitchen where Billie was in the process of making bangers and mash with thick onion gravy. As he read the news, he debated in the back of his mind whether there would be peas and a large Yorkshire pudding on his plate, or would he have butter beans instead of the peas. He loved butter beans.

The past week had been a typical one for him. Tonight was his last shift before the weekend off. Not that it mattered. The weather meant that Tyne Dock was quiet. This meant that the usual whores and local spivs had kept clear of the area – which also meant that he had nearly nothing to do apart from listen to the radio and read papers and magazines. There was always something to read in the cabin, some of it questionable.

Saturday had brought the announcement of power cuts in the Midlands. A couple of days later saw the closure of a couple of roads near to the shipwreck due to the volume of sand that had been blown from the beach onto the roads by the gale force winds. The temperature had soared to nearly three degrees, giving the impression that a thaw was in the offing. But that hadn't mattered to The Queen as she flew out of the country to visit Australia and New Zealand as part of an official tour. More worrying for Tommy was the report of more people trying to escape from East Germany to West Germany. What was so horrible there?

The door opened and Sebastian walked in. "Mmmm! Something smells good."

"Sit yourselves down at the table," said the voice from the kitchen. "It's nearly ready."

Tommy heaved himself from his chair and allowed the paper to fall on the floor. Sebastian sat opposite him. He picked up the knife and idly inspected it. Then he did the same with his fork. Tommy looked at him with curiosity.

"What are you expecting to find?"

Sebastian shook his head. "Nothing. I don't know why I did that."

"You've been a bit distracted in the last few days, son. Everything alright?"

Sebastian nodded then said, "Yeah, business is OK. Could be better, could be worse. The weather's not helping."

The food arrived. No butter beans – just peas with two medium sized Yorkshire puddings each. Billie sat down and they started eating.

Tommy said, "Sebastian's just saying that business is OK. Does he look like everything's OK?"

Sebastian ate a sausage without comment but saw his mother giving him a searching look. Billie waited for a reply that wasn't forthcoming.

She said, "Is anything the matter, son?"

Sebastian put down his fork and said, "I have got something on my mind. And before you ask it's got nothing to do with the business and even less to do with Alice. I think I need to speak to Jack."

Billie froze, and even Tommy hesitated a moment.

"You're not in any trouble are you, lad?" said Tommy, his voice gaining an edge that wasn't there before.

"No, nothing like that. I need some information. Some *official* information I mean. I need to know about a bunch of people that you might have heard of, grandad, but I don't want folklore or speculation. I want the truth."

"You'd better spit it out, lad. You're beginning to worry me a bit. And I can see your mother getting a bit anxious as well. C'mon, let's have it."

Sebastian put down his knife next to the fork. Most of the food remained uneaten. The other two plates on the table weren't seeing much action either. He wiped his mouth and took a drink of water.

"What are Sand Dancers?"

Both Tommy and his daughter let out an audible sigh of relief.

"Are you taking the piss, son? We're all Sand Dancers. We were born in South Shields."

"I'm not talking about us, or our neighbours. I'm talking about the Sand Dancers gang.

Billie dropped her knife onto the plate. Her Yorkshire pudding catapulted onto the floor spraying gravy over her pinny. Tommy deliberately sat back on his chair and wiped his mouth, giving him some time to think.

"What's brought this on?"

"What do you mean?"

"Exactly as I say. You don't bring something like that into the conversation unless you have a point to make."

"I'm just asking who they are, that's all."

Billie retrieved her Yorkshire pudding from the floor and asked, "Why do you want to know about them?"

"So you know about them as well?"

Tommy said, "Sooner or later everybody in town knows about the Sand Dancers. They're a mostly foreigners although there are one or two locals amongst them."

Billie grabbed her son's hand. "Why do you want to know, son?"

Sebastian told them the story of Shafiq and his seemingly innocuous meetings. Tommy and Billie slowly finished off their dinner as the tale unfolded. Neither showed any sign of wanting to interrupt him. When he'd finished, Tommy and Billie stared at the centre of the table.

"So? What do you think?

Tommy said, "Just watch yourself, lad. These people can cause you a hell of a lot of damage. Be careful."

Billie said nothing.

Later that night Sebastian lay in bed and contemplated the conversation he'd had with his mother and grandad. They knew something that he didn't, but he got the distinct impression that they didn't want to talk about it. The advice was to wait and see. That was probably good advice. What he didn't want to do was to antagonise any situation, or any one person or group, least of all the Sand Dancers. He had a business to run, which depended on the good will of the Yemeni community. If the Sand Dancers wanted to exert some muscle, they could put him out of business. Yet he was intrigued that the gang had 'allowed' him to trade without any concessions or obvious 'protection'.

As the clock swept towards midnight Sebastian reflected on the month since New Year's Eve. It was an unusual habit. On the last day of every month he lay in bed and did his review. It wasn't a process that allowed him to justify his actions or reactions. It was a process that allowed him to remember what had gone on in his life, and how it affected him. It had started when he was on National Service and he found himself reminiscing on a regular basis. He'd ask himself two questions. 'How did I get here?' and 'What have I done recently?' Sometimes he'd ask the supplementary question, 'What have I learned?' The answers provided him with enough thoughts to give his own verdict on the month. The decisions were either 'good', 'bad' or 'indifferent'. Eventually, he decided that meeting Alice was the best thing to happen to him for a long time. Business was OK, and the wreck of the Adelfotis II an exciting event. The only real downside to the month was the appearance of the shady Shafiq. However, Sebastian's official version of January 1963 was that it was a 'good' month for him.

February 1963

9

Friday 1ˢᵗ February 1963

Alice was wrapped up against the severe cold. She wore a full-length mock fur coat with a Russian type fur hat and leather boots. It was early. The milkmen were out and about delivering their daily pints for hundreds of people yet to know that there had been a heavy fall of snow. She pointed the Wolseley down Ocean Road towards the sea front and carefully negotiated the suburban terrain. As she passed the junction with Woodbine Street she glanced to her right and caught a glimpse of the terraces that had stood for years.

These houses were old, cold and damp. A hundred years of dust and grime caked the walls. A thousand voices had lived, laughed and screamed in these houses during that time. Comedies and tragedies abounded. Yet despite the accumulated poverty they embraced, there were remnants of a culture that was in terminal decline. Alice had seen a report recommending the demolition of these properties. Once these houses were emptied and the echoes of family empires extinguished, there would be a fleeting moment when they would resemble the scene of a crime after the cleaners had been, and before the demolition men came to dismantle the walls of history.

The older generations were dying or were being moved on. The passage of time was moving relentlessly forward casting aside the ill, the infirm and the old. The war had been over for nearly seventeen years but some people from hereabouts still lived their lives as though it was an enduring distant conflict. Their environment hadn't changed. Some of the buildings and houses were remnants from before the previous war. The landscape was testament to the trials and tribulations of the developed industrial carnage that had provided sustenance to an impoverished workforce eking out an existence. A dirty heritage of rotting wood, cobbled roads and a rat infested riverside kept progress at bay. Yet, the new generations wanted it all but weren't prepared to wait like their parents and grandparents.

They wanted it now. The new generations wanted to tear down their heritage and replace it with something modern, whatever that was. 'New' meant modern, and to get 'new' you had to tear out the heart, which was firmly entrenched in 'old'. The government had a phrase for it – slum clearance. They behaved like the Sorcerer in Aladdin by offering the equivalent of 'new lamps for old.' New was better, wasn't it?

Alice knew she was being stupid by coming out at this time of the morning after a heavy snowfall. It was an unnecessary risk to her safety – she could skid off the road or be trapped in a drift, but she figured that the main town centre roads would be comparatively free. She was partly right. The Council snowploughs had been out for several hours already. However, the idea of capturing the stark contrast of the wreck amidst a beautifully white unsullied carpet of snow was a photographic opportunity not to be missed. Photography was a hobby of hers. The photograph would be a metaphor for the politics of the day; the rusting wreck of the current Tory regime being surrounded by the cleansing purity of socialism. The prospect excited her. She parked the car at the bottom of Lawe Road and made her way through the North Marine Park carrying her *Leica III* camera. She was captivated by the serenity of it all. Momentarily, she forgot about the wreck and stood observing the pristine splendour of nature. Her concentration was spoiled by a noise from behind a bush. A few moments later, a cat sauntered towards her then turned and scampered away in a flurry of powdered snow. Strange to see a cat, she thought. She moved on slowly through the pathways, the light becoming dimmer, all the time casting huge shadows.

Suddenly, there was another sound, similar to the first, but closer. She turned and scanned a full 360 degrees but saw nothing. She was now distracted and decided to hurry out of the park to fulfil her plan. Just as she got to the exit she saw another set of footprints in the snow going in the opposite direction. Curious, she thought I haven't seen anyone ...

Before she could complete the thought, she was knocked violently to the ground. A short stocky figure dressed in black leapt on her and covered her mouth before she could scream. Screaming wasn't an option. Alice could hardly breathe; the air having been expelled from her lungs during the initial assault. She struggled and then saw the flash of steel as it was waved before her eyes. Her assailant didn't speak. His face was covered by some sort of woollen hat that had slits in it for eyes. The blackness of them seared through her mind and she instantly stopped struggling. Her captor was breathing heavily laden alcohol fumes at her He pressed the point of his knife to her throat. Alice thought that this was the way she would die.

The man fumbled beneath her coat and felt her breasts. A few seconds later his hand was between her legs. Fear ripped through her. She was going to be raped before having her throat cut. From deep within, her primordial ancestry rebelled. She bit down hard and her teeth cut through his finger to the bone. *He* was the one that screamed. She tried to throw him off her, but he slapped her across the face – hard. She tasted the dull iron of her own blood. Her fear intensified and she writhed around the ground trying to unseat her attacker. She sensed him pause, then saw the knife coming towards her face in a huge arc. She closed her eyes knowing that death was imminent. She felt the impact near her temple and her consciousness immediately disappeared into a black hole.

The Ingham Infirmary in South Shields was named after the town's first Member of Parliament and dealt with all of its accidents and emergencies. It stood less than a hundred yards from Ede House, where the Constituency Labour Party was housed and where Alice was now employed. The ninety-year-old main building had been redeveloped and extended over the years but there was talk of it being replaced by a new General Hospital on an existing site a couple of miles away.

Sebastian sat in a pea green painted room. He'd been there for two hours waiting for updates on Alice's condition. He replayed the sequence of events, as told to him, over and over again.

He'd been awakened by the loud rapping of the door knocker. Jack Tozer stood there.

"Your lady friend's in the Ingham. She's been assaulted."

It took Sebastian a few seconds to absorb the information. Eventually he said, "What happened?"

"Someone attacked her in the North Marine Park early on. She was found unconscious. They've taken her to the Ingham. Last I heard she was still unconscious. By the way, this is all unofficial. I didn't tell you this."

Sebastian nodded. "Thanks, Jack. I'll go straight up there."

It took Sebastian nearly an hour to get ready and walk through the snow to the Infirmary. Traffic was light. Buses were almost non-existent. He'd entered the hospital through the vehicular entrance and found out where Alice had been taken. He'd only gained access because he'd described himself as her 'next of kin,' a title he claimed by declaring her as his fiancée.

A nurse entered the room – breaking his reverie.

"Mister Crawley?"

"Yes."

"You can come through now. Please bear in mind that Alice has had a severe bang on the head and suffered other contusions and abrasions to the face. I wouldn't advise visiting for more than ten minutes or so. The police have asked us to inform them when she regained consciousness. We'll be doing that shortly. They'll want to interview her."

A nod was all he could muster.

He followed her through to a room off the main ward. Alice lay still on a bed, her red hair a stark contrast to the white sheets and pillowcases.

"Alice?" said the nurse. "Your fiancée's here?"

"Who?"

"It's me, love," said Sebastian as he leaned over and kissed her lightly on the lips.

The nurse said, "Ten minutes, no more," and left.

Alice's face was discoloured, with one or two scratches over her nose and cheeks. Her bottom lip was cut and swollen. Her hair was matted and dirty.

"I'm not looking my best," she said in obvious discomfort.

"What happened?" he asked.

She related the story as best she could. Sebastian felt himself getting angrier at each word.

"The nurse said I was found a few seconds after I was attacked. Apparently, a policeman saw my car parked in the street and followed my footsteps into the park. The man who attacked me had already run off. I don't know what would have happened if that policeman hadn't been suspicious. The man who attacked me took my camera and my coat." She smiled briefly before the pain reminded her to take it easy. "Anyway, when did we become engaged?"

Sebastian coloured. "I'm sorry. I had to tell the nurse some story, didn't I?"

"Well that must be the shortest engagement on record."

Just then a burly man swept through the door. "I'm Detective Sergeant Smith from South Shields CID." To Sebastian he said, "And who might you be?"

Sebastian identified himself.

"I need you to leave, sir. I have a few questions to ask this lady that are quite delicate. I'm sure you'll understand."

Sebastian didn't understand at all, but he kissed Alice on the lips and told her he would visit later.

He walked up to Dean Road and found a cafe. Two bacon sandwiches and a mug of tea later, he was walking down Laygate Lane towards Holborn, where he called in to see Sammy.

They sat in the front room. Sammy's parents were out. Sebastian told him of this morning's events.

Sammy said, "What kind of twisted bastard assaults women at that time of the morning?"

Sebastian shrugged. "I don't suppose we'll ever find out, unless the police get lucky."

Sammy shook his head. "The police should put a lot more effort into catching these sorts of criminals. It's a bloody disgrace."

Sebastian smiled. "They've got a special squad trying to catch you."

Sammy sat up straight. "What?"

"The police are looking for you. They're working nightshifts specially to catch you. You've become a pain in the arse to them. They want you."

Sammy was more than a little proud of the fact that he had been so successful that a special squad had been assembled to catch him. Public enemy number one. That was him. The criminal mastermind of South Shields: Samir al-Aziz. But at the same time, he was concerned that the chances of him being caught had risen significantly, although he'd not been active since the turn of the year. However, funds were getting low and he needed to bring some money in soon.

"I'll have to be careful."

"It would be better to stop doing it altogether and think yourself lucky you got away with it all this time."

He grinned. "I am a lucky person, Sebastian."

"You're a jammy bastard, I'll give you that, but I still think that you can't go on forever. You're bound to cop it sooner or later."

"Thanks for the information. I'll be careful."

Sebastian left the house and trudged his way back to Catherine Street He was determined to have forty winks before his trip to see Alice at visiting time.

Steven 'Bull' Cowell waited outside High Shields Railway Station. To all intents and purposes waiting for a taxi, but that was just a ploy to outwit any nosey parker or passing policeman. He was waiting for Sammy.

He had followed Sammy's advice and wore shoes with a good grip for climbing, leather gloves for comfort and to stop fingerprints, black trousers, shirt and a black donkey jacket. He'd argued that wearing black was stupid when there was snow all over the place, but Sammy told him he'd been successful because he had planned everything properly. These were his rules, so Bull had given in.

It was just after midnight when Sammy appeared, looking as fresh as a daisy. He was dressed completely in black with the addition of a black hat. He threw a black balaclava to Bull and told him to wear it.

"Are you ready? Or do you want to scrap the idea before you start?"

"No. I need to do this. I've got debts."

"I'll tell you again. You do exactly what I say at all times. The last thing we need is for you to go off on your own. This isn't a game, Bull. This is dangerous. If we get caught it'll mean that we both go to prison."

"I know that, Sammy. Let's cut the cackle and get on with it." He started walking towards the Town Centre.

Sammy shook his head. "You're not listening to me. I decide when and where we go. Listen!" He grabbed Bull by the arm. "Sebastian came to see me today. He said that the police have got a special squad out working nights to catch me. I've given it some thought, and I've decided that I'm keeping away from the Town Centre for the time being. We'll be going to the Laygate area. And before you start shouting your mouth off, I know it's closer to home, but I also think it's better to steer clear of the police for the time being. Besides, if they're looking in the Town Centre then they're not looking at Laygate."

Bull shrugged. It made sense. He followed Sammy's lead and headed under the bridge towards Laygate.

Half an hour later Sammy and Bull were crouched in the back yard of a shop in Frederick Street. They had been there for a full five minutes allowing their night vision to kick in. A frost was forming over the snow making it crisp ... and unreliable. Their breath hung in the air.

Sammy whispered, "This place should be easy. There's no alarm and the back door's rotten."

Bull nodded and followed Sammy to the door. Sammy put his ear against the wood and listened for a few seconds. He peered through the window. When he'd visited the shop that afternoon, one of four he'd visited, he'd made mental notes on the layout as best he could. He knew there was a storeroom and office at the rear, although he didn't know what was kept there. He tested the resistance of the door and jammed his foot in the bottom to create extra tension. A short, powerful shoulder charge caused the lock keep to collapse and leave the door ajar.

Bull smiled. Surely it wasn't that easy. He moved to enter the shop

Sammy put his finger over his mouth to silence him. "Wait to see what happens," he hissed.

After two minutes had passed, Sammy entered the shop and started looking around. "Don't touch anything unless you have to," he ordered

He went from room to room and eventually picked up a cash box. He smiled to himself. What was the point of having a cash box if you leave the key in? He opened it and took around £20, which he stuffed in his pocket. There was little else. He signalled to Bull that he was finished. Bull nodded towards some cigarettes. Sammy shook his head. Despite his instructions, Bull picked up five packs of cigarettes and put them in his pockets. Sammy's eyes flashed in anger. Bringing Bull was a bad idea.

They made their way into the back yard and stood for a few seconds just in case anyone was walking past. They climbed back over the wall and made their way up the back lane. Even if the police stopped them now, what would they find? One man would have a few quid in his pocket and another far too many cigarettes for his own health.

Jack Tozer sat on an old battered car seat in a local taxi office supping a cup of tea. He'd talked to one or two of the drivers and mentioned that there was an initiative going on to catch burglars, and if any of them saw anyone acting suspiciously, they should report it to the police. He knew it was a shot in the dark. A lot of the taxi drivers sailed close to the wind themselves, and he felt nothing would come of it. However, there was one or two who were decent men trying to do an honest day's work. He'd also given the same message to some milkmen the previous morning. If he didn't catch this mysterious burglar, then it wasn't for the want of trying. His men were out there combing the Town Centre, front and back, always on the alert, though he knew that these were experienced police officers, and experienced police officers had a habit of finding themselves nice warm places to hide during weather like this. There was an old saying that said a good policeman never gets wet. He grimaced to himself. He was sitting in a taxi office and he could feel it in his bones that his team would be in similar places, out of the cold night air.

Sammy shuffled up onto the factory roof. A panting Bull clambered up beside him. They crouched low against the skyline. They had already burgled four shops and offices and taken cash and office equipment, and a couple of rings and a necklace found in a drawer. The haul was wrapped and hidden in a special place ready for collection during daylight hours. This was their last job of the night. It was nearly four o'clock. They hadn't seen any patrolling police officers. In fact, in four hours they had only seen two cars moving down Frederick Street.

"Be careful here, Bull. These flat roofs are OK to walk on but they've got loads of skylights and air ducts and things. You have to watch where you're going. We need to get into the middle to get access to the main skylight. There's a maintenance ladder just inside. Once we're in, we can access the manager's office. I have some good information that there's going to be a few hundred quid there over the weekend. I was going to do it tomorrow by myself but seeing that there's no police about we might as well do it now."

Bull nodded vigorously. A few hundred quid! That would enable him to pay off a big part of his debts.

They traversed the roof quickly and reached the large skylight in minutes. Sammy examined the catch and found it to be padlocked.

"Damn!" he said, "I didn't expect that."

"But it's only a small lock. We can snap it off."

Sammy shook his head. "No. It'll cause too much noise. Someone might hear us."

Bull looked at him in desperation. "I'll find something."

"No, Bull. Come on, let's go. We'll come back some other time."

"But a few hundred pounds, Sammy. That's a lot of money."

"It's too dangerous."

Sammy started to retrace his steps back to where they had reached the roof. He was about halfway across when he realised Bull wasn't behind him. He was still over by the large skylight levering the padlock off with some sort of pole. Sammy cursed under his breath and started back. Just as he reached him, the padlock snapped. Bull lost balance and fell against the skylight. Sammy saw a brief look of pleasure on Bull's face turn to surprise before the skylight collapsed and he fell through the hole. A split second later he heard a crash of glass and a dull thud. Sammy scrambled to the hole. A nightlight partially lit the scene below. Bull was lying immobile on the floor, his head at an impossible angle to his body. A pool of blood spread around him.

Sammy gaped in horror. He could see quite clearly that Bull wasn't breathing and he was very badly hurt. He started to descend the maintenance ladder knowing that he would leave traces of his visit behind, but he couldn't do nothing. What if Bull was actually alive and needed help? Then a torch beam cut through the night sky and a security guard appeared. Sammy crouched back on the roof, calculating that the security guard would not spot him from the ground, but his egress from the factory was cut off and there was no way he could get to Bull. He would have to wait it out. If Bull was still alive, the security guards would call for an ambulance.

The pool of blood surrounding Bull had stopped broadening. Torch beams crisscrossed the factory. It started snowing. Sammy began to cry. Small, snuffling sobs at first, followed by deep, frightened, silent screams. He sucked in air and held it until he couldn't hold it any further. He gasped it out and refilled his lungs again and again until panic subsided. He began shivering. He didn't know if it was the cold or shock.

A second torch beam joined the first.

"What have we got here?" said a voice with authority.

"Hello, officer. I heard a noise like a window being smashed. I reported it and came out to check. I can't find anything, though, unless there's something on top."

"You can't check up there in this weather. You sure it was breaking glass?"

"Absolutely positive. It *might* have come from somewhere else. But it was too close for that. I was speaking to Sergeant Tozer the other day. We worked together when I was a constable. He told me about some break-ins that were going on. Maybe this is one of them. We need to get the keyholder out to check the premises."

"You go and call him out and I'll look around here."

The security man left, and the unknown constable switched off his torch.

Sammy lay on the roof a few yards above the policeman's head. After a few seconds he caught the whiff of cigarette smoke as the officer occupied the silence. Sammy was doomed. Should he surrender himself or make a dash for it? He didn't have the heart to try and escape. He would give himself up and tell the truth to the officer. He was heading for prison anyway, but he needed to explain how Bull had met his maker.

A car pulled up outside the factory. Sammy heard the officer below him utter some profanity and saw the cigarette arc into the snow when it was discarded. The officer walked slowly to the car and spoke to the driver. It became obvious that the driver was another police officer when the constable got into the vehicle. The car idled. Sammy saw two cigarette ends burning inside it.

This was an opportunity to make his escape. The two policemen were in the car at the front of the premises. The security guard would be in the office at the side of the premises calling the keyholder, and Sammy's point of egress was at the rear. With one last glance at his friend, Sammy crawled over the roof and lowered himself down to the ground through a series of gradually lowering levels. He quickly entered the darkness and remained there for a few moments until the strength and feeling returned to his body. He kept to the shadows and took a circuitous route back to his home via Templetown.

He collapsed on his bed but was unable to sleep. The image of Bull spread-eagled on the factory floor haunted him. The police would find out who Bull was and make enquiries, so it would be only a matter of time before they knocked on his door. And while he was in this state, he would crumble and tell them everything.

He thought back on the evening's events. He'd been careful as usual. There was nothing for the police to grab hold of, at least nothing that would lead them directly to him. No fingerprints. No stolen goods. Nothing. Except for Bull.

He looked around his room. What would the police find if they did come for him? The answer was - lots of things. He leapt from his bed and feverishly gathered together things that he thought would be incriminating. He put them all in a suitcase. The suitcase gave him an idea. He gathered some clothing together and grabbed the last remaining cash from his secret hideaway. He scribbled a note to his parents saying that he was going away on a business trip to Leeds. He dated it yesterday and said that he would be back probably in a week.

He walked out into the cold morning air and hurried over to High Shields Station to wait for the next train. There was one other person on the elevated platform.

"There must be something funny going on over there," he said pointing in the general direction of Laygate. "A couple of police cars and an ambulance came by a few minutes ago. Somebody's in the shit."

Sammy said nothing.

10

Sebastian left the house early to set up the stall in Market Place. He was expecting some new stuff today after one of his suppliers had left a note at his home yesterday afternoon. He was glad of it really. It would get him out of the house while the telephone engineer was installing the telephone in the passage. It had taken him months to convince his grandad that it would help in his business. Grandad's reluctance was centred on the 'fact' that nobody ever rings to tell you good news. Other arguments were that people would stop meeting and just talk on the phone, and then there was the cost factor. Sebastian's reassurance that all cost and the bills would be paid by him had swung the argument just before Christmas. Today was when the Heath and Crawley families joined the communications network.

By the time Sebastian reached the stall, Jackie had already got things under control. The box of new stuff had been delivered in a van about thirty minutes previously. Jackie knew from past experience that Sebastian liked to assess all new stuff straight from the box. It was the only way he could keep tabs on what was coming in and be sure that it tallied with the manifest.

Jackie said, "The police are busy today. There's something going on over in Laygate."

"An accident?"

"No, no. I mean something big."

"Like what?"

Jackie drew closer and whispered out of the side of his mouth. "I heard somebody died." And then added "in suspicious circumstances." He said it as though it was being announced on the BBC news.

"And what do you think these suspicious circumstances are, then?"

Jackie stopped what he was doing. He looked over both shoulders to make sure that no-one was in earshot before speaking. "I live in John Williamson Street, and I walk through Laygate to get here. Well, this morning I was passing one of the factories up there when I saw loads of policemen around one of them. One of my drinking pals is the security man there. An ex-copper. He told me that a burglar had fallen through the roof when he was breaking into the factory. He's dead."

Sebastian stood with his mouth open staring at Jackie.

"Boss? Is something the matter?"

Sebastian's brain froze. Sammy. He had only spoken to him yesterday. He hadn't mentioned he was going out burgling, although he wouldn't have said so anyway. He sat down on Jackie's chair.

"Boss?"

Sebastian shook his head. Jackie was looking at him with a half curious – half frightened expression.

"Sorry, Jackie," said Sebastian, "I get a shooting pain through my head every now and then. It's nothing," he lied.

Jackie nodded. "Got to keep an eye on things like that," he said as he started loading more goods onto the stall.

"Listen, Jackie, I'm going to meet a friend. I'll be back in about an hour or two. Can you manage?"

"Well" said Jackie drawing a deep breath, "I suppose so."

"I'll make it worth your while. Thanks."

Sebastian walked quickly away from Market Place and made the comparatively short journey to Sammy's house in Holborn within fifteen minutes. He rapped vigorously on the door but received no answer. He knocked again and waited. Still no response. The next-door neighbour opened their door and recognised Sebastian as a frequent visitor of Sammy.

"They are away for the weekend," The neighbour said in a thick accent.

Sebastian bit his lip in frustration. "And Sammy?"

"I have not seen Samir since yesterday." She paused. "Since you came."

Sebastian thanked her and wrote a note on a piece of paper he had in his pocket. It said, *Need to speak to you urgently about your business, Sebastian.* He shoved the note through the letterbox. He would have to call again later.

He walked slowly back to the stall.

Jackie was surprised to see him so soon.

"He was out," Sebastian said.

The rest of the day moved at a snail's pace. Sebastian checked his watch every few minutes, but it didn't help the time to hurry on. Eventually, he left Jackie to close up and paid him his wages, and a bonus.

Sebastian walked slowly down King Street although he could have been in his own world. The past thirty-six hours had been awful. He had visited Alice last night, but she had slept most of the time. The trauma of the incident was taking its toll. The likelihood was that she would be released today after seeing a consultant. That had been at the insistence of Uncle Jim, who had telephoned the hospital from the Houses of Parliament, which had given Alice immediate celebrity status, which she tried to play down.

And now Sammy, possibly dead after a burglary gone wrong. That had kicked the stuffing out of him. But it could be someone else. There was hope. There was more than one burglar in South Shields, and Laygate wasn't Sammy's preferred area. Not being able to contact Sammy made things complicated. He needed to know.

He bought a *Gazette* from the vendor at the end of the street and quickly scanned the pages. There was a small mention of an assault in the North Marine Park. It didn't mention who the victim was. Probably the result of another telephone call from Uncle Jim. It mentioned that the police were still making enquiries. There was nothing about a body being found, although that might appear in later editions. The *Gazette* wasn't printed on a Sunday, so unless the story was picked up by the regional Sunday papers it wouldn't appear until Monday. He couldn't wait until then to find out if Sammy was alive or not.

When Sebastian got home, he saw the new telephone on a small but elegant semi-circular table in the hall. He picked it up and heard a dial tone. He replaced the handset and walked into the living room.

Tommy sat in his chair and Billie on the settee. They were watching *Grandstand* on television.

"How's business?" said Tommy.

"OK"

"How's Alice?"

"OK"

Tommy glanced at Billie and she returned a quizzical expression. As far as Tommy was concerned, he had gone through the formalities of a conversation. Sebastian's replies had indicated that he didn't want to talk. He handed over the responsibility to his daughter.

She said, "Anything the matter, pet?"

Sebastian shrugged. "There's always something the matter these days, but nothing more than usual. Are you seeing Jack tonight?"

"As a matter of fact I am. I rang him with the new telephone. I made the first call about half an hour ago. He was due to be working night shift, but they've called it off. The burglar they were looking for has been found. Jack didn't say how or why, but he was a very pleased man when I spoke to him."

"Is he picking you up?"

"He is. Why?"

"You already know why. It's the Sand Dancers thing."

Tommy shook his head but said nothing.

"All I'll need is a few minutes alone with him. He might not tell me anything, but he never will if I don't ask him."

Half an hour later, Billie went into the kitchen to make sausage, egg and chips, another favourite of Tommy's. She then disappeared upstairs to put on her face and glad rags.

Within the hour, Jack Tozer stood in the living room in Catherine Street. It looked like he'd already had a whisky or two. His face glowed. "Your mother says you want a word with me," he said warily.

"I just want a bit of information, Jack, that's all."

"Oh yes? And what might that be?"

"I want to pick your brain about the Sand Dancers, in a criminal context, that is."

Jacks eyes blazed suspiciously. "Why?"

Sebastian frowned. "A guy called Shafiq has shown up on three occasions where I've been. He had a funny little tattoo on his hand. I was just wanting to know about them."

"Shafiq eh? Well, well, well. What did he want?"

"Nothing. Just conversation, that's all."

"Has he asked you to do anything for him?"

"No."

"Hmmm. They're a sly bunch. And that Shafiq fella is a smarmy bastard."

"So? What about the Sand Dancers?"

Jack sat down and reclined in the chair as if he owned the place and told Sebastian much the same as he already knew.

Sebastian said, "So as long as they just pass the time of day I'll be OK?"

Jack nodded, then said, "But watch out. If they've got an eye on you, it's only a matter of time before they ask you to do a favour for them. In your line of business, it might be something to do with importing something or exporting something. I can't for the life of me think why they would need to ask you to do anything else. You're not the biggest businessperson in town and you have as much influence as the man in the moon."

Sebastian disregarded the jibe. "What do they do?"

"They intimidate people. They persuade people to do things. They have a little bit of influence, though they rarely resort to outright violence. Their boss is a strange bloke who you don't often see. He has a few captains who organise things and do his dirty work. Like Shafiq. They're never in your face unless they need to be, and if they need to be, you're in trouble."

"I still don't see what they do? How do they make their money?"

Jack shrugged. "Nobody knows, but they have plenty. The local thugs rarely put up much of a resistance – not in the same league you see. But some of the gangs from Newcastle have shown some interest in the Sand Dancers, although nothing ever seems to come of it."

Sebastian wasn't getting the answers he wanted. Perhaps his grandad was right. Perhaps it was just as easy to let things go rather than stir up something that wasn't even a problem – yet. He decided to change the subject.

"Thanks for that, Jack. It's much appreciated. I hear you've caught your burglar."

Jack laughed, "I suppose you could say that, although he's not exactly admitting his crimes at the moment." He laughed even louder at his own joke.

"You mean he's clammed up?"

"He's not speaking at all."

"I don't know what you mean?"

"He's dead. The stupid bastard fell through the roof of a factory in Laygate. Landed on his head and snapped his neck like a twig. Serves him right. Now we can go through our records and write off our crime wave as being 'detected'. The Chief Constable and the Watch Committee will be pleased."

Sebastian tensed and tried to give the impression that he was underwhelmed by the whole thing. "So, no court case, then. I suppose the burglar's body has been taken away and the family informed."

Jack gave Sebastian a suspicious look. He said "I don't know. His family have been informed. The body will go to the morgue. There'll have to be a postmortem examination to establish cause of death, and then there'll be an inquest."

Sebastian thought, if Sammy was the burglar then Jack was saying his parents had been informed. But they were away for the weekend and, as far as he knew, no-one knew where that was. Perhaps it wasn't Sammy after all.

"One thing was funny, though," Jack added.

"What?"

"He was a big lad for a burglar. He had the build of a bloody rugby player."

"Perhaps you've got the wrong man."

"No. We're satisfied that we've got our burglar. There were a few other burglaries nearby, so we're running forensic tests to see if they tie in. We're confident, shall we say. Anyway, this is eating into my drinking time." He stood up and in a lowered voice said, "You let me know if that Shafiq fella asks you to do him a favour."

"OK."

Jack opened the door and shouted "C'mon, Billie, let's get going."

Billie came downstairs in a pall of perfume and kissed Sebastian goodbye. "See you tomorrow, love."

Sunday 3rd February 1963

Sebastian lay in bed trying to come to terms with the hangover that insisted it had a right to be recognised. Last night had seen his grandad break open a bottle of rum and they had consumed most of it between them. It had been good to spend some time with him. He was full of the old stories that Sebastian had heard many times before, but he had a knack of rehashing them to provide a new slant on things.

The evening had started badly. Sebastian had spoken to the hospital and discovered that Alice had been discharged. She wasn't at her usual address, unless she just didn't want to answer the phone. So, without an alternative, grandad's rum was much the better option, although he now regretted it.

He'd once been told by an alcoholic at his stall that alcohol is not normally thought of as a depressant, but it was. It depresses that inbuilt safety switch inside your head. That's the switch that stops you from putting yourself in danger or doing stupid things. But when the switch is flipped on and off constantly, it wears out and you cease to be in control. Eventually, you come across a green light that allows you to travel downhill towards a black tunnel. That's when you find out that gravity's taken over and the brakes don't work. And when you enter that dismal tunnel you can't tell where you're going because the only light you see is the light at the end of the tunnel, and it comes straight out of the roaring fires of Hell.

Sebastian hadn't got anywhere near that stage, but he did think that Jack Tozer was sailing pretty close to the mark. His lifestyle seemed to focus on alcohol and sex. Sebastian was absolutely sure that Jack loved alcohol more than he loved Billie.

He recalled the conversation with Jack.

His fears over the possibility of Sammy being the dead burglar had been unfounded. The description given by Jack didn't even remotely sound like Sammy, so whoever the unlucky man was didn't have any other significance to Sebastian, other than as a passing interest in another wasted life, but it was a hazard of his chosen profession, like a building site accident or a train crash.

Sebastian turned over in bed and waited for the pain to subside in his head. He glanced at the clock and decided that it was time to get up. A bacon and egg sandwich would put him back on the road to recovery. An *Alka Seltzer* wouldn't come amiss either.

Half an hour later, Sebastian wondered whether the egg and bacon had been such a good idea. He was considering making himself sick when there was a knock on the door. He eased his way along the passage and threw open the door to find Mick Monroe standing wide eyed on the step.

Mick said, "Bull's dead."

They stared at each while time stood still. When it decided to move on, Mick added "He fell through a skylight on a factory roof. They say he was burgling the place."

Sebastian staggered back into the passage. Mick took that as an open invitation to step in. He shut the door behind him. They both went into the living room just as Tommy came downstairs in his dressing gown and saw the ashen face of his grandson.

"What the Hell's this about

Sebastian answered. "Bull died while burgling a factory."

"Bloody Hell! I thought he was a nice lad. They're a nice family."

Sebastian said to Mick, "What happened?"

It took fifteen minutes for Mick to describe how the police went to Bull's house yesterday morning and took away his father to identify the body. The story about the burglary had been told to Mick by Bull's younger brother Alan. The family were stunned, as were Mick, Sebastian and Tommy.

Sebastian was putting things together. He knew that Bull wasn't a burglar, but he also knew that he owed money to a few people. It was hard to imagine that Bull would do something like that by himself so Sammy must have been with him when Bull had plunged through the skylight. He imagined that Sammy had been unable to save him and then realised at some point that Bull was dead and had left. Was he in hiding? And if so, where would he be?

"Bull's no burglar," Sebastian said.

"That's what I said to Alan. But he says the police are convinced that he was up to no good. Why else would you be on a factory roof at four o'clock in the morning?"

"I don't know, Mick, but Bull isn't a burglar, although we do know someone who is."

Tommy shot a glance at both of them, "And who might that be?"

Sebastian shook his head at him. "Sorry, grandad. It's none of your business. Better you don't know."

"So that's how it is, is it?" he growled. "I'd better go and make the tea, then." He stormed out of the room.

Mick said quietly. "We know Sammy is, but not Bull, never in a month of Sunday's. Surely you don't think they were working together?"

"I don't know," confessed Sebastian. "But I need to speak to Sammy to find out. I can't believe that they were working together. I'll smack his head if they were."

The next hour was spent in memories of times together in school, the difficult periods of teenage angst, and their development into young men. They were both agreed that Bull hadn't been gifted with intelligence, but he had been a loyal and devoted friend.

Sebastian imagined Bull's body in the mortuary of the hospital - it was next to the nurse's home. Yards away from the broken corpse, excited chatter and shrill laughter would filter through the walls to break the atmosphere. Nurses wrapped up against the weather would exit by the side door on their way to or from their shifts. It didn't matter to them. Death was a part of their working day. One body was just as dead as another; yet all around the country, people were feeling exactly as he felt at that moment.

Other people were praying, making love or giving birth. Many more were sleeping or eating or driving their cars. Some would be thinking that the world they lived in was difficult to fathom. They were right.

A few miles away from Catherine Street, Jack Tozer was lying in post-coital bliss while Billie was rustling up some breakfast downstairs. It had been a good few days so far. Firstly, the burglar had died because of his own incompetence, which meant that a whole lot of evidence gathering and painstaking enquiries wouldn't be necessary anymore. Secondly, he'd had a good drink, and, thirdly, Billie had surpassed herself last night. She never failed to satisfy him, though he had the solicitor's receptionist in mind when ravaging Billie. He smiled. Life was good at the moment. Tomorrow, he was back on dayshift, so he would pay a visit to the solicitor's office as part of his robust attention to criminal investigation.

Billie bustled into the bedroom carrying a tray with tea, and bacon sandwiches. Her housecoat had become undone and a pendulous breast hung free. Jack reached across and took the weight of it in the palm of his right hand.

"Now now, Jack," said Billie, "I've brought you breakfast in bed."

"Breakfast can wait," he growled as he pinched her nipple. "This can't." He pulled aside the sheets to reveal his readiness for action.

11

Monday 4th February 1963

Sebastian walked towards the town from Holborn. He was in a reflective mood. His life had been touched by exciting and violent events in the last week or two. It demonstrated that life at times, was fickle. He was thinking that there wouldn't be a man alive who hadn't considered his own mortality at one time or another, or their own sanity, or the sanity of a loved one. Any man who said he'd never thought himself mad at some time was, by definition, mad, because he was lying to himself.

What on earth was Bull thinking? Did he have a moment of insanity? Was his judgement flawed? Was he coerced?

Only Sammy would know what had happened, or at least he would be able to give some insight into the matter. However, another visit to Sammy's house had again proven fruitless. That, in itself, was suspicious. Something was very wrong. He needed to know 'why?'

Sebastian felt himself becoming emotional. He had lost control of his life. In a couple of days his world had become a mess, like he was inside one of those Christmas things with a yuletide setting and all someone had to do was shake it and the white flakes would be swept up into the water and settle like snow. He stopped at the top of Mill Dam and looked out over the river. Welder's arcs twinkled in the shipyards and the sound of riveting and windy hammers reverberated from afar.

His gaze swept through the people around him. They were part of the factory system. They clocked on and off, and in between they became part of a process that started with raw materials and churned out a definite article. In this case, the raw materials were the vibrant, eager workhorses of apprentices, and the definite articles were clapped out ghosts of weary, scarred men who coughed out spit and phlegm from damaged lungs that were blackening from the inside. Their pleasures were pigeons and pubs, football and fags, and the rituals of a visit to the town centre and market on Saturday mornings dressed in a suit and tie that had seen better days. They were like old paintings in a forgotten art gallery. Row after row of ancient frames carrying cracked canvasses of elderly men in their prime. Their names written beside them. And no-one remembered who they were.

Sebastian had once read that knowledge was about providing the right answer, but intelligence was about asking the right question. He figured that was just about right, but he also thought the two came together on occasions. Life wasn't that simple. If you thought too much about something, sometimes you forgot what it was you were thinking about. The world was too complex. He didn't need to know about things like nuclear fission or what lived in the sea. He cared even less about far flung places like Bolivia or Honduras. These were just places on the back of cards that came with a square of bubblegum. For some people, the right question was 'where is the next pay packet coming from?' The answer, in this case, was far more valuable.

He'd always thought that education in the formal sense ends by the time you are fifteen or sixteen. You have around ten years from starting to learn the ABCs to taking your final exams – if you make it that far. Most people got through life with what they learnt during those ten years, because they had eyes set on a job long before leaving school. Yes, some went on to university, albeit very few from this part of the country, but the intellectual development of most people was directed right from the start. We are told where our father's footsteps are, and we are expected to follow them. The factories, mines and shipyards applauded this. For every retiring journeyman there was a relative to take his place. The companies fed the ego of the working man and told them that their workmanship was the best in the world. They may be right, but the belief that countries and companies would continue to invest in their future was the equivalent of the community as a whole putting all its eggs in one basket. They never ever catered for the intrusion of some foreign egg collector or a potential rise in the population of cuckoos.

He watched the industry of the people thinking how, to them, education wasn't the same as schooling. Everyone needs to make a living, and sometimes schooling stands in the way of education. An apprentice endured the classroom only because they were required to by law. The writings of Shakespeare or Jane Austen failed to capture the imagination as much as wood or metal or the feel of tools in their hands. Verbs, adjectives and nouns were not the same companion as a hammer or saw or chisel. The battle between contemplation and a wage packet was an easy one for the working man. Contemplation didn't feed the kids and education was all about the certainty of a job well done and a thick brown envelope at the end of the week.

Sebastian trudged homeward down Coronation Street and then into Keppel Street. Before he crossed Fowler Street into Catherine Street, he looked up towards the Town Hall clock as it struck midday.

The building was a showpiece. It was a magnificent example of Edwardian engineering in its planning and construction. It had all the architectural bells and whistles, foibles and frippery anyone would expect in a fine community palace of power. It was ostentatious and graceful at the same time. It was imposing but practical. Yet the whole thing was pointless if the aesthetics of the building overshadowed or undermined its function, or the pretentious clamouring of the elected body failed to serve the needs of its people. The only other building in the Borough that offered to serve the needs of the public was the hospital. Nobody wanted to go there either.

Sebastian tramped up the street and entered the house. He made his way to the living room and opened the door. Tommy sat with a beaming smile on his face.

"Hello, son," he said. "You've had a visitor."

"Oh! Who might that be? Sammy?"

"Not even close. It was your lady friend, Alice. She's a smart lass for a socialist, I'll give you that. And she's quite easy on the eye, if you know what I mean, even with the bruises."

Sebastian's spirits lifted immediately. "When was that?"

Tommy glanced at the clock on the wall. "About an hour ago. She's got our telephone number now and she's going to ring you this afternoon. By the way, she told me about what happened the other day. That was a bit naughty. I hope Jack Tozer and his mates catch the bastard and put him behind bars."

"Yeah. I'll speak to Jack about it when I see him again. He's probably out making enquiries as we speak."

Jack Tozer *was* making enquiries. Although the questions he was asking related to the current status of Sylvia, the receptionist at the solicitor's office. Jack's eyes gleamed as she flounced around the office. He knew she was interested in him by the way she sat with a straight back and breathed deeply to accentuate her curves. For a forty-year-old woman she was definitely in the Diana Dors mould; a blond bombshell with a cleavage that stopped her feet getting wet in the rain.

He'd told her that enquiries were continuing into the office burglary, but he'd had little time over the weekend because he'd been out catching other burglars. Sylvia was enthralled. Real action excited her, and the rough, tough world of a crime-solving copper appealed to her sense of adventure. It wasn't long before they agreed to have a meal in a Newcastle restaurant later in the week. Jack couldn't stop himself from grinning as he made his way back to the station. He'd have to put off Billie this weekend. She would understand. She wouldn't ask too many questions. He'd make sure of that.

Later that evening, Sebastian sat in the Grosvenor Grill opposite Alice, eating a steak with all the trimmings. She ate chicken with some vegetables. He thought it had been a risky strategy on her behalf to arrange a meal here after the farrago of their disagreement a couple of weeks or so ago. Nevertheless, it was good to see her again. He noticed she was wearing make-up. It made her look even better. He never asked whether she was wearing it for aesthetic purposes or to cover up any blemishes caused by bruising or the effects of her assault. She looked relaxed. The nightmare scenario of a few days ago didn't appear to be lingering. Sebastian thought that she must be made of stronger stuff than he.

She had picked him up an hour previously and negotiated the weather again. Thank God for living near the sea, where the lying snow wasn't causing too much trouble, unlike the rest of the country, which was paralysed in some places. The first part of the conversation had covered the period of non-contact between him seeing her in hospital and her calling to see him earlier today.

It had been a political and safety-first decision by 'Uncle Jim' to remove Alice from the hospital. She'd been cared for by a nurse, but she'd dispensed with her services within twenty-four hours, such was the rapid improvement in her health. She now considered herself to be "fighting fit" and "ready to go back to work."

"So what have you been doing?" she enquired.

Sebastian had already decided that his worries over Sammy and the death of Bull wasn't something for their conversation. He'd though about it so much that he wanted to give his mind a rest. Anyway, nothing had been resolved yet. Any conversation would be pure speculation, and he didn't want any more wild ideas screaming for attention inside his head.

He said, "Nothing much."

Alice gave him one of her interrogation type looks, so he said, "I was too busy worrying about you to do anything."

She grinned. Sebastian wasn't sure if she knew he was lying or not but was glad that, whatever she thought, she played along. "You softy. I presume everyone gets a bit upset when their fiancée gets attacked."

He grinned back. "It's a strange feeling being engaged. When are we getting married, then? I'm looking forward to the honeymoon."

She laughed out loud. One or two other diners glanced across at her. She smiled back at them in a 'piss off' kind of way. She was a sassy woman alright. Even so, the mention of a honeymoon meant that sex had raised its head and a few moments silence descended on them while they considered it.

Sebastian said, "Sorry. Forget I said that."

She laughed again then whispered, "Don't you want to come to bed with me?"

Sebastian almost choked.

Again she laughed out loud. She was teasing him. She said "You should've seen the look on your face. It was a picture." She reached across and took his hand. "Really, Sebastian, you need to loosen up. Sometimes you think far too deeply. Just let things happen."

Sebastian squirmed a little, then nodded. "The steak's good," he said.

Alice shook her head in bemusement.

A waiter appeared with a tray in his hand. A silver dome on it reflected the dining room and its customers.

"What's this?" asked Sebastian. "I didn't order anything else." He turned to Alice and said, "Did you?"

She shook her head.

The waiter said, "A gentleman in the lounge asked me to bring you this." With a great flourish he whipped off the dome to reveal a *Leica III* camera.

Sebastian was confused. "What's this got to do with me? It's a camera. It's not mine. It's not even new. I don't even…" He saw the look on Alice's face. She was ashen. "What is it? What's the matter?"

"Sir?" said the waiter. "What do you want me to do with it?"

Alice picked up the camera. "It's OK," she said, "It's mine. Is the gentleman who asked you to do this still in the lounge?"

"Yes, Madam."

Alice rose from her seat and walked towards the lounge. Sebastian leapt to his feet and followed her. The waiter ran after them.

Once inside the lounge, Alice waited until the waiter scanned the crowd.

"I'm sorry, Madam. He's not here now."

Sebastian said, "What's this all about, Alice?"

"It's my camera," she said. "The one I had with me when I was attacked."

He turned to the waiter "Are you sure he's not here?"

"He's not here, sir."

Sebastian glanced around the room. His gaze settled on a man sitting in an armchair next to the fire. He had a large glass of brandy in one hand and a cigar in the other. The black-haired man with a pencil thin moustache nodded slowly in his direction and raised his glass in salute. Alice didn't see him.

Sebastian said to Alice, "Go back to the table and order me an apple crumble and custard. I'll be with you in a moment. There's someone here I need to say hello to."

Alice bridled a little. She didn't take too well to being given orders. She wanted to know who the person was and what was so important.

"Please," Sebastian said. "Trust me."

Alice bit her lip but then smiled and said, "OK. I trust you." And left with the waiter.

Sebastian made his way through the couple of dozen patrons to the fireside.

"Good evening, Mister Crawley. Are you enjoying your meal with the lovely lady? She is pleased to get her camera back, no?"

"Shafiq. What the hell has this to do with you?"

His smile broadened so that his moustache appeared to be a horizontal line above his top lip. "I have arranged so that a colleague of mine has returned the camera to its rightful owner. That is a good deed, yes?"

"How did you get hold of it?"

"Ah! That is another story to be told some other time, my friend. Let us be grateful, for the moment that Miss Alice has had her property returned."

"You know how she lost it, don't you?"

"I know lots of things, Mister Crawley. And yes, I do know about the unfortunate incident that resulted in Miss Alice being hospitalised. A very nasty incident I'm sure. But all is well that ends well, Mister Crawley. Is that not so? By the way, your friends lovely fur coat is hanging on a peg next to the door there." He indicated a row of pegs at the other side of the room. "You must retrieve it before it goes missing again. It is expensive, no?"

Sebastian leaned in closer to Shafiq. "I'm warning you, Shafiq. Stay away from Alice. Stay away from me."

"There is no need for warnings, Mister Crawley. I mean you and Miss Alice no harm. Indeed, I only wish for you to be living happily ever after. That is what they say in fairy stories, is it not? And now I must leave you." He got up and stubbed out his cigar. He drained his glass and whispered, "Have a good evening, Mister Crawley. We shall speak again very shortly. We have things to discuss."

Shafiq buttoned up his jacket and assumed his fixed smile as he exited the room.

Sebastian rejoined Alice carrying her coat just as his apple crumble arrived. The surprise at seeing the coat was written all over her face.

"Where did you get this?"

"It was hanging in the lounge."

"How did it get there?"

"I don't know," he blustered, "It just appeared. Like your camera."

Alice examined the coat and found it to be undamaged. In fact it had been cleaned.

"So, who was your friend?"

"A client of mine."

"I see. Business then," Alice said unconvincingly

Sebastian nodded and started to demolish his apple crumble.

Neither spoke during the dessert although Alice reached across the table and fingered her camera, obviously consumed with thoughts about her attack and the man who had done it. Sebastian was thinking about Shafiq.

Alice spoke first.

"How did he get hold of my camera? How did he know where I was? How did he know it was mine?"

Sebastian briefly wondered if Alice was talking about Shafiq. Had she seen them talking? Had she worked out the connection? He shook his head and decided to play a straight bat. "I don't know. Surely it wasn't returned by the man who attacked you. I can't see anyone doing that at the risk of being caught. It doesn't seem credible. Perhaps he got a friend to do it."

Alice seemed a little disappointed by that reply.

She picked up the camera and examined it again. "The film's still in it. I remember I had taken about six photos the day before and I see that the dial shows six shots have been taken. Whoever took it hasn't used it. And judging by how it looks, the camera hasn't come to any harm."

"You'll have to tell the police."

"I suppose so. But they'll ask an awful lot of awkward questions that I can't answer."

"All you can tell them is the truth. You don't know how it was returned to you other than the waiter bringing it on a silver platter."

"And nothing else?" she inquired.

"You can only tell them what you know."

Alice nodded. ""There's no time like the present."

They drove to the police station and asked for Detective Sergeant Smith, only to be told he had a couple of days off. She left a message and they got back into the car.

12

Wednesday 6*th* February 1963

Tommy Heath sat in the pub bar with a pint of beer on the table in front of him. Unusually for him he hadn't been able to sleep so he'd got dressed and wandered along the road to the pub. The nightshift had been completely uneventful because the bad weather had limited traffic and the ships were few and far between. The dock's fortunes were declining and all the businesses associated with it were living in trepidation of another economic disaster. The news on Monday that the Admiralty had ordered three new ships for the shipyards on the Tyne was a shot in the arm for the industry, but it didn't auger well for the future. The newspaper lying on the table next to his pint announced that it had been the coldest January for twenty-three years. For Tyneside, the outlook was cold, bleak and miserable.

Buckingham Palace had announced the forthcoming marriage of Princess Alexandra to Angus Ogilvy, whoever he was, but mostly it was bad news. There had been a fire in Cleveland Street, just a hundred yards away. Luckily no-one was hurt. A spark from the fire had ignited the carpet. Tommy shook his head. It was an event that could happen to anyone. Why don't people use a fireguard?

It looked like the *Adelfotis II* was going to be sold for scrap. They had better get a move on or the sea will claim it, thought Tommy. His eyes moved to the rear page for the sport. Most football teams hadn't kicked a ball this year due to the weather but Manchester United had managed to pay Celtic £50,000 for the services of Pat Crerand, a player Tommy had heard of but never seen play. Moving from one Catholic club to another, Tommy said to himself. Tommy was a Sunderland supporter and they were doing alright. Promotion was a distinct possibility this year, even though their leading goal scorer, Brian Clough had done his knee in at Christmas.

Tommy sighed and had another swallow of beer. He glanced at his watch and saw that it was nearly three o'clock. Last orders would be called shortly. Time to go home, have a bite to eat and a snooze in front of the fire before getting ready for his last shift this week. He sat back and allowed his thoughts to wander. Sebastian's interest in the Sand Dancers was natural. There weren't that many young men who hadn't been interested in what they saw as a 'glamorous' lifestyle. Tommy blamed Hollywood for corrupting young minds through 'movies'. What Tommy hadn't told him was that his mother, Billie, had flirted with the gang before the war, but it hadn't amounted to anything, primarily because war broke out, but there was also the fact that she'd gotten herself pregnant by Reg Crawley. However, the appearance of this middle-eastern bloke in Sebastian's life was a bit ominous. He didn't like that. Hopefully, it would blow over, although he had grave doubts.

Sebastian's girlfriend was a revelation. Tommy had seen Sebastian with the occasional girl and had actually met one or two. Sebastian didn't seem to be that bothered about them, something that, at the time, made Tommy think Sebastian could have been a bit of a 'nancy boy' Alice was different. Sebastian's eyes lit up when she was around. It was obvious that he was trying to be nonchalant, but he wasn't fooling anybody; his eyes seemed to be magnetically attracted to her. Whenever she was within sight, Sebastian was looking at her, and what's more, she was aware of it. That made her powerful and gave her clout.

The situation with Billie wasn't the best. Tommy didn't have much faith in the idea that Billie had met her beau, and all would be OK for the rest of her life. She didn't have a good track record when it came to love, but then again who did? He wasn't a great admirer of Jack Tozer either. He was a cocky bastard who thought he was God's gift. Tommy wasn't sure it was because of his upbringing, his personality, or just being a policeman that made him jar the nerves a bit. He'd met people like him before. Almost every one of them had got their face pushed back at some time, although hardly any of them seemed to learn their lesson.

He drank up and folded the paper under his arm. He braced himself against the cold and launched himself into the outside world. A quick scamper along the street saw him seek the warmth of his living room before the cold managed to make him feel too uncomfortable. Soon, the fire was built up and blazing. He placed the fireguard in front of it, mindful of the newspaper story. He slept in his favourite chair.

Blanche Fada spooned the last of the ice cream into her mouth. A cup of tea sat on the table in front of her. She was sitting in Minchella's ice cream parlour on Ocean Road, passing the time away. She'd been shopping in King Street, buying one or two things from Binns so she could entertain a friend or two over the weekend. She lit a cigarette and blew a cloud of smoke towards the ceiling. She considered herself a social smoker, mostly when in bed with one of her friends.

The door opened and a customer was swept in with a shock of cold air. An elderly woman wearing a green head square and matching green coat lumbered in to join the other dozen or so patrons. She glanced at Blanche and quickly looked away before scuttling to the back of the shop. Mrs. Fletcher was a neighbour of Blanche's although they never spoke. She didn't approve of Blanche's lifestyle obviously. Blanche smiled. Mrs. Fletcher probably didn't have friends - certainly not the kind of friends that Blanche had.

She considered ordering another cup of tea but decided against it. It would be dark soon and she wanted to be in the warm safety of her home before the ice and frost re-formed. Captain Robert Duncan was due at eight o'clock and he was a stickler for time management. He liked things to be precise. He was a committed Scottish Presbyterian and lay preacher. He wore starched collars and highly polished boots. He rarely spoke but indicated with hand signals what he wanted, which was usually the same every time. He was courteous, friendly and tender. He liked to be stroked – slowly. He always wore his cap in bed. At ten o'clock he would exit the house after bowing to Blanche and leaving a ten-pound note on the mantelpiece.

She made her way home and built up the fire, all the while telling herself how friendships were part of her business relations, and how acquaintances were not. What did she care for Chinese Whispers and nosey neighbours? What did they know?

She took a long, hot bath and lit several perfumed candles that Sebastian had managed to get her. Captain Bob liked the smell of spices, especially cinnamon. When her friend knocked on her door at precisely eight o'clock, Blanche was ready, willing and able. He smiled broadly as he entered her home. He removed his coat and hung it on a peg in the hall. Without a word he deliberately brushed against Blanche as he went past her and started up the stairs. It would definitely be 'Aye, Aye, Captain' tonight.

At ten o'clock Captain Bob strode out of Blanche's house and headed down the bank to the train station. At two minutes past ten a black car pulled up outside and a man with a pencil moustache climbed out and went to the front door. He rapped on it twice and waited a few seconds before the door was opened by Blanche. A brief conversation took place and the man was admitted.

It was another freezing night, the worst winter since 1947.

Saturday 9*th* February 1963

Sebastian waited in his grandad's house to be picked up in Alice's Wolseley. He'd invited her to go with him to the Empire Theatre in Sunderland to see Helen Shapiro, who had had several chart hits in the last couple of years, including his favourite, *Walking back to happiness*. Alice had been more interested in the support acts, which included a group called The Beatles who had sung a couple of catchy tunes that made the charts. The alternative of a visit to the Majestic Ballroom didn't appeal to him. He thought that the cover charge of five bob was a bit pricey anyway.

"Bloody stupid sod!" said Tommy who was sitting next to him reading the paper.

"What?" said Sebastian.

"An Indian fella got killed on the sports field."

"Doing what?" said Sebastian.

He read aloud. "A judge at a sports meeting at Howrah near Calcutta was killed by a javelin which pierced his chest as he was supervising events."

"He couldn't have been doing much supervising. He must have been on the field when the athlete threw the bloody javelin," Sebastian remarked. "Anything else in the news? Anything interesting, that is."

Tommy skipped back to the front pages and scanned it. "The Prime Minister of Iraq's been killed in a coup, but I don't suppose anyone's bothered about that. There's been more men laid off at Palmers shipyard due to a slackening in the ship repair world. That's three hundred and twenty men – no – that's three hundred and twenty families who are affected."

Just then a car horn sounded in the street outside the house. Sebastian peered through the curtains and saw the Wolseley idling outside.

"I'm off," he said.

Tommy grunted a goodbye and said, "I'm off soon as well."

Sebastian closed the front door behind him and just as he reached the car he heard someone shout his name. He paused and looked up the street towards the town centre. Sammy was walking as quickly as he could towards him. Sebastian opened the car door and said, "Won't be a minute," to Alice.

"I need to talk to you, Sebastian," Sammy said.

"I've got a few things to say to you too." The anger and sarcasm obvious. "But it'll have to wait until tomorrow. I'm going out tonight."

"But I need to speak to you. It's important."

Sebastian gave a quick look in Alice's direction and swore at the sky. "Look, Sammy. I know. Bull's dead. He was with you. But I've got other matters to deal with just now. How about we meet up tomorrow?"

"I saw it, Sebastian. I saw him die." The anguish in his voice was tangible, the look on his face was pure horror.

Sebastian decided he had to speak to Sammy now. His friend needed emotional support. He walked back to the car and opened the door.

Alice rolled her eyes as if she knew what was coming. "What's up?" she said. "Do I need to trust you on this one as well?"

"Sorry, Alice. It's important. I need to talk to him."

"Business?"

"Well ... no ... maybe ... yes. Personal. A friend."

"Are you serious?" she asked incredulously. "Do you hear what you're saying?"

"I'm sorry, Alice. This is important."

"And what happens between us is not? Is that your priority in life, to support your friends first?"

Sebastian sighed. This wasn't going well. "I'll explain sometime. Trust ..." He didn't finish the sentence; he knew they were the wrong words.

"Someday you'll learn to trust me. Alright, have your secret life. I know my place in it."

Alice slammed the car into first gear and released the handbrake. Sebastian managed to slam the door shut before she drove away.

Then he swore at the sky again.

"I'm sorry, Sebastian," said Sammy when Sebastian returned to him, "but you're the only person I can speak to. I need help."

"You need a bloody good hiding if you ask me. Come on."

They both went into the house and met Tommy on the way out, who barely raised an eyebrow at Sebastian's apparent change of plan. He was on his way, as usual, to the pub.

Sammy accepted Sebastian's offer of a large whisky, and as he poured one for himself, he listened to Sammy's garbled account of the past seven days, occasionally losing the thread as he thought about Alice's reaction. The glasses were refilled twice before the full story emerged and Sebastian had reasoned he'd be able to make up with Alice.

He sat in his grandfather's throne and gazed into the fire like a wizened shaman. Sammy sat on the settee waiting for him to speak.

"It's a bloody mess, Sammy. Why the hell did you take Bull of all people? One of the reasons why we called him Bull was because he was like a bull in a china shop. You knew that. So why?" Sebastian couldn't sit still. He stood and stalked around the room

"He...He asked me to." Sammy stammered, feeling totally inadequate.

"Oh come on, Sammy. Bull's never a burglar. He's too clumsy, too big, too bloody headstrong to be a burglar."

"He needed money."

"He always needed money."

Neither spoke for a few moments. Sebastian paced the floor while Sammy hid his head in his hands.

Sebastian said, "Who else knows about this?"

"No-one."

"Really?"

Tears sprang to Sammy's eyes. "Who can I tell?"

Sebastian sat down again and spent a few minutes collecting his thoughts. If no-one knew outside this room then Sammy was safe – unless he had left evidence at the scene of the crime, or crimes. If Sammy had been as careful as he usually was on these occasions, then the likelihood of him being discovered was remote.

In conversations with Jack Tozer he had found out that the greater the crime warranted the greater investigation by the police. A theft of a bottle of milk from the doorstep received less attention than the theft of a car. It stood to reason. The attack on Alice was being thoroughly investigated because it was a serious assault by an anonymous man, and of course she was ... connected. The assault hinted at something more sinister than a domestic dispute or a pub fight. Any burglary was a serious matter, but domestic burglaries were more serious, especially at night. And, if a death occurred, then the full weight of justice was used to squeeze out the truth and prosecute any offenders. The only difference in Bull's case was that, to all intent and purposes, he had died while being involved in a criminal act. There was no real victim. Natural justice had been served.

Sebastian stared at Sammy, who withered in his seat. His voice was steely as he said, "I can't bring myself to speak to you properly, Sammy. I'm so angry at you. I just can't help wondering about what went through Bull's mind or the pain he experienced. What about his family? They've been left without him in their lives anymore; and they have to live with the stigma of having a burglar in the family. And as for you." He pointed his finger at him. "You get off scot free. It's not fair, Sammy. I'm not saying I would rather it had been you who died. All I'm saying is that, in my eyes, Bull was just an innocent bloke who made a wrong decision. But you're a career criminal. It's an occupational hazard, a calculated risk."

Despite the heat from the fire Sammy shivered. "Help me, Sebastian," he pleaded.

Sebastian drew in a huge breath and exhaled slowly. His mind fell into problem solving mode.

"In my opinion, you do nothing." He watched as Sammy's confusion deepened. "If the police had any evidence that linked you to the burglaries then they would've been knocking on your door before now. I take it no-one's done that?"

"No-one's knocked on my door except you, according to my neighbour."

"Okay. I've only heard snippets of information about the case from Jack, but the police seem to be treating it as a burglary gone wrong. In fact they might even chalk off some other crimes they've put down to Bull because it'll improve their crime figures. So, unless they're waiting on some sort of forensic test, and I doubt it, or they have a witness, which I again doubt, they'll probably not look at it as intensely as they would in other crimes where someone has died."

Hope registered on Sammy's face.

"Don't expect too much, Sammy. It'll take a long time for this to die down, and even longer for me to forgive you."

Sammy muttered, "Thanks," and made to leave.

Sebastian said softly, "I think it's best if we don't see each other again for some time. If I get to know anything concrete, I'll get word to you. But..." his voice trailed off.

Sammy nodded and without saying a word left the house.

Sebastian kicked at a cushion that had fallen onto the floor. It sailed through the kitchen door and clattered some pans on the bench. A box of eggs fell to the floor in a scrambled mess of yolk and broken shells.

Sebastian swore at the ceiling.

13

Sunday 10th February 1963

Sebastian dialled a number he had memorised. He heard the ring tone call out a half a dozen times before it was answered by a female voice.

"It's me," he said.

Her response was cool. "And who might that be? Is it Richard? No, it must be Simon. Didn't we have such a lovely time last night? The Beatles were fantastic, weren't they?"

Sebastian frowned. She'd still gone to the theatre without him. And who were these other men? Was she playing him?

He didn't respond. There was a pause. A long pause. The line went dead.

He debated whether or not to ring again but decided against it. Alice was angry, and she had a good right to be. He'd dropped her at the last moment for a mate who'd appeared out of nowhere. He couldn't tell her why. As far as she was concerned, she'd come off second best. She wasn't his priority.

Old anxieties from the past emerged again, coalescing into a single question. Was she worth the effort? She was far too independent to be treated like other women he'd known, and she wouldn't stand for being side lined or relegated to an inferior position. Other women he'd known would have simply accepted their lot in life, and in this day and age that meant being ... it meant being ... what did it mean? He couldn't treat her the way Jack treated his mother, and he hated the way boyfriends and girlfriends fell into specific roles. That was why he'd never been able to have a lasting relationship. Alice was different. She challenged those roles without being argumentative about it – she just acted - and it confused him. He wanted something different but found it hard to get himself out of the gender role he despised so much ... but knew came all too easily to him. He had to try harder. He had to treat her as an equal, as a partner. It would be the only thing that would work. And it dawned on him that her behaviour was probably more about her training him up than it was about female petulance. That made him smile despite the image of him being a lab rat.

It needed more thought. Safety first, he said to himself. I'll call back later.

Blanche Fada lay in bed enjoying the luxury of having had a friend-free night. The *Teasmade* came to a boil at her bedside and soon she was propped up and sipping tea with a plain biscuit in hand ready to dunk.

She enjoyed the company of her friends, but on the rare occasion that no-one arrived, she indulged herself with a glass of wine, a deep hot bath and an early night. Sometimes, she played records of her favourite singers. Her taste in music was eclectic. It ranged from Frank Sinatra to Jim Reeves and included Elvis, Billy Fury and Adam Faith. The singers were inevitably men. Some were mysterious, some were 'bad boys' but most were just bloody good singers. Last night she'd listened to Cliff Richard. She'd seen him in *Summer Holiday* last month and enjoyed it so much that yesterday she'd bought the soundtrack LP of the film from *Saville's* in King Street. Her favourite was *Bachelor Boy*.

For some reason the song reminded her of Sebastian Crawley. He could have played Cliff's part of Don in the film. He had the looks and charisma to carry it off. She didn't know if Sebastian could sing, but that didn't matter, that wasn't what the girls wanted.

She put down the cup and brushed one or two crumbs onto the floor. She rearranged the pillows and lay back. The Town Hall clock struck the half hour. She glanced at the *Teasmade* and saw the time was half past nine. She wasn't ready to get up yet.

She heard the letterbox open in the passage downstairs and the familiar thud and flutter of the newspapers as they landed on the floor. Outside, she heard a neighbour collecting the milk bottles from the step and slamming the front door. She guessed it was Mrs. Johnson across the street. She had three young kids who wouldn't be lying around in bed. They would need their breakfast now. Blanche knew that their father would still be in bed, though. He would get up just in time to have a cooked breakfast, a wash and shave and then venture out for the workingmen's club opening at midday.

Her mind bounced between one subject and another. She enjoyed the aimless, random thoughts that visited and departed. It was a mood that reflected her personality. Some days she was quiet and introspective while others saw her brash, brassy persona emerge and perform. Over the years she'd managed to identify triggers for these moods and could sometimes generate them. But, on occasions, she was prone to bouts of instant depression. When this happened, she had to hide away in her home and let it take its course. Usually, these negative moods lasted only a few days before something else burst to the front and swept it away. People had that effect as well. Sebastian was one, a positive person. He charged the atmosphere just by being there. His mother was the same. Jack Tozer was a negative person. It was as if the air chilled when he entered the room.

And another was Shafiq.

Despite his almost permanent smile, his presence sucked energy from the room, and anybody in close proximity lost the will to continue. When Sebastian had described the shady character that had been cropping up in his daily life, one of the prime suspects as far as Blanche was concerned had been Shafiq. She'd denied knowledge of him to Sebastian, but she'd known him years ago when he was a weedy runt living in the West Holborn area of South Shields. He had been embraced by the Sand Dancers and rapidly became an effective 'soldier' in their organisation.

Last Wednesday, after Captain Bob left, Shafiq had arrived and asked to chat to her. She'd reluctantly admitted him and shown him into the lounge. After the usual pleasantries he'd enquired about her 'business'. Her protestations that she wasn't running a business, but entertaining friends only caused his smile to widen.

"You would miss your friends if they stopped coming, yes?"

"Why would they stop coming?" It was a genuine question. She couldn't see any reason why that would happen. Of course, as she grew older it was inevitable that some of her friends would seek someone younger or desire fresh fields to plough. At the same time, some friends found comfort in the semi-domestic life she offered.

Shafiq lit a cigar without asking permission and blew a column of blue smoke into the air. He watched as it rose to the ceiling and curled back on itself.

"Your friends may tire of you," he suggested. "They may not want to walk up the bank to this fine house because they may encounter ... obstacles."

Blanche frowned. What the hell was Shafiq on about? "Obstacles?"

Shafiq blew another layer of smoke in the air. A thin cloud eddied around them.

"Oh there are many potential obstacles, Miss Fada. Your friends may get lost, or fall down, or become discouraged from keeping your company. Who am I to predict what possible mishaps might occur to them? I am not a clairvoyant. I do not have a crystal ball." His smile was like a cold fragment of steel.

Blanche took a few moments to compose herself.

"What's this all about, Shafiq? Why are you saying these things to me? I haven't done anyone any harm."

"You are one of us," he said evenly. "We have known each other since our days in school, have we not? It is right that we should look after ourselves, and each other, is that not so?"

It was true they had been at the same school, but Blanche spoke like a local while Shafiq had kept his clipped, accented dialect that was a remnant of living in a house that didn't speak English. She eyed the dancing figure on Shafiq's hand. She wasn't a member of the Sand Dancers, but her ancestry, and Shafiq's, could probably be traced back to the Middle East through the engine rooms of countless ships. She knew some of her relatives had flirted with the group in her younger days. Some had sported the tattoo. It was a male orientated gang. Women weren't trusted enough. Their role was to serve their men folk.

Blanche answered carefully. "We share a common heritage, I suppose. But I can look after myself. I've managed pretty well so far."

Shafiq nodded. "But things change. Nothing lasts forever. Am I not right in this?"

Blanche leaned back in her chair. "What's going on, Shafiq?"

Shafiq leaned forward and lit another cigar. "We like to help each other through difficult times," he said in a business-like tone. "We would like to make sure that your business remains your business."

"Stop talking in riddles, Shafiq. What do you mean?"

"Your friends are important people, no? They talk to you?"

Blanche nodded slowly.

"It would be of interest to my employers if any useful information could be passed on to us. We would be very grateful. And, of course, we would make sure no unexpected obstacles presented themselves." His smile became thinner. He obviously loved his job.

Blanche said, "The next time Captain Bob's auntie wets the bed I'll be sure to let you know. I'll send you a telegram."

Shafiq's smile froze on his face and he stood up. The sudden movement caused Blanche to shrink into her chair.

Shafiq said, "I do not appreciate your sense of humour, Miss Fada. You would do well to accept our friendship. We will be waiting for your messages."

He handed her a small card with a telephone number and a local address. The address would be an ordinary house with an ordinary family whose service to the Sand Dancers was like that provided by the local Post Office.

Shafiq buttoned up his coat and left without saying another word.

The memory of that meeting had caused her deep consternation. She'd thought about the type of information the Sand Dancers would appreciate but couldn't form any cohesive criteria. In the end, she decided to write down whatever her friends said about the future, their jobs or just any gossip she didn't fully appreciate herself. It would be something. It would also show the Sand Dancers that her information was almost meaningless. Of course, she would still record everything in her diaries. And only Sebastian knew about those. She'd already written a few things down, but when she'd looked at them in the cold light of the next day, she'd torn them up. She would set her own criteria, and one of those was to wait at least a day before sending anything to the Sand Dancers. Blanche was frightened. Not in the context of quivering in a corner waiting to be attacked; it was more subtle than that. She had a gnawing portent of a future mishap, a fundamental feeling of insecurity. Perhaps it was unfounded, but she knew enough about the Sand Dancers that you had to find a way to accommodate them ... or else.

A couple of miles away, in Harton, Jack Tozer sat at the kitchen table reading the seedy court report stories sensationalised in the *News of the World*. A particularly lurid case involving a reporter entering a brothel in London had caught his attention. He laughed when he read the line 'our reporter made his excuses and left.' Jack's opinion was that he was lying. No red-blooded man would decline the offer of a shag if it was free, or if someone else was paying for it. If he had been the reporter, he would have shagged a few of them and covered up the cost in his expense claims and lied about it. Most people were gullible. Who would believe the words of common prostitutes against the word of an honest, hardworking copper like him?

Billie put a plateful of eggs, bacon, sausage and beans in front of him. A smaller plate contained three slices of highly salted fried bread. Jack folded his paper and threw it onto a chair next to him before attacking his breakfast. Billie sat next to him and watched. A solitary egg sandwich waited to be eaten next to her cup of tea.

He decided that she mustn't be that hungry. Her stomach cramps had given way to a period during the night and he wasn't too happy about it. He expected to be sated when she slept over, otherwise what was the point of her being there. A woman was there purely and simply to cater for the needs of her man. It was pointless giving a woman brains. She didn't need them, unless it was used to experiment in the bedroom or the kitchen.

He glanced at Billie as he chewed a huge mouthful of fried bread and sausage. A thin trail of tomato sauce escaped from his lips and headed towards his chin. He wiped it off with the edge of the tablecloth. They had been together for almost a year. It had been good. She was great in bed, cooked a decent meal and was honest. She still scrubbed up well but there were signs that middle age wouldn't be kind to her. Moreover, she was starting to say things that suggested she was a permanent fixture in his house. That wasn't going to happen. There were plenty other people out there who could warm his bed. People like Sylvia, for instance, his new receptionist friend. She had the added bonus of having her own house and an insurance settlement to maintain her. She didn't need a job. Sylvia had everything that Billie had, and more.

Jack felt the faint stirrings in his groin and thought about bending Billie across the kitchen table before remembering she had her period. Nine months ago he wouldn't have cared less about the mess, but he decided it wouldn't be worth the hassle going for it now. He took a fresh piece of bread, buttered it and used it to wipe his plate clean before popping it into his mouth.

"That was a good breakfast. At least there are still some things you can do."

Billie gazed out of the window.

Jack said, "What I mean is that there are still things you can do for me." He pushed himself away from the table and opened his legs to show her a bulge in his trousers.

"No, Jack. I'm not feeling very well."

"You don't need to feel well to use your hands."

Billie continued to stare out of the window. A robin was bouncing around the garden chasing sparrows away from his patch.

Jack waited a few seconds then stood up in disgust. He had a good mind to throw her onto the floor and take her anyway. The floor was polished wood and any mess could be cleaned up without a problem. She would object at first, but she would let it happen. He decided against it. He'd save himself for Sylvia later in the week. By then he'd be ready to explode. And if she didn't let him have his way, then Billie would be clean by then. He picked up his paper and stalked into the lounge leaving Billie to clear away the dishes and tidy up. She continued to gaze out of the window. Her uneaten egg sandwich curled up at the edges and wallowed in a puddle of congealed fat.

14

Thursday 14th February 1963

Alice sat at a desk with a large typewriter in front of her. The waiting room outside the office was full of people who wanted to complain about one thing or another. Alice had learned early on that people complained about anything. They were mildly concerned about Russia and the Conservative government, but their priorities were more likely to include the increase in the number of seagulls or the fact that the trolley buses were giving passengers mild electric shocks when they got on them. Mrs. James from Marshall Wallis Road in the town wanted to know why potatoes were selling for fivepence a pound and Jaffas were seven for a shilling. Mr. Rogers from Salmon Street was concerned that Tony Curtis had unwisely married and what was Shirley Bassey going to do with the £2400 she had been awarded in her defamation suit settled in a Sydney court, in Australia. Alice wanted to scream.

A chat with a knowledgeable party member earlier in the week had reinforced her view that the Labour Party in this constituency didn't need to try very hard to win over the hearts and minds of the people. They would vote Labour no matter who was running. In her view, that was one of the reasons why society was in desperate need of change. The Prime Minister, Harold Macmillan, had said a few years ago that Britain 'had never had it so good.' Given that the austerity of the war years had given way to a relatively free society, he was probably right, but why was everything compared to life when the country was at war? Change was needed and change was what the people of Britain were going to get with a Labour Prime Minister at the next election. She looked forward to the leadership election between George Brown and Harold Wilson. Gaitskill would have been better, and she would prefer Brown to Wilson, but the country would be better off with either of them.

Within the office the talk amongst the girls was Valentine's Day. Only one had received a card from an admirer and an entire parade of likely candidates had been examined and rejected as suitors. One of the other girls was discussing an invite to a Beatnik party at the weekend and whether or not she should go. Beatnik parties were what young, nonconforming people did these days. The idea of wandering around wearing a black, turtleneck sweater, dark glasses and a beret while reciting poetry to the sound of bongo drums, didn't appeal to Alice.

She shook her head. She needed to go for a walk, so she volunteered to take the post to the Post Office down the road.

It was cold, although there had been a bit of a thaw in the last few days. Rutted slush was blackening by the side of the road. She was frustrated. Not only because of her job not fulfilling expectations, but with her relationship with Sebastian. Relationship? You couldn't even call it that. There wasn't one; at least not one that she could tell anyone about. Last weekend just about summed it all up. He was ready to go on a date with her and an old mate turns up. So he instantly cancels her date with him. What kind of man did that? An old man, that's who. A man with out-dated ideas, a man who thought he had right to be self-indulgent. He obviously considered himself to have some kind of divine right to command women and to keep them from worrying their sweet little heads with weighty masculine matters. She snorted involuntarily, to the surprise of a passing old lady who gave her a spectacled stare.

Ok, she didn't always react well, but she didn't want to nag him into doing the right thing by their relationship; he had to come to that realisation in his own time, under his own steam. If he didn't own the change, he wouldn't commit to it.

She felt a little guilty about her reaction to his telephone call the other day. Well, she was angry, and he had to know it. She'd got angrier when he didn't call her on Monday, and the anger had turned into annoyance by Tuesday, and ambivalence by Wednesday. Today she was concerned more than anything. Was the relationship over? Had she scared him away or did he really not give a damn about her?

She waited in the queue to be served and completed her business in a few minutes before stepping out into the cold. On the slow walk back to the office she considered her career stepping stone into the future, and again dreamt about a job on Kennedy's staff, something like being in a team of advisors on foreign affairs would be ideal, or maybe she should pursue a higher degree, become a professor, teach politics, write books. Soon, though, her building came into view and her mind ticked back to Mrs. James of Marshall Wallis Road, and some disembodied echo of Sebastian saying something along the lines of her having far more options than that woman or any member of her family were ever likely to have. Her mood hit rock bottom as she wandered into the office and she was greeted with subdued giggling from the girls. Give me strength, she thought. They were huddled around a huge bouquet of red roses that made even Alice gasp in astonishment. They were beautiful.

"Wow," she said. "Which one of you girls has an admirer that can afford to buy you flowers like this?"

The girls giggled even more uncontrollably. It was enough for a rather large Councillor to poke his head around the corner and clear his throat theatrically in admonishment.

The Beatnik party invitee handed Alice the card that came with the flowers. She read it. It said: 'To Alice, Sorry' and was signed with a capital S.

She felt the blush fill her face. She sat at her desk and whispered to herself, "God bless you, Sebastian," and blinked back tears.

Jack Tozer smoothed down the lapels of his best suit and appraised himself in the mirror. "Looking good. lad. Looking good." The suit had been his fathers, who had a keen eye for good cloths and sharp design. The colour was a deep brown with flecks of black. Officially, the colour was 'nigger brown' according to the old Jew who had ordered and cut the cloth when his father had commissioned it on a business trip to London.

Jack patted his breast pocket to make sure that his packet of Durex was still there. Being prepared was one of Jack's mottos. He liked to cater for all eventualities. His new woman was an experienced widow who knew the game. He might 'get his end away,' but then he might not. He didn't want to miss an opportunity if it presented itself. He knew that some women wouldn't have sex unless the man wore 'a blob.' He preferred not to wear one. He liked the skin to skin approach. He knew the woman would enjoy it more if she just let him do what he did best.

He smiled. "Looking bloody good." His hand pulled the comb from his back trouser pocket and he drew it down the parting of his *Brylcreem* covered hair before sweeping its bulk to one side. His other hand pushed the hair slightly forward to create a quiff. He replaced the comb and checked his wallet. This evening was costing him a packet. A posh restaurant in Newcastle, with a bottle of wine would impress the lady, but would it be enough to get inside her knickers?

He grinned. A bit of authority, a touch of charm, lots of compliments and a free meal worked on most women. Shagging the woman was just reward for all the effort he was putting into it. He hoped she would appreciate it. He felt himself getting hard. "Not yet, lad," he whispered to himself, "your turn comes later."

Sebastian stood outside 'Uncle Jim's' house with a bunch of flowers in one hand and a box of chocolates in the other. He'd taken the time to go to a very busy florist in the town centre to choose some red roses for the bouquet he'd sent to Ede House that morning, and to select a smaller, less traditional bunch of flowers to give to her tonight. She wouldn't be expecting that. The roses had produced the desired effect. He'd received a phone call from Alice to thank him, and he'd taken the opportunity to ask her out for a date so they could talk through their problems. Alice had sighed a lot, and wavered, and made up an excuse, but in the end had said that she really did believe he was worth the effort, and finally said yes, ok, but no more secrets. He'd winced at that and shook his head but had verbalised an OK. The truth was, he'd decided to tell her as much as he dared tell anyone about his friends and their activities. He'd play it by ear. He'd answer her questions but would be vague with answers. He booked at a restaurant in Newcastle, annoyed that their prices had increased for Valentine's Day, but accepted the premium if it meant that he could sort his differences out with Alice.

Alice opened the door and stepped to one side to allow him in. She looked gorgeous in a figure-hugging green dress that seemed far and away from her usual attire. The last vestiges of bruising had been camouflaged by a little light makeup. Sebastian felt a surge of pure lust scorch its way through his veins, and it showed.

Alice grinned.

Sebastian stepped over the threshold and woodenly shoved the flowers and chocolates towards her. The power of speech seemed to have left him as his gaze wandered up and down.

"Well thank you, kind sir," said Alice as she curtseyed and proffered her cheek for a demure kiss.

Sebastian dutifully obliged.

Alice's gaze swept over him and took in his charcoal grey suit, coloured tie and gleaming shoes. "You look quite the gent, and handsome, to boot."

Sebastian eventually composed himself and, almost with a sigh, said, "And you look simply ravishing."

They smiled the smile of lovers.

"Look, Alice, I need to apologise for ..."

"No. Don't. Not here. Not now."

"But, I feel the need to apologise, or at least give you an explanation ..."

Alice shrugged. "I have to say I was annoyed. I came home after seeing the Beatles and vowed never to see you again."

"But you changed your mind."

Alice took a few seconds to reply. "I changed my mind because of something you say all the time. I asked myself 'Is it worth all the effort?' And the answer was that it was too early to say, so I decided to err on the side of safety. You're still not totally forgiven and, yes, I would like some explanation, even if it's something dark and sinister. If we are to be a couple, we should share our lives." Then she changed her sails and said, "The flowers were beautiful."

Sebastian shuffled, unsure what to say next.

Alice took on the pose of a film star and breathed, "Kiss me, you fool."

Sebastian grabbed Alice by the shoulders and kissed her hard on the mouth. Any tension between them gave way to passion, and for a few moments they were lost inside a romantic novel.

Alice broke the moment, her eyes wide and moist, her lipstick smudged.

Sebastian coughed to clear an imaginary frog from his throat. "Sorry. I didn't mean..."

"Sebastian. Will you please stop apologising for everything? Half of every conversation we have starts off with you saying 'sorry' for something."

"Sor..."

Alice burst out laughing and took a step towards him. She touched his face and said, "There's something maddening about you that confuses me. The way you go on ... you're so naive in a lot of ways, but so self-assured in others. You've got hidden intelligence. There's something. I don't know what it is. I'm baffled. I've never met anyone like you. You're just a mass of contradictions. You treat me with respect and pay me attention, but then blow me off as if I were just so much fluff. But deep down, behind those beautiful eyes, your mind is whirring away thinking about something else, and I'd wager there's only good intent in those thoughts. What the hell is going on inside your head, Sebastian? I want to know. It fascinates me."

"What can I say? I'm just a local lad who's doing okay. And ... If we are going to be honest, I've never met anyone like you. I don't know how to act with you sometimes. I can feel myself changing the way I look at all sorts of things because of you. You're not like other girls. You're ... I don't have the words ... heavenly. You make *me* feel special. I don't know. I really don't know. No, that's not true. I do know something. I know that I can't go very long without thinking about you."

She shimmied closer and held his arms by his side. She kissed him again, but when he showed signs of responding, she stood back again.

"No, no, no, Mr. Crawley. That wouldn't do at all. I've taken the time to get ready for this evening and I'm determined to have that date we missed out on the other day. Let's go."

A few minutes later they were driving towards Newcastle.

Tommy Heath was sitting in front of the television with Billie on a chair beside him.

"I presume Jack's working?"

"Why do you ask?"

"It's Valentine's Day. People who love each other go out and pretend that they're enjoying themselves. Like Sebastian and Little Miss Marx."

"Her name's Alice. And, yes, Jack's working. It's one of the problems with courting a policeman."

"Courting? Is that what it's called these days?"

Billie ignored the jibe.

Tommy continued. "What's he doing these days now that his burglar's been found dead?"

Billie sniffed and said "I can't tell you. It's all hush hush."

"Bloody hush hush. That man's full of his own self-importance. He thinks that what he does really makes a difference. He's bloody deluded. What's more, he's bloody dangerous."

"There's no need to swear, dad. Jack's got a difficult job and he does it well. He's very well respected amongst his bosses."

Tommy tutted and picked up the Gazette. "I just hope he does alright by you. I don't give a toss about him. What's going to happen in the future? Is there any chance you might get married?" He peered over the newspaper anticipating an answer.

Billie snuggled into her chair before answering. "We've talked about it. But Jack isn't quite ready to settle down yet."

Tommy spat a little laugh. "Not ready to settle down? Good God, woman, can you not see that it'll never happen? He's stringing you along. Just like all the others."

Billie said nothing, her lip trembling.

Tommy saw the tears forming at the corner of her eye.

"I'm sorry, love. I didn't mean it like that. I know you've not had the best of times, but you do have a history of picking men who take what they can and dump you. I know that because I've been the one to pick up the pieces. I hate to see you hurt."

Billie wiped her eyes. "I think Jack's different. You'll see." She stood up. "I'm going upstairs to have a bath and then go to bed and listen to the wireless."

Tommy sighed as she exited the room. He scanned the paper for his customary news fix. Harold Wilson was the new leader of the Labour Party. Tommy sighed again. Wilson would never win a General Election against MacMillan. The country was in safe hands even though they had failed to get the UK into the Common Market a few weeks ago. Bloody de Gaulle. One day we'll be there, and we'll stay there forever.

Jack Tozer sat in the lounge of the Royal Turks Head in Grey Street, Newcastle. The theatre crowd were arriving after their evening in the Theatre Royal opposite. He was savouring a Cuban cigar after a meal that had featured the best steak he had ever tasted. A large brandy was warming in his hand. Opposite him sat Sylvia looking goddess-like in a peach coloured dress that revealed an enticing portion of shapely leg. Her figure reminded him of Jayne Mansfield.

Sylvia had allowed him to do the talking over dinner. He'd extolled his prowess as a crime fighter and let her know that he had his finger on the pulse of South Shields. 'Nothing ever happens without me knowing about it,' he'd said.

Her reply wasn't what he expected. 'You haven't found out who burgled our office.'

His reply was 'Not yet. But we will.'

Jack sat in a chair with his back to the door. It wasn't his favourite position because he liked to see who was coming in and going out. In South Shields he wouldn't dream of doing that. His local knowledge fed off the comings and goings of local people. But here, Sylvia had requested his preferred seat because she wanted to see if anyone famous came in or out.

He glanced at his watch and calculated the time he would need to get Sylvia back home.

Sebastian put his arm around Alice's waist and guided her through the hotel doorway into the overwhelming heat and fug of the swirling tobacco smoke of the lounge. Well-dressed people sat and conversed, mainly couples celebrating their love for each other. Although Sebastian wondered how many of them were actually married, or even partners.

They were shown to a table in the far corner of the room and Sebastian ordered some drinks.

They ate a pleasant meal. Alice introduced him to pasta. His difficulty with the spaghetti bolognaise was evident, as a close inspection of his tie would testify. It wasn't until Alice showed him a technique to get the spaghetti onto his fork and into his mouth that he became comfortable. Secretly, he wasn't that fussed on pasta. The tiramisu was more to his liking, but he would have preferred jam roly-poly and custard any day.

The honest display of affections a few hours before acted as an undercurrent to the meal. They dined as if they had been lovers for years. Every nuance was acknowledged and stored. Every glance meant something deep and passionate. Wit and wisdom were traded in equal measure. They both accepted, by their body language, that they would be lovers sooner rather than later.

Sebastian raised his glass and scanned the room as he drank. Sober suits and muted dresses abounded. The homogenised blandness was broken by a shock of peach from the dress of a striking, mature lady who was sitting demurely facing the door. He couldn't see her escort, but whoever he was, was a lucky man.

Alice said, "So where were we? Something about sex, wasn't it?"

Sebastian smiled. She was as eager as him. He summarised their conversations so far that night then said, "Having decided to escalate our relationship." He paused, anticipating a contradiction, but none came. He continued. "We're here to discuss how we can arrange a period of time together where we are unlikely to be interrupted. During that time, we will attempt to overcome some of the tension that has occurred between us and accelerate a deeper understanding of what we're about."

Alice laughed. "That's as unromantic as it comes. What we're about is trying to shag each other without people finding out; and setting ground rules from here on in."

Sebastian shrugged. "In a nutshell."

They both giggled

Sebastian said, "Are you sure about this?"

"Are you trying to be gallant?"

"No. I'm just trying to make sure you know what you're doing."

"Sebastian, I'm not a virgin. I don't have any preconceived, romantic ideas of love and marriage. I'm a woman."

Sebastian was thinking he knew that but wasn't sure if he could say it without causing some comment about objectification.

Alice frowned. Looked past Sebastian. "Isn't that your mother's boyfriend."

"What?"

She pointed across the room. "I thought he was your mother's boyfriend."

Sebastian turned to see Jack Tozer with his arm around the peach dressed woman as he headed towards the exit. Several pairs of eyes followed the woman and Jack's hand as it slid down to her backside and give a gentle squeeze

The colour drained from Sebastian's face.

Alice's thoughts coalesced into one word. "Bastard."

15

Friday 15th February 1963

Sebastian was in a quandary. A universal problem faced by people every day all over the world battled for supremacy inside his head. Should he tell or keep his mouth shut? Was it right to tell his mother and see her distraught, or watch as she deluded herself by fabricating a story in his defence? Should he forget about the whole thing and let the dice fall the way fate had designed it? Should he have to decide which scenario resulted in the least harm to all concerned or did his mother's wellbeing reign supreme?

He'd discussed it at length with Alice in the Royal Turks Head, and consumed too much alcohol in the process. Their conversation about a night of passion had dissolved, to be replaced by the torture of his mother being wronged by Jack 'The Bastard' Tozer. Alice had helped him all the way, standing by his side and appreciating his concerns for his mother. She'd brought him home and left with a casual "I'll give you a call." Although, when he thought about it, he wasn't too sure which one of them had said it. And there was an empathetic kiss in there, too, which seemed to be some sort of seal of friendship.

Did he need to discuss the situation with his grandad? Would he be more able to supply a solution? Or would he walk round to the police station and demand to see Jack with a view to punching him on the nose?

Eventually, after a fried breakfast and a cup of coffee to soak up the hangover, Sebastian walked around to Blanche's house, where he was welcomed with open arms.

He spent fifteen minutes telling her about the previous evening and its possible ramifications. Blanche listened intently without comment. Then, when Sebastian had finished telling his tale, she stood up and looked out of the window at the stone-cold streets that still glistened with frost and the remnants of a snowfall earlier in the week.

Her voice was sad and tired. "It always happens to your mother."

"What's your advice, Blanche?"

"It's difficult to know where to start. It's happened so many times to her it's easy to say that she'll cope, and cope well. But I think she's getting to the end of her tether now. She's not getting any younger and the opportunities for settling down are getting more limited. But she's resilient."

"What do we do about Jack Tozer?"

"What can you do? He's a policeman."

"But they have codes of conduct and disciplinary procedures."

"And where will that get you? Enough trouble from the local constabulary that would last you a lifetime, that's what you'd get. You can't afford that bother, Sebastian. Not in your line of business."

"So he gets away with it?"

"I hate to say this but there could be a rational explanation."

Sebastian stared incredulously at her. "Are you joking?"

"I've met and mixed with an awful lot of Jack Tozers in my time, and sometimes they're asked to do all sorts of weird things in the line of duty. This could be one of them."

"You mean like spies?"

Blanche smiled. "No, not like spies. I don't think Jack Tozer is South Shields' answer to James Bond. But I do know that there can be some strange goings on in the name of security and justice."

"The only justice in this case is for Jack Tozer to be kicked in the balls so hard he ends up with three Adam's apples."

"You asked for my advice, Sebastian. Well here it is. Let sleeping dogs lie. It's never good to have a knee jerk reaction to any situation. These things have a habit of sorting themselves out."

"But in the meantime, my mother still panders to the whims of that bastard."

Blanche gave Sebastian a hug. He was rigid with tension. "Calm down, Sebastian. It'll do you no good getting yourself worked up like this. Your mother's a big girl. She can handle herself. She'll find out in due course and she'll handle it in her own way."

Sebastian left shortly afterwards. Blanche watched through the net curtains in her front room as he walked down the street. When he'd disappeared from view, she picked up a pen and paper and wrote: 'A minor local businessman has a grudge against the police. A policeman is double-crossing his girlfriend.' She put the note in an envelope. Information for the Sand Dancers, suitably obtuse and nondescript, an everyday occurrence and unimportant. But at least Blanche was doing what she had been asked to do by Shafiq. He could file that away for future reference any way he wanted.

Sebastian entered his grandfather's house to raised voices. Tommy was sitting in his usual chair. Billie sat at the table. Her eyes were red and she clutched a hankie in one hand.

Sebastian raised a querying eyebrow to his grandad.

Tommy shook his head. "The world's turned to shit again."

"Mam?"

She shook her head and dabbed her eyes.

Tommy said, "It looks like Jack's two-timing her."

Surely last night's episode at the Royal Turks Head couldn't have been brought to his mother's attention already.

Tommy said. "Jack was seen last night with a woman in Newcastle. He told your mother he was working."

"Who's to say he wasn't. He doesn't need to be wearing a uniform and funny hat to be at work," Sebastian said, but it sounded even more unlikely than when Blanche had said it.

Tommy said, "That might be so, but I doubt whether the police would condone an officer touching up a fellow officer in public."

"What?"

"He was seen feeling this woman's arse. He was all over her."

"Who's been saying this?"

Billie said, "I've got a friend called Freda. She's a horrible woman with a vicious tongue, but what she says is usually true. It's why she can be so horrible. Freda saw Jack with a woman in a hotel. He wasn't working. He drank a lot and made it obvious what he wanted from her."

"Have you spoken to Jack?"

She shook her head. "He's at work."

"Maybe," Tommy added sarcastically.

Sebastian glared at him. The telephone rang in the hall. Sebastian was closest and answered it.

"Sebastian?"

It was Jack Tozer.

"Yes."

"Can you pass a message on to your mother?"

"She's here."

"No. No. Don't disturb her. Tell her I'm at work and something's cropped up that I need to deal with. I'll be working late. Tell her I'll call over the weekend. Thanks."

"Jack, I think…"

But Jack had ended the call.

Sebastian wandered back into the lounge.

"That was Jack on the phone." He turned to his mother and said, "He's working tonight. He'll call you over the weekend."

Billie started crying again and Tommy harumphed. As Sebastian walked into the kitchen, he heard his grandfather say, "Here we are three generations of one family living under the same roof. Not one of us has someone to love other than each other. So what does that make us? Losers? I have to admit that I've been lonely all of these years, even though you two have been here. I miss someone to cuddle at nights or someone to tell me off when I come back from the pub. Maybe even someone to tell me to get a haircut or call into the butchers for a half pound of mince. But I can tell you this. I would rather have that hole in my life rather than go through all these troubles that other people can cause you."

No-one responded so he continued.

"When I think of dying I think of who'll come to my funeral. Who knows me well enough to organise it. What music do I want? What prayers? Who knows me? The real me. In fifty years' time the world will never know I existed. My schools will be gone. My church and workplace gone. This house, gone. Sebastian might still be here. An old man sitting in a chair like this talking to his children or grandchildren. But the world that I know now will be, like me, gone forever."

"Shut up, grandad," said Sebastian as he re-entered the room carrying a glass of milk and a biscuit. "What's that got to do with Jack and my mam?"

Tommy didn't reply. Everyone knew that it was frustration that was causing his diatribe. He loved his family but rarely showed it, and when a member of his family suffered, so did he.

An awkward silence descended, and everyone tried to behave normally. However, the atmosphere was stifling, and Sebastian debated whether or not to fuel the fires of discontent and anxiety by relating his own story of the Royal Turks Head. He decided against it. If the truth came out later, he could be discredited. Blanche had been right. Billie had to discover the truth in her own way and in her own time.

Alice arrived to pick up Sebastian and take him out. Their planned evening of lust, or love, hadn't materialised. The impetus was gone, or at least having a hiatus. There was a strangeness about them. Sebastian explained what had happened earlier today with Blanche and, latterly, with his grandad and mother. Alice listened as she drove. By the time he had finished the story she was parked outside *The Ship* in Harton Village.

Sebastian said, "Are we going in here?"

"No, but it's a decent place for me to park while you get out and go around the corner to Jack's house to see if he's home or not."

Sebastian stared at her. He knew that his grandfather was inclined to go to the police station and smack Jack across the face; it was the way that things used to be settled. Smacking a policeman wasn't a good idea, though Sebastian knew that sometimes it was the only way to make your point. He wasn't a great lover of violence and was rarely the aggressor, but if the Army had taught him one thing it was to fight. A strong sense of injustice meant that every blow he landed was justified. He had a cut-off point; he couldn't beat someone to a pulp. He could recognise when someone was defeated, and he'd stop at that point.

"You're as a gentleman fighter; a man of principle and respect. You'll do the right thing," Alice added.

No-one had seen Sebastian lose control, but he knew that if there was sufficient cause, he was capable of engaging with an opponent and acting like a screaming banshee released from a hitherto unknown corner of Hell.

She was right. It was pointless debating the matter if he could gather some evidence for himself. Without further discussion, he got out of the car and walked with purpose towards Jack's house. Within minutes he was standing at his gate. His car was parked on the road and the curtains in the house were closed. A light was on downstairs. Jack sometimes didn't take his car to work and another sergeant would collect him in a police car, so that meant nothing. The light could be a security measure, especially with the curtains closed.

Sebastian walked up the path and debated whether to knock. Before he could decide, he heard a woman's laughter and a manly guffaw. Sebastian moved towards the window and put his ear to the glass. A music programme. Radio. Two voices. He identified the man's voice as Jack. The woman's voice he did not know.

Sebastian looked around the street before moving to the front of the window. No-one was watching him. There was a small gap between the curtains. He peered through the gap like a peeping tom, but he felt no guilt. He saw Jack Tozer half sitting, half lying on his settee with the woman-in-peach from last night. She was wearing a loose-fitting jumper and a skirt that was riding up her thighs, exposing stocking tops. They were kissing enthusiastically. Sebastian watched for a few more seconds before walking stealthily away. On impulse he picked up a stone and embedded it into a snowball. He threw the snowball at Jack Tozer's front window and ran. The sound of smashing glass told him that his aim was perfect. When he arrived at Alice's car he was breathing heavily and laughing hysterically and shouted, "Drive. Drive. Drive."

Alice laughed and drove off south through the peaceful village towards Cleadon. By the time he arrived at a hotel in nearby Seaburn, Sebastian's adrenaline rush had subsided into mild elation.

"You've turned into an anarchist," Alice grinned. "Now you know how I feel when I protest against nuclear disarmament."

"Please don't talk about politics, Alice. We've had so many bad starts that we need to relax and enjoy ourselves."

Alice continued smiling and stroked his face. "I know. Why do you think I brought you here?"

Sebastian was momentarily confused, then he realised he was at a hotel and not a pub.

"I booked us in this afternoon. I wasn't going to leave anything to chance. All I needed was you."

"I haven't brought anything, you know, to wear."

Alice laughed again. "If you're talking about pyjamas, or sheaths, then you don't need them. I've catered for everything. There should be a bottle of champagne on ice and a buffet supper as well. Anyway, if anyone says they saw you throwing a brick through the window of one of our local constabulary then you have an alibi. You've been here with me since at least five o'clock."

16

Friday 22nd February 1963

It had been nearly three weeks since Sammy had seen Bull fall to his death through the factory skylight. His initial reaction of leaving the scene of the incident had been right; no-one had made enquiries of his whereabouts, except Sebastian. It still cut him deeply that Bull had died – because of his own greed and taking unnecessary risks, he kept telling himself. He shouldn't have taken him. It was as simple as that. Despite Bull's insistence. He should have been stronger. A persistent thought kept nagging at the back of his head, a thought he continued to resist; he wanted to show off. Sammy wanted to show how brilliant a thief he was. No. No. Bull had pleaded with him. He'd thought it was easy money. It was, if you took out the risk factor. But it took experience to reduce the pitfalls of crime. If he'd listened, if he'd done what he was told …

The authorities had declared that Bull's death had been a burglary that had 'gone wrong'. The police were hanging all sorts of crimes on his name. It appeared that every previously undetected burglary in the Borough was being analysed for its *modus operandi*, and those that were similar were being written off as detected. A police spokesman had declared that they were no longer continuing enquiries into a 'substantial' number of burglaries. It was wrong, but Sammy saw that it actually helped him, as long as he stopped now. To continue would be stupid. It was only a matter of time before he got caught, maybe distracted by something, a misplaced step. If it can happen, it will happen. He'd heard that said before. But he was good at what he did. He was very good. There was a reason he had never been caught.

Sammy sat in his bedroom clutching a glass of water while looking out into the dark. The spicy aroma of his mother's cooking was beginning to fade away. However, the tastes still lingered on his tongue.

Outside, the weather remained freezing cold, but snow hadn't fallen since Monday, meaning that there had been snow on the ground for sixty-four consecutive days. There was no wind. The advantages of that for the burglar were the same as for a patrolling policeman. It meant that sounds travelled. Breaking glass, the crack of a door being forced open or a burglar alarm could be heard easily. The footsteps of a policeman or the engine of a car could be heard just as easily.

These were conditions he liked.

He donned his dark clothing.

He was careful not to carry anything which could incriminate him. The police were fond of arresting someone for 'Being found by night armed or in possession of housebreaking implements'. The offence was a felony which could mean being sent to prison for up to five years on first conviction. Although he had never burgled a house, the police would conjure up a worst-case scenario just to give themselves 'reasonable suspicion' which was necessary for them to employ 'a power of arrest'. Planning was everything. He had secret stashes of small knives and tools in a number of locations that he could gain access to, rather than carry them around.

He walked across the road past the entrance to High Shields railway station and headed up the street towards Laygate. He passed the police box and the entrance to New Green Street and stood outside *Allens* department store. That wasn't his target. But to any casual observer he would be just a local lad out late minding his own business.

He stood there for a few minutes watching his breath dissipate into the cold air. The sound of breaking glass came from the rear of the shops in New Green Street. It had been muffled, but to a practiced ear like Sammy's it was obvious. He now had a dilemma. Should he investigate and find out who it was, or should he mind his own business? The trouble was that if anyone had seen him in the area, he would become a suspect. That would be completely ironic – to be arrested for a burglary he hadn't committed. He waited a few moments as he suspected the burglar would've done to reassure himself that he hadn't been discovered. People lived nearby who may have heard it and phoned the police.

He quietly made his way to the opening that led between the shops and the department store and stood listening intently. He heard nothing.

Suddenly, he felt a hand on his shoulder, and he was whipped around and flung against the wall. A policeman pinned his arms against his body.

"And who might you be?" the policeman enquired, his voice firm, hard, deep.

Sammy mumbled his name.

The policeman eased his grip but kept his hand on Sammy's chest, pinning him against the wall.

Sammy saw that the policeman wouldn't stand for any nonsense and tried to relax. He hadn't done anything wrong. Just then a police car drew up alongside them both and a sergeant got out.

"Hello, Sarge, I was on my way to ring in at the box when I saw this fella acting suspiciously."

The sergeant stood next to Sammy, towering over him.

"So why are you here at this time of night, lad?"

Sammy said, "I was walking home when I heard the sound of breaking glass. I went to see where it was coming from."

The constable glanced at the sergeant and said, "Pull the other one, son. Do you expect me to believe that load of shit?"

"I'm telling the truth, officer."

The sergeant said, "Well, PC Richardson, we'd better check it out." The tone of his voice was sarcastic. If he believed Sammy, then it wasn't obvious.

PC Richardson let go of Sammy and pushed him into the dark lane leading to the rear of the shops. He lit up his torch and scanned the premises. The beam searched high and low and eventually settled on some glistening fragments of glass. The officers became more interested and left Sammy standing alone. If he had wanted to, Sammy could have run away, but he followed, slightly behind them.

Suddenly, a face with a shocked expression appeared at a window. The officers relaxed.

"Come on out, son," said PC Richardson. "You are not obliged to say anything unless you wish to do so, but anything you do say will be taken down in writing and may be given in evidence. I'm arresting you on suspicion of burglary under the Larceny Act 1916."

Sammy saw the sergeant raise an eyebrow. PC Richardson was being very formal, presumably for Sammy's benefit as a member of the public.

PC Richardson hauled his prisoner out of the window as the sergeant brought the car into the back lane. The prisoner, a sorry looking man twice the age of Sammy, smelled of alcohol and urine, and said that he only wanted to find a place to sleep. The fact that his pockets contained ample packets of cigarettes and chocolate made Sammy decide that the man wasn't a career burglar.

"I'm sorry if I roughed you up a bit, son," PC Richardson said to Sammy, "but you can't be too careful these days."

"I'm happy to help," said Sammy.

"We'll need you to make a statement."

Sammy nodded reluctantly. If there was any time to be given a licence to burgle shops, it was now. He knew the beat officer would be off the streets, and so would his supervisor. If tomorrow morning a few more burglaries were discovered, it wouldn't take a stretch of the imagination to envisage them being pinned on the middle-aged drunk heading towards the police cells.

An hour later, Sammy was ushered into the police car to be taken home after giving his statement to PC Richardson. The prisoner was due to be put before the court the next morning. A friendly conversation developed between Sammy and the sergeant about crime in South Shields, burglary in particular. Sammy decided to take a chance and pump the sergeant for information.

"I thought it would stop after that one was killed the other week."

The sergeant laughed. "Aye, he did a few, and there's not many been done since."

"You mean there's more than one burglar out there?"

The sergeant gave him a strange look. "Och aye, of course there is. It's just that this one was a bit special."

"Special?"

"Aye. He was prolific. It's a bit strange, though. I've never seen a burglar that big before. He was a big lad alright, if you know what I mean. Most burglars are wee lads."

"I read in the Gazette about the group of burglars who were convicted and sent to prison."

"Aye, we've had a few successes recently. Burglars beware eh?" He laughed.

"So the long arm of the law has solved the burglar problem," Sammy said, joining in the joke.

"You could say that. We've not got a problem now."

Sammy was relieved to hear that and decided to ask questions in another direction. "So the burglar that died was by himself, then?"

"As far as we know. There's no evidence otherwise."

Sammy saw a quizzical look come across the sergeant's face and decided it was time to stop asking questions.

"You're a regular nosey parker, aren't you?"

"Just passing time, that's all."

"By the way, what were you doing walking around the streets at that time of night?"

Sammy felt his throat tighten, although the sergeant wouldn't have noticed in the gloom of the night. "I was on my way home."

"From where?"

"I live here, sergeant. Thanks for the ride."

"Och, aye. Okay. Well thanks for being so public spirited."

The car slowed to a halt and Sammy climbed out of the car and waved as it drove away. Despite the cold, he was sweating. He entered the house and made his way to his bedroom. As he lay in bed, he reflected on the night. It had been rewarding. Not in the conventional way of money and goods, but in the intelligence way. The police weren't looking for him. As far as they were concerned, he didn't exist, except as a helpful and concerned citizen.

Saturday 23rd February 1963

It had been a week since Sebastian had thrown the snowball brick through Jack Tozer's window and his night of passion with Alice. The smashed window had caused Jack a great deal of embarrassment, according to Billie, who had eventually met up with him on the Sunday. He had called in his colleagues because a crime had been committed. They had come and wandered around a bit, then decided it must have been kids playing, even though Jack had pointed to the size ten footprints in the snow outside his front window. Obviously, Jack had kept the presence of Sylvia out of the story. He'd told Billie that he had been feeling unwell and had come home early.

He'd seen Alice every day for a week. They had lunched, walked and snuggled up on couches and in her car. There hadn't been a moment when she was missing from his thoughts. She was a wonderful woman and he wanted to spend more time with her. He despised the fact that she had to go to work. Her presence in his mind had erected a barrier to everything else that was going on around him. Gone were thoughts of Jack's betrayal of his mother and of the mysterious Shafiq and the Sand Dancers. Even Sammy's burglaries and the catastrophic death of Bull seemed to wane in prominence. On more than one occasion he had caught himself thinking of a future with Alice. But the idea had been tempered by a realisation that Alice herself had a say in all this. He knew she had dreams and ambitions of her own and they may not yet feature a Tyneside trader of knick-knacks. He was realistic enough to know that glitz and glitter that looked wonderful on a Saturday night was just a colourful mess of mulch in the gutter on a Sunday morning, like wet confetti after a wedding. He would have to find ways of making some of Alice's dreams come true. Possibly including a Prince Charming from South Shields.

Today was an early start for Sebastian. Jackie was ill so Sebastian had to set up the market stall himself. He'd sent word to a couple of people who occasionally lent a hand at the stall to attend when they could. It was a long cold day tending the stall when you were by yourself. The air was crystal clear and shocking to the lungs if you drew a deep breath. Temperatures were expected to reach a high of three degrees. People were moving about to keep warm rather than to do business. Sebastian read through a few newspapers to stave off boredom, mainly looking for snippets of political news that he could drop into a conversation with Alice.

Five hundred people had been killed in a Libyan earthquake and there had been an announcement that the 1962 Commonwealth Games had created a profit of twenty thousand pounds. Nationally, the teacher's union were upset about proposals to change their salary structure and South Shields police had been boosted by an increase of twenty-one staff.

By nine o'clock the market was in full swing despite the cold. The aptly named Winter sisters, Joan and Elsie, turned up and took over the running of the stall. They were fine dealing with the public and selling goods, but they didn't like closing down at the end of trading. Sebastian would have to be there then.

He rang Alice from the telephone box next to the public conveniences. She agreed to meet him for lunch at a local café at one o'clock. He filled in the time wandering around the market looking at what was on offer and noting how other stall holders did their business and presented their wares. The hubbub of regulars and visitors was transcended by the ribald patter of the stall holders calling out and hollering like fairground barkers enticing customers to buy. This was something that Sebastian had never tried to copy. These people were natural salesmen, while he just displayed goods without trying to kid or cajole anyone. He nodded at his fellow traders and they returned a nod. See and be seen had been a motto of his for years. It was important to know who was doing what. It was also important to show he was keeping tabs on people and prices.

Sebastian took some time out to lean against the police box in the marketplace and pour himself a cup of beef tea from a flask. The salty, meaty drink, a universal remedy for keeping the cold at bay at football matches up and down the country, scorched its satisfying way down his throat and warmed his stomach. A pall of cigar smoke clouded by. He looked around the corner of the box to see where it had come from.

"Hello, Shafiq. Isn't it a bit cold for you today?"

Shafiq grinned and blew another cloud of smoke into the air, watching it dissipate into the atmosphere before speaking. "Good morning, Mr. Crawley. It is indeed cold. But it is still a lovely day. No? How are you this morning? I see your regular employee is not at work today."

"You don't miss much, do you?"

Shafiq's smile broadened. "I like to think that I am a keen observer of life, Mr. Crawley."

"Of life? Or me?"

"You are undeniably an interesting man, Mr. Crawley, but you are one of many men that interest me. It is my job to be interested in people."

"Why? What have I done to make you interested in me?"

Shafiq thought a moment and said, "Every man has the choice in life to walk in the light or crawl in the dark. Sometimes the light dims, but that does not make it dark. Sometimes the light cuts through the dark and all you see is people who make the wrong choices crawling along blindly."

Sebastian frowned. Eventually, he shook his head and said, "I have no idea what that means. Why is it I can never get an answer that I understand from you?"

Shafiq looked pained. "There are many answers to a single question, Mr. Crawley. You will have to think about it. Here is another saying. It is an Arabic proverb. Take wisdom from the wise – not everyone who rides a horse is a jockey."

Sebastian shook his head. "I'm wasting my time here. You're wasting your time watching me. I'm just trying to make my way in life. There's nothing unusual about me."

"It is my time to waste, but I assure you that we mean you no harm."

"We?" said Sebastian, "I take it you mean the Sand Dancers?"

Shafiq sucked on his cigar for one last time and threw the butt into the gutter. The smile faded.

"I see you have been making some enquiries. About me perhaps? Has your mother's boyfriend been advising you? A policeman's view is possibly not the best interpretation of us. We are a quiet group of people who like to meet and talk with people. Your politicians have a word for it – lobbying. We like to talk to people and persuade them about what we consider to be right."

"Right for whom?"

The smile returned. "If we are happy, everyone is happy, Mr. Crawley. If we are unhappy, we tell people. Sometimes they act on our advice and then we become happy again."

"What about the blackmail, intimidation, violence?" Sebastian had no evidence of these accusations but wanted to see Shafiq's reaction."

Shafiq's eyes narrowed. His voice lowered. "Those are serious allegations, Mr. Crawley. I warn you not to repeat them. It is unhealthy. Accusations such as those make us very unhappy. You should listen to people other than those in law enforcement. Their views are biased. Our brotherhood wants nothing more than to exist in peace and harmony with our fellow men. We may have different religions, but our God is the same."

Sebastian didn't think that was a strictly religious quote. It was more along the lines of 'there is more than one way to skin a cat.' But Shafiq's demeanour showed that his brotherhood didn't take kindly to being attacked. He opened his hands in appeasement. "You've said before that you're interested in me. I have no idea why. I mean you or your organisation no harm. I've lived twenty-odd years without you, and I see no reason whatsoever for needing you in the future. I don't understand what you do and I haven't got time to play games."

Shafiq offered Sebastian his hand. Sebastian took it and shook. It wasn't friendly. It wasn't business-like. It was as if they had made an agreement. In fact it felt as though there was a bonding. Whatever it was, Sebastian felt relieved somehow. He glanced down at their hands, at the tattoo rising and falling, like a man performing a waltz.

Shafiq said, "Our paths will cross again, Mr. Crawley. It is destiny. Destiny involves choosing paths. It is not the same as fate. Fate is something that does not have a choice. I bid you farewell ... for the moment."

Sebastian watched him walk briskly through the market and down King Street, where he was lost among the Saturday shoppers. He poured himself another cup of beef tea and emptied the dregs into the gutter.

17

Monday 25th February 1963

Jack Tozer was surprised to find himself in bed.
"I made it this far, then," he mumbled to himself. Then consciousness began to assert itself. The room swam. He lay in bed with his eyes shut, assessing the strength of his hangover. It was a mighty one. The worst he could remember. It had been years since he'd experienced that swirling room effect.

He broke wind. It was a long and resonant fart that almost lifted the sheet from the bed. He waited a few seconds and then smelled the stench as it seeped around the room. His mouth was dry and sticky. It had been some session, some weekend.

He remembered that much. The beer hadn't stopped flowing since Friday. Billie had been kind and loving and more than active in the bedroom. She'd been Plan B; Sylvia was visiting relatives in Edinburgh and hadn't been available.

On Friday, drinks in a Workingmen's Club and a fish supper had ended in sex. Saturday's session had started when the pubs opened at eleven, and when they closed at three he had gone home and slept until six. Billie had made him a meal and they were both out again by seven. She'd mentioned that thirty Bingo halls around the country had taken part in a competition and a Boldon man had scooped the prize at the Odeon

"He told reporters that he was going to buy himself a car and use the rest to put down as a deposit on a new house," she'd said.

So they'd tried their luck. A small win had meant that the evening had cost almost nothing. Then it was home again. Another coupling with Billie.

He remembered waking up on Sunday. And Billie had stayed to make Sunday lunch when he went the club at midday. He remembered returning to a roast lamb dinner, which he polished off with relish, and the two bottles of whisky nestled in a bag by the door – a gift from a 'friend.'

Jack farted again. He clutched the sheets and blankets around his neck in an attempt to stop the foul gas reaching his nose but all it did was delay the inevitable by a few seconds. He debated whether to get up or stay where he was.

He remembered watching *Wagon Train* with Billie around five thirty. That was when she'd mentioned someone had seen him with another woman in Newcastle on Valentine's Day.

"So who was she?" she asked.

"I'm sorry I can't tell you. It's police business."

It was his stock reply. It gave him time to think. Who the hell had seen him? He hadn't seen anyone he knew. Not that it mattered. In a week or two Billie would be history as far as their relationship was concerned. He was tiring of her and Sylvia was looking good as a replacement. She was a touch of class compared to Billie.

"That won't wash, Jack. I need to hear more than that. You owe me that much."

Jack growled at her. He owed her nothing. He had given her a good time for nearly a year. She had done well out of the relationship. "That's all you're going to get, woman. I don't need to tell you anything about what I do."

"But, Jack, we're together. It's common decency to give me an explanation."

Jack leaned over to her and spat out the only reply he would give her on the matter. "It was police business. It doesn't concern you. Now shut up about it. And look, we've never been together. It's been convenient for both of us. You've got more out of this than I have. You're a slag, Billie. Nothing more. Nothing less."

No-one was more surprised than Jack when Billie slapped him across the face. At first, he was stunned, then he stood up and cuffed her with his right hand and sent her sprawling on the floor.

"Get up and make me some tea. And watch your mouth. What gives you the right to talk to me like that?"

He snatched up the bag that contained the whisky and relieved it of one bottle. He screwed off the top and took a huge slug as Billie crawled up the chair and went into the kitchen. Who the Hell did she think she was demanding answers like that?

Ten minutes later Billie carried a tray of salmon sandwiches into the sitting room and placed it beside Jack. He said nothing. He ate three sandwiches and then tossed the remainder and the tray onto the floor.

"These are shit! Can you not do anything right? You're bloody hopeless."

He swigged from the whisky bottle again. Billie bent down to pick up the sandwiches. Jack smacked her again. The blow caught her nose and a spray of blood danced up the sideboard. Jack roared with laughter.

"Stupid cow. Now you look like a real slag. You could get yourself a job as a whore down the docks at any time. Ask your father. He's seen plenty of them."

Billie ran upstairs. Jack took another swig of whisky.

Jack shuffled into a new position in bed and realised he was fully clothed.

"Bloody Hell," he grumbled, "it must've been quite a bender.

He swung his feet onto the cold floor and lurched towards the bathroom. The light was already on. Out into the landing, he caught sight of Billie's coat at the bottom of the stairs. He squinted into the gloom. There was something else down there – something that he couldn't quite make out. It was a few moments before his brain sorted out the bits of information and fused them together into decipherable form.

"Christ!"

Adrenaline surged through him and camouflaged his pain and discomfort. He scampered down the stairs and saw Billie lying there – disjointed, pale, broken. Her face was smeared in blood from two scratches across her left cheek and a broken nose.

"Christ Almighty!"

He reached out to feel for a pulse, but he already knew she was dead.

Billie was dead.

God! How was he going to deal with this?

He sat on the bottom stairs gazing at her body until panic gave in to professional calculation. He slowly constructed a story of what could have happened. Billie was careless. Yes, that was it. A simple accident. He'd be the selfless, loving partner. Crestfallen. A sudden and unexpected loss of a loved one.

He started to tidy up the house, momentarily surprised by the remnants of salmon sandwiches on the floor and a television with a broken screen.

"Jesus!"

Then he remembered his Frankie Vaughan impersonation. 'Give me the moonlight, give me the girl.' And the trademark kick that sent the tray sailing into the television. The screen popping and *Wagon Train* dissolving into the cathode ray tube at the back of the set. He turned the television to the wall and cleaned up the salmon sandwich debris. He went back upstairs. Halfway up another fragment of memory surfaced.

He was at the bottom of the stairs, salmon sandwich sticking to his feet.

"Where are you, whore? Get down here and clean up this bloody mess."

Whisky. He was carrying the whisky bottle.

"Billie! Billie! Where the bloody hell are you?"

Billie appeared out of the bathroom at the top of the stairs holding toilet paper against her nose. She looked at him, terrified, and ran into the bedroom. Jack staggered up the stairs. Billie came out of the bedroom carrying her coat and a bag.

"Where th'ell d'you think you're going?" Jack slurred, swaying like a tree in a gale.

Billie squeezed past him and said, "Home."

As he washed and shaved, he remembered grabbing at the bag. He put on his best suit. He had to maintain an air of authority. His colleagues would want to inspect his house from top to bottom. He made himself a pot of strong tea and a few slices of toast.

Had they tussled?

He picked up the phone.

He stared at the top of the stairs for a moment. Had he heard a scream? Or was he now just imaging that? She must have fallen, he said to himself.

He rang 62222 and reported the tragic accident that had resulted in the death of his fiancée.

Blanche Fada wrote another note for the attention of the Sand Dancers. A friend had mentioned a special cargo that was arriving at Tyne Dock at the weekend. He'd told her the ship's name but not what was special about the contents of the hold.

Her plan was to drop the note off at the given address and then go down to the market and browse. She'd been in the house all weekend and needed a breath of fresh air. The sun was shining but it was still very cold. She wrapped up well and set off towards Eleanor Street. She turned left and crossed over Shortridge Street to Alma Street, where the note was left with a young woman with ginger hair who accepted it without comment. Her journey took her from there into Woodbine Street and down onto Ocean Road, where she turned left and kept on walking to the crossing at King Street. She looked up Fowler Street and saw what appeared to be a convoy of marked and unmarked police cars heading up towards the Town Hall and beyond. Something was going on. Perhaps she'd be told by somebody in the know, or, more probably, read about it in the Gazette tomorrow. She continued her walk to the market.

It didn't take much for the locals to decide that they needed a visit to the market. A bit of sunshine had brought them all out. It was busy. She meandered between the stalls until she came to the one owned by Sebastian, who was in the process of selling some kind of shisha pipe to a well-dressed woman. He was charming her, although it wasn't necessary. She was going to buy it anyway. Blanche caught Sebastian's eye and waved. He returned the greeting. She gave him the thumbs up and he nodded. She moved on. She decided she would call in to see Billie on her way back home. Old Tommy would be out somewhere, Sebastian was here, so Billie would be by herself. It was an excellent opportunity to have a chinwag and a cup of tea with a mate.

An hour later she turned into Catherine Street on her way home. She carried a string shopping bag with a few groceries. She paused outside Tommy Heath's house and knocked on the door. There was no reply. She knocked again but there was still no answer. She was just about to leave when a police car entered the street and pulled up next to Blanche. She watched as a big burly policeman rapped on the door.

"There's no-one in," said Blanche. "I've been knocking for a couple of minutes."

"I see," said the copper. "Do you know where I could find Mr. Sebastian Crawley or Mr. Thomas Heath?"

"Why? What's it about?"

The officer smiled briefly before donning his official face. "I'm afraid I'm not at liberty to say. I need to speak to one, or both, of those two men as a matter of urgency."

Blanche sensed that the policeman was adamant and decided to tell him what she knew.

"I don't know where Tommy is, but Sebastian runs a stall in the Market Place. I saw him there about an hour ago. It's the one that sells all the foreign pipes and stuff."

The policeman nodded as if he recalled the stall. "Thank you. I'll go there now."

The officer climbed back into the car and drove off. Blanche carried on along the street and up the bank to her home. She was worried. A policeman coming to your door was never a good thing. Of course Billie was seeing a policeman, maybe he'd been injured and they wanted to tell Billie straight away. No. The copper had said he wanted to speak to Tommy or Sebastian. Maybe Jack Tozer had been killed and they wanted to speak to the men of the house for them to tell Billie about it. That was a police procedure wasn't it? In truth, she came up with a dozen scenarios each of which could have been viable. She would have to speak to Sebastian or Billie as soon as possible to find out the true story. And, depending on the outcome, write a note in her diary and a little message for Shafiq and his brotherhood.

Sebastian was relieved when Jackie turned up from his sickbed. Jackie said that his wife was 'doing his head in' and decided that he would rather be here than at home. Sebastian told him he could pack up and leave anytime if he started feeling unwell, but Jackie produced a hearty mince pie and told him he had all the medicine he required right there.

Sebastian was just about to leave when a police officer made his way to the stall. He said, "Are you Sebastian Crawley?"

"I am."

"You are Sebastian Crawley from Catherine Street?"

"Yes."

"Mr. Crawley, I'm afraid I have some bad news for you. Can you please come with me?"

Bewildered, Sebastian said, "Yes, of course."

They made their way to the car and got inside.

18

Tuesday 26th February 1963

The flowers had started arriving the previous afternoon and there had been a steady flow since. Some people, too shy or too poor to buy flowers, had pushed cards or notes expressing their condolences and sympathy through the door. The first lot were read with interest, those that followed were given a cursory glance. Tommy and Sebastian sat in a darkened room behind closed curtains, silent. Women usually hugged and wept, men were stoic. Both knew they had shed tears in private but had never thought to talk about it. They didn't know how to act. Their job had been to comfort their women, to show resolve and fortitude. But what do you do when the woman was gone? Who made the tea in moments like this? Or the sandwiches? Who would do their washing now? These mindless questions filtered through their grief. Their world had changed – but it hadn't in so many ways.

The clock on the sideboard ticked harrowingly. Tommy sat in his chair wearing a dark suit. Sebastian was his mirror image. Both stared at the fire, which had crumbled into a single mass of barely glowing embers. Both recognised the need for more coal. Neither had the will or the energy to remedy the situation.

Visitors were few. The police, a minister and Blanche Fada had displayed the full gamut of emotions they were likely to encounter in the next few weeks or months. The police were professional and courteous with a hint of sympathy. The minister was caring and thoughtful with a hint of other worldly salvation. Blanche epitomised the deep emotion and irrational guilt of a deeply loved friend. An undertaker from the Co-op had received his commission with gratitude and professional reverence. There was a slight hitch. A post-mortem was due to be held, and that would be followed by an inquest.

As far as Sebastian was concerned the biggest surprise was that Jack Tozer hadn't paid them a visit, after all his mother had fallen to her death in Jack's house. A suggestion had been made that Jack might have been too overwrought by the incident to call on them. Sebastian was, in many ways, glad that Jack hadn't turned up. It would be too much for three men to be sharing these emotions; three men who loved the same woman, for different reasons, in their own individual ways.

The telephone had rung on a couple of occasions but neither of the men had been inclined to answer it. It was possible that one of the callers may have been Jack, so he may have to be given the benefit of the doubt. Sebastian didn't know if Alice was aware of the situation, and at that moment didn't particularly care. Tommy was lost. He had loved two women in his life – his wife and his daughter - both had died before their time, both cut down before they could dote on grandchildren or become harridans to their henpecked spouses.

The sound of the letterbox opening and post dropping on the floor stirred both men from their tainted reverie.

Sebastian said, "I'll get it."

Tommy said, "I suppose I'd better get some coal."

Both shuffled out of the room looking ten years older than they were.

Sebastian found three cards on the passage floor. He ripped them open and read the sentiments. He carefully arranged them on the sideboard with the others. Tommy came in with a scuttle of coal and tipped it onto the embers. It would be touch and go whether they would regenerate the fire or put it out.

Suddenly Sebastian felt the need to go out of the house.

"Are you ok, grandad? I need to get out and clear my head a bit."

Tommy nodded and slumped into his chair, not saying a word.

"I'll be back soon."

Sebastian stepped out into the street and strode up the hill hoping that he wouldn't see anyone who wanted to commiserate with him. Fifteen minutes later he stood outside Ede House where Alice worked. He debated whether or not to go in and tell her his news or ask someone to tell her that he was outside. His deliberations were decided when Alice came out of the door clutching a handful of mail.

"What's the matter?" she asked when she saw him up close. "What's happened?" she said when he didn't answer.

Sebastian leaked tears. His shoulders shook. A pitiful whimper escaped from his throat. Another worker from the office appeared at Alice's side and eyed Sebastian curiously. Alice thrust the post into her hands and told her to post it. Alice embraced Sebastian and ushered him into a small reception room where councillors normally saw voters. Sebastian slumped into a chair and bent over, head in hands. It was a controlled cry, reminiscent of a silent movie from fifty years before. He took huge, gulping breaths and swayed backwards and forwards. Alice was frightened. She leaned in towards him and held his head to her chest. Tears began streaming down her face in sympathy.

Outside the window, the virgin snow had been covered with a faint dusting of industrial grime, intruding, maligning, tarnishing the once pristine vista.

After a few minutes, Sebastian composed himself enough to say, "Mam's dead."

Colour drained from Alice's face.

"Oh my God, Sebastian. How?"

"She fell down the stairs at Jack's house yesterday morning. She was drunk."

Alice hugged him harder. Sebastian stared out the window into Westoe Road, and beyond to the Ingham Infirmary where his mother's body lay.

"How's your grandad taking it?"

It was a silly question, and she knew it, but saying how sorry you were at times like this was trite at best.

"He's been there before with grandma, but nothing can prepare anybody to have to cope with the death of a child"

"Where is he now?"

"At home."

"Shouldn't you be with him?"

"I had to come out. I had to see you."

She pulled him closer and hugged him tightly. After a few moments thought she said, "Right. We're going back down there now. I'll tell work that I need to leave. Give me a couple of minutes."

Alice left the room and came back two minutes later wearing a red coat. She held his hand and guided him through the door to the cold outside and to her car parked nearby. The next few minutes were spent in silence as she drove through the town centre and into Catherine Street.

Half an hour later, Alice had made tea for Tommy and was trying to get the two men to engage in conversation. Perhaps it was too painful or too soon, she thought, because neither of them was inclined to talk about Billie.

Thursday 28th February 1963

Blanche Fada was devastated. Her close friend was dead and now she had a letter informing her that her house was to be demolished as part of a slum clearance scheme. The area was going to be redeveloped. Her section of Broderick Street, along with Eleanor Street, Wouldhave Street, Shortridge Street and Alma Street were going to be wiped from the local landscape.

Blanche had spent the afternoon crying and wailing. She wanted to comfort Sebastian and his grandad, but she needed comforting too. She hadn't the strength to be steadfast and stiff upper lipped and didn't have the domestic soul capable of making endless cups of tea and sandwiches. She needed to scream and shout – so that's what she did. She threw herself onto her bed and punched and kicked and tore anything she could lay her hands on.

Poor Billie – she never had a life worth living. She rarely complained. All she ever wanted was to love and be loved. Everyone outside her family had taken all she had to offer and hadn't shown her the decency and respect she was owed. She was a lost soul - and now her soul was lost forever. She looked at the clock, expecting it to stop. She almost willed it to stop as a portent, a sign that demonstrated that Blanche was aware of her thoughts. The clock ticked on dismissively.

When Sebastian went to bed, he realised it was the last day of the month and, as usual, reflected on the past month and give it a rating on his personal scale of 'goodness'. He already knew what the answer would be – the worst month of his life. It was hard to imagine that a month where he had moved from having a relationship with a casual girlfriend to that of an intense lover could figure so low in his estimation. That rich, passionate and powerful feeling paled into insignificance when measured against the loss of Bull Cowell and the accidental death of his mother.

He took his time re-examining every painful and thrilling memory. He considered his business life, social life and personal life. There was an inclination to isolate each section and pass judgement. And that's what he did. It ended up like a school report where each subject was marked separately with a score and a comment. His business was fine, although that remained largely due to the goodwill of the Yemeni people. The news yesterday that the Yemeni government had made an official complaint about the 'aggressive' nature of Britain towards their country was of concern to him and something that might have ramifications later on. He'd also read of the demolition of nearby streets and realised that his childhood was about to be obliterated in the name of progress. His grandad had said weeks ago that it was only a matter of time before the whole area was razed to the ground. He didn't believe him at the time, but here was official confirmation that he was right. Soon, he guessed, the house in which he lay, the house that had witnessed his childhood, would be condemned and bulldozed and ready to be taken to a landfill site. A century of memories erased.

February had been a bad month.

March 1963

19

Friday 1st March 1963

Detective Sergeant Smith sat in his office with his feet up on the desk reading the *Shields Gazette*. It was partly his job to feed the newspaper with crime details and he took a particular interest to see if they got the details correct. On more than one occasion he'd had to speak to the editor about discrepancies, but, credit where it was due, they usually reported what he told them. He accepted that sometimes they used the information with a big dose of artistic licence. That was fine. After all, they were in the business of selling newspapers.

The item about Tip Pickers taking coal from Marsden Colliery was there. The prolonged bout of bad weather had eaten up supplies of coal and coke for the average family and a lot of people had been laid off work. One way to reduce household expenditure was to scour the slagheaps for coal that cost nothing, unless you were caught and prosecuted. Many a man had found himself with a criminal record when all he was doing was to fend for his family.

He read the other news items. The local MP Chuter Ede had been made head of a committee to investigate the modernisation of parliament. He smiled at that one. Ede was coming to the end of his career. By the time the report was ready, he would have retired. Still, Ede was a clever bloke – a former Home Secretary and Leader of The House. He scanned further. Workers could now be paid by cheques rather than cash. Again, he shook his head. It would take more than a piece of paper to reassure the common working man that it was the best way forward. In his experience, the working man liked to get his hard-earned money in a little brown envelope and count it – all £15 17s 3d a week they said were the average wages, a quarter of what he was getting. The ritual of giving the wife her housekeeping money was how it had happened for generations, and that's how it would be for generations to come. The wife would take the money and run to the shops. Although, not to Liptons in King Street it would seem, given the article announcing that it was to close for 'uneconomical' reasons. He shrugged his shoulders. Shit happens.

DS Smith heard the sound of heels approaching his door. By the time it opened and a secretary poked her head into his office, he was sitting upright reading crime reports.

"The Super wants to see you. Five minutes. In his office."

Smith groaned inwardly. The Superintendent never wanted to see him unless there was something amiss. He couldn't think of anything that had needed to be prepared, so maybe it was a compliment. CID had had a good month and the crime figures were lower than normal. He quickly scanned the Daily Log to make sure he was up to-date with events before heading towards the Super's office.

Superintendent Archibald Balfour was a wiry, slim, moustachioed man from Dundee, in Scotland. No-one knew how he managed to become a Superintendent in South Shields. It may have been his background in the Scots Guards, or his childhood as the son of a Scottish laird, or his wife being the sister of the Mayor, but as far as operational police officers were concerned, he was a waste of space. He didn't know one street from the next, or one estate from another. He could find his way to the beach or to Tyne Dock but anywhere else required a driver to take him. He was very good at knowing Police Regulations, Terms and Conditions of Service and every member of the Council.

"Take a seat, Sergeant."

Smith sat on the other side of the Super's desk.

"It was an unfortunate business the other day, wasn't it?"

"Sir?"

"That business with Tozer."

Smith nodded his understanding

"It's certainly a bit of a do," he said. "Not like Sergeant Tozer to be involved in something like this. My sympathies are with him at the moment." He smiled an appropriate smile.

"How well do you know him?"

The question put Smith on his guard. It wasn't one that he expected.

"Professionally? He is an effective enough police officer. As a man, a private individual, I hardly know him."

Superintendent Balfour nodded, acknowledging the distinction.

"Did you know his fiancée?"

Smith rubbed his chin as he thought. He'd seen Jack with the woman called Billie on a couple of occasions, He'd been surprised to find she was his fiancée. As far as he knew she was just the latest in a long line of woman, none of whom had lasted twelve months. Jack was a womaniser. A love them and leave them type of man. Smith didn't understand his success with women, but successful he was. Tozer was a little bit too much of a braggart for his liking. CID work was about subtlety and finesse, two words that were never levelled at Tozer.

"I didn't know her at all. I was introduced to her once. I know that her father is an old soldier from the Great War and her son has a stall on the market. They're an unremarkable family, sir, none of whom are known to the police."

Superintendent Balfour leaned back in his leather chair and half turned towards the window that looked out over Keppel Street towards Binns. He opened a packet of cigarettes and lit one. Almost as an afterthought he offered the packet to Smith, who declined, although he dearly wanted to fill his pipe.

Balfour said, "You attended the scene, didn't you?"

"I did."

"Did you find anything untoward?"

"Sir?"

"Did anything strike you as a bit odd?"

"The television had a broken screen and was facing the wall. There was some glass in the carpet."

"What about Tozer?"

"He was a bit subdued."

"Subdued? Would that be your reaction under those circumstances?"

"Sir, are you trying to get at something I'm not aware of?"

The Super ground out his cigarette and leaned forward with his elbows on the table. "What I'm trying to get at, Sergeant, is this: was there a sufficient investigation into Mrs Crawley's death?"

"Investigation? There was a domestic death as the result of an accidental fall due to the lady being intoxicated." Anxiety was beginning to creep into his voice.

Balfour picked up a report from his desk and handed it to Smith.

"There was a post-mortem on the body. That's the report."

Sergeant Smith took the report and hurriedly scanned each page. After a few minutes he put the report back on the desk.

Balfour said, "We appear to have taken some things for granted, Sergeant."

Smith nodded reluctantly, saying nothing.

Balfour continued. "It's the old conundrum, isn't it? Billie Crawley died as the result of her injuries after falling down the stairs. The question is, did she fall or was she pushed?

Smith shook his head. "I can't believe for one moment that Jack Tozer pushed her down the stairs. Jack's a lot of things but he's not a…"

"Murderer?" said Balfour without a smile.

Smith shook his head again. "This is not a murder, sir. Jack wouldn't do this deliberately."

"I thought you said you didn't know him as a man."

"I don't. But I do know that Jack wouldn't allow himself to get into this situation."

"The report says that some of Mrs Crawley's injuries were received before she fell to her death. Was Sergeant Tozer responsible for them, I ask? And if so, what were the circumstances that led to those injuries? What did Tozer say when you arrived at the scene?"

"He gave a concise account of events and said that he last saw her the previous night prior to going to bed. They'd had one or two drinks and gone to sleep. He found her when he went to the toilet the next morning. He presumed she'd overbalanced and fell to her death."

"The toxicology report says there was no alcohol in her blood, only on her clothing."

Smith shrugged. "That doesn't mean she didn't lose her balance and fall."

"How do you account for the injuries?"

"I can't. But he wouldn't be the first person to have to put his woman in her place during an argument."

Balfour frowned and drew another cigarette from his packet. Smith was sweating profusely and gasping for his pipe.

Smith said, "There was one thing that I thought very strange. Tozer was wearing his best suit when I got there. There was also the smell of toast. It was as if he had taken his time before reporting the accident. It never occurred to me at the time that he was *prepared* when he called it in."

Balfour stood up. Smith leapt to his feet, as was the convention within the service.

"That's all for now, Sergeant. You must keep this to yourself, you understand."

"What's the next step sir?"

"Nothing at the moment. And I do believe that when the Chief Constable is appraised, he will take no further action against Sergeant Tozer simply because there is no evidence to support a crime having been committed. We might have to give Sergeant Tozer the benefit of the doubt. Although I don't suppose that he will be promoted any further than his current rank. We don't like unexplained things. We don't like people to make waves. Sergeant Tozer is batting on a sticky wicket from now on. Remember, tell no-one outside this room. You are dismissed, Sergeant."

Smith hurriedly decamped and almost ran back to his office. He fumbled for his pipe and tobacco and was grateful for the rich blend's soothing properties as he slumped into his chair. He picked up a pen to write a few notes about the meeting, another habit he'd learned over the years when dealing with senior officers. Many had hazy memories when asked to recount conversations that were now being questioned. He noticed his hand was shaking. This was a load of shit. It had nothing to do with him other than he attended the scene. There weren't any suspicious signs. He opened his pocketbook and reread the notes he had made at the time. He saw the entry which concluded his observations as 'no suspicious circumstances' and put the book down. Was there nothing suspicious? Had he missed something? Sure, there'd been a few odd things, but nothing that would cause anybody to suspect a fellow officer of the law. The Super was reading things into the report that weren't there. Bastard.

Sebastian responded to the ring of the telephone. He still wasn't used to it being there and dimly wondered what the noise was before recognition dawned.

It was Alice.

"Sebastian, it's me." Her voice was soft and husky as if she'd been smoking. "I have to drive south today. My mother's ill."

Alice had received her own phone call less than an hour before. Her mother had collapsed. Her father had called to say that she was being taken to the local hospital. They thought it was a stoke or something. She promised to attend as soon as possible.

Sebastian sighed, "Yes, you must go. You never know when they'll be taken from you."

He didn't want to elaborate. Of course, she must go. Even though he felt tiny twinges of frustration. He needed Alice here. She was a steadying, different voice amidst the local frenetic ululations of the past day or so. He could tell that she was reluctant to leave him in his hour of need, but the threat of suffering her own catastrophic loss assumed supremacy on her list of priorities.

"I don't know how long I'll be. I…"

"Alice, just go," Sebastian said, "Let's just get through all this shit and see what happens."

They said their farewells and Sebastian trudged back to his bed on the verge of tears.

Shafiq squinted at the collection of notes laid before him on the table. A cup of tea with a piece of lemon loitered near his right hand, his gold ring reflecting off the china. He donned a pair of spectacles, a recent necessity when reading, and sifted through the messages. Most were meaningless – at the moment. Sometimes these snippets of information could be dropped into conversations with people, who would wonder where the knowledge came from and how Shafiq had got hold of it. It also made them think 'how much more about me does Shafiq know?' It gave him an edge when speaking to people. It also helped in feeding crucial information up the line to his boss. Shafiq had taken a man called The Collator as his role model, a policeman in the area who collected intelligence about known criminals and disseminated it to all the other officers. The difference between them was that Shafiq passed the serious stuff upwards and kept the rest to himself.

He was an important man within the brotherhood. He had a high profile. He was the 'fixer'. His bosses were almost anonymous in the local community; they preferred to keep a low profile. The brotherhood thrived by putting pressure on people, businesses and organisations, but rarely became involved in major crime. All they asked from criminal organisations was to be informed of what was happening and to be paid a fee for allowing it to happen. If no fee was paid, enquiries would be made, and a 'tax' levied. The initial problems in setting up such a scheme had involved a show of violence, but the Sand Dancers were usually regarded as 'friendly' by most criminals. An individual thief was almost immune to the power of the brotherhood unless he cropped up in information supplied through notes. On occasions, an individual's crime spree went undetected by either the Sand Dancers or the police.

Shafiq prioritised the notes. He kept a card system in a filing cabinet behind his desk. He usually spent two hours a day reviewing, analysing and updating his system. He was confident that he was probably more acquainted with everyday life in South Shields than any other person in the borough. Despite what the police said. On occasions, he received the same information from different sources. That was useful for cross referencing. Sometimes the information was gossip – and no more than that – but it was all written onto his cards.

A piece of information he'd received from several sources was the most prominent in his mind at that moment. He'd passed it up the line as soon as he'd received it. It was the death of Billie Crawley. He knew his boss had a special interest in the Crawley family. He didn't know why, but he had been told to report anything he heard about them. Indeed, he had received a note from the boss for him to 'make acquaintance' with Sebastian Crawley a few months ago. The boss had to be obeyed without question. Shafiq knew his place in the brotherhood and wanted to keep it. He did as he was told but at the same time, he was free to do what he liked.

His information said that Billie Crawley had died as the result of falling down the stairs at her lover's house. One person had used the term 'boyfriend' and another 'fiancée', however lover was the most appropriate in his eyes. The lover was Sergeant Jack Tozer of South Shields Police, which was interesting in itself.

Tozer wasn't a favourite of the brotherhood. He was a man who trod a fine line between being on the right side of the law and operating on the wrong side of it. It was a case of someone who knew the rules and being in the position to bend them sufficiently to get his own way. The brotherhood had tried to influence him some time ago. That hadn't been successful because of his arrogance. It made his inclusion a liability. Inducements had been withdrawn and a watchful eye had been kept on him instead. Tozer thought that he was above the law because he *was* the law.

Shafiq opened a draw and took out one of his cigars. He rolled it between his finger and thumb and licked one end before lighting it. He thought about his last meeting with Sebastian. It had been almost prophetic. That conversation last Saturday had been a crucial moment, and his relationship with Sebastian had undergone a subtle change. Sebastian Crawley had accepted the fact that Shafiq and the Sand Dancers were interested in him in a non-sinister way - almost in a fraternal way. They had shaken hands. Shafiq had done his master's bidding. He wasn't sure what his involvement would be from now on. His boss would decide that. He would have to wait until word came down the line. He smiled, that was fate.

Tommy Heath wandered aimlessly down Catherine Street, over Woodbine Street, and made his way to the bottom of Broderick Street, where Blanche Fada lived. He stood at the junction and surveyed the houses and surrounding streets. This was where he was born and lived most of his life. This was home. This was where he'd learned the rules of survival. And he had survived. He had survived the Great War. He had survived the death of his beloved wife. He had survived the trauma of bringing up a baby daughter almost by himself. He had survived his daughter's flirtation with the Sand Dancers, her pregnancy, marriage and death of her husband. He had survived being the father figure to his grandson. But now he felt no longer like a survivor. His daughter was gone. Billie had developed many faults over the years and made many mistakes in her brief life, but he loved her like no other.

The biting wind caused Tommy to gather his coat more firmly around himself. The cold seeped through the soles of his shoes. Tommy couldn't have cared less. He had lost the need for living. He was an old man. It was wrong that he had outlived his daughter. There was no reason to live.

He turned a full 360 degrees. These homes were part of his youth and now it was to be demolished. To an outsider these homes were slums. To him every blackened brick carried a memory, every cobbled stone had witnessed him growing up. The roads had taken him to fight for his country as a young firebrand and echoed to his footsteps when his haunted frame stumbled back home. A hundred years of smoke and grime rested on the slates that formed the roofs. A hundred years of sweat and tears were the mortar keeping the chimney pots and stacks together as they gorged out plumes of smoke into steely skies. The corner shops still showed traces of current and previous owners. Their hoardings proclaimed their own death knell. The streets were jaded, worn, faded and torn, leeching their colour and character into the gloom and grey. Generations had lived here. The community was dying. Inside, so was Tommy. He stood there and wept – for himself, his way of life, and his history.

20

Thursday 7th March 1963

For a week or more after his mother's death Sebastian had received sympathy from a multitude of people, a lot of whom he didn't know. He stood at his mother's graveside and gazed at the flowers. Rain fell softly, causing the ink to run on the messages of condolence written on the cards, and some beautiful blue/black words and tributes were in the process of being eradicated, lost forever, draining into the cold earth.

They say that time lasts forever - however that was measured – and it waited for no man. It always wins in the end, they said. Nobody can stand nose to nose against time and be successful. They also say that time's a great healer. It is. Eventually, it cures everything with death.

Sebastian raised his head and gazed into the greyness above him. The rain was light and gentle, dampening his face. He wanted to scream at the world and its creator. He wanted to punish someone, seek revenge, hurl accusations and lay the blame for his mother's death at their feet. But it had been an accident. The police had told him that no-one was to blame. He couldn't even point his finger at Jack Tozer. He felt completely emasculated.

He turned away from the grave and began walking towards the cemetery's exit. His mother's final resting place was less than half a mile away from where she'd died. Jack hadn't turned up for the funeral. He was 'too upset to attend'. He had obviously also been too upset to speak to Sebastian or his grandad since the accident. No words expressing grief or loss had been conveyed to them at any stage. His final communication, a huge floral wreath, dwarfed the family flowers. Another wreath, majestic in construction, quality and colour had also drawn the eye. An anonymous donor. Sebastian assumed the card had become dislodged and lost.

Alice had also sent a lovely wreath. A telephone call two days ago from Surrey confirmed that her mother had suffered a minor stroke and there was every likelihood she would make a substantial recovery. It was her father that needed looking after and Alice had promised to stay with him until domestic help could be arranged. She also promised to return to South Shields as soon as possible. Their conversation had been strangely comforting – loving even. They were missing each other.

As Sebastian neared the cemetery exit he saw a figure standing on the path near the gates. The figure was smoking a cigar, and unusually, the thin grin was missing. The last thing Sebastian wanted was a meaningless chat with Shafiq, so he ignored him and walked straight past.

Shafiq followed.

"Mr. Crawley, sir. I am sorry to impose during this very sad time. Please forgive me. I cannot apologise enough for this intrusion."

"Go away, Shafiq. Not now, please." Sebastian continued walking.

"May I offer my condolences to you and your grandfather."

"OK, thank you, just go." He quickened his pace.

Shafiq followed suit.

"Mr. Crawley, sir, I need to speak to you."

"Go away, Shafiq. This is neither the time nor the place."

"I agree it is indelicate, Mr. Crawley, but it is a matter of importance."

Sebastian stopped and glared at Shafiq.

"What the hell is so important that you need to violate my mother's grave to tell me."

Shafiq bowed his head and his enunciation became dull and drawn. "I do not wish to violate anything, Mr. Crawley. I have every respect for the dead. I too have suffered the loss of a beloved mother. It is indeed the most painful of experiences."

Sebastian took a deep breath and shook his head. He said, "OK, Shafiq, I appreciate your best wishes and accept that you're not here spying on me, or whatever …"

Shafiq interrupted him by raising his hand. "Mr. Crawley, I have come here because it has been decided that you should know something about your mother's death."

Sebastian's brow furrowed. "What? What's that mean? Who has decided?"

Shafiq shrugged his shoulders. "My employers."

"The Sand Dancers? Why would a bunch of criminals decide what I should or shouldn't know?"

The pained expression returned to Shafiq's face. "We are not your enemies, Mr. Crawley. Indeed, we would like you to consider us as your friends."

"You know what they say, Shafiq, 'who needs enemies when you have friends like you.'"

Sebastian started walking away.

Shafiq hurried to catch up.

"Anyway," continued Sebastian, "what is it that is so important that you have to tell me today of all days?"

Shafiq fell in beside him and matched him pace for pace. "We have friends, Mr. Crawley. Friends in the know. Friends who help us."

Sebastian stopped. "Shafiq, I have no time for nods and winks and innuendo. Just tell me straight."

It was Shafiq's turn to take a deep breath. He stared across the cemetery. When he spoke, his voice was cold and low. "Your mother's death may not have been an accident."

Sebastian stepped back and grabbed a street sign for support. "How? Why? What do you mean?" he spluttered.

"We have friends. We have friends in most places, including the police force. One of those friends has given us information that casts some doubt on how your mother met her ... ah ... officially explained death."

Sebastian thoughts raced in tumbling confusion of images and people and relationships It took him a few moments for everything to register. His response was to grab Shafiq by the lapels of his overcoat. Shafiq offered no resistance.

"Listen here, you bastard. What are you trying to tell me?"

Shafiq fought to maintain his composure. He opened up his arms as a sign of open compliance. It was obvious that he was not going to resist so Sebastian released his grip and Shafiq adjusted his coat.

"Mr. Crawley, I understand you are upset. This news is remarkable. It changes perceptions."

"For Christ's sake, Shafiq, tell me what it is."

Shafiq was back in control. He hesitated and took a cigar from his pocket. As he lit it Sebastian noticed a slight tremor in his hands. Sebastian waited, seething inside.

Shafiq glanced around them to make sure no-one else was in earshot before speaking.

"Your mother was visiting her boyfriend, Sergeant Tozer, was she not?"

Sebastian nodded.

"She fell down the stairs and unfortunately died?"

Sebastian nodded again."

"Our contacts in the police force say that there were some unanswered questions about her death."

"Like what?"

"It appears that some of your mother's injuries were sustained prior to her falling down the stairs. If indeed that is what happened."

Sebastian stared at him. A thousand questions demanded an answer all at once, but he said, "Go on."

"The police report says that her injuries were caused 'ante mortem' but it does not speculate how that may have happened."

"Anything else?"

"Yes. Everyone was told that your mother had been drinking alcohol and that was the main reason she fell to her death." Shafiq stared into Sebastian's eyes without blinking.

Sebastian could feel pressure inside his head. If Shafiq didn't tell him what he knew in the next ten seconds, then he would punch him as hard as any man had ever punched another human being.

"Mr. Crawley. This was a misrepresentation of what actually happened."

"Just bloody tell me, Shafiq!"

"The report says that alcohol was a contributory factor …"

Sebastian readied his right fist.

"… but that your mother was completely sober when she died."

Sebastian staggered to a nearby wall and sat on it. The rain instantly soaked his trousers. He shook his head as if the action would shake away all his troubles. His breath became shallow and rapid. He felt nauseous. "Mr. Crawley?"

Sebastian said nothing.

"Mr Crawley. I will take you home."

Again, Sebastian said nothing. His head was spinning. He couldn't marshal his thoughts.

Shafiq raised his arm in the air as if he was a child wanting to answer questions in a classroom. Within seconds a black car drew up by the side of the road and the door opened. A man of middle-eastern appearance climbed out and stood awaiting instructions from Shafiq.

"Mr. Crawley has been taken ill. We need to take him home."

As they drove away, Sebastian's blank face peered out of the back window and watched as a man in overalls closed the cemetery gates.

Tommy Heath was surprised to see Sebastian back so soon. He had only been away an hour. He looked dreadful and disorientated. Tommy sat him down and made a cup of tea and some toast – always a good start when raw emotions were on show. Tommy waited for Sebastian to say something.

Eventually, Sebastian said, "Mam didn't fall down the stairs because she was drunk."

Tommy's face creased in confusion. In his experience death had a way of messing with people's minds. Everyone reacted differently. Some people screamed and shouted while others sought a dark place to hide; some people wailed and wept, and others gritted their teeth and became emotional robots. He'd seen plenty of it in the trenches during the war. Sebastian was usually a rational thinker rarely disposed to making rash comments or knee jerk reactions, so it wasn't easy to assess which category Sebastian fitted into with this outburst. His son was the type of man who accepted the facts as they were presented to him. He wouldn't have expected anything else. So what was happening here?

"Sebastian, the police said …"

Sebastian thumped the table and jumped to his feet. The chair teetered on two legs and a plate leapt in the air in surprise. "The police say a lot of things. It's not always true."

"What do you mean, son?"

"Mam wasn't drunk. In fact, she was stone cold sober when she died."

"Who's told you this?"

"Shafiq."

Tommy's eyes widened. "The Sand Dancer fella?"

Sebastian nodded. "Yes, Shafiq. He also said that my mam had been beaten up before she died."

Now it was Tommy's turn to stand. There was no point in questioning the veracity of what Sebastian had told him. He knew that the Sand Dancers had a way of getting information. If they said something, then they meant it. And that could only happen if their information was true. Their organisation existed because of their access to accurate intelligence.

Tommy stood next to the fire. Sebastian leaned against the sideboard.

Tommy said, "We've been led up the ..."

"Jack Tozer has some explaining to do."

Tommy shook his head. "Is that why he hasn't been anywhere near us?"

Sebastian nodded. "Seems likely."

They stared at each other for a few moments before Tommy sat in his favourite chair. "So, what are we going to do about it?" he said.

Friday 8th March 1963

Tommy walked towards Laygate, not actually thinking, just ruminating on what he'd read in the *Gazette* before leaving the pub. *Liptons,* the grocers in King Street, was closing. A man called Beeching had submitted a report about closing railway stations and doing away with some lines. The railways were losing one hundred and fifty million pounds a year. They were uneconomical. Everything seemed to be uneconomical. The council had approved plans to build a huge housing estate at Simonside. It was progress at the cost of the past. Seven hundred and twenty-five men had been laid off in the shipyards.

Tommy remembered a picture of ice flowing down the River Tyne from a couple of days ago and thought the atrocious weather had something to do with the lay-offs. There was a water shortage in town. He shook his head. It had been snowing for months and there was a water shortage.

These were bad times. South Shields was a desperate place to live. It was old and tired. It needed some action by the council. Industry all along Tyneside was based on old machinery and old practices. The unions were far too many and were likely to call a strike at the drop of a hat. The threat of a docker's strike in Newcastle was a typical example. Tommy wondered why these people didn't realise that their strike affected whole swathes of people who just wanted to earn a crust for their families.

The brooding streets of Laygate came into view and Tommy's pace slowed a little. He found himself humming along to a tune in his head 'Say wonderful things to me' – the latest Ronnie Carroll song. Singing while Rome burned, flitted across his brain. Images of Londoners in the Tube during The Blitz. Into the Valley of Death. Charge of the Light Brigade.

This was a rough part of town.

He became aware of several sets of eyes watching him, and when he turned a corner, he was confronted by three men. They stood evenly balanced with their feet apart. Hands held away from the body like gunslingers; fingers curled into fists, ready for action. They were smoking Capstan full strength cigarettes to emphasise how hard they were. Two of the men wore hats that were meant to show they could've stepped out of a George Raft movie over twenty years ago. Tommy hated these guys and what they stood for. They had all the trappings and mannerisms of hard men, but they hadn't earned the right to intimidate him. Neither of them had stood on the wrong side of a rifle barrel like he had during the Great War. Neither of them had stood toe to toe and swapped punches in a fair fight. And neither had experienced the kind of fear that threatens control of the anal sphincter. Both were flick knife, razor and knuckle duster types. Both were used to working together to thrash vulnerable and frightened locals to enforce unwritten rules. Both were men by gender only. Neither had gained his balls as part of a journey scarred by the mistakes and brutality of real life.

The third one, who wore a pencil thin moustache, smiled at him.

"Mr. Heath. Welcome. Please step inside." He pointed to the back door of a pub.

Tommy had been in here once before. It was one of many pubs in the area. It was common for people to finish work and walk into the pubs with their overalls reeking of sweat, oil and burnt metal.

Here, factory and shipyard smells were swamped by the smells of tobacco and cheap perfume. He noticed a woman sitting in the corner of the room drinking half a pint of some frothy beer. There was no other way to say it, she was the type of woman who looked better in the dark. She was ugly. God had obviously been having a lie down when she was born. Her saving grace was that she was the most attractive person in the room.

Tommy declined a drink and came straight to the point. "You told Sebastian some news."

Shafiq nodded.

"I want you to confirm to me what you told him."

Shafiq slowly lit a cigar. He then told Tommy what he had previously told Sebastian.

"And all of this is true? You're not trying to manipulate us?"

With as great a flourish as he could muster, Shafiq clicked his fingers and one of his thugs produced a few sheets of paper clipped together at the top left-hand corner. It carried the letterhead of South Shields Police.

"Here is a copy of the report, Mr. Heath. You may read it, of course, but you may not have it. We will deny that we have even seen it. As we will also deny that this meeting ever happened."

Tommy glanced around the room. There were maybe twenty people there. Shafiq read Tommy's mind.

"These people are not here, Mr. Heath. They are all somewhere else."

Tommy nodded. Shafiq handed over the report.

The muscles in Tommy's face tightened and he started grinding his teeth as he read through the pages. It was a dispassionate account of his daughter's death, full of phrases such as 'it appears', 'it is possible,' and 'in all probability'. Facts and figures were conspicuous by their absence. He wanted to read something that said his daughter's death was 'an accident', or someone was responsible, but it didn't. It mentioned Billie having injuries 'consistent with an assault'. The only fact that Tommy could glean from the report was that Billie was not intoxicated. It stated that most of the content had emanated from the verbal account supplied by Jack Tozer and it mentioned inconsistencies that needed investigating. A handwritten note, signed by the Chief Constable, had scrawled 'NFA – inform Coroner' at the base of the page. Tommy presumed NFA meant No Further Action.

He handed the report back to Shafiq. "Thank you"

"It is my pleasure to do you a service, Mr. Heath. We do not want you to be told a lie by the police."

"Why's that?"

Shafiq shrugged but didn't answer the question directly. "I must insist that you do not mention this report to anyone, Mr. Heath. Your grandson is aware of it but has not seen it. Also, it would advisable that you do not pursue any action that may compromise our part in this matter."

"What's your angle on this?"

"I'm sorry Mr. Heath. What do you mean?"

"What do the Sand Dancers get out of this?"

Shafiq smiled his thin smile. This was more familiar territory for him. "We like to help people. We like to take care of our friends."

"We aren't friends with any Sand Dancers."

"My information is that you became friends with us many years ago, Mr. Heath. Through your daughter. We are maintaining that friendship. Once you are our friend, we will be your friend always. That is what friendship is about, is it not?"

It had been a long time ago. Billie and Blanche had been caught up with a group of Yemeni youths who were a bit older than them just before the Second World War. Some of the Yemenis had been extended family of Blanche, and one of the youths had taken a particular shine to Billie. At one stage it looked as if the relationship was becoming serious. Tommy remembered taking the youth aside and speaking frankly to him, spelling out his hopes and dreams for Billie and suggesting that their relationship would do neither of them any good in the long run and Billie was too young. The youth agreed to step back a little until Billie was an adult. His maturity had surprised Tommy at the time, and they had shaken hands on the matter. His parting remark had been 'we are friends, sir'.

Tommy had been pleased with the result, only to be thwarted a couple of months later by Billie becoming pregnant and marrying Reginald Crawley.

Tommy held out his hand. He didn't want to be involved with the Sand Dancers, but events had overtaken him. This report had shed new light on his daughter's death, and he wanted to find out the truth. He couldn't do it by himself. He needed the resources of the Sand Dancers.

Shafiq's handshake was firm and strong. The eye contact never wavered. They were friends, at least in Shafiq's definition of the word. For Tommy, they were joined one to the other in mutual benevolence. They had mutual goals. Although what exactly they were had not been decided.

Tommy tramped home with new thoughts and old conversations in his head. Arthur Jones, his commanding officer during the war had said to him, 'It's absolutely pointless worrying about someone who is dead. They can't harm you anymore, nor can they influence anything that you do. By all means, think about them and remember the times you spent together. It's those that are still living that you have to worry about. They can influence what you do or say or how you react in certain circumstances. They can harm you in a whole host of ways. But as you grow older what these people say or do stop having any consequences. What you thought was critical earlier in your life becomes inconsequential to the point that they don't matter at all. And once you're gone, every material thing that you valued becomes someone else's rubbish. Everything in life is temporary – including life itself.'

Things changed all the time. Women had taken over the traditional roles of their husbands in the factories. They had donned overalls or drove tractors while their men folk had fought in the trenches. When the men returned, they discovered their old life had new rules. Women were forced to return to domesticity. The 'land fit for heroes' was a slum infested hovel. The world changed. It never stayed the same for long. And in the future, the new would become old, kids would be pensioners.

It was the circle of life.

Tommy was grieving for his daughter now. He had grieved for Vivien. It wasn't fair that a man could lose his wife and only child before his own death. But that was how life dealt its cards. The people didn't even know which game was being played.

And here he was. An alliance with the Sand Dancers. On the brink of new battles. Shafiq was his new commanding officer. His enemy didn't carry rifles, now they used lies. The new foxholes had a blue light dangling ominously above them.

21

Saturday 9th March 1963

Jack Tozer sat at his desk in the Sergeant's office with a frown on his face and a steaming mug of tea warming his hands as he gazed out into the street. His desk was covered in sheets of paper, files and notes. This was not the usual organised chaos that gave the impression that he was busy. This was darker than that. These papers were the result of his inability to organise his thoughts into a coherent pattern. This was him unable to decide where things went and what he should do. This was inertia rather than procrastination.

It had been twelve days since he'd found Billie's body at the bottom of his stairs. In those twelve days he'd received the commiserations of his colleagues and acquaintances in abundance. He'd managed to appear crestfallen most of the time, but he needed to move on. The last thing he wanted was an air of permanent pity surrounding him. Some of the 'chats' he'd had were like minor interrogations, with his peers and superior officers, and he'd bluffed his way through them as best he could. It was time move on.

Sylvia wasn't replying to his telephone calls. A visit to her office proved unsuccessful too. He concluded that she'd heard all about the commotion surrounding him and had distanced herself from it. He shrugged and put his feet up on the desk.

He hadn't been in contact with Tommy Heath or Sebastian. That was an area he was slightly nervous about - although he didn't really know why. Billie was gone, so the relationship with both those men was gone as well. Sod them for making him feel like this.

Sod them all.

He picked up a report, more burglaries, and stared at it, trying to assimilate its contents. His eyes strayed to the Modus Operandi, or MO – the way a crime was committed. Its familiarity intrigued him and something of the old Jack Tozer returned. It was the same as those burglaries earlier on in the year, the ones that had resulted in the death of that Cowell lad. Even in its turgid state his mind grasped hold of a thought. Was the burglar he had been seeking still active? Was Cowell a random burglar? It certainly made sense. Cowell wasn't the right profile for your typical burglar. He recalled the check he'd made on Cowell with The Collator's intelligence records. It had said that Cowell was previously unrecorded and therefore had no known associates. He got up and walked along the corridor and up the stairs to the CID floor. He found the secretary who had typed up Cowell's case notes and persuaded her to let him look through them. He sat down at a desk and read.

The report on Cowell's background listed several worrying traits. He was a gambler. His favourite hobby was horse racing and he had a flutter every day. Although he had enjoyed moderate successes, he frequently lost money. It appeared that when he won money he usually splashed out on a meal and a lot of alcohol. The rest would be ploughed straight back into horse racing through the recently legalised betting shops, although he still managed to lose some in card games. Words like 'dim-witted' and 'slow' alluded to his level of intelligence. Phrases such as 'easily led' and 'quick to lose his temper' also appeared.

Jack shook his head. Cowell wasn't the burglar he had sought. Someone else was out there. He scanned Cowell's list of friends and his eyes lit up on one name – Sebastian Crawley. He grabbed a pen and wrote down seven names and addresses on a piece of paper and put it in his pocket.

He heard someone singing *Crazy*, a song by Patsy Cline who had been killed in a plane crash in the USA a few days ago. The voice belonged to Detective Sergeant Smith.

Jack nodded. Smith stopped singing and nodded back.

"Can I help you, Jack?"

Jack shook his head and walked briskly out of the office and back down the stairs. He could feel Smithy's eyes following him. It wouldn't take him long to find out what he had looked at.

His chair creaked as he sat back down at his desk. He glanced at the names he'd written down. He knew Sebastian didn't have any criminal record, but he would check out the others. Fifteen minutes later, after a telephone call to The Collator's office, the sheet of paper had a few more scribbled notes written on it. Chief amongst them was a note about Samir al-Aziz, who had been checked in the Laygate area during the early hours of the morning on Saturday 23rd February. He had assisted the police in catching a burglar. Jack frowned. That was unusual to say the least, but what was he doing out at that time of night anyway? The report said he was returning home after seeing a friend – plausible, uncheckable – his friend would have been alerted by now.

Jack picked up his helmet and the piece of paper. Samir al-Aziz was about to get a visit from the police.

Half an hour later he was standing outside the al-Aziz household in Holborn rapping on the front door without getting an answer. The booming sounds of drills and triphammers violating metal hulls in the nearby shipyard permeated the air. Jack stood and looked around the street and detected a few twitching curtains. His visit would be noted and relayed to many ears before the end of the day.

An old woman wrapped up tightly against the cold wandered down the street. As she drew near, she said, "There's no-one in. It's a Saturday. They'll be down street."

Jack nodded to himself. 'Down street' meant the Town Centre. Everyone in South Shields appeared to visit the market and wander down King Street on a Saturday morning.

As she passed him, the old woman said, "Except for Samir. He'll be lying in bed upstairs in the back room. But he might as well be dead the hours he keeps."

Jack walked after the woman. "What do you mean 'the hours he keeps'?"

The old woman continued at the same pace. "He's out all hours of the night, and sleeps during the day. I don't sleep you see. It's the pain in my back. I'm up and look out of the window most nights. Sometimes I see foxes around the bins. And hedgehogs. Although it's been a long, long winter this year."

The woman withdrew a key from her purse and put it in the lock of a door four houses down from the al-Aziz house.

Jack Tozer said, "Can I ask you a few questions?"

The old woman entered her house and said, "I don't talk to the Police." She slammed the door behind her.

Jack scanned the street and saw more twitching curtains. He resigned himself to gaining no further information from this community. However, Samir al-Aziz was now a suspect in his eyes. Jack would have to make more enquiries about his nocturnal activities. The only drawback was that he would have to keep it to himself. If he informed the CID, they would want to take it off him. The CID were glory seekers and Jack was in desperate need of a little bit of glory himself.

Sebastian stared out of his window. The grey skies matched his mood. He'd spent hours trying to think of some strategy to find out the truth behind his mother's death. His grandad had told him of his meeting with Shafiq. That was a surprise. Like a lamb visiting the lion in his own lair. He didn't think his grandad would know where to find Shafiq never mind go and visit him. But his grandad never ceased to amaze him. He wasn't just a big mouth. He had a cool brain capable of identifying problems and then coming up with plans to overcome them.

Sebastian's first reaction had been to confront Jack Tozer on his doorstep. He didn't want to visit the house where his mother died so that idea was out of the question. His second idea was to waylay Jack and beat the truth out of him, or at least arrange for that to be done. That wasn't realistic.

He'd spoken to Alice about it. Alice was down south at her parent's house, although promising to return next Friday to go to work on the following Monday. She'd offered sympathy and caution when he garbled his thoughts about retribution. She'd already broached the subject with Uncle Jim, and the police had reacted to an enquiry from their local MP, but she would need more evidence than Sebastian's accusations to take matters further.

"What about getting a copy of the report?" he suggested.

Alice said she'd see what was possible. That Uncle Jim might be able to pull a few strings to get the report from the pathologist.

Sebastian, however, then thought it would be a bad idea. The Sand Dancers might not like that because it might lead to an investigation about how Sebastian knew there was something in it. Besides, the fewer people who knew anything the better at this stage. Sebastian sighed. There seemed no way forward.

There was a knock on the front door. Sebastian walked down the passage and threw it open. Blanche Fada stood on the doorstep.

"Hello, Sebastian. Have you got a cup of tea for an old mate?"

He led her through to the front room and invited her to sit down while he made the tea. Blanche almost cried at the remnant memories of Billie's tributes that adorned every flat surface. There were obvious signs of neglect everywhere. Dust was gathering in corners. A small cobweb hung near the light in the centre of the room. Finger marks littered unwashed windows and through the door into the kitchen she spied a scruffy looking towel.

"How are you getting on?" she asked knowing what the answer would be.

Sebastian came into the room carrying two cups, one of which was cracked. His answer was a shrug.

"I've come to offer my services."

"In what way?"

Blanche waived her hand around the room. "I think it's fairly obvious that this place needs a woman's touch." She waived his protestations away. "Just until you get back on your feet or organise something else. It's the least I can do. Billie was my closest friend and I care about you and your grandfather. These are rough times, Sebastian, and they'll probably get worse before they get better. All I'm trying to do is give you one less thing to worry about."

It had never occurred to Sebastian that the house needed to be cleaned or that somebody actually spent time doing it. He now noticed the dirt for the first time. "You're right. It could do with a bit of a clean. I'll have a chat with grandad and let you know."

"Ok. So what else is going on?"

The enquiry had been a general one, but Sebastian saw it as an opportunity to unload his worries and fears to a trusted friend. He told her everything, including his meeting with Shafiq and the police report. He also told her about some of his ideas for getting back at Jack Tozer.

Blanche laughed.

"You're sounding like the plot of an Alfred Hitchcock movie. I don't think you'll get away with it somehow. You need to be a lot more subtle than that."

"I know. I need to get a copy of the pathologist report. Any ideas?"

Blanche shrugged and shook her head. "I know a lot of people and there's even more information in my diaries, but I don't know anyone connected to the pathologist's office. Can't help you there."

Silence filled the room for a few moments before Blanche raised an eyebrow and said, "If you know that the records are kept there then it should be a simple matter of stealing it."

Sebastian's stony gaze settled on her. After a few moments he said, "And how do I get into the office?"

Blanche said, "I'm not suggesting that you break into the office yourself. Don't you know anyone who would do it for you?"

Sebastian squirmed a little, unsure whether Blanche knew something more about his friends than she should, but that wasn't such a bad idea. It would be a piece of cake for Sammy. He didn't think there'd be any security on the building. Why would there be? Who would want to break into a mortuary?

After five minutes of silence, Blanche got up and left and Sebastian plunged deep into a plan that involved one of his best friends.

22

Tuesday 12th March 1963

Sebastian knocked on Sammy's front door. It was answered by Sammy's mother, who smothered him in kisses and offered him all sorts of sweets, meats and drinks before he had even made the living room, all of which he refused. Sammy wandered in and commanded his mother to make them some coffee and leave them alone. They had business to discuss.

After ten minutes of apologies and revisiting what had gone on since Sebastian had last been there on New Year's Day, Sebastian said, "I want to run an idea past you."

Sammy smiled. He knew that Sebastian didn't like being involved in illegal activities although he wasn't averse to profiting from them as long as the risk was undertaken by someone else. This was interesting. "Go ahead."

Sebastian told Sammy about his plan for someone to break into the mortuary office and steal the report about his mother's death. He put it in a way that suggested it was a sentimental, albeit macabre, motive that fuelled his desire to have the report.

Sammy said, "I know you, Sebastian. That's bullshit. There's something else."

Sebastian shook his head. "I only want the report."

"So why have you come to me?"

"I want to know if the plan is viable and that there is no undue risk for whoever does it. I came to you because you're the expert in that particular field."

Sammy smiled again. "You want me to do it for you?"

Sebastian looked long and hard at Sammy, then nodded. "Yes, I had you in mind. I know I was less than happy about you and Bull, and before we go any further, I still am upset about it, but I understand how and why it happened. It's done. It's over. And you're right, there is a reason why I want this report. The report will show that my mother wasn't intoxicated and that she had injuries which were received before she died."

Sammy's eyes widened. "Bloody Hell! That means the police haven't done their job properly. Somebody's responsible for her death. Who could've ..." Realisation dawned on him. "Tozer?"

Sebastian said, "There's no proof of course. But he might have a few questions to answer, and at the moment he's not speaking to anyone."

Sammy got up and wandered around the room, thinking things through. After a few moments he said, "I presume you want the report as soon as possible. I can't just turn up tonight and break into the place. I'll need to know what security is in place. It would be helpful if I knew the layout."

The way Sammy spoke demonstrated that he had taken the commission of stealing the report, and Sebastian was grateful for it. The next hour saw them discussing and dismissing proposals until they came up with a workable plan. They left Sammy's house and called in at a local shop to buy a *Gazette* and a note pad. They caught the bus up to Harton Lane and then they separated. A casual observer looking out of the nearby nurse's home would have seen a young man of Middle-Eastern appearance walk up and down Harton Lane and through the hospital grounds as though he was lost and trying to find his way around. The same observer would have seen another young man who looked like a reporter entering the mortuary block with notepad in hand and a *Gazette* in his jacket pocket.

It was already dark when Sebastian arrived back home. He had spent a couple of hours with Sammy and he was satisfied that their plan was an effective one with little chance of discovery. Having said that, there was always the off chance that something could scupper the whole thing. Sammy already knew that, to his cost.

A fire blazed in the front room and Sebastian's grandad sat glumly next to it. Next to him sat Shafiq, trademark smile smirkier than ever at the surprise shown by Sebastian.

"Sit down, son," Tommy said.

Sebastian did as he was bid without comment.

Shafiq said, "I am honoured to meet you in your home, Mr. Crawley. Your grandfather has been so kind as to make me some tea."

Sebastian glanced at Tommy. His expression hadn't changed.

"What can I do for you, Shafiq? It must be something important for you to come and see me here. It's obviously not a social call."

"That is very observant of you, Mr. Crawley. I will come straight to the point."

"That'll be something new, then."

Shafiq grinned. "You have an excellent sense of humour, Mr. Crawley. You remind me of Groucho Marx. An extraordinary comedian, if I may say so."

"Get on with it, Shafiq."

"Ah, yes. Today you have been playing detective have you not?"

Sebastian's brow furrowed. How could Shafiq know about what he did today so quickly?

"You have been making enquiries under the guise of being a reporter for the newspaper. After you left the mortuary, the lady you spoke to wanted to give you some further information. She rang the *Gazette* and asked to speak to Robert Stevenson, the reporter. There was no such person, of course. Suffice it to say that my contacts in the *Gazette* and in the community soon identified the reporter as you. That information was conveyed to me this afternoon." Shafiq appeared smug. "You are not made to be a Sherlock Holmes, Mr. Crawley. Now my questions are these. What were you doing? And for what purpose?"

Sebastian's reaction was immediate. "It's none of your business."

"Come, Mr. Crawley, we have covered this ground before. Everything you do is my business. We have a new relationship. Am I right?" He waved at Tommy. "Your grandfather is also my friend. It appears he does not know what you were doing either."

Tommy regarded his grandson but still said nothing.

"I wanted to see where they took my mother when she died." He shook his head to feign anguish. He wrung his hands to suggest distress. He hoped his performance as a wretched, devoted son was better than that of a reporter.

"But her last resting place was at the Chapel of Rest at the undertakers," Shafiq said

Sebastian nodded – slowly and deliberately. "I wanted to get it fixed in my head. I've been to Tozer's house before, so I know what it looks like and I've been to the Chapel of Rest before. I've never been to the mortuary. The unknown inside my head was troubling me. I had to see it. I knew I couldn't just walk up to it and demand entry. I didn't have the bottle to pretend to be a detective or other official. A reporter was the first thing that came to mind. It was amateurish, I know, but it was all I could think of."

Shafiq's inimitable smile reappeared. "Indeed, it was amateurish. You should have come to me, Mr. Crawley. I could have made arrangements for you. It would have avoided all this suspicion and I would not have had to appear at your front door to surprise your grandfather. I would prefer, in future, if you asked me to help you, Mr. Crawley. I can arrange things."

Sebastian nodded. "I'm sorry, Shafiq. I'm not in the habit of asking other people to do things for me. I know now that in the future, if I ever need help again, to come to you." He thrust out his hand.

Shafiq raised his eyebrows in surprise.

They shook.

Shafiq stood.

"I am glad we have sorted out that little problem, Mr. Crawley. I will trouble you no further. I bid you goodnight." He nodded at Tommy, who returned the gesture.

Sebastian ushered him to the door and returned to Tommy who was staring into the fire.

"So what was that all about?"

"What do you mean, grandad?"

"All that bullshit about needing to visit the mortuary. The false grief."

"I don't know what you mean."

"You can't kid me, son. And I'm not even sure if Shafiq, there, swallowed it. I've seen enough bullshit in my time to cover half of England. And you know the old saying 'If it looks like bullshit and smells like bullshit, then it probably is bullshit.' And from where I sit the stench is terrible. What's going on?"

Sebastian sighed. There was no point in pretending anymore. But it was pointless telling him the plan he had formulated with

Sammy. He didn't need to know the details, because he would worry. And, secondly, he couldn't be used as a witness against them if things turned awry. He could even be arrested as part of a conspiracy if he knew too much

"Ok, grandad. I won't go into details, though. I've made arrangements to get hold of that report."

Tommy's face darkened. "Don't take unnecessary risks, son. I couldn't do with losing you as well."

He shuffled out of the room and Sebastian heard him climb the stairs. Tommy was an old man and a seasoned pro who understood that sometimes you had to work in the dark and trust others to do what they had to do. He didn't like it, but he recognised there was a bigger picture that necessitated him being kept on the side lines. He was well aware of the 'need to know' concept from his army days. And Tommy knew he didn't need to know at this stage.

23

Friday 15th March 1963

Samir al-Aziz slipped out of his house just after midnight. As far as he was concerned the misty night was ideal for breaking and entering. The upside was that the mist hung around and swallowed everyone and everything; visibility was down to about twenty-five yards. The downside was that sound travelled easily. But even that had an upside; he would be able to hear anyone approaching and make his escape.

Sebastian had sent a message to him to delay the plan for a few days, or even a week or two. Sammy, though, had the final decision, and he had decided that tonight was their best chance for success.

The mortuary had a bell alarm, and only the front door was connected to that alarm. None of the small windows were alarmed, but entry through any of those was impossible in the time frame he had allowed himself. If the alarm was activated, there were plenty of people within earshot. The residents of Harton Lane would hear it and some of them would have a telephone and call the police. The close proximity of the nurse's accommodation was another hazard. There were additional risks in that nurses being nurses, they came home at all hours of the day and night and might report someone lurking in the area, which is why he decided to make his move after midnight on a weekday. There would still be people on the street, but fewer than at any other time.

Sammy's plan was to disable the alarm. It could be done in two ways. Firstly, a cushion pad of some description could be attached to the bell so that when the clapper was activated, the impact was negated, and no-one would hear it. The second option was to cut the clapper arm so contact could not be made. There were other options. All rejected for one reason or another. The lock on the door was a straightforward mortise lock, and, as anyone would know, the lock is only as good as the frame it is attached to. In this case, the mortuary was an old building with rotting window frames and an equally unserviceable door and jambs. The problem for Sammy would be when he entered the building. Sebastian had given him a simple plan of the office area and the filing cabinets, although he didn't have any information as to how the reports were filed. He hoped it was a straightforward alphabetical system.

Sammy hung around in the shadows watching, waiting and listening for footsteps or the sound of vehicles. He was absorbing the atmosphere and confirming the intelligence he had collected of what was usual in this area at this time of the night. After half an hour he walked briskly up to the mortuary and as nimbly as he could climbed the cast iron drainpipe that give him access to the alarm. He stuffed a wodge of folded newspapers between the bell and its clapper and shimmied down the drainpipe again. He returned to the shadows. It had taken less than thirty seconds. He waited to see if there had been any reaction. This was the testing time. The 'high alert' time when seconds seemed like minutes. The familiar sensations emerged. He tried to calm his breathing. His temples pounded. His mouth was dry.

Ten agonising minutes came and went without incident. It was time for phase two.

Sammy walked up to the door of the mortuary and pressed his foot against the bottom of the door to create pressure on the lock. Although slightly built, he knew that his body weight was sufficient to increase the pressure. He crouched slightly then threw his body weight through his shoulder onto an area just above the lock. There was a splintering sound and the door keep snapped the wood from the frame. The door swung open with the lock still intact. Easy. He glanced at the alarm. It was completely immobile. Success. He smiled, waited a few moments to see if the shattering of the door had created any reaction. There was none. Good. He closed the door behind him.

Sammy slid inside and was immediately greeted by the smell of antiseptic. It didn't bother him. The prospect of a body being in the next room didn't bother him either. He moved towards the window where the filing cabinets stood and tried the top drawer. It was locked. Bugger. He turned to the desk and tried the draws. Locked. All of them. Not a problem. Easily dealt with, but the noise might be an issue. He scanned the desk. A letter opener in a cup with pencils and pens stood at the top of a pad. Sammy thought that if someone seated at this desk wanted to secure the cabinet behind them, they would lock it and put the keys in a handy place. The top drawer of the desk? He took the letter opener and prised the drawer open. The key was there. The drawer fell to the floor. It was only a small drawer half the size of the rest. Sammy had pulled it too far. The noise echoed around the room and the contents spilled across the floor. Sammy froze. He picked up the drawer and hastily replaced its contents before shoving it back into the desk.

"I'm sure I heard the noise coming from here."

The blood drained from Sammy's face. He searched for a place to hide. Nowhere in the office. Another door. He tried it. It opened. He guessed this was where the bodies were kept, where post-mortems were carried out. The darkness was disorientating. No windows.

"The doors been smashed open." Deep voice. Male. Security guard?

"Leave it, Ronnie," said a shrill female voice, "Lets tell security in the main building, or ring the police. There might be someone inside."

Just two people. Boyfriend and girlfriend?

"We'll soon find out."

"Ronnie!"

"Shush, Sandra," said Ronnie, then in a loud, brash voice shouted "Is anyone there? Come on out. I've informed the police and they'll be here in two minutes."

The door moving. Ronnie entering the building.

"Ronnie!" pleaded Sandra, "Come back."

Switch. Light under door.

"Doesn't look as if anything's been touched. We must've scared them off."

"Ronnie, come on."

"Might as well have a look around while I'm here."

More footsteps.

"What's in there?"

Sandra closer.

The sound of drawers opening.

"Keys for the cabinet."

A metallic screech. Filing cabinet opening.
"Nothing in here but files and paper." Ronnie.
"That's a lovely typewriter." Sandra. Closer.
"I'm not taking that," Ronnie said.
Opportunists. They would take something and leave.
Sounds of rummaging. A little laugh of triumph. Found some money? Footsteps just beyond the door.
"Where are you going, Ronnie?"
"To see what's in here."
"That's where they keep the bodies."
"Uh, ok. Let's leave that, then."
"What's this, then?"
A new voice. Authoratative. Security?
"Shit!" says Ronnie.
Sandra crying.
Sammy groaned. He was caught, surely.

Two hours later Sammy was still in the mortuary having listened to the protestations of Ronnie and Sandra as they explained why they had been found on the premises. The security men, Bob and Bert, had called the police, and two constables had turned up and taken the despairing burglars away. The keyholders for the mortuary were the hospital security, so the door jamb had sustained a temporary repair by Bob, and Bert had pronounced the premises secure once more. The newspapers had been removed from the alarm bell but the alarm could not be reset because of the temporary repair. The alarm company would attend first thing in the morning. No-one had entered the mortuary clinical area. As far as Sammy was concerned, he could've had a tea party there and no-one would have been the wiser. Nevertheless, he was shaking like Yuri Gagarin would've been when he was launched into space two years previously.

Fifteen minutes after the departure of Bob and Bert, Sammy re-entered the office. He immediately retrieved the keys and opened the filing cabinet. The reports were filed in folders marked by the appropriate month. Sammy sighed with relief. His search took barely thirty seconds before he found the file bearing the name of Billie Crawley. He snatched the report and folded it twice and placed it in his pocket. He shoved the cabinet shut and went to the front door.

Bob's skills as a joiner were worse than his skills as a security officer. Within a minute, the mortuary door was wide open, and mist was filtering through into the office. Sammy couldn't contain himself any longer. He galloped down the back streets away from the hospital. He crossed Stanhope Road and into the West Park. He found a shelter next to the bowling green and started breathing adrenaline.

He would be glad to get home.

It had been a close call. The second in a few weeks. He must be losing his touch.

Jack Tozer climbed into bed after a nightshift of mixed fortunes. It was his second nightshift of the week. The first had been a very quiet night. His shift had started quietly, and he'd managed to direct his constables to their beats after their usual briefing, before parking his police car in a street where he could monitor movements in the Holborn area. He'd been lucky at first. Just after midnight he'd seen someone fitting the description of Samir al-Aziz walking from Holborn towards Laygate. He'd managed to follow discretely for a mile or so before the man disappeared into the West Park. Despite patrolling the streets around the park, Jack never saw him again.

A while later, he heard the Control Room sending two officers to the hospital mortuary where staff reported that they had apprehended a burglar. He was making his way there when the officers reported back that a man and his girlfriend had been detained. The man wasn't Samir al-Aziz. Jack turned around and made his way back to the station via Laygate and Holborn on the off chance that he would come across the man. He was unlucky. The nightshift ended without any other notable incidents.

24

Monday 18th March 1963

There are some people who can't face the world or the challenges it presents. Their traditional response is to stick their head in the sand and hope the situation disappeared of its own accord - or they waited for someone else to take care of it. Tommy Heath didn't like people who did that. He always said that if he ever saw someone stick their head in the sand, he would walk right up to them and kick them up the arse. That's all they deserved. And yet that was how he felt about himself. Recent events had left him with the feeling that he was allowing the world to dictate to him what he should do. He was being passive. Was that the equivalent of sticking his head in the sand? Did he need someone to kick him up the arse?

Sebastian was obviously up to something. Something was going on and he needed to feel part of it. Or at least be consulted about it. Was he being sidelined because he was too old? Could he do something? If so, what? Would anything he did compromise whatever anyone else was doing, or about to do? He stamped his feet, partly in anger and partly because he was feeling the cold.

He stood at the top of the South Marine Park, a few yards from Seafield Terrace and looked out beyond the lake and the fairground over the road to the cold grey North Sea lapping against the Sandhaven Beach and the pier that curled in front of the mouth of the Tyne. Ships and boats bobbed and surged through the waters to do their business; seasoned mariners demonstrated their experience and skill in navigation; fishermen cast lines from the pier into the water. Whether it was for sport or, more likely, to provide a meal for the family, wherever there was a river and sea, men would seek to use it to provide food or income. The river was dirty and industrial and teeming with waste, yet it was the life blood, the main artery, of Tyneside's heart.

Despite the cold, Tommy sat on one of the benches on the terrace that hosted the 'Titty Lizzie's'. The bronze statues had been the decorative companions to Queen Victoria outside the Town Hall for years before they were taken to their current location some years ago to spare the blushes of women and visitors.

Tommy was in a quandary. He didn't need to work, but he liked to. He didn't need to work nightshifts, but he did. He could spend the rest of his days listening to the radio and reading newspapers, have a few beers and sleep, but his nagging fear was that he was succumbing to the 'head in the sand' scenario. He was nearing his three score years and ten, so time was running out. Most people felt the need to relax and enjoy retirement, if that was possible. The pension was OK, not enough to have a wonderful life, though he was fortunate enough to have the remnants of Arthur Jones's legacy to eke out the last of his days.

His breath billowed into the cold air and he stamped his feet again. It had been years since he'd needed to think clinically, and it was an effort to do so, but he knew the time for action was drawing close. He needed to be mentally alert to assimilate any plan and to offer advice should it be necessary. He certainly needed to know what was going on in the mind of his grandson.

Blanche sauntered confidently into a pub in the Laygate area of South Shields. The old idea of a woman walking into a pub on her own would still frighten most women, but Blanche had done it many times and endured the scorn of both sexes. Two women sat on stools at the end of the bar. They were at different ends of a spectrum. The older woman was bold and forthright, bordering on brassy. Her luxuriant hair was swept back to reveal a straight neck, jutting jaw and a wide forehead that any footballing centre forward would die for. She held herself straight and tall with her statuesque figure promising an evening in heaven. She oozed maturity and sexuality in her leopard-skin blouse and brown leather skirt. The younger woman was similarly dressed, still learning her trade by the look of her: coy, reserved, awkward. She aspired to be her older companion, and, in time, it would be her who would become the expert, while the current holder would be sat at the entrance of some hovel collecting money. It was a cycle that Blanche had seen many times before. These were local girls, without qualifications, lacking direction or good advice, resorting to traditional methods of supporting themselves. They were pariahs in the community. The hazards of pregnancy, venereal disease or violence were a constant threat lurking at the back of their minds. Blanche knew the game and played by the same rules – on a different pitch.

It had been years since she'd visited the area and a glance around the room saw that she was being regarded with suspicion. Two large men sat next to a door in the far corner of the room. She made her way around the tables towards the door. As she neared it, the two men stood up and threw out their chests to suggest their importance and the unlikelihood of Blanche making it beyond them.

"Tell Shafiq that Blanche is here."

The taller of the two men glanced at his partner and nodded almost imperceptibly. The smaller man turned and went through the door only to return in less than one minute. Neither of the men spoke. A few seconds later, the door opened again and the swarthy face of Shafiq with his permanent smile appeared.

"Miss Fada. How lovely for you to come and see me. It is unusual, no? You need not have come here. I would have come to you." His voice was warm and welcoming, yet his message was cold. It really meant 'don't come here. I am the one who turns up unannounced to catch *you* off guard.'

Blanche returned the cold smile. "I have something for you that I couldn't write down."

"Then come through to my office and tell me all about it. I will organise some tea."

Blanche followed Shafiq into a long dark passage. The ill fitted door at the far end was framed by an oblong of light that blinded Blanche as it was opened.

Shafiq said, "You are not impressed?" He shrugged. "It is not a comfortable place. It is a place of work. It is one of many places of work. I confess that none of them are as comfortable as the offices of a bank manager or a solicitor. I do not need to impress."

Blanche dismissed his apology with a flick of her head. "I'll come straight to the point. I have a friend …" Shafiq's grin widened, "... who tells me that there is a shipment arriving on Friday."

Shafiq's eyes joined the grin on his face. "Let me order some tea. Then we can discuss this further."

Shafiq leaned back in his chair and lit a cigar whilst he thought of what Blanche had told him. Her information was sound. He had heard rumours from other sources; Blanche's information had merely confirmed it and added another dimension. He had a dilemma. The Sand Dancers' business was usually confined to having a finger in everybody else's pie. They prided themselves on knowing who did what, when and to whom. They rarely got themselves involved in the actual deeds of crime because it carried too much risk. They weren't a crime syndicate interested in pulling off the crime of the century. They didn't get involved in financial embezzlement, drugs, or the seedier sides of violence, such as murder, although the organisation had flirted with all of these things when it first emerged as a brotherhood over thirty years ago. Their business was information. They gathered it. They made sure that the right people became aware of it – for a fee. They allowed people to plan and carry out crimes – for a fee. Those who failed to pay their dues were visited and asked politely to comply with the unwritten contract. Those who subsequently failed to deliver would somehow find that their activities had been detected by the police. The Sand Dancers were respected and feared. Their demands weren't too onerous, and the crime families of the North East held them in high esteem as professionals.

Shafiq blew a huge cloud of blue smoke into the air and coughed vigorously. He hadn't realised that he'd been drawing on the cigar like a cigarette. He ground it out on the pedestal ashtray at the side of his desk and poured himself some water from a jug.

The dilemma was an unusual one. If the information he had gathered was to be believed – and there was no reason why it shouldn't – then, as far as Shafiq knew, it was beyond the capability of local criminals. Regional crime syndicates would need to be informed. Which one? Such decisions could lead to conflict and gang rivalry. Fortunately, that wasn't Shafiq's brief, although it would be left to him to liaise with the chosen gang.

He picked up the phone and dialled a number that he rarely used.

Sebastian Crawley smiled to himself. He'd picked Alice up from Newcastle Central Station when she'd returned from her visit down south and they'd gone to the Station Hotel, where they were booked in as Mr. and Mrs. Crawley.

The whole weekend had been like an oasis in the desert; a glimpse of heaven in the middle of hell. The initial fury of his lovemaking had acquiesced to delicacy and tenderness like a soothing balm applied to an inflamed abrasion. In the trials and tribulations that surrounded him, the presence of Alice by his side drew the poison from his life and gave him a semblance of normality.

He'd taken her to Uncle Jim's house last night and he'd found it difficult to say goodbye, but she'd said she needed a good night's sleep because there was important business going on at work the next day. He'd delayed the inevitable, but she'd insisted. It was a nice game they'd played.

Sebastian supped his tea. His grandad was out for a walk in the park. He would be back soon and go to bed because he was working every night this week at his security post at the entrance to Tyne Dock. Sebastian didn't know why he did it. Grandad had often talked about retiring, and the day for him to step down was surely coming soon. Tommy Heath was an old man.

Sebastian read the pathologist's report for the umpteenth time. The words never changed, though he kept expecting them to evolve into what the police had said happened. It was clinical and almost matter of fact. The police version of things was there, yes, in an erroneous sort of way that bordered on complete fabrication. The truth lay somewhere in between. Billie Crawley had already been injured before she died – and she had been stone cold sober. As far as Sebastian was concerned, the only person who could clarify the circumstances and answer any questions was Jack Tozer, and he had been conspicuous by his absence.

25

Wednesday 20th March 1963

Wednesday was half day closing and Alice had time on her hands. She was tired of the trivial – the everyday nonsense that seemed so important to the local people. Why on earth were they more worried about dustbin collections than the atom bomb? It was incomprehensible that they didn't care. Perhaps Sebastian was right, the people knew that South Shields was low on the list of Russia's international strategic targets. An infestation of rats was more likely.

Her frenzied weekend of passion with Sebastian had reminded her of what life could be like in here. The pragmatist Alice knew that sex wasn't everything. Her dreams and ambitions still focused on America in the short term and who knew what else after that. Sebastian was a distraction, a welcome one, but a distraction nonetheless. Sometimes he consumed her every waking thought, but on the other hand, he was so frustrating. He obviously had strong beliefs but his lack of 'get up and go' annoyed her. Why wasn't he more proactive? Why didn't he just get on with things? She needed to know. And the only person she could think of who could give her the answer was Blanche.

Alice knocked on the broad wooden door and waited. She heard a light clip-clop of sandals on wood before the door was heaved open.

Alice said, "Hi, my name is…"

"Alice," said Blanche as she raised an eyebrow in surprise. "Hmmm, this is interesting. You'd better come in." She stood to one side and allowed Alice entry. Blanche caught the whiff of a delicately expensive perfume and made a mental note of what it was.

"I'm sorry for bursting in on you like this but I need to talk to someone…"

Once again Blanche finished off her sentence, "about Sebastian?" She smiled. It was a knowing smile liberally sprinkled with affection for him. "What makes you think I can supply the answers?"

"If anyone can, it would be you. You know him better than anyone else I can think of. I didn't get the chance to ask his mother."

Blanche's eyes clouded at the mention of her best friend. "She probably couldn't have told you anyway. They were different. Billie was an open book. What you saw is what you got. Sebastian is a closed book. In fact, he's a volume of books hidden in a dark place. You'll have to find him, dust him off and search every page to see what makes him tick. I don't think anyone's capable of that. Not even you. And I have heard you're a bit of a live wire yourself."

Despite herself Alice blushed. Sebastian had been talking about her to Blanche. "So, what's your advice then?"

"First of all, we'll have tea." Blanche loped into her kitchen and Alice heard her preparing the pot.

Alice let her eyes swing around the room. It was traditionally decorated with one or two items of furniture that looked well-made and highly polished. There were no pictures or photographs and the overall impression was one of faded elegance. The house had seen better days, but Blanche kept it clean and tidy.

Blanche poured the tea and settled back into a large armchair. She rested her head on a crocheted antimacassar. She didn't wait to be asked a question.

"This isn't about Sebastian though is it?" she asked. "It's more about you. From what I've heard you're much more forthright in your views than most people around here, although I have to say I haven't seen any obvious signs of it. Nevertheless, I think you need to look in the mirror and ask yourself the questions you're considering asking me."

Alice smiled to herself. Blanche was the first woman she'd met up here who looked as if she had 'balls' and wasn't afraid to speak her mind. She could see immediately why Sebastian liked and respected her. She was a woman after her own heart. Alice relaxed.

"I think I've already asked myself those questions but I'm not happy with some of the answers."

It was Blanche's turn to smile. "That's what happens when you involve men. Don't get me wrong, Sebastian is a good guy. One of the most decent human beings I've ever met. He would never do anyone any harm if he could do them a good turn. Having said that, if push comes to shove, he is capable of 'doing the right thing', and if that meant someone getting hurt, then so be it. He has a strong sense of justice. At least his kind of justice."

Alice nodded, "Just like the Sand Dancers?" It was a provocative comment meant to test Blanche.

Blanche paused to consider a response. Eventually, she said, "The Sand Dancers have their own codes and I admit that some of what I've said about Sebastian applies to them. I think that's down to the leadership of the organisation. Anyway, you're not here to talk about them. Are you going to America or not?"

Alice sipped her tea before replying. "Yes, I am. It's an open invitation. It's about timing really. There's such a lot going on there. I mean the way they treat the negroes over there is terrible. They won't allow them…"

"I read the newspapers and watch the news bulletins. Don't forget I'm mixed race. I've experienced some of the problems."

"No, this is different it's not just that. It's about…"

Blanche waved her hand in dismissal. "Sorry Alice, I've no time for conversations like this. They ultimately lead to nowhere. If you think you can make the difference, then go to America and do it now. There's no point in trying to argue the toss with me. My days of trying to make someone see my point of view are long gone. There are people out there who *can* make a difference and perhaps you're one of them, but for me, the party's over."

Alice stared at Blanche. Perhaps she wasn't the strong woman she first thought she was. Is this what time does to you? Does it grind away and wear you down? Or was it like the effect old age has on the body where the taut fitness of youth is replaced by the pudgy flab of middle age or the atrophic hollowness of immobility and infirmity. Blanche was still a good-looking woman even though she was nearing middle age. What had caused her to lose her spark? she wondered.

After a few moments Blanche said, "Live your life Alice. Live it like you want to live it and don't get side-tracked by the emptiness of love and promises. I can speak from experience when I say that. I've loved and been left high and dry by empty promises. All it does is distract you from your goals and leaves a vacuum where your heart used to be. It also starts shredding your mind. You can't think straight. You can't see straight, and suddenly one day you wake up living someone else's dream and wondering how you got there. If you love Sebastian then go for it, but know this, he'll never leave South Shields for the bright lights of London, never mind New York or Washington DC. He's a home bird. That's what makes him reliable, and predictable and one of the best friends a woman like me could ever have."

It was an emotional speech and one Alice didn't expect to hear. Blanche loved Sebastian in a different way to how she felt about him. She could see why Sebastian loved her back.

"Thank you," said Alice in hushed tones. "I'm grateful for your insight." She stood to leave and walked towards the door. Blanche followed suit. Alice turned and surprised herself by embracing her. Blanche responded. At that point they were two women with a shared soul.

26

Friday 22nd March 1963

Tommy Heath sat in the security cabin at the entrance to Tyne Dock. The huge, ancient grain silos surrounding him created an air of decayed grandeur. It was just after midnight – two hours into his fifth shift in a row. It was overtime. He was helping out a mate who had family matters to attend to. It was as silent as the grave. All things had to pass him to get into the Dock. At least that was the theory. All vehicular and pedestrian traffic had to register their presence, but there were ways and means to get by him and there had been many occasions when seamen, or prostitutes, had scaled the walls, and some had concealed themselves in cars. Tommy, and the whole world, knew the system wasn't infallible. If someone wanted to get into the dock, it didn't take a great deal of effort to do so.

The Tyne Dock arches, built a hundred years ago to house the gravity railways carrying millions of tons of coal from the Durham coalfields, loomed beside him in a splendid display of Victorian opulence. Any approaching vehicle from the Jarrow end announced their arrival well in advance as the engine noise reverberated through the arches and exited near the public toilets over the road.

He stretched his legs and opened the cabin door. He walked to the road and listened. Nothing. He crossed the road to the public convenience and relieved himself while keeping an ear open for the sound of an engine or hobnailed boot. It was cold, though not unpleasantly so, not after the winter the country had just endured. He retraced his steps and settled into the cabin. He opened a bag and retrieved a cheese sandwich. This was his life: permanent nightshifts fortified by cheese sandwiches and the occasional pint of beer supplemented by a pipe full of tobacco.

Less than a mile away, Samir al-Aziz walked in the shadows of Holborn towards Tyne Dock on his way to Phillipson Street just off the Jarrow Road. This was where his latest stash of tools was hidden. The vast industrial estate beyond there was his new playground. Most of these commercial premises were modern and usually alarmed, but some weren't, and he'd pick off those first and see what happened. The estate was deserted at nighttime save for the occasional factory that worked nightshift, or a sleeping security officer. The scares he'd had to endure in recent times made him ultra-careful. If he set off an alarm, he would hear it, if it was a delayed response, he'd hear the police cars approaching, and hide. There were plenty of places to hide. His only problem would be dogs, but they were rarely used.

As he neared the entrance to Tyne Dock, he peered around the gatepost to see if the security man was alert. He recognised Sebastian's grandad.

"Shit!" he muttered to himself. He was in a predicament. He could casually walk across the entrance and pretend he was looking up Hudson Street, but there was no guarantee that he would go unrecognised. The very act of doing that would be suspicious in itself. He decided to backtrack and cross the road. If he made his way towards Tyne Dock railway station, he could follow the railway line and get back onto the main Newcastle road near the football ground at Simonside. It was an unnecessary diversion and would delay him an extra half an hour.

He heard a vehicle approaching.

Sammy stepped into the shadows and hid. A van came through the arches and turned into the dock and stopped at the security gates. The front seat passenger handed over some sheets of paper to Tommy, and Tommy scratched his head. Obviously, the visit wasn't expected and there'd be some questions and answers to be negotiated. Sammy seized the moment and ran across the dock entrance, partially hidden by the van. As he reached the other side, he glanced back at the security cabin. Tommy wasn't happy with the paperwork.

"I don't give shit, son. This isn't right."

The passenger was a shifty looking man in a muffler and black flat cap and dark overalls. His face was thin, accentuated by a pointed chin and nose, that stared straight ahead, declining any sort of eye contact with Tommy. This bloke was up to no good. The driver was smoking a cigar. Sammy wondered how a man working nightshift as a van driver could afford to smoke cigars. He continued to watch and listen.

"I'm not responsible for the paperwork, grandad. I just do as I'm told. Me and him just do as we're told," said Pointy Nose jabbing his thumb at Cigar Man, who nodded his agreement.

Tommy said, "I'm going to have to check with the ship."

He reached for the sheaf of papers hanging on a hook at the side of the window to see the communication protocols for the ships berthed in Tyne Dock.

Pointy Nose said, "Mind if I get out of the cab and stretch my legs while you do that?"

Tommy shook his head. Sammy smiled, as far as Tommy was concerned the man could shimmy up a lamppost if he wanted, but he wasn't getting past him without proper authorisation.

Pointy Nose got out of the cab and walked around to the driver's side and had a muted conversation with Cigar Man, who also got out. They both wandered casually to the security cabin door as Tommy reached for the telephone.

Suddenly, Sammy saw Pointy Nose reach through the window and grab the phone out of Tommy's hand as Cigar Man went into the cabin and pushed Tommy into the corner, take a leather cosh from his pocket and hit Tommy on the side of the head.

The two men dragged Tommy out of the cabin and put him in the back of the van. Pointy Nose got in with him while Cigar Man got back into the driver's seat and drove off into the gloom inside the dock.

Sammy stared at the cabin not knowing what to do. He considered ringing the police, or an ambulance. Tommy was an old man and he'd been coshed. He was sure to need medical attention. As for the police, they were a suspicious lot and they would wonder how Sammy had been the witness to two crimes in just a few weeks. They would certainly start investigating what he was doing there at that time of night. The telephone was off the cradle and swung like a pendulum. Invoices, receipts and papers littered the floor. There was no sign of any blood. Sammy breathed a sigh of relief. He retrieved the phone and tapped the cradle until he got an open line. He dialled 999.

After a brief moment a female voice said, "Emergency, which service please?"

Sammy deliberately lowered his voice and said gruffly, "Help. I need help at Tyne Dock." Before the female could respond, he hung up the phone.

Sammy hurried away from the cabin and stood over the road. He watched for a moment and then reality kicked in and he scampered up Hudson Street and eventually gained access to the railway lines above the arches. A police car eventually appeared and drove up to the cabin. A sergeant and a constable got out and looked around. They were inside the cabin for several minutes and used the telephone. The constable investigated the area bordering the dockside, some thirty yards away. Some ships were berthed nearly half a mile to the west overlooking the Jarrow Slake. The inky black river slithered by. Distant shipyards made the sounds of work.

After half an hour, the sergeant left the scene in the car and the constable remained at the cabin. Security was their issue. There was no evidence of foul play and nothing to suggest that a struggle had taken place apart from the paper on the floor. The constable would remain at the cabin until he was relieved either by a colleague or the nightshift security man's replacement. The police weren't interested in anything beyond what appeared to be a basic security problem.

So, Sammy now had a different problem. Tommy had been attacked and taken into the dock by what appeared to be two thugs. The men had been in there for about forty-five minutes and Sammy's troubled mind had already ran through a variety of scenarios that ended up with Tommy floating face down in the river.

He was sweating profusely despite the cold. These near misses were playing havoc with his body temperature and probably turning him grey before his time, but he had to follow this through, and the only way he could do that was to enter the dock and find out where the hell that bloody van had gone.

It took him about half an hour to locate it. A small ship was berthed near the staithes at the end of the dock. Its night lights burned and it looked deserted. The van was parked near the gangplank. Sammy timidly approached and tried the driver's door. It was unlocked and the keys were in the ignition. He opened the rear doors. Tommy Heath lay motionless on the floor, bound and gagged. Sammy held his breath and touched Tommy, who flinched. Sammy breathed again.

"Mr Heath, it's Samir, Sebastians's friend. Please be quiet and I'll get you out of here."

Tommy grunted in response.

Sammy pulled the gag off Tommy's face.

Tommy said, "I've got a knife in my pocket."

Sammy searched and found a Swiss Army Knife in his jacket. It was the same make and model as the one Sebastian carried. He quickly sawed through the ropes.

"Come on, Mr Heath, let's go."

They both scrambled away and into the darkness.

"Are you OK, Mr Heath?"

Tommy nodded; his breathing laboured. "Need to get back to the main gate. Alert police."

"Mr Heath. You're in no fit state to do anything at the moment. It's a long way back there."

Tommy gulped a lungful of air and nodded again.

Sammy thought hard. Tommy Heath just wasn't physically able to make it to the security office without rest or assistance after what he had endured in the last hour or so. He noticed a small office building close by.

"Mr Heath. Does that building have a phone?"

"Yes. But it's locked."

Sammy shrugged. He helped Tommy to his feet and supported him to the front door of the building. Even in the gloom Sammy saw that the door was a standard construction and therefore easy to force.

"What are you thinking, son?" said Tommy, regaining some composure.

"There's a phone in there. I can get us in, but you'll have to make the phone call. There's a policeman sitting in your cabin. Call him.

Tommy was no mug. "What about you?"

Sammy saw the comprehension on Tommy's face. "I'll not be able to stick around ... problems might arise, if you know what I mean."

"OK, son. I understand." He reached out to Sammy and offered his hand. "I owe you that much."

The noise of the breaking door reverberated around the room. Sammy hoped it hadn't carried out into the dock area itself or it simply mingled with the far away sounds of the shipyards filtering through the mist. "Are you OK, Mr Heath? Can I leave you to it?"

Tommy said, "Thanks again, Samir. I'll take it from here."

Sammy smiled, nodded and left. Tommy reached for the phone and dialled the security office.

Sergeant Jack Tozer drove towards the staithes and jetty to the west of the security office with three constables beside him in the car. Another police vehicle with two more officers was *en route* to the dock from the police station a couple of miles away. He was following up the allegations relayed to him by the constable he had left at the cabin, that the night watchman had been kidnapped and assaulted by two men who were still in the dock area, in a van. The night watchman himself was hiding in a building towards the staithes. He had his doubts. Nothing like this ever happened in South Shields. Someone had got the wrong end of the stick – but it had to be checked out. He knew from experience that strange things happened against all the odds.

The car slowly glided through the patchy mist without lights. There was an air of excitement in the car even though two of the constables were as long in the tooth as their sergeant. The youngest constable, PC Tobin, had less than three years' service, so he would be the officer who got the shittiest job. In this case, it was looking after the night watchman. An ambulance had been summoned as a precaution.

As the car neared a small building on the left, Jack Tozer saw the front door was ajar. He told PC Tobin to wait with the caller. In his rear-view mirror, he saw an ambulance enter the dock with its blue lights flashing.

"Shit!" said Tozer. "Now everyone in the dock will know something's going on." He flicked on his lights and moved forward more quickly.

Sammy crawled through and over the stacks of timber stockpiled near the staithes. He had a good view of the ship, the van and the main road through the dock from the security gate.

The mist was eddying backwards and forwards so at no time did he see all of the dock all of the time. He waited.

There was some movement at the top of the ship's gangway. The man who had coshed Tommy was carrying a briefcase, closely followed by his mate who was carrying a slightly larger case. They edged their way to the dockside and walked towards the rear of the van. They paused when they realised the van was open. Cigar Man threw open the back doors. He muttered to his friend and a muted argument took place between them. The two men scanned the area around them but couldn't see anything. They placed the larger case in the van and secured the doors. Pointy Nose held on to the briefcase.

As the men got into the van, a flashing blue light cut through the gloom away to the east. Pointy Nose and Cigar Man saw it at the same time. The doors to the van flew open and the two men ran into the dock in different directions. Sammy watched Cigar Man wheeze his way directly to the nearest wall, a few hundred yards away. Scaling that would lead to the road outside. A pile of wooden pallets was stacked against it. It would be risky, but Cigar Man had no choice. The blue light was getting nearer and there was another vehicle that looked like a police car a few hundred yards in front of it.

Cigar Man proved to be quite nimble for an overweight smoker, perhaps aided by a surge of adrenaline. He scrapped his way to the top of the pile and glanced down to the path on the other side. It was nearly fifteen feet – too far to jump without injury. He lowered his bulky frame down the other side and dropped the last few feet to the path.

Sammy's attention turned to Pointy Nose who had run the wrong way. It was a few seconds before he realised he was heading towards the river. It soon dawned on him that there was no escape that way so doubled back, saw where Cigar Man was and headed that way, still clutching the briefcase.

"Stop! Police!" rang out, but Pointy Nose ignored it and clambered over the pallets. A police officer was hard on his tail and the briefcase was getting in his way. He threw it to the ground, reached the top and vaulted into the road below.

Sammy peered through the thinning mist as the police officers spoke to each other and a couple of them wandered off, and he hung around as the office-in-charge discovered the briefcase and tried to open it – without success – and then take it to the van, where he tried again There was nothing Sammy could do but wait until the police had done their job. He settled in for a long and uncomfortable night.

Jack Tozer was a frustrated man. First, the ambulance had scuppered his silent approach to a possible crime, then both of the suspects had escaped over the perimeter wall, probably without any property. He'd nearly caught one. Ten years ago he would've had him. His constables were wandering around the dock giving the appearance of searching for accomplices or stolen property, but in reality they knew that if they ever got within earshot of their sergeant they would end up with a job that would mean standing around in the cold for the rest of the night. On top of that, he had recovered a suitcase and a briefcase, both locked.

Jack sat on the edge of the van's floor and gazed around him. So what had he got? An anonymous tip off that there had been an assault on a night watchman that had yet to be confirmed; intelligence that a crime had been committed, although he didn't have a complainant, or a prisoner; an abandoned van containing a suitcase and a briefcase that were locked. It wasn't exactly cut and dried. He still had to establish that a crime had occurred and one way to do that was to find out what was in those cases. He reached inside his greatcoat pocket and withdrew a penknife, which he used on the locks, becoming more frustrated the longer he picked at them. Eventually he hacked through the leather strap on the briefcase, which snapped open after a few minutes. Inside were dozens of small, soft bags containing small, hard objects. He chose one at random to open. Three tiny, sparkling stones used whatever light that was available to them to wink at him.

Diamonds.

Jack knew nothing about precious stones or gems. He'd only ever seen them as rings or earrings, although he knew there were some stones worth millions of pounds. He carefully put them back into the pouch and selected another bag at random. More gems. Each bag the same. He pulled the suitcase towards him and renewed his efforts to open the lock. Again he failed. He searched around for a heavy stone or a piece of metal and found a thin pole rusting in a bucket on the dockside. He returned to the van and levered the two clasps away from the case. As sure as hell one of his senior officers would question his methods for opening the case, but stuff it – they weren't here. The ends justified the means as far as he was concerned.

Jack recoiled in surprise. The case was crammed full of bundles of pound notes, £5 notes and £10 notes.

"Bloody Hell. Bloody, Bloody Hell."

He picked up a bundle and riffled through it. The notes were used and therefore untraceable. It looked as though each bundle had been packed by someone in a bank or post office and neatly stacked into the suitcase. There were thousands of pounds there.

Jack heard a sound about twenty yards to his right. He quickly shut the suitcase squinted into the darkness. A small shape scurried into the gloom. He shivered and re-opened the suitcase and stared at the banknotes. He glanced around the docks again and saw no-one except his two officers, who were straying even further away from the van, their efforts seriously lax, one of them was even smoking a cigarette.

Jack slowly formulated a plan and decided it was good.

27

Saturday 23rd March 1963

Blanche washed her hands and draped the towel over the sink, her mind occupied by the proposed 'slum clearance' in the town centre and talk that alternative housing would be found for her in the new Whiteleas or Simonside areas. She wasn't happy. Those places were too far out of town and away from her natural haunts. Business would suffer. Indeed, her line of business would probably cease altogether. She was a comfort to her friends, but they probably wouldn't bother travelling out to the sticks to see her.

She picked up her coat and handbag and told Tommy Heath that she was away.

Tommy blinked up from the television as if he'd just come out of a trance, and then he stood. "Thanks, Blanche. We really appreciate you doing this for us."

"I do it because I want to, Mr. Heath. Sit down, man, you've been through a helluva lot in the past day or so."

Tommy sat. Blanche watched the old man settle. He was almost indestructible. She recalled the many occasions he had mysteriously appeared when she and Billie had got themselves into a bit of bother during their teens and trouble was smoothed over by the unflappable Tommy Heath. He always gave the impression that he was unconcerned about what Billie got up to, but he could never hide his true feelings from Blanche. She was one of the few who could read him like a book. And, like a book, he was a hard covered first edition full of facts and useful information. He was an original. His knowledge was a handbook for life.

As she walked to the shops, her thoughts competed with the traffic noise. A train lumbered into South Shields railway station on the bridge above her.

King Street was where everyone went. That was the hub of the town. It was full of suited men wearing hats and caps, and women wrapped up against the cold. The younger folk were carbon copies of their parents with slightly longer or greased back hair. Their attitude was different. Maybe it was the same for every new generation. They entered puberty and the teenage years full of pent up romance, anger and rebellion. They wanted to change the world. Every acne faced youth felt as though he could impregnate several females a day for the rest of his life, and every female thought that Cliff Richard, Adam Faith or Billy Fury was looking for her. Yet Blanche knew that the majority of them would grow and flourish, but eventually die within this borough's boundaries, and they'd work in the shipyards and factories and shops and offices along the river and settle for something less than their dreams promised. They were under educated, under trained and destined for failure. Their work and social circles would define them. A few would escape, like from a PoW camp during the War. Few made it, but those who did were legends.

Most people yearned for fame and fortune but the closest they'd get to a fortune would be winning the Pools, like Vivien Nicholson had done a couple of years ago. She said she'd spend, spend, spend. And wouldn't you? A hundred and fifty thousand pounds was a huge amount of money by any standards much less for these people.

This was life: spotty teenagers grew up to become fathers of spotty teenagers. Coy, fresh faced girls became mothers to the next generation of fresh-faced girls. And so it ground on, and, eventually, everything that had lived would die.

Blanche reached the market and wandered from stall to stall. She wasn't looking for anything in particular, she just liked to breathe the atmosphere of the place. Everyone in town gravitated here at some stage. Drinkers hovered around the many pubs, travellers swept in from the nearby ferry from North Shields, and day trippers got off the train at the end of the line. The economy was dying but no-one had told the bargain hunting folk of South Shields.

She paused next to the Old Town Hall, where parliamentarians and councillors from the past had addressed the people from the top of the stairs. Blanche knew her history, most people around here did. They knew about Roman settlements and how South Shields became little more than a thin town edging the filthy River Tyne and not grown until shipbuilding and mining had built it up into a thriving Borough. Its association with the sea hung on the very air the people breathed, from the squawking of gulls to the saltiness in the breeze, and most kids knew that the town had produced the first lifeboat and had a world famous Marine College, and in the pubs and bars and around the market stalls there would be many a tale told by weather-beaten men.

A voice close to her shoulder jolted Blanche from her reverie

"A very good morning to you, Miss Fada"

Shafiq grinned at her.

"I'm sorry if I startled you, Miss Fada. That was not my intention. I was wondering if I may have a private word with you."

Blanche nodded. "Over here," she said, pointing to St. Hilda's churchyard.

Shafiq followed her at a leisurely pace lighting a cigar as he went and acknowledging the recognition of people who had received, or given, small favours in the past. They made their way to a substantial tree and stopped.

Shafiq blew a column of smoke into the air before saying, "The information you gave us was acted upon and some friends from Newcastle made an unsuccessful bid to appropriate the property."

Blanche said, "You mean they cocked it up."

"Shall we say that things did not quite go to plan."

"That still amounts to a cock up. What's that got to do with me?"

Shafiq said, "There is something specific we need from you."

Blanche sighed and looked away. Why was life suddenly more complicated? "Look, I've given you the information I received. I don't have anything further and I'm not scheduled to see my friend for weeks, months if he's gone back to sea. I can't see how I can help you there."

Shafiq took another draw on his cigar. "There were other matters that came to light during the regrettable failure in the docks."

Blanche shot him a suspicious glance.

"It appears that a mutual acquaintance became involved."

Before Blanche could tell him she knew, Shafiq said, "Mr Heath had the misfortune to be working at the security office when the matter took place. Thankfully his injuries were superficial. We have told our friends from Newcastle that his involvement was unnecessary and unwarranted."

"I'm sure Tommy will be happy to hear that"

"There is no need for sarcasm, Miss Fada. I merely wish to point out that Mr Heath's involvement was undesirable. However, it allows us to make some delicate enquiries." Shafiq's smile reappeared as he threw his cigar butt onto the grass.

Blanche was suspicious, and it showed on her face. She managed to say, "That's someone's grave."

Shafiq immediately bent down and picked up the butt and ground it out before placing it into a handkerchief and putting it in his pocket.

Blanche said, "What kind of delicate enquiries?"

"You are friends with Mr Heath and Sebastian."

"From what I understand, so are you"

"But your position is more familiar."

"My position?"

"You enjoy their confidence while I am only really an associate. They still regard me with suspicion."

Blanche nodded and wondered if there anybody who didn't.

Shafiq continued. "We have a mutually beneficial friendship, Miss Fada. I look after your interests and you supply me with information."

"You haven't done anything for me except threaten to destroy my source of income."

Shafiq's smile widened. "We are in the early stages of our friendship. I have been unable to help you so far, but I think I can remedy that soon, as long as you continue to be amenable to me."

Blanche was intrigued. "What do you want me to do and what do I get out of it?"

Shafiq lit up another cigar. "The incident on the dock was, as I said, unsuccessful. It was unsuccessful because our Newcastle friends did not get what they came for. I have contacts who will try to find out what happened to the goods, but Mr Heath may be an alternative source of information."

"You want me to pump him for information?"

"Not exactly. But you are in a very good situation to make suggestions or to ask apparently innocent questions."

So, Shafiq wanted her to be a mole in the Heath household. Her first thought was to tell him to go to hell. But the question still remained, what was in it for her?

"You want me to chat with Tommy and Sebastian to find out if they have any idea where the goods are. Is that right?"

"That is correct."

"And what will you do for me?"

"We are aware that your house has been listed for demolition. We are also aware that people in your predicament are to be offered houses out of the town centre. We understand that this will have an impact on your business. As we have already discovered, your business is also a very good source of information, and to lose that would be unfortunate … for both of us. I have mentioned before, Miss Fada, that we have lots of friends in lots of different areas. I am able to suggest to people that your relocation to a house on the other side of Ocean Road, or to Beach Road, would be an excellent result for you. I can make this happen."

Sunday 31st March 1963

Blanche sat in a comfortable chair opposite Alice who had attended her home on request. A plate of biscuits sat on top of a crocheted doily on the table, surrounded by a blue-tinged tea set. Tea was 'massing' in the pot.

Blanche said, "I've got a bit of a dilemma that I need to talk to you about."

Alice raised her eyebrows. She had thought about their last meeting many times – looking at it from several angles before deciding that Blanche was trustworthy and a 'decent sort'.

"Go on," she said.

"I've been approached by Shafiq." Alice nodded to acknowledge she knew who he was. "And he's asked me to essentially, spy on Sebastian and Mister Heath."

"Spy? In what way?"

Blanche related the conversation she had with Shafiq in the grounds of St. Hilda's Church the previous week. "The question is, what do I do?"

Alice took her time to reply. Blanche poured the tea and shoved the biscuits towards her.

"My first reaction is to tell him to piss off. But, having said that, I realise that he represents the Sand Dancers, and they can manipulate the lives of ordinary people and make it difficult for them. I have to say that I can't help you. Normally, people can say yes or no to any request but what we're talking about here is something like blackmail. If you don't do something for them then there will be repercussions. Can you go to the police? No, I don't think so. You haven't got the confidence in them anyway. I don't know Blanche. But what I do know is that you have to tell Sebastian and his granddad. But you know that don't you?"

Blanche nodded slowly. "I can't go to the police and I'm passing scraps of information to Shafiq in any case. This is a bit more specific and I would feel like a traitor to two people I care about dearly."

Sebastian lay in bed contemplating the month of March. There had been highs and lows; life had become a seesaw of emotions and experiences. He was undecided; a good or bad month? He was too tired to pick through each event in turn and mark it with a plus or minus. He wavered, then abandoned the month in his mental archive as 'undecided' as he fell into a deep sleep.

April 1963

28

Monday 1ˢᵗ April 1963

Sebastian was pleased with his grandfather's progress. It had been over a week since he had been attacked while at work at Tyne Dock. The aches and pains had abated, and the bruises were losing their colourful bloom. Sebastian hoped that the two weeks sick leave Tommy had been given would stretch even further and perhaps give him a taste of what retirement would bring. Spring was around the corner and the warmer weather over the weekend was a welcome relief from the dire winter. Of course, nothing could ameliorate the pain of losing Billie, but putting the clocks forward yesterday heralded British Summer Time and seemed to bring a new focus. Life was being repaired as it marched on into a new month.

Having said that, Tommy's incessant newspaper reports about the state of the country brought a sense of doom and gloom. Teachers were asking for a pay rise. £620 a year wasn't enough. The Beeching Report said that the railways were an important nationalised industry but had to be solvent. Recommendations included the closure of 2363 railway stations around the country.

"Uneconomical," Tommy said. "Everything's bloody uneconomical."

"A bet on the Grand National wouldn't've been, grandad."

"Ayala. 66/1."

"A pound would've got you a month's wages."

"If you could afford to bet that much."

Tommy sucked on his pipe. The fire roared away in the hearth. He inched his chair away from it. He blew a cloud of smoke towards the lightshade.

He said, "*The King and I* is on at the Regent. You might want to take your lass there."

Sebastian smiled, wondering how Alice would feel about that reference.

"I don't suppose she'd be into *The Bridge over the River Kwai.*" Before Sebastian could reply, Tommy continued. "Richard Burton's separating from his wife Sybil. I'm not surprised. He's obviously playing around with Elizabeth Taylor."

Sebastian raised his eyebrows. "It just goes to show that there's a cost to being rich and famous. Last week it was Bobby Darin and Sandra Dee."

"It doesn't matter who you are. If you can't keep your dick zipped up you're heading for trouble."

Sebastian smiled. "It works the other way as well. Anthony Newley and Joan Collins are getting married."

"I've never rated either one of them. What have they ever done?"

The question remained unanswered. Sebastian shrugged. He couldn't care less either way.

Tommy continued.

"I don't suppose those poor bastards who've been paid off at Smith's Dock in North Shields are bothered either. Four hundred men. Shipbuilding on the river is going down the pan at a rapid rate."

"It's one of those things, grandad. Britain's modernising itself. It's called progress. Just look at the slum clearance programme. It's happening all over the north east, not just here in Shields. They're even developing an airport at Wolsingham, between Ponteland and Newcastle. They're building for the future."

"Progress, you call it? Tell that to the thousands of families being moved from their friends and neighbours."

"Their friends and neighbours are going with them."

"Into high rise flats? No, thanks." Tommy sucked on his pipe. "Take a look around you, son. In a year or two's time, all of this will be gone. Progress? Bah!"

The wind outside rattled the windows. Tommy had a saying: 'When the wind's from the east, the weathers a beast. When the wind's from the west, the weather's the best.' And sure enough, a fierce easterly gale had caused drifting sand to block the promenade at the sea front, and there was still some snow on the

Pennines, so although the ice flows on the Tyne had ceased, winter hadn't quite gone to bed yet.

There was a knock on the door.

Sebastian shot a glance at his grandfather to ask if he was expecting anyone. Tommy shrugged.

It was Blanche.

Sebastian kissed her on the cheek as she entered and followed her into the living room. Without delay she said, "I'm glad I've managed to get you both together."

Tommy glanced at Sebastian. Sebastian shrugged.

"Do you want some tea, Blanche?" asked Tommy.

"No, thanks. Not at the moment."

"So, what have we done to offend you?" joshed Sebastian.

"It's about Shafiq and the Sand Dancers."

Both Tommy and Sebastian rolled their eyes.

Sebastian asked, "What about them?"

Blanche took a deep breath and blurted out a dirty secret. "I'm one of their informants."

Sebastian was dumbfounded. The silence hung heavily for a few moments as the news found its place.

She continued. "Shafiq approached me some time ago and asked me to supply him with information. He wanted any kind of information about anyone and anything. Gossip if you like. He threatened me ... no ... he... suggested certain events might take place if I didn't comply with his request. So, I did what he asked. He can destroy my lifestyle."

Sebastian knew exactly what Blanch meant. "He's a tricky bastard alright. But what did you tell him?"

"Just bits and pieces of gossip from the neighbourhood, and snippets of conversations I have with my friends."

Sebastian shot another glance at his grandfather and wondered if he understood the nuance behind Blanche's mention of her friends.

Blanche carried on regardless. "Shafiq used to say that every piece of information was a piece of a jigsaw. He collected the pieces and tried to fit them together to make a bigger picture. He gets information from a whole lot of people so he can cross reference and double check to see what's going on. None of what I passed had any value at all, I saw to that ... until two weeks ago. I told Shafiq about a shipment that was coming into Tyne Dock. I didn't think much of it until ..."

"I was assaulted," said Tommy, finishing off her sentence.

Blanche nodded.

Sebastian said, "You *knew* about what was happening and didn't say anything to us?"

"That's not what she's saying, son," said Tommy. "She's saying that it was she who told Shafiq and he who organised the attack."

"Not quite, Mr. Heath. Shafiq passed the information on to a gang in Newcastle and they carried it out. But they cocked it up. You weren't supposed to get hurt."

"Bastards," said Sebastian.

Tommy spread his arms and flapped them at Sebastian in a calming motion. "Let her finish."

"Shafiq told me that the Newcastle gang were disturbed when the police came, and they ran away. The shipment was abandoned. They don't know where the shipment is."

Tommy nodded. It all fitted in with what he knew. He hadn't told anyone about Sammy's involvement in his rescue and he was unsure whether to say something now. Blanche was revealing what she knew, but if he revealed Sammy's involvement would she report it to Shafiq? If she did, then Sammy was a goner.

Silence filled the room as they all contemplated the news and worked out how much it impacted on their lives. It was Sebastian who spoke first.

"Did Shafiq tell you to come here?"

"No. If he knew I was telling you this, he would get really mad." She licked her lips. Her mouth was dry. "He asked me to spy on you."

It was a profound statement. Spying was the stuff of James Bond wasn't it? And James Bond had never been to South Shields. What's more, Blanche Fada wasn't *Mata Hari* either.

"You'll have to explain that one, Blanche," said Tommy.

She fidgeted with a button on her coat. "Shafiq knows I come here to clean and do a bit of tidying up. He knows we chat on about things. All he was asking was for me to stimulate conversations in certain areas and feed them back to him."

Tommy said, "So you haven't got to rake through our drawers or inspect letters that are lying around?"

"Mr. Heath, I wouldn't do that."

"Well we don't know what you would do now, Blanche. I don't know if you can be trusted anymore."

"I understand how you feel. But the reason why I'm here today is to tell you what's going on. I can't bear the dishonesty. I have very few people in my life that I love and respect. Your family, Mr. Heath, contained those people who I care about the most. Billie was my best mate. Sebastian is a dear friend, and you are the person who I respect more than any other living person. You're the closest thing I've got to family."

A tear forced its way from the corner of an ear and trickled down her cheek.

It took Tommy a few moments to analyse her words, then he got out of his chair and embraced Blanche.

"It's okay, love. Life is full of shit. Only the depth varies. We need to stick together."

Sebastian thought he heard gears clunk as the world changed again.

Tommy went into the kitchen to make tea.

"You haven't said much," said Blanche to Sebastian.

"I'm still taking it all in," he replied.

"We have to do something," she said.

"Like what?"

"Come on, Sebastian. You need to air some of those thoughts you have. You need to galvanise yourself into some sort of action. Don't you care anymore or is your mind being distracted by your girlfriend?"

Sebastian tensed. He wasn't the one causing all the bother. He had felt the need for action for some time and he thought he'd started the process with the raid on the mortuary. Action was certainly needed, but how was he supposed to move things forward if everything constantly changed?

Tommy brought the tea in on a tray and set it down on the table. He announced that he had something to say. "This musn't go beyond these four walls, mind you."

Blanche nodded. "I promise I won't repeat it to anyone."

"Okay. The night of the assault, I was looked after by your mate Sammy. He called the ambulance and police."

Sebastian couldn't believe it. What the hell was going on? First there was Blanche the spy. Second was his secretive grandfather and now Sammy was a crime fighting angel of mercy. How had he not known all this? Was Blanche right? Was he so mixed up in his life with Alice that he was missing the important things that were raining around him?

"Christ Almighty," he said, and ran a hand over his face. "Has anyone got anything else to reveal. It seems like I've been living in a bubble. Why am I just finding all this out now?"

"You kept the mortuary thing to yourself," said his grandfather.

"That was different. It was a criminal act that I didn't want anyone else mixed up in."

Tommy shrugged. "We all have our reasons. What's important now is that we pool our secrets. As individuals we are powerless. We all have an axe to grind in some form or another. We all suffered a loss when Billie died. And we know that her death was suspicious We all have a feeling that we should do something to mend that grief or avenge her death."

Fire blazed in his eyes and a faraway expression descended on his face "We need to identify our enemies and march against them. Engage them when we can and retreat when the occasion deman...."

"OK, grandad. We get the picture. But it's not like Dunkirk yet"

Blanche smiled at Sebastian. "What you're saying is that we must pool our knowledge, talent and resources to do something constructive, and maybe even manipulate the situation to our advantage."

They all exchanged glances and found themselves nodding at each other.

29

Saturday 6th April 1963

Sebastian ordered two coffees and sat in the window seat. Sammy joined him two minutes later. A thin film of sweat glistened on Sammy's brow.

"So what's the matter, Sebastian?"

"I wanted to thank you."

Sammy leaned back in surprise. He wasn't expecting that. "Thank me? What for?"

"Helping my grandad when he got attacked at work."

Sammy sighed. It was a combination of relief and shock. Relieved that he hadn't been discovered or caused Sebastian problems, and shock that Tommy Heath had revealed his involvement in the Tyne Dock incident.

"You've been a good friend to me over the years, Sammy. I don't pretend to like your lifestyle and I'm still coming to terms with your stupidity over Bull's death. but you've done me two massive favours recently. I think it's about time we pooled our knowledge."

Sammy's brow knitted. "Pooled our knowledge?"

Sebastian nodded. "I need to know exactly what you saw and what you did when my grandad got attacked."

Forty-five minutes later, having refilled their coffees, Sebastian gazed out of the window into the packed street deep in thought. Sammy waited. The cafe was almost full, and condensation trickled down the window. Sebastian took a deep breath and exhaled audibly. "There's something not quite right here; it doesn't add up.

"As far as I can see, this is how things panned out. What I'm about to say can't go any further you understand. Like my grandad says, 'walls have ears', and certain people overhear conversations and report them to people who can do something about it."

Sammy was momentarily puzzled. Then it dawned on him. He squinted over both shoulders before saying, "You mean The Sand Dancers?"

Sebastian nodded. Sammy's worry returned.

Sebastian said, "If you'd rather not hear this then I'll keep it to myself."

Sammy shook his head and looked over his shoulder then leaned forward conspiratorially. "OK, but keep your voice down."

"The Tyne Dock job was executed by a gang from Newcastle. They cocked it up. They were to take receipt of a shipment of something by fair means or foul and take it back to Newcastle. Nobody knows what the shipment is but we know it came in a briefcase and a suitcase. The gang was disturbed and got chased by the police. They lost their merchandise. It was found by a copper, who took it away. The assault on my grandad was obviously part of the cock up. He sends his regards by the way."

Sammy nodded his acceptance.

Sebastian continued.

"I know from a friend that the Newcastle gang were upset by what happened and they've asked The Sand Dancers to help them get their shipment back. The Sand Dancers are using their network to find out what's going on. It'll only be a matter of time before they have an answer."

Sammy said, "I presume The Sand Dancers have contacts in the police?"

Sebastian nodded.

Sammy's eyes widened. "Well, there's no way that they'll recover the cases from the police station."

Sebastian agreed. Once it had been checked in it became part of the official records, even though it might not have been part of a crime.

"I'd love to know what was in those cases," said Sammy. "The Sand Dancers will find out but there's nothing that they can do now."

"We'll all hear about it eventually. Remember, Sammy, not a word of this conversation can be repeated to anyone."

"Who would I tell?"

"Loose lips sink ships."

As Sebastian walked back to the market, he continued to mull things over in his mind. There was something missing. Something lying around inside his head that didn't add up, but he couldn't drag it out into the open. It was something crucial, but it refused to be discovered. By the time he reached the stall he had given up. Perhaps he could sleep on it.

Blanche was weary, and troubled, and anxious, and distracted. She was having a bad day. The depression, the hormone imbalance or whatever it was had descended on her on Thursday and had never left. It was a bad time to meet with Shafiq. The only thing she had to tell him was that there was nothing to tell him. Not a single word about the shipment had been spilled onto the street, or the bed sheets.

She stood in Fowler Street waiting for the bus to Laygate. She had a headache and was considering whether it would be wiser for her to go home, but the arrival of the bus made the decision for her and she climbed aboard and paid the fare. She was still feeling jaded when she arrived at her destination. She alighted and wandered across the road towards Allens department store. A car drew up at the side of the road next to her and the window wound down.

"This isn't your normal neck of the woods," said Jack Tozer.
"What ... what do you mean?" she stammered.
"You don't look well, Miss Fada. Can I help?"
"I'm sorry. I'm not feeling very well at all."
"Where were you going? I'll give you a lift."
Even in her contrary state Blanche knew that to continue to see Shafiq would be a mistake. "I ... just visiting. I think I should go home, though."
Jack Tozer got out of his car and supported Blanche by the elbow and gently guided her to the back seat of his car.
Barely five minutes later Blanche was lying on her sofa while Jack Tozer rummaged around her kitchen preparing a pot of tea. She had begged him to leave her at the front door, but he had insisted on making sure she was safely home and resting. She hadn't the resolve to fight him. All she wanted was for him to go. If he would leave after making a pot of tea, so be it.

"Get that down your neck," said Jack as he placed the tray on a small table beside an armchair. "Do you need any tablets or something?"

Blanche kept her eyes shut and shielded with her arm but managed to say "No thanks, Sergeant Tozer. I just need to rest in perfect quiet. If you pull the curtains as you leave, that'll be fine. Thanks."

"I can't leave you like this. You're not well. And call me Jack. I'm not in uniform and I'm not on duty."

Blanche stayed silent for a few moments. All she wanted was for him to leave her in peace. She ignored him for a moment, then said, "Thanks for doing this, but as you can see I'm in no fit state to carry on a conversation. Perhaps some other time."

Jack Tozer suddenly stood and said, "Some other time" And quickly made his way to the front door, which he closed with more force than was necessary.

Blanche groaned, but was feeling too ill to worry about it. Soon, she was sleeping.

Tuesday 9*th* April 1963

Sebastian listened distractedly on the phone as Alice told him about deciphering scrawled notes a Councillor had made in the margin of the Council Minutes and how tedious she found it compared to the big issues being debated elsewhere in the world where some people were trying to make a difference. The march this weekend at Aldermaston was her attempt to make a difference. Even the leaders of the civilised world recognised that something had to be done. The news yesterday that the United States of America and the Union of Soviet Socialist Republics had set up a 'hot line' telephone between the countries was hugely satisfying. The fact that Kennedy and Krushchev could pick up a phone and talk things over before sending bombs all over the world was evidence of fresh thinking. No-one wanted another stand off like The Bay of Pigs incident in Cuba, last year.

The *Beeching Report* had antagonised people too. Hundreds of people were complaining about the proposed closures of their local railway stations. The unions had called for a three-day strike in protest. That came hard on the heels of the pay award to bus workers of six shillings a week. Their demand for a reduction to a forty-hour week had been rejected. The people were railing against the Government. Harold MacMillan was having a bad time of it and the Labour Party was licking its lips in anticipation of government.

Sebastian was quiet throughout the monologue and thinking how disinterested he was feeling at that time. These last couple of days his thoughts had been anywhere but on Alice, and now he found this debriefing role a bit exhausting. He had things to do rather than listen to this.

Alice told him about a conversation she'd heard from some girls in the next room at work. Their subject, as usual, was men. Aspiration was redundant, she said. Parochialism reigned supreme in South Shields if these girls were to be believed.

"You haven't said anything about me going away this week."

"If it means something to you, go do it," he said.

In truth, he was ambivalent about the whole protest thing.

"You trying to get rid of me?" she teased.

He told her he was busy, that something was going on and he needed to concentrate on that to the exclusion of everything else.

There was a long silence on the other end of the phone.

Even to Sebastian it sounded lame.

An authoritative voice called Alice's name and broke the uncomfortable silence.

"I have to go," she said, her voice a little more detached than it usually was. "Someone wants to tap into my broad understanding of international politics."

That, or they wanted her to write a withering letter to some idiot who complained about the state of the flower beds in North Marine Park, Sebastian thought.

Later that day Alice knocked on the door of Blanche's house and was admitted immediately. She was frustrated with Sebastian and wanted to discuss the situation with the only other woman who knew him well. She recounted the days conversation and her plans to protest at Aldermaston this weekend. Blanche sat and absorbed it all. She was in listening mode only. Something she was practiced at.

Eventually, Blanche said, "We've had a conversation like this already. You've decided to go and do something that your passionate about and can't understand why Sebastian isn't as passionate. That's life for you. That's what happens. When you only have yourself to worry about, it makes life easier to make sacrifices."

"Sacrifices?"

Blanche nodded, "I'm not sure what you know, or if you know anything at all, but Sebastian has things on his mind at the moment. Forget that. It's probably stuff you really shouldn't know anyway."

Alice immediately became concerned. "Is he in trouble?"

"No, not at the moment. Look, I probably shouldn't tell you this but...1

"I'm a big girl Blanche. I can make decisions for myself."

Blanche sighed. "You mustn't tell a soul about this and what I plan to do about it."

A hour or so later and about a mile away, in Catherine Street, Tommy and Sebastian sat with Blanche. A curious atmosphere hung in the air, where Tommy continually glanced at his grandson and 'I don't know what's going on' shoulder shrugs were passed around like cakes at teatime. Sebastian waited for Blanche to get to the point knowing she would only get there when she was ready. Blanche, for her part, wanted to say something important about the Sand Dancers but was having difficulty doing so.

Blanche stirred her tea, as she had done since it had been poured over five minutes ago. Tommy coughed. Blanche jumped and almost spilt her tea. She placed the still full lukewarm cup on the table. She cast her gaze between Tommy and Sebastian.

"I have a plan," she said without drama.

Neither of the men responded.

"I had a visitor last night."

That wasn't enough information for the men to get excited about.

"Sergeant Tozer," she added.

Tommy shot a glance at Sebastian who nodded slowly at Blanche, encouraging her to continue.

Blanche told them of her encounter with Jack Tozer the previous Saturday when she'd been unwell and he'd taken her home.

"I thought you and him didn't get on?" said Tommy.

"We didn't."

"Past tense. That means you're getting on now." The level of disgust was evident in his voice.

"Not so, Mr. Heath. I'm pretending to get on with him."

Tommy twisted his face in disbelief, but Sebastian nodded again. The penny had dropped. He said, "Listen to what she's saying, grandad. She's pretending. I presume that is part of your plan?"

She nodded vigorously in relief. "Yes, that's exactly what I'm doing. It all came to me on Sunday. You know I hate Jack Tozer as much as anyone else, but he's always had a liking for me, even though he's tried to get me arrested on a few occasions, and even though he was with your mother. He's tried to grope me before as well, but I've never given him any encouragement. He hated that."

Tommy muttered, "He's a bastard".

Sebastian was thinking fast. "So Jack Tozer did you a favour and you saw that by reacting to it in a positive way we could use it to our advantage."

"That's what I thought," said Blanche.

Sebastian shook his head. "I appreciate what you're saying, Blanche, but I don't think you've thought this through. It's unlikely that Jack would tell you anything about anything. And you'd be putting yourself in danger. Jack Tozer has no scruples, and he would expect an awful lot of, shall we say, personal sacrifices on your behalf. I can't ask you to do that for us. It's not an option."

Steel entered Blanche's eyes.

"I know what I'm doing, Sebastian. I know what Jack is like and I had enough conversations with your mother to know what he's likely to be like in private. It's not as though I've not had enough experience in this line of work, is it? You won't believe some of the things I've done when the means are justified. What's more, you're not asking me to do it. I'm volunteering. I thought about it all day on Sunday and yesterday I went into the police station to see Jack. He was as surprised as Mr Heath is at this moment".

Sebastian could see that his grandad was more than surprised; he looked astonished at Blanche's proposal. His grandad had always thought of Blanche as a 'tart with a heart'; a well-meaning woman who had resorted to what she did because of a lack of opportunity to do anything else. This was obviously a step beyond the imagination of the old man.

Blanche continued.

"I told him I was grateful for his kindness and consideration when I was unwell and was there some way I could repay that kindness by making a donation to a police charity or something."

Sebastian involuntarily smiled. A police charity would be the last thing in Jack Tozer's mind.

Blanche ignored Sebastian's smile.

"We discussed charitable options. He said he was a genuinely caring person who happened to be a policeman and his act was not because he was on duty. It was a personal response to someone who he knew, someone who was in need of care and attention."

"He's a bastard," Tommy spat.

Sebastian said, "OK. So let's cut through all the bullshit. What was the end result?"

Blanche stared straight at Sebastian.

"He's taking me out on Friday night."

There was silence for a few moments as Sebastian and Tommy thought through the ramifications of this arrangement. Sebastian tried to balance the pros and cons of such a dicey relationship. His trust in Blanche was unequivocal, but he knew Jack Tozer was a scheming, selfish manipulator who wouldn't think twice about harming Blanche if it suited his purpose. He recalled a conversation with his mother about Jack in which she said that he was forever conscious about how he was perceived by his bosses. He checked out everyone he came into contact with through police files to get a background picture of his target and any unsavoury information about them resulted in their dismissal from his life. He was very much aware of the police discipline code that association with a person of doubtful character came under the title of Discreditable Conduct. If that was the case, surely Jack would have checked out Blanche already. Her 'profession' couldn't be described as professional, in ordinary social circles. He certainly couldn't take her to the Police Club without raising a few eyebrows amongst the hierarchy.

Sebastian hugged Blanche. As he drew her close, he whispered, "You don't have to do this."

He felt her ease against his body.

"I need to do this for Billie, and me. All my life I've pandered to the whims of men. I'm good at it. I've taken everything a man can shove at me and begged for more just to make him feel good. I've lied and cheated and twisted the truth to get my way and at the same time made it seem that the man in my bed was in complete control. It's how I get through the days, weeks and months of my miserable life. Billie was my friend, a very special friend. Some of the happiest days of my life were with her. She was a wonderful person and I loved her. Jack Tozer used her, but she knew it. She hoped he would like her enough to eventually fall in love with her. That was never going to happen. I need to take her place. I need to find out as much as I can about her death, and if Jack was responsible in some way."

A tear trickled down her cheek and soaked into Sebastian's shirt. Tommy steepled his fingers, touching his nose as if in prayer. Another long silence followed before Blanche detached herself from Sebastian's arms. She stared into his eyes.

"I'm going to do this, Sebastian. With or without your blessing."

Sebastian decided that there was nothing he could do to change her mind. The best course of action for him was to support her in any way he could. "What do we do about the Sand Dancers?" he said.

"I don't know. I can only play one game at a time. You'll have to handle them. I'll go on feeding them little bits and pieces, but when they know I'm with Jack Tozer they'll want something more. They always want more. At least Shafiq does."

Tommy said, "He's another bastard, but he's a tricky one."

30

Good Friday 12th April 1963

Tommy was in his usual chair listening to an American radio station as Sebastian entered the room. Something was up.

"What is it?" asked Sebastian.

"Another bloody disaster," said Tommy. "An American submarine, the USS Thresher, has disappeared in the Atlantic. It was a nuclear sub."

Sebastian understood the significance of that immediately. "Was it the Russians?"

"No, no, no. It wasn't sabotage or war or anything. At least that's what they're saying at the moment. We just don't know. It's scary to think that there might be some atom bombs lying on the ocean floor."

"What about the crew?"

Tommy shook his head. "Gone. All gone. Poor bastards."

"I wonder if Alice knows?" said Sebastian.

Tommy didn't see the connection at first, but he nodded vigorously when he remembered she was on the CND march at Aldermaston. "Oh yes. They'll know alright. They'll be screaming to high heaven. Ban the bomb. Ban the bomb." Tommy punched the air in mock tribute. "How is she anyway?"

It came as a bit of a surprise to Sebastian that he'd not given Alice much thought these past few days, but he smiled despite the possible significance of that and the doom and gloom the newscasters were relaying through the Bakelite wireless on the sideboard.

He reached across and switched it off. The Yankee voice was replaced by the faint brass tones of a band that was passing by the end of the street fifty yards away. The Good Friday tradition of dozens of mainly juvenile bands marching down nearby Fowler Street and Ocean Road was in full swing. Sebastian himself had marched many times as a child. It was the start of the Easter weekend. The Amusement park would be open, and the chip shops would be frying all day. South Shields was a seaside town, and a good start to the summer was crucial to local businesses.

Tommy said, "I wonder what Winston thinks about the sub?"

Sebastian shrugged. Churchill had just been made an honorary citizen of the United States of America. "I suppose he'll be as concerned as any other former leader of the free world. Nuclear capability is worrying at the best of times, never mind when it's at the bottom of the ocean."

"At least it can't do any harm down there."

"That depends on whether it's intact or leaking radiation. I'd hate to think there was some sort of mutated monster being born down there."

Tommy laughed. "You've been watching too many *Quatermass* programmes on the telly. Bloody mutated sea monsters. Ha!"

Shafiq stubbed out his cigar against the wall, threw it into a wastepaper basket, turned away from the parade and walked towards his car. The parades were usually joyous occasions and people were in a happy mood. The day trippers and tourists had started arriving and soon the town centre would be thronging. Good Friday was a long and fruitful day. People were generally happy, and happy people talked a lot. Moreover, the to-ing and fro-ing of crowds could be used to camouflage the Sand Dancers' activities. There was money to be made and Shafiq would make sure that it was channelled to the right places.

There was only one dark cloud on his horizon: the botched shambles of the Tyne Dock raid by the Newcastle gang. It still hadn't been sorted. The Geordies had acknowledged that the Sand Dancers had acted entirely within their remit and the incompetent gang had been disciplined. Shafiq shuddered to think what that meant. He was no stranger to violence, and he knew that some gangs were ruthless when met with non-compliance or incompetence. The plain fact remained that the shipment had not been recovered; at least not all of it. His informants in the police station had told him that Sergeant Tozer had found a case in the Dock and recorded as 'property other than found property' and 'owner unknown'. The property had been listed as 'precious stones'. Shafiq also knew that a comprehensive search of the Tyne Dock area had failed to reveal where the precious stones had come from. And there had been a *second* case. The Newcastle gang had been reluctant to divulge that information. Part of the shipment had been a sizeable amount of untraceable, used banknotes.

Shafiq's network had sprung into action. People were told that a case was missing, although no-one was told what was inside it. Shafiq had made it known that the Sand Dancers would be very grateful to the person finding the case. And the rumours had started. So far, the case hadn't been located. To Shafiq that meant one of a few options had occurred. Firstly, there hadn't been a second case at all, and he could think of a few reasons why the Geordies would want people to think that. Secondly, the gang members who had committed the crime were lying about the second case. Thirdly, the case was still in the Dock, hidden from view. Lastly, someone else had found it and was keeping hold if it.

Shafiq thought the last option was most likely. Maybe someone had it in their house and was deciding what to do with it. Every day, that person's options were being limited. It took a disciplined man to find a crock of gold and not tell anyone about it. The temptation would be to spend some of it. He would spend a few pounds at first to see if the money was real, but when that was proved to be ok, greed would take over, and a typical dock worker wouldn't be able to resist buying himself a car or something grander. The news would filter through the neighbourhood and sooner or later one of Shafiq's informants would hear about it and pass it on to him. Shafiq would prefer that to be sooner rather than later.

He slid into the car and drove a circuitous route back to Laygate to avoid the bands and parades and arrived at his office fifteen minutes later. There were several messages waiting for him. None contained information about the Tyne Dock raid. However, there was one message that intrigued him. It was from Blanche Fada. 'Having dinner with Jack Tozer in Newcastle tonight.'

Shafiq was surprised and intrigued. Blanche and Tozer didn't get on – so what was happening here? He glanced at the clock on the wall and thought about going around to see her, but he decided he could get all the information he needed after the event rather than trying to assuage his curiosity today. Nevertheless, a smile crossed his face. Blanche and Jack Tozer? Something was definitely up here.

Blanche was having second thoughts. During her recent conversation with Alice, Alice had declared her plan as too dangerous but admitted it was so unusual that it might work. A night with Jack Tozer probably wasn't the best way to start the Easter weekend. All of her 'friends' would be busy with their families until Monday, so she didn't expect any of them would be contacting her until Tuesday, by then the festivities would be over and the normality of routine would have started to consume everything else.

The hot bath had relaxed her, but she expected the tension would return when she met Jack. She'd pondered on what to wear, like any woman would on a first date, deliberating on how far she should go if Jack became amorous. Would he expect to have sex? And would that be based on his own desire or his knowledge of her past? Surely Jack would know that the relationship was a temporary arrangement? Though that being the case, why did Jack want to wine and dine her when he could just create a moment to satiate his lust? It was confusing. Yet Blanche knew that she had to gain as much information as possible in a very short time. If Jack was a wham-bam-thank-you-ma'am lover, then the whole thing would be over in days rather than weeks because he would move on to someone else who was more acceptable for his social circle. Blanche reminded herself that she was an accomplished lover. If she could keep him interested by a combination of variety and adventure, the relationship could be extended indefinitely. Moreover, she could exercise a certain degree of control. She'd said it before on more than one occasion, if you have a man's balls in your hand, you can control him by squeezing them or stroking them. Even so, Jack Tozer would be a challenge.

Jack Tozer stalked up and down Ocean Road as the parade progressed. He was on double time so he didn't care. Whenever anyone approached him to complain about something he signalled to a constable or special constable to take details. He was far too busy to deal with rubbish, supervising the parade and talent spotting, his phrase for seeking out females who he designated as potential lovers. He would move in and show his authority before 'interviewing' them. A wide smile and a wisecrack would be his opening gambit followed by lots of eye contact, more smiles and seemingly intelligent chit chat. It worked quite well. A lot of women were in awe of authoritative men in uniform. Maybe it was a legacy from the war, or maybe it was an inbred respect for policemen. Whatever it was, he was good at using it to his advantage.

Despite seeing one or two possibles, Jack's thoughts kept returning to Blanche Fada. Despite his abrasive relationship with her in the past he had always acknowledged that she excited him. He'd thought about it quite often yet couldn't fathom what it was that sent a chill down his backbone. He'd had sex with Billie many times in the past, sometimes thinking of Blanche while he did it, and now he had the opportunity to do it for real. He was slightly apprehensive – an unusual feeling for him. Blanche was an experienced woman, sexually, a prostitute in all but name. Would she find him wanting – in size, shape or experience? Would he be compared to others? It would only be the one night. He could argue that the evening hadn't worked out and that the relationship had therefore to ended, but he didn't want her to be anything than less than impressed by his prowess.

It had occurred to him that Blanche might think that a genuine relationship was on the cards. Let her think that. It was no skin off his nose. How could she think that a half-caste common prostitute was in the same class as a well off, white, police sergeant who held a position of respect in the community? No, this was a quiet meal with a shag at the end of it as far as he was concerned. He was off duty tomorrow so he could shag her again and again. He grinned and felt himself getting aroused at the mere thought of it. Blanche was in for a treat. He hoped she made a good breakfast.

It was a middle of the road restaurant. Not too grand but not the worst place in the world. Blanche settled on the old standby of a black dress that emphasised the glow of her olive skin, while

Jack had gone for a dark blue pinstriped suit with blue tie. Their conversation since he had picked her up in his car had been about the parade, and the traditions of the folk of South Shields. None of the traditions seemed to include anything from her Yemeni heritage.

Jack had been sweet and courteous. Blanche could see why he was successful with women. He frequently managed to brush his hands against her without apparently intending to do so. There was plenty of eye contact, and she could occasionally feel them surveying her body. If she didn't already know he was a bastard, she wouldn't have believed anyone who told her.

It was over dessert that he first mentioned his relationship with Billie and the seeming hostility between Blanche and himself. He was apologetic and remorseful, but Blanche could tell that the words were for the benefit of the evening and didn't reflect his true feelings. He talked of Billie as an item from his past and life had to move on. Yet Billie had been dead only seven weeks and he was already seeking bedfellows.

Blanche remained passive, letting Jack go through his animalistic seduction routine. It was obvious that he was expecting to have sex with her, but the more he talked and preened, the less likely sex became for Blanche. She would have to bait her hook, though, to tease and tantalise, then draw him in slowly. She concluded that Jack was a man who took the lead in everything. For her plan to work she needed to reverse the roles.

Jack was talking about the importance of intimacy in a loving relationship.

"For a couple entering into a life together, however long that may be, they need to make sure that they are sexually compatible. I know the Church and conventional society says that people shouldn't enter into sexual relationships until they're married, but I think that mature adults should be able to make those decisions themselves, don't you? I think it's nice that when a man comes home from work he can sit down to a meal and put his feet up. And if he wants to exercise his conjugal rights, then I can't see any reason why his woman would object. After all, he brings in the money."

Jack almost leapt out of his chair when Blanche's stockinged foot came into contact with his crotch.

She said, "You don't half talk a lot, Jack. I've often thought that actions speak louder than words."

Jack was flustered. "I... I... errrm... Bloody Hell, woman."

"Move closer," she instructed him.

Jack glanced around to see if anyone was watching. The answer was no. Although it was a Bank Holiday weekend, the restaurant wasn't full and they were partially screened at a table in an alcove towards the rear. He shuffled forward. Her foot re-established contact with his crotch. Jack was hard – and red in the face. He squirmed to accommodate her touch. Her big toe travelled the length of his penis causing Jack to open his mouth and suck in a lungful of air. She repeated the exercise several times, then, just as suddenly as it had started, she retrieved her foot and put her shoe back on.

"I think I'll have some coffee, Jack."

Jack was open mouthed with astonishment. She'd done enough for the moment to hint at heaven later. Jack adjusted his trousers to make himself more comfortable. He seemed to have difficulty in concentrating on the remnants of his ice cream.

"Coffee? Oh yes, coffee."

The journey home was a bit more subdued. Jack seemed a bit preoccupied. When they reached Blanche's house, Jack started to open the car door but Blanche stopped him. She grabbed him by the balls and massaged him. He became hard again. She undid a couple of buttons on his fly and slipped her hand in to grab his penis. He groaned. She undid two more buttons and put her other hand in to cup his balls. A combination of squeezing and stroking brought Jack to the point of orgasm – a sign that Blanche recognised – so she stopped and withdrew her hands.

For the second time in half an hour Jack was left almost speechless with astonishment.

"You ... you can't ... Christ!"

Blanche opened the door and slid out of the car. "Goodnight, Jack. Keep in touch." She slammed the door shut and sauntered up to her front door, inserted the key and disappeared into her home. A few seconds later she heard Jack's car tear off up the street. Round one to me, she thought.

31

Saturday 13th April 1963

Blanche was expecting it. A knock on the door at nine o'clock in the morning. It had to be one of three people. The unlikeliest would be Sebastian Crawley because he would probably be on his stall in the market, but he usually entrusted that task to Jackie. The second guess would be Jack Tozer demanding an explanation about last night, or to finish off what he was expecting. She would have bet all the money in her bank account that he would have finished himself off when he got home. The most likely knocker would be Shafiq. After her note to him the previous day, Shafiq would be more than mildly curious about her night out with Jack Tozer, and he would wait until this hour to allow Jack to quietly leave without being noticed.

Shafiq's grin was wide and natural. His eyes glinted with curiosity and intrigue.

"Good morning, Miss Fada. Today is a good day, yes? And may I say even better after a good dinner?"

Blanche said nothing. She stood aside to let him in.

Shafiq sat down without being invited and removed a cigar from his jacket pocket. He was settling down for an epic event like a child waiting for their grandfather to read them a fairy story while they scoffed some chocolate.

A swirl of cigar smoke headed towards the ceiling.

"Tea?" asked Blanche.

"I've no time for tea, Miss Fada. I'm more interested in your evening with the splendid Sergeant Tozer."

"I thought you might be."

"Correct me if I am wrong but I believed that you and Sergeant Tozer were not on friendly terms. I am curious about how that relationship has changed. It is unusual. No?"

Blanche sat in an armchair and told Shafiq about how Jack had helped her and how she had decided that it wouldn't do her any harm and actually be a benefit to the Sand Dancers if she managed to squeeze some information from him. She noticed a momentary flash of disbelief cross Shafiq's face.

Shafiq said, "We have people who can tell us such police work."

"I know that, but they're mainly typists and administrators, aren't they?"

Shafiq said nothing.

Blanche continued. "I did this because I wanted to show you that my information about the Tyne Dock raid wasn't an isolated incident. I know things didn't go according to plan and I know that Jack Tozer was on duty that night. I have to be honest; I have selfish reasons as well. I want to know a little bit more about Billie Crawley's death. Jack Tozer seems to have all the answers and I wanted to know some of them myself."

Shafiq weighed up Blanche's explanation before saying. "Will you be passing on any of this information to Sebastian Crawley and his grandfather?"

Blanche feigned surprise, then said, "If I hear anything about Billie, then yes. I couldn't not tell them."

Shafiq nodded.

Blanche said, "Mr. Heath was knocked about in the Tyne Dock incident. I don't suppose there would be any merit in telling him anything about it as it's a police matter, and there's nothing Tommy can do about it now, but still, if I can tell him something … well, he deserves to know."

The answer seemed to satisfy Shafiq. "This puts you in an impossible situation with Sergeant Tozer, does it not? He will want something in return."

"This is not a formal arrangement, Shafiq. He doesn't give me information for services rendered. And nothing has happened yet."

Shafiq raised an eyebrow.

"Last night we had a nice dinner and he brought me home. He didn't come in. Suffice to say that I gave him enough incentive for me to expect a future visit, soon."

The smile returned to Shafiq's face.

"And you will keep me informed, Miss Fada, of course?"

"I'm not going to give you a blow by blow account of what we get up to, but I'm sure you'll be happy with what I pass on to you."

"So be it. I look forward to your notes." Shafiq stubbed out the cigar and fastened his jacket to signify he was leaving. "One thing more. Whatever you pass on to Mr Crawley needs to be run by me first. I do not like to be surprised by people who have more information than me."

Blanche saw him to the door and closed it behind him.

Tommy Heath was in the pub talking to Lily the barmaid about the recent divorces of film stars. Seen at a distance, the woman appeared to be a very attractive, full figured, mature woman, however, as you moved closer, her mystique dissolved. Her clothes were worn and stretched, their lustre fading. Her face was lined, her skin blotched and sagging, her hair coarse and brittle. A diet of gin, cigarettes and chips had taken its toll. She had obviously been lovely once, but her feet embodied her appearance; no amount of red nail varnish could distract you from the calluses and bunions accumulated through trying to be something you're not. To some men, a few drinks would replace their circumspection and she would regain her lost allure and her vibrancy, and glamour would creep out of the shadows to tease and seduce, resulting in a frenzy of discarded clothes and sweat.

The conversation had turned to love, and with the benefit of a few beers inside him Tommy said, "If you consider love, think of it as a colour. When it's young it's like a newly painted canvas, full of vibrant colours with splashes of vivid reds, velvet blues and vibrant yellows. After a few years, some of the striking aspects of colour lose their appeal. They can become dull and lacklustre. But you learn that when you mix some colours together you get a different colour altogether. You become aware that vibrancy is not always the best. You start to appreciate pastel shades and the effects of light and shade. Through time, you flirt with maroon, mauve and magenta before you eventually settle on inoffensively soft hues like beige and magnolia. When you're old, they are deeply satisfying colours. The colour of love is beige."

Lily finished off polishing the glass and said, "That's what you think, Tommy, and it's very nice and all, but as far as I'm concerned the colour of love is a dirty brown and looks like shit."

Tommy sniggered. To Lily, romance was something you read about in a novel. In reality, in South Shields, it always ended up with a bloke trying to shag you.

"Lily, my love, you have a way with words that would put Shakespeare to shame."

"Piss off, Tommy"

Tommy laughed. "I'll say farewell, my lovely. Now it's time for home, a meal and a nap."

The walk to his house took less than one minute. The dying embers of the fire were hastily restored to a domestic furnace. The meal was a couple of pies from the butchers. He decided that he didn't have time to heat them up, and he was hungry, so he dumped dollops of tomato sauce on them and ate them cold. Soon, a combination of food, beer and heat sent him to the Land of Nod.

A little while later, Sebastian ushered Blanche into the baking hot lounge. His grandad was slumped in his chair snoring loudly. Blanche smiled. Sebastian shook his head. He didn't blame him. What did he have to live for other than the small mercies of life like a pie and a pint on a Saturday afternoon? He'd probably wake up in time for the football results at five o'clock.

Blanche went to the kitchen and filled the kettle. Sebastian dumped his money bag behind the settee to be counted later. Blanche had met him at the stall and walked with him to Catherine Street as she told him about her night with Jack. Her description of the previous night's events was a more colourful version of that disclosed to Shafiq.

She went through it all again when Tommy spluttered to consciousness.

"You're playing with fire," Tommy said. "The bastard's not a man you can treat like an idiot."

"He's right, Blanche. If Jack thinks you're winding him up, he'll tear you apart."

"I know that. And I also know what I'll have to do in the future. I'm prepared for it. I haven't met a man yet who's taken advantage of me – except possibly the first guy I ever loved. At least he taught me a lesson I'll never forget. I can't say I'm not a little bit apprehensive, but I know I can play Jack Tozer for all he's worth. You see, I have what he wants, and I know that it's only a temporary thing, but I also know that the Jack Tozers of this world keep coming back for more until the novelty wears off or they find something different. I can promise you this, he will not be getting bored and he won't be looking elsewhere for a few weeks."

Tommy and Sebastian exchanged glances, neither knowing how to respond.

Blanche continued. "By the way, I've told Shafiq the same thing. He's expecting to be kept informed as soon as anything is known. Obviously, I'll tell you the truth, and I can't risk telling Shafiq something that isn't the truth, but we need to be completely secret about this." She looked squarely at Sebastian. "And you can't tell Alice. I'm sorry, Sebastian. We don't know what she would do or how she would react. We can't afford the risk. In any case, if anything happens, we wouldn't want to compromise her or her uncle. It wouldn't be right." She didn't reveal that Alice already knew part of her plan.

Sebastian thought for a moment, then nodded. Blanche was right. Alice couldn't be mixed up in this. He had kept her well and truly at arm's length for some time now, to the point where he felt a little bit divorced from her, and he'd felt a similar reflection coming the other way, though he knew that this was because he'd reverted to his old secret ways and Alice didn't react well to that, and she'd had her head turned by politics on the world stage.

Jack Tozer walked towards his local pub with the *Football Pink* under his arm. This one was from Newcastle, where Jack had spent the afternoon. His team was Sunderland, and he was beaming after today's one nil win over Portsmouth, which had kept them in third position in the league with a glorious chance of promotion to the first division.

As he crossed over Harton Lane his mind examined the previous night for signs and subtleties that indicated the evening would end up like it had. There was something strange about Blanche Fada that he couldn't put his finger on. She made him feel unsure and insecure. She undermined his authority. Her directness had surprised him, even though she was a borderline prostitute. Some time ago he had tried to have her arrested, but he couldn't find anyone to give evidence against her and she was never ever found in circumstances that warranted her detention and the case was dropped. She'd snubbed him after that. She'd always been cool and articulate, her intelligent eyes cutting through his veneer of power. It should have filled him with the determination to overcome her insolence, but all it had done was stir his lust. This was one woman who had not succumbed to his charm or acquiesced to his authority.

All discreet enquiries he'd ever made had failed to uncover any dirt on her. For a woman of her occupation it was surprising that no-one was prepared to say anything against her, apart from a few gossiping neighbours.

He'd lain in bed most of the night thinking about her. He'd resisted the temptation to pleasure himself so he could keep the erection for a few hours. Eventually he'd succumbed. He'd decided to wait a few days and then go back to her. Was she playing a game? He didn't think so. What was there to gain? She knew there was nothing long term. A shag was a shag. It may be that her business pleasure was different from social pleasure. Maybe she was a bit of a fetishist and this was all foreplay. Her clients weren't exactly the strong virile type and she was looking for something different. Perhaps poor Blanche was a bit frustrated and had recognised him for the buck he was. Yes, all she wanted was a good old shagging, like most other women. He smiled to himself and started whistling. His stride lengthened and became more purposeful. Sunderland on the way up and a woman crowing for his body. Life couldn't get better.

"Blanche Fada, my love. You're in for a bloody good time sometime soon."

32

Easter Monday 15th April 1963

Sebastian put the phone down. He was happy that Alice was back safe and sound. She'd described her seventy two hours away with the protesting multitudes and she'd managed to convey her excitement about the march, but there was something not quite right. Her voice was croaky and she was obviously tired, and that's what she told him, but her insistence on wanting to see him tomorrow was odd. He had expected longing or desire or something personal – but that's not what he felt. There was a distance there. An arm's length detachment that was a bit disconcerting. He shook his head. A sense of foreboding entered his mind.

He went over the conversation again in his head.

She was tired and restless. The weekend had been tremendous. Her arms were aching. Had they been successful? Who could tell? The Tories now knew the strength of their argument and woe betide them at the next election if they failed to heed the voice of the people. She'd met lots of people who shared her views on politics and life in general. They accepted her for who she was and recognised her intellect and ambition. This was her world. These were her people.

He was well aware that life in South Shields was a far cry from what she'd wanted, and it had been her intention to make South Shields a step on the ladder to success. She'd often questioned why she was there in the first place, that it was a chance to work on the 'coal face' of politics in a downtrodden, industrial, working class area. It gave her middle class upbringing some acceptability. She'd once told him that she hoped people would welcome an intelligent, resolute woman to fight in their corner, like Ellen Wilkinson had done at neighbouring Jarrow some years ago. The offer from Uncle Jim had been a godsend. And often enough Sebastian had listened to her describe the mundanity of local politics and being administrative support to a bunch of well-meaning old Councillors, and that had never sat well with her style of politics. She wanted to work with people like Kennedy. The prospect of work with the

Democratic Party in America appealed to her. And so it should, he'd agreed.

Sebastian was now thinking that he was an obstacle to her ambitions. Something was about to give.

"Something up?" Tommy asked.

Sebastian gave a stoic grin. "I don't think so. Alice's had a good time in London changing the world. She's tired and aching but she'll be alright tomorrow."

They both sat and watched television in silence. The national anthem finished off the programmes for the night, and after a few minutes Tommy said, "Have you given any thought to what Blanche is doing?"

"Time and time again. I think she's taking too big a chance and something unexpected might happen. I think she's got it all wrong, but we're out of options, really. She thinks it's worth a try and she's the one who's doing it." He shrugged. "All we can do is give her a bit of support when she needs it."

Tommy nodded. "What about Shafiq?"

"I doubt the Sand Dancers will want to be involved with anything like this. They'll appreciate any information, of course, but I don't think they'll want to dirty their hands."

"Unless they can find another angle they can work. Shafiq's a strange one. He likes you, you know."

Sebastian shot his grandfather a glance. "What do you mean?"

"I don't really know. But whenever he talks to you, he's almost reverential. It's like he knows you're in a position on a pedestal above him."

"Don't be daft."

Tommy said, "Mark my words. There's something that we're missing here."

Sebastian, though, had turned his mind to other messages that were hidden between other lines.

Tuesday 16th April 1963

Blanche stood at the rear of the police station in Keppel Street and waited. Jack Tozer was about to finish his shift and Blanche had crimped and preened herself in preparation for greeting him when he came off duty.

There was a genuine look of surprise on Jack's face when he exited the station car park and found her waiting.

He pulled alongside her and said, "Are you waiting for me or is this just a coincidence?"

She opened the passenger door and slid in beside him.

He said, "And what do you think..."

She kissed him hard and long as the revs on his car increased to a crescendo. She pulled away from him, leaving him confused, astonished and confounded by her behaviour.

"I've come to finish off what I started the other night. Come on, Jack, take me back to your place and show me what you've got."

Jack tried to engage gears and stalled the car. He tried again, successfully this time, and screeched his way up Garden Lane.

Blanche reached across and rubbed his groin, nearly causing an accident as they passed the Labour Party Headquarters in Westoe Road. By the time they reached the bottom of Sunderland Road, Blanche had Jack growling. By Harton Village he was whimpering. She sat regally as Jack parked on his drive. She watched as he tried to comport himself with his usual display of superiority to his neighbours. He then invited Blanche, by gesture, to enter his home. She agreed. Game on, she thought.

It was a masculine house. There had been a little bit of titivation, presumably by Billie, but it favoured function rather than aesthetic pleasure. Blanche sat down in an armchair and waited for Jack to react in some way.

Inside his own house and with the full knowledge that he was about to have sex, Jack became his old arrogant self. He swaggered almost nonchalantly from the lounge to the kitchen to pick up a couple of glasses. He made his way to the drinks cabinet and poured two large glasses of whisky. Was this his idea of foreplay, wondered Blanche?

Jack offered the drink to Blanche. She took it and placed it on a small table to the side of the chair. She had no intention of drinking it. Jack gulped his in two swallows and poured another.

Blanche said, "Do you need a stiff drink, or do you need a drink to make you stiff?"

Jack smiled. He liked it when women talked dirty. He took another swallow and put the glass down on the table. There'll be a ring there tomorrow morning, thought Blanche absently.

Jack said, "Come on, Blanche, you started this, now let's get some action. His eyes were gleaming, and he rubbed his hands together in anticipation, rather like a schoolboy having been asked to bowl in his first cricket match.

Blanche stood and dropped her coat onto the chair. She walked slowly towards Jack and paused beside him. "You had better be worth it, Jack." She then sidled past him and began to climb the stairs.

Jack waited a moment and finished off his second whisky.

Blanche reached the top landing as Jack said, "The master bedroom is to the right."

Blanche entered the room and saw that the bed was unmade. She turned and walked out as Jack was halfway up the stairs.

"I'm not lying in an unmade bed," she said and went into the next bedroom just as Jack shouted.

"Not in there, Blanche." There was a note of urgency in his voice.

Blanche entered the room. It was sparsely furnished. It had a full-sized bed that was covered in a green candlewick bedspread. There was a wooden chair, an old oak wardrobe and a matching chest of drawers. On the drawers were three bundles of banknotes in various denominations. An old case was on the floor half concealed under the bed.

Jack burst into the room behind her. He was furious. He grabbed Blanche by the shoulder and spun her road. "I told you not to come in here."

Blanche shrugged him off and poked him in the chest. "Get your hands off me. You don't touch me unless I say so." She pointed to the master bedroom and said, "If you think I'm going to lie in that, then you have another thing coming. You may not like the person I am, Jack, but there are certain standards that I like to maintain, and one of them is cleanliness." She waved at the room behind her. "This looks like a better room for what I had in mind, but I seem to have stumbled on your family fortune. Why don't you keep it in a bank?"

Jack snarled, "It's none of your business what I do in my own home. You're just like your mate Billie. She couldn't do as she was told either. The only thing she was good at was pleasuring me in the bedroom." His face was red, his eyes were wide and glazed.

Blanche decided that it was time to leave.

"Where do you think you're going?" He grabbed both her shoulders and threw her onto the bed, which, in turn, knocked the chest of drawers and three piles of banknotes fell to the floor like confetti, covering the mat.

Jack held Blanche's wrists and threw his whole bodyweight on top of her, breathing whisky soaked fumes into her face. She struggled, but years of fighting drunks on the streets allowed Jack to easily subdue her

"Get off me, Jack," she shouted.

"You can't tease me, you bitch. You came here for a shag and a shag is what you're going to get."

Blanche kept struggling, but a hard slap across the face stunned her and she momentarily lost all strength. Jack held her wrists together in one huge hand. His other hand went up her dress and started stroking her vulva on top of her knickers.

She screamed.

Jack slapped her again.

"Do that again and I'll give you something to scream about."

He eased aside her knickers, using his thumb to search deep inside her. After a few moments, he removed it and started fumbling at his flies.

This was her moment. His attention was on his own penis. With an explosion of self-preservation, she freed both of her hands from Jack's grip and thrust a thumb into his left eye socket. Jack howled in pain, slapped blindly at Blanche's hand, while clutching his eye. Blanche made use of Jack's movements to shove him off her. He fell to the bed and banged his head on the chest of draws. Stunned for just a moment, he lay there with his penis and balls exposed. Blanche snatched up her shoe and whacked his balls with everything she had. Jack's scream had never been that high since he'd been a soprano in the school choir, and he rolled over and vomited on the floor.

Blanche quickly picked up a wad of money wrapped in a small red paper sleeve and fled.

33

Wednesday 17th April 1963

Sebastian ate a crumpet in front of the fire. He was surprisingly upbeat given that his girlfriend had told him last night that she was going to America. He didn't know yet how he felt about that. He hadn't realised just how prepared he had been for the news and how easily he accepted it. Perhaps it was because of all that had gone on lately and Alice's absences. The overwhelming love he had felt just a couple of weeks ago had faded and blurred under the weight of his family tragedies.

Alice had stolen his heart for a few months. No, not stolen, she had borrowed it and refashioned it. It was now an updated version of the one he'd had a few months ago, somehow more able to deal with change. The final break up – was that even how to describe it? - had been as low key as if she were simply saying goodnight. It was almost like a mutual acknowledgement that they wouldn't be seeing each other again, an understanding that what had gone before was some sort of bonding experience that would keep them tied until they met again in the future. It certainly bore no resemblance whatsoever to the romantic ideals and the tears of Hollywood. It was as if he had known all along that their relationship was destined never to survive and there was a natural cut-off date where they would go their own ways, still connected but distant in time and space.

She was a high-flying whirlwind of a woman with dreams and ambitions far beyond the boundaries of South Shields, while he was nailed to the area by his business, by birth, by history. Alice had certainly opened his mind to women's issues and world politics, and somewhere in all that he knew that he had to let her go to pursue her dream, and she'd cried when he'd said that, that she had a right to dream.

"You're a wonderful man, Sebastian Crawley."

Alice was a wonderful woman.

But so was South Shields.

Tommy ambled into the room carrying a paper bag wet with saveloy dips.

"Lunch," he said.

Sebastian said nothing. He wasn't going to mention Alice to his grandad at the moment. There were still a few things he had to come to terms with first.

"I met Blanche in Ocean Road," said Tommy. "She said that she's coming around here at eleven to talk to us. She said it was serious, that she had arranged for Shafiq to be here as well, which I thought was a bit of a cheek."

Blanche and Shafiq arrived at the same time. A veneer of nervous energy infused the room. Sebastian had images of the final scene in *High Noon,* a movie he'd watched with Alice on tv, who had given a running commentary on male chauvinism throughout the feature.

It was Blanche who started talking first.

"You all knew that I met Jack Tozer last weekend and that I was going to meet him again soon. Well, yesterday I met up with him again and went back to his house."

They all nodded.

No-one commented.

Blanche continued.

"I fully intended to have sex with Jack as part of a plan I came up with."

Shafiq raised an eyebrow and pulled out a cigar which he lit despite Tommy coughing theatrically, although he didn't say anything.

"However, things didn't go to plan. I went into the wrong bedroom by mistake and Jack went berserk. He threw me onto the bed and then ... er ... he ... er ... molested me."

Tommy hung his head.

Sebastian stared into the fire.

Shafiq blew smoke rings at the ceiling.

"Jack was going to rape me. I managed to get him off me as he was getting his cock out. When he fell on the bed, I whacked his balls with my shoe. He didn't have the energy to get up."

Tommy said, "I hope his balls rot and fester."

Sebastian said, "Are you all right, Blanche?

She nodded. "I was a little shaken up at the time and he's given me a bruise." She pointed to her cheek.

"This is most interesting, Miss Fada," said Shafiq. "I am a busy man. There is more you wish to say?"

"You're right, Shafiq. When I was there, I took some money from the bedroom." Blanche reached for her handbag and drew out the wad of banknotes. She placed it on the table.

Tommy whistled soft and low, "There's a few quid there."

Sebastian's brow furrowed. "Are you saying you stole Jack's money? Is that what this meeting's about?"

Shafiq said, "I do not think so, Mr Crawley. I believe Miss Fada has further revelations."

Blanche said, "It wasn't until I got home and started thinking about the incident that I realised that the money that Jack had in his bedroom was probably more than he should have. Fair enough if he doesn't like banks and wants to keep his money in cash under the bed. There's no harm in that. But I think he's been up to no good."

The men in the room swapped suspicious looks and asked themselves the same questions. Was Jack Tozer bent? Was he on the take?

A few moments passed whilst they all considered the possibilities. The wad of red wrapped money brooded on the table before them.

"Well?" asked Blanche. "Am I right or am I way off the beam?"

Tommy said nothing.

Sebastian said, "I think you may be right. It's a pity we don't know how much was there."

Shafiq stubbed out his cigar and said, "About fifty thousand pounds I would guess."

Tommy said, "That's a helluva guess. Where did that come from?"

Shafiq made an instant decision to tell Sebastian and Tommy the rudiments of the Tyne Dock raid.

"Mister Heath, you were a victim in the unfortunate incident at your place of work. Those men who assaulted you were meant to receive two cases containing, shall we call them, remuneration. One case contained jewels and the other cash. I know this, although the owners of the property did not fully keep me informed. A grave error if you ask me. However, when the police intervened, the cases were abandoned inside the dock. Sergeant Tozer found one of the cases, the one containing jewels, and took it to the police station. The other case is still classified as missing."

Tommy whistled softly again.

"Jack kept the ..."

"That is my conclusion. Sergeant Tozer has a case full of money in his house."

"Had a case full of money. If he's got any sense, he'll have stashed it somewhere else by now. You sure it's the same money?"

Shafiq pointed to the table. "I happen to know that the money that was stolen was wrapped in red sleeves, just like that."

Blanche said, "So what do we do?"

"An interesting question, Miss Fada. I will take charge of the money and return it to the rightful owners."

Tommy eyed Shafiq suspiciously.

Shafiq feigned pain. "Mister Heath, I am an honourable man. I am not a thief. I will do as I say. I am a man of my word."

They all digested that in different ways.

Eventually Blanche broke the growing silence. "Forgive my ignorance," she said, "but couldn't we just go to the police station and ask to see a senior officer? I'm sure that they have official ways of dealing with things like this. Jack Tozer wouldn't be the first bent copper they've ever had."

Shafiq winced. "That would be a mistake. We don't know, for instance, if Sergeant Tozer has an accomplice, although that is highly unlikely. And a police investigation would not be healthy for my friends in Newcastle. This has to be dealt with carefully."

Sebastian had been listening to their discussion in thoughtful silence. Shafiq was right. A lawful intervention and investigation by the police would take too long and would involve a lot of people. Jack Tozer had to be sorted, and sorted quickly.

Shafiq almost read Sebastian's mind. "We cannot allow for anyone to take action on their own initiative. That would be unfortunate for all concerned. This is a serious matter that needs to be dealt with by people who know what they are doing and have the resources to carry it out."

Tommy said, "I don't like the sound of that. You're not talking about topping him surely?"

Shafiq smiled. "We like to keep our options open at all times. I do not think that the death of Sergeant Tozer, accidentally or otherwise, would serve our purposes. I will report these issues to my superiors, and they will decide what is appropriate."

Sebastian said, "And who might they be?"

Shafiq's smile widened. "I am not at liberty to say, Mister Crawley, but be assured he has you best interests at heart."

Shafiq picked up the money from the table and put it in his coat pocket. His eyes searched the faces of those present and didn't see any dissent. He nodded and left.

Suddenly, Blanche burst into tears. Sebastian went to her and comforted her. After a few moments she raised her head and said, "I have to get away. Jack will come for me; I know he will. He'll not let this go. I've hurt his pride."

"I think you hurt more than that from what you say." Tommy said. "You can stay here if you want. Billie's room's free."

Sebastian said, "That's fine, but she can't be a prisoner here. It'll not take Jack long to figure out where she is and then he'll come chasing like a bat out of Hell. I think you should go away somewhere else until we deal with Jack."

"What have you in mind, son?"

"Shafiq said we can't inform the police, and I agree with that. He also said that he was going to inform his boss, whoever that is. The Sand Dancers are just another organisation with a chain of command. By the time they've discussed what their options are, we could've done something about Jack Tozer ourselves. Once Blanche is safe, I'll sort out Jack bloody Tozer."

Blanche wiped tears from her cheek, smudging her make-up at the same time. "Don't do anything stupid, Sebastian. Jack's an animal. I can't go away. As long as Jack Tozer's around, I can never be safe. I'll have to stay put."

Sebastian stood up. "OK, then it means I've got to get on with it now."

Tommy said, "Get on with what exactly?"

"I'm going to Jack's house."

Tommy stood in front of Sebastian. "You can't go there, son. It'll come to no good."

"I have to, grandad. Jack Tozer's responsible for the death of my mother and molesting my friend. I can't allow that to go on."

Tommy said, "Act in haste – repent at leisure. I'm not letting you out of this house in your present state. I have a better plan."

"And what's that?"

"Just give me twenty-four hours."

Twenty-four hours can be a long time, Sebastian thought. It separates yesterday from today, and today from tomorrow. Some people are alive one day and not the next. It's the space that separates girl friend from girlfriend.

34

Thursday 18th April 1963

Detective Sergeant Smith stroked his stubbly chin and stared at the glass of brown ale on the table before him. He slowly shook his head. It couldn't be, surely. Here he was, eight months from retirement and then for someone to drop this on him was his worst nightmare. This pub was a regular port of call for him. He made himself known to his informant, who he referenced as Accra. He then went to the toilet where he was joined by Accra. A brief conversation usually led to the informant getting a packet of cigarettes or a ten-bob note, depending on the value of the information received. Yet if this informant's information was correct, he was entitled to at least twenty quid.

The detective reached for his notebook and wrote down the conversation word for word.

    Smith - What have you got for me?
    Accra - I need big money.
    Smith - Big money demands big news. So what have you got?
    Accra - I have information about a policeman.
    Smith - Yes?
    Accra - I believe you are looking for some money in a case.
    Smith - And?
    Accra - The policeman has this case. How much you give me?
    Smith - Tell me what you know and I'll see what I can do.
    Accra - I have heard the policeman has the case. I do not know his name but he went to the crime and took the case.
    Smith - That officer took the case to the police station.
    Accra - No, he took one case only to police station.
    Smith - How do you know this?
    Accra - I have heard from man who was there.
    Smith - OK. Get me some evidence. Let me speak to the man who told you.
    Accra - That cannot happen. He not want to be involved. I have to go. You give me big money.

The brief conversation had resulted in Detective Sergeant Smith giving Accra a pound note, with the promise of more when further information or evidence came to light. Smith now had a problem. What should he do with the information? It was idle gossip based on fact. Hearsay. It wouldn't have taken long for the jungle drums to tell the world that a quantity of jewels had been recovered from a crime that went wrong in Tyne Dock. Smith was used to gossip. It had brought him just reward in the past. He usually knew when gossip was good. It was a gut feeling – and that feeling was gnawing away at his insides. However, a gut feeling wasn't evidence and the Super would agree, so he'd try and tap into other sources first to see if there was any corroboration anywhere.

He left his beer and made his way back to the station. The Collator's office was unoccupied, so he spent the next fifteen minutes looking at recent intelligence. He was about to give up when he came across an item from PC Richardson, a Laygate bobby, which said:

Information received that there is another case missing in the Tyne Dock area in relation to a burglary/theft on Friday 22nd March 1963. The case is alleged to contain a quantity of cash belonging to an unnamed person in Newcastle. Informant believed to be related to perpetrator.

Smith saw that the information hadn't been given a high priority and had never made it to the CID office. It was probably put down as low-level unconfirmed gossip and left in the files. Smith's gut grumbled again. Detective work was about taking pieces of a jigsaw and putting them together without the lid to tell you where things were likely to be placed, or more importantly, what was in the picture. Now he had two pieces of the jigsaw.

He then went to the Incident Log and scanned the messages for 22nd March into the early hours. He came across a message from an anonymous male caller who had said "Help. I need help at Tyne Dock." The person who took the call said an attempt had been made by the caller to disguise his voice. The call had led the police to discover that the night watchman had been assaulted and damage had been done to the night watchman's office. Later,

Jack Tozer had found a case of jewels in the dock after disturbing two men who were acting suspiciously and who were believed to be the people who had attacked the night watchman.

More pieces of the jigsaw.

Far from being a good old-fashioned copper, Jack Tozer was looking more like a gamekeeper turned poacher. Smith hated bent coppers. He'd done nearly twenty-five years trying to put criminals behind bars, yet every year was wasted when a bad penny turned up and made a mockery of the system. He needed evidence, and the only evidence that would work would be either a witness or the case of money. The former was unlikely. So, Jack, being the main suspect at this time, if he had the money, where would he hide it? Jack wasn't stupid. He wouldn't put it in a bank or trust anyone else to keep it for him. Most likely, at least initially, he'd have it at home, secreted away where no-one else had access.

He picked up the phone and dialled a number in Newcastle.

"Crime Squad, Sergeant Miller," said a gruff voiced Glaswegian.

"Glad to see you're still working there, Jock," said Smith.

"Is that you, Smithy? How's life in the sticks?"

Smith smiled, Rory Miller and he had joined the police on the same day. Their careers had run almost in parallel since then, their paths crossing every now and then.

"Listen, Jock, I haven't got time to chat at the moment. I need to tap your brains about a Newcastle gang that might have done a job in South Shields."

"I'll see what I can do, Smithy. What's the story?"

Smith told him what he knew, leaving out the suspicions about Jack Tozer.

Miller said, "Aye, that fits in with what we know. We have someone on the inside of a gang who tells us that two of their lads were given … correctional guidance … after cocking a job up. They ended up in hospital. We also had a whisper that there was a heavy payment going down last month that involved jewels and cash. The money never arrived, and one or two local people were a bit put out because they hadn't got what they were promised. Corruption levels are pretty high at the minute. There's a lot of backhanders being bandied about."

"So we have the jewels but the cash is still missing?"

"Aye, it appears so. We reckon on between forty and fifty thousand pounds."

Smith blew a long low whistle. "That's a lot of money."

"Aye, it is. More than I've ever seen. But there's an awful lot of people's palms that need to be greased here."

Smith finished the conversation and returned to his notes. The jigsaw pieces were mounting. Then there was the Coroner's report about the death of the woman at Jack's house in February. That didn't show Jack Tozer in a good light either. There were certainly questions to be asked, but he didn't want to be the man to ask them. He would see Superintendent Balfour tomorrow and hopefully he'd pass it on to someone else. Smith didn't want this one on his hands, not with retirement just around the corner.

Tommy Heath wandered up the street where Jack Tozer's house stood. His mouth was dry. His confidence of the morning ebbed like the tide covering Jarrow Slake. His plan was almost the same as Sebastian's plan. He was going to knock on Jack's door and take it as it came. He would tell Jack he was grieving over Billie and had been disappointed that Jack hadn't attended the funeral or been to pay his respects. It was a simple ruse, but he wanted to see Jack's reaction.

The Tozer house was a double-fronted detached house with a five-foot high hedge around it. Tommy strode up to the front door and knocked twice. He waited. There was no answer. He knocked again and listened through the letter box. No-one was home. Plan A was defeated before it even began. Plan B was more dangerous. He reached into his pocket and pulled out a key. It had a little blue truncheon as a fob. It had been given to Tommy as part of Billie's possessions when she died, and everybody assumed it was the key to Jack's front door. He knocked once more just to be sure. Hearing nothing, he put the key into the lock and turned it. The door opened. He stepped inside.

There was no time to waste. According to Blanche the money was in a case in a bedroom on the left at the top of the stairs. He paused briefly before ascending. This was where Billie died. He shivered.

"This is for you, Billie."

At the top of the stairs he went into the bedroom on the left and went straight to the space underneath the bed. There was nothing there. He searched the wardrobe and drawers. Nothing. He extended his search to the other rooms upstairs. No luck. Panic began to set in. The money was gone. Tommy raced downstairs as fast as he could and flung open cupboard doors to see if he could find the case. No case.

Tommy walked away from the house and into Harton Village, where he stood at the bar of *The Ship* and ordered a pint of beer. His breathing was laboured, and he was sweating heavily. The bar maid gave him a worried look.

"Are you alright?"

Tommy said, "I am now, love. I am now."

Two hours later Tommy walked into his house to find Sebastian waiting for him.

Sebastian said, "Looks like you've had a few."

Tommy sat down in his chair and breathed out heavily. He said, "I have, son. I needed a few after what I've done."

Sebastian's brow knitted together. "And what might that be?"

"I did what you said you were going to do yesterday. I went to Jack Tozer's house."

Sebastian stood up. "What!"

Tommy told his story.

Sebastian shook his head. "You stupid old man. What would you have done if you were caught?"

"I wasn't caught. Look, it needed to be done. Now we know that the money isn't at Jack's house."

"And now we have no chance at all of getting the bastard."

"Oh yes we have," said Tommy. "I met a bloke in the pub who gave me a lift down to *The Brunswick* at Laygate. I had a couple in there and when I came out who do you think I bumped into? You're mate Sammy. We had a bit of chat. I wanted to buy him a drink, but he doesn't do alcohol much, does he? Anyway, we got talking about how he saved my skin in the Dock the other week and when I mentioned that the police had found a case with jewels in he said, 'what about the other one?' He says he saw the policeman, I'm presuming Jack Tozer, open two cases and take both of them away." Tommy's ruddy face positively beamed.

"Must have a piss," he said as he got up and went to the toilet.

Sebastian was stunned. Jack Tozer had taken the money. His grandad's reckless act had reaped dividends. Now it looked for certain that Tozer was a criminal masquerading as a policeman. The question now was how to bring Jack Tozer nearer to justice? Sammy was a key witness, but he would never be able to give evidence in a court of law as he was actively involved in committing crimes himself. He would be discredited immediately, so any testimony would be useless.

Tommy re-entered the room. "What do you think?"

Sebastian said, "It all points to Jack Tozer being corrupt. But this is bigger than us, grandad. I think we need to inform the Sand Dancers. I think we need their help."

"Shit," said Tommy.

35

Saturday 20th April 1963

Blanche, Tommy and Sebastian had gathered in Shafiq's office. They had run the gauntlet of a bunch of heavies to gain access to his inner sanctum, but they had been friendly enough. Blanche had smiled at those she recognised, and one even smiled back. Shafiq offered the trio drinks, but they all refused. He appeared a little nervous, which to Sebastian seemed odd. When does someone get nervous in their own office? Sebastian briefly outlined the events leading to them seeking an audience with him. He didn't mention Sammy by name.

Shafiq said, "I am pleased you have come to me, gentlemen," and almost as an afterthought added, "and lady."

That was a bit formal, thought Sebastian.

"I am grateful that you have confidence in our friendship. I am sure that we can do business together."

And that's what it was, thought Sebastian. Business. It wasn't about what Sebastian wanted it to be about – a criminal responsible for his mother's death and for forcing himself on Blanche. "Look, Shafiq, we've told you what we know. So how are we going to bring Jack to justice."

"Ah! Justice," said Shafiq, "Justice comes in many forms. Some people say an eye for an eye is justice. Some people say imprisonment is justice. Justice is many things to many people. Our friends in Newcastle would see justice as getting their property back and eliminating the rogue Sergeant Tozer."

Tommy said, "What? You mean like ... kill him?"

Shafiq gave one of his thin smiles. "In a perfect world Sergeant Tozer would get what he deserves, but I think on this occasion we can be fairly certain that that will not happen." He looked Sebastian squarely in the face. "We have to ask you how much involvement you want in this matter. I would advise none at all. You have already suggested that the Sergeant is a professional. That is so. It would be better to leave it up to us. We are professionals also. However, some of our methods may not be entirely within the law. We need not be confined by the rules of evidence or the balance of probabilities. Whatever outcome we need to befall Sergeant Tozer can be delivered. It just needs to be organised properly."

Blanche said, "I want him to go away forever."

Tommy said, "I'd like to see him convicted in a court of law and sent to prison. They won't tolerate blokes like him in there."

Sebastian said, "I believe he was responsible for the death of my mother. I accept that he probably didn't murder her, but he was responsible for her injuries and the way she died. He's telling lies, or at best avoiding the truth. Like grandad, I would like to see him go to prison, but there's no way he would be convicted over my mother's death. The money is a different matter. That's stealing. That's a crime, and policemen should be solving crimes not committing them."

"That is so, Mister Crawley. We will see what we can do."

The telephone rang. Shafiq picked it up and listened. He said nothing before replacing the phone in its cradle. He stood up. The nervousness returned.

"We are about to meet my superior. I beg you to give him respect. He is a powerful man."

The door opened and a middle-aged man with a swarthy complexion, wearing a blue, perfectly tailored, three-piece suit entered the room. He paused briefly to survey Shafiq and his visitors. He wore a genuine smile on his face as he gazed long and hard at Blanche, then Tommy and, lastly, Sebastian.

Sebastian felt real warmth emanating from him. Shafiq had portrayed him as a man to fear, but Sebastian couldn't see anything other than a friendly chap who happened to drop into the office. It was hard to believe that he was the head of a crime family. Sebastian held out his hand.

"Pleased to meet you."

The man took a step forward and grasped his hand. It was unexpectedly firm and friendly. The man had penetrating eyes that twinkled 'I like you'.

The man let go and turned to his grandad offering his hand. Tommy shook it, a strange look on his face.

The man spoke for the first time. "Hello, Mister Heath. It has been a long time." His voice was authoritative and cultured.

Sebastian saw his grandfather wrestling with confusing memories and emotions, and a glance in Blanche's direction revealed a face almost drained of colour. The man kissed Blanche on both cheeks.

He said, "Hello, Blanche."

The man sat down in Shafiq's chair. Shafiq perched himself against a filing cabinet.

Sebastian said, "I'm a little confused here. You seem to know Blanche and my grandad. What the Hell's going on?"

Tommy spoke first. Without taking his eyes off the man he said, "I never thought I'd ever see you again. Twenty-four years, it must be. Twenty-four years."

"That is so, Mister Heath. I kept my promise. I always keep my promises." He turned to Blanche. "And how are you Blanche?"

Blanche breathed out audibly. "Is it really you?"

The man laughed. "It is me, Blanche. It really is, after all these years."

Sebastian said, "Will someone explain to me what this is about?"

Blanche said, "This is Jaden Hameed. He was one of a gang that your mother and I used to knock about with when we were teenagers. He was your mother's first real boyfriend."

Hameed nodded to confirm what she had said.

Tommy said, "Your mother fell in love with him, but I asked him to leave her alone. She was too young ... and he was a Sand Dancer."

Hameed grinned, showing a row of even white teeth.

"Again, that is so, Mister Heath. Billie was a simple girl with simple dreams and ambitions. I loved her deeply, you know." He waved his hands in the air. "Who knows what would have happened if we had defied you. We may have drifted apart and gone our separate ways, we may have married and had ten children. No one will ever know. You told me to leave Billie alone and I did. It broke my heart, but I recognised that you loved Billie as much, if not more, than me. You said you wanted her to have the best opportunities that life could offer her. Yet within months she was pregnant and married to Reginald Crawley. Tell me, Mister Heath, was that the best opportunity you could give her?"

Tommy shook his head. A tear formed in the corner of his eye. "Billie was Billie. You couldn't tell her what to do. She was headstrong. She was running around with Blanche here. I didn't know whether that was a good thing or a bad thing. I tried to do what I thought was best. And when she got pregnant ... Reginald Crawley was a good man. Billie liked him."

"Liked him?"

Tommy stared at Haseem. "I'm not apologising to you for my actions. What I did can't be changed. I don't know whether I was right or wrong; I made the decision based on what I thought was in Billie's best interests."

Haseem said, "I know that, Mister Heath. That is why I stayed away. I remember Billie with fondness, and I was sad when I heard of her death. I sent a wreath to her funeral. Of course, I couldn't put my name to it." Haseem stared at his memories in the corner of the room for a few moments until the silence was broken.

Sebastian said, "So where have you been for twenty-odd years?"

"I have been busy, Sebastian. I have been building the business that employs dedicated workers like Shafiq here."

Shafiq smiled at the praise from his boss.

"My organisation has interests in a variety of legitimate businesses, but unlike most organisations we have developed a culture of getting things done. Sometimes that means we have to cross the boundaries of legality. We do that very infrequently, I should add. Sometimes all we have to do is mention our name, and that usually suffices." He changed the subject. "These are matters that we can discuss at a later date. We have a more pressing problem on our hands. I have been kept up to date by Shafiq. I have spoken to our friends in Newcastle and they are happy for us to address the issues that have arisen on our doorstep. As long as they get their money, less our commission, they will be happy. I am aware of the problems that you face with the policeman. And I have a proposal that I think will be acceptable to all parties."

Jack Tozer examined his face in the mirror. His left eye was bloodshot and still painful. He'd taken to wearing an eye patch in public, as recommended by his doctor, who had told him that there was no lasting damage. The doctor also said that the violent criminal who had done this to Jack when he had arrested him should be sent to prison.

Jack had organised his work in order to spend more time in the office until the eye cleared up a little more. He told everyone at the station that he'd got oil in his eye when he was doing an oil change on his car. It also helped to ease the discomfort in his groin. His testicles had swollen to twice their normal size and were painful to the touch, even walking was a chore. The doctor had said there was probably no long-term damage and he'd been lucky that the blow hadn't caused a major rupture, although he should come back if the pain persisted. In essence, Jack had to lay low for a week or so and hope there was no need for surgery.

But he hadn't been idle.

The fight with Blanche had brought him come to his senses. The money was his future and it couldn't remain in the house. He'd also decided to see if he could leave the police with a medical pension. An old injury sustained years ago could be reinvented, enough for him to cite it as the cause of his suffering. It would be supported by his doctor. And the police surgeon, the doctor who signed these things off, could easily be manipulated by reminding him of the instance Jack found him driving his car while drunk. On that occasion, Jack had taken him home knowing that someday he may need a favour in return.

Those decisions made; Jack needed to set the ball rolling. There was still one outstanding matter he needed to sort out. Blanche Fada. He looked again at his eye and gingerly felt his balls. She had to pay for humiliating him. Blanche Fada would suffer.

36

Tuesday 23rd April 1963

Blanche lay in bed wide awake. It was just after four o'clock in the morning and a blackbird was singing outside. The Town Hall clock had bonged and the cold world outside was still resting. Two days ago, her Sunday friend had expressed his disappointment on leaving, complaining that she was distant. She claimed to be unwell but, in truth, she was completely distracted. It seemed that her whole world was focussed on Jack Tozer. She regretted ever getting involved with him.

The reappearance of Jaden Hameed after so many years was another event that unsettled her. There were too many ghosts associated with him. She knew that Billie had loved him. She had talked about their future together and had been desperately sad when he disappeared. The last thing Blanche heard about him was that he'd gone to the Aden Protectorate area of Yemen at the outbreak of World War Two. Billie had thrown herself at plain old Reg Crawley to compensate.

Blanche sniffed the air. Could she smell smoke? She sat up. Yes, it was smoke. Where was it coming from? She jumped out of bed and pulled on her dressing gown. She looked out of the window and saw nothing. She walked to the bedroom door and opened it. She saw smoke drifting up the stairs. Bewildered, she descended slowly. When she neared the bottom, she heard the crackle of fire. "Oh, God," she said, and her first thought was that she had forgotten to put the fireguard up. She threw open the door into the passage and saw flames licking under the kitchen door. What? There was no fire in the kitchen. She was certain that the gas had been switched off as she hadn't cooked anything for three days. Despite her instincts to run out of the house and call the fire brigade, Blanche marched up to the door and opened it. A roar of hot air blasted her back into the hallway. Flames flared through the door frame and instantly started spreading. Blanche scrambled to the phone near the front door and dialled

999. The operator told her to evacuate the building immediately. She ran into the front street shouting "Fire! Fire!"

Curtains began twitching and lights came on. A few seconds later a man appeared half dressed and asked Blanche if she was alright and if anyone else was in the house. Blanche was numb. She shook her head.

The Fire Brigade arrived shortly afterwards. By then every house in the street was up and viewing the spectacle. The police arrived and started establishing a linear sequence of events. Someone gave Blanche a hot cup of tea and a blanket. After a while she saw a fireman talking to a constable, who approached her.

The policeman said, "The Fire Brigade have found out that the back door has been forced and an accelerant ignited in the kitchen. Can you explain this?"

Blanche said, "Back door ... accelerant? What does that mean?"

The constable recognised shock. "It means that someone broke into your house and used something like petrol to start a fire. Do you know who could've done that?"

Blanche was unable to answer.

The fire was extinguished in a relatively short space of time. It had been contained at ground level. Upstairs was damaged but not burnt. She would be able to salvage a lot of things, but it wasn't habitable, and as it was in the area to be demolished it would be boarded up until the relocations began. She stared at the smouldering bricks and timber that once was her house, her home and her livelihood, and began sobbing.

The telephone rang and Sebastian heaved himself out of the chair and stretched as he walked to the hallway to answer it.

"Hello?"

"I need to see you."

It was Alice.

"Have you changed your mind?"

There was a pause

"Do I need to change my mind if I want to see you?"

Sebastian said, "No, but is there any point in prolonging the agony by seeing each other?"

"Is that what it is? Agony?"

Sebastian wondered. He'd given the matter very little thought lately as other things seemed so much more important. Hearing her voice again, though, reminded him of the good times they'd shared.

"I miss you."

"I miss you, too, but you do see why I'm doing this, don't you?"

Sebastian's tone softened. "Of course I do. I probably knew at the back of my mind that someday soon you would go somewhere a bit bigger than dear old South Shields."

"We can still write to each other and maybe you could come over to America on holiday."

Sebastian sighed. That wasn't going to happen. He'd rather make a clean break than have a long-distance relationship, that way was surely doomed and would be strewn out over months, or years, until it became a sham.

"Look, Alice, we both know that when you go to America that's us finished. If we can have a good time together until you go, then that's fine. Let's make some memories and part as friends. When are you going?"

There was silence for a few moments, then Alice whispered, "Friday."

"Friday! You mean this Friday. In three days time?"

"Yes, when they found out that I was coming, they said there was an opportunity to start next Monday, and did I want it. I said 'Yes'."

"Christ, Alice! You don't do things by halves do you?"

"Sebastian, can I see you? I can be there in fifteen minutes. We'll go for a drive somewhere or you can come here ... or a hotel?"

Desire filled him. Desire to see Alice and desire to feel her body for the last time.

He said, "Pick me up in fifteen minutes."

Just as he replaced the phone there was a knock on the front door. A woman who he recognised but couldn't name said, "Somebody's set fire to Blanche Fada's house. She's out on the streets. Just thought you would like to know."

Sebastian thanked the woman and grabbed his coat. He slammed the door behind him and hurried across Anderson Street and up into Broderick Street. The fire brigade was leaving, and a Council van stood outside Blanche's house. A kindly neighbour directed him to where Blanche stood sobbing. Sebastian slowly put his arms around her and held her close, allowing his body to absorb her grief.

An hour later, he led Blanche back to Catherine Street carrying a suitcase containing some clothes and her precious diaries. This would be her new home for the time being. He would contact Shafiq later and get him to exercise some of his alleged magic to get another house for Blanche.

He picked up a note as he entered the front door. It read 'I thought you were better than this. I loved you Sebastian. Goodbye.' It was signed 'Alice'.

The small office was full. Superintendent Balfour and Detective Sergeant Smith were hosting a meeting with three detectives from Newcastle. The focus of their meeting was Jack Tozer.

Superintendent Balfour said, "Gentlemen, you've seen the report from Sergeant Smith, and you've had the opportunity to peruse other documents and reports concerning Tozer. You've also seen his service record. Comments please?"

A sandy haired detective coughed politely and said, "There's no direct evidence to link Tozer to any crime. It is all suspicion and nuances. We've no witnesses. I can't see this going anywhere?"

Balfour nodded. "I agree so far. Anyone else got ideas?"

A large Yorkshireman said, "There's no smoke without fire, though, is there? I mean as far as I can see, this Tozer fella is a wrong'un. He sails close to the wind, that's for sure, but I agree we've got nowt on him."

The third detective, a thin, sallow man with dark hair and brooding eyes said, "We have enough grounds to dig deeper. A man like this thinks he's untouchable. That leads to complacency, and complacency leads to mistakes, and if this man has made mistakes then it shouldn't be that difficult to find them if we look close enough. We could forensically examine everything he's done, everywhere he's been. We could also keep discreet observations on him. If he's bad, we'll find it."

Balfour said, "Thank you, Detective Chief Inspector. I trust you can handle this yourself? Please come back to me if you need anything. One more thing, this investigation must be completely secret. No-one must know about it outside these four walls."

Two floors below Superintendent Balfour's office, a middle-aged cleaner entered the sergeant's office with a brush, mop and bucket of water. She picked up the detritus of office life and put it into a rubbish bag. She emptied the bin and started dusting the flat surfaces with a cloth. She brushed the floor and gave it a once over with the mop. Near the door was a hat stand with uniform jackets and coats hanging from it. She reached into the bucket and picked out another cloth and a bottle of colourless liquid. She rubbed one of the coats as if she was removing a stain, placed all her tools into the bucket and left the room.

At 6pm Jack Tozer returned to duty. As usual he read the Daily Log, the record of events covering the twenty-four-hour period from midnight to the following midnight. It had the usual reported mixture of annoyance caused by youths, domestic disputes and disputes between neighbours. The primary item was a house fire in Broderick Street, the dwelling of Blanche Fada. The Log said there had been no injuries, but the house, although not destroyed, was now uninhabitable.

Jack grinned. "Oh dear. What a pity."

The house would never be lived in again so Blanche would have to take her business elsewhere. By the time he had had a word with someone on the Housing Committee, Blanche would find herself well away from the centre of town. The fact that she was a woman past her prime meant that living on a suburban housing estate would never be conducive to a profitable client base again.

He looked at some reports left for his attention. He scribbled comments, signed papers and placed them in the out tray to be returned to the officers who'd submitted them. He stretched and decided to make a cup of tea. While he waited for the kettle to boil, he picked up an old newspaper and scoured it for something he cared about. The only item worth noticing was the announcement that the President of the United States's wife, Jackie Kennedy, was pregnant. Jack growled. She was worth a shag alright. He unconsciously touched his balls ... and winced.

In total contrast, there was an item that announced that the old St Thomas's Church at the junction of Catherine Street and Fowler Street was to be knocked down. Jack grinned again. Bit by bit, South Shields was being taken apart and remodelled. The old communities would go and so would all their problems.

By that time, he would be long gone, living it up in some tropical paradise with girls on tap, but maybe Scotland would be better, he couldn't live among foreigners.

37

Wednesday 24th April 1963

"Every time you look into the mirror you see a different person to who you were yesterday. Something is different. It may be a blemish of some sort, or the length of your hair. If you look closely you'll see it. Watch your face – it changes. I've got a mirror with one side that's ordinary and another side that magnifies everything. It's still your face but the details are different. You notice every pore of your skin, every hair on your head, every small crease etched over the years by your lifestyle. Your experiences and mistakes shape what you see. And it doesn't matter what you put on your face, once you look into your own eyes you know that whatever's been said or done has already been judged. You can't fight it. One day I'll look in the mirror and see an old woman. And my eyes will ask 'What the hell did that woman do to my face?'"

Sebastian said nothing. Blanche had been distant and unconnected to the real world. He knew that she had 'funny days' when she was just like this – disjointed, abstract and living in a void between sanity and irrationality. He got up and switched the television on. After a few moments the smiling face of Princess Alexandra filled the screen as she walked down the aisle to meet her future husband, Angus Ogilvy.

Blanche whimpered, "That'll never happen to me."

Sebastian ignored her. "I'm off to a meeting, Blanche. Will you be alright by yourself? Don't answer the door to anyone. Nobody needs to know where you are."

Blanche nodded; her eyes fixed to the pageantry of a royal wedding.

Sammy had called the meeting.

To Sebastian, Sammy was a nervous wreck. They sat in the same café in Laygate, at the same table where they had spoken to each other a few weeks ago. "Did your grandad tell you I saw him?"

Sebastian nodded.

"Did he tell you that I saw a policeman take two cases away?"

Sebastian nodded again.

"Then that makes me a witness, doesn't it?"

"Only if the police know you were there."

Sammy wrung his hands. "Listen, Sebastian. I've made mistakes. I was responsible for Bull's death. I'm all over the place. I'm taking too many chances. I don't think I can take any more. Help me, Seb."

His hands started shaking. This was a man on the edge, thought Sebastian. "What do you want me to do?"

"I need to get all this off my chest. I can't handle it anymore."

"You've got to get a grip of yourself, Sammy. You look as though you're going to explode."

Sammy's eyes widened. "I am. I am."

"Ok," said Sebastian, "Let's talk this through and see what we can come up with."

Three hours later, Sebastian called on Shafiq and asked to speak with Jaden Hameed. Shafiq was, at once, nervous.

"I need to tell him what this is about, Mister Crawley. He cannot be surprised. He does not like surprises."

"It's you who doesn't like surprises, Shafiq. I need to see him. I have a plan. It's too important. I don't need any of it to be filtered. I admire your honesty and integrity, but I need to see Mister Hameed face to face."

Shafiq made the call and arrangements were made for Saturday morning

Sebastian walked from Laygate to the police station in Keppel Street. He asked for Detective Sergeant Smith and was shown up to the CID office, where Sergeant Smith sat smoking his pipe.

"How can I help you? Is this about your mother's death?"

Sebastian had forgotten that this was the man who had attended Jack Tozer's house when his mother died. He had been mentioned on the report connected to the death certificate.

"No, not directly. I have some information that you might be interested in. About one of your colleagues. Sergeant Tozer."

Smith leaned back in his chair. "I know he was your mother's boyfr… err, sorry, I mean fiancée." He paused taking stock of

Sebastian. "How do I know that what you're going to tell me is not just sour grapes?"

"You don't. But it's not."

Smith said and did nothing, waiting for Sebastian to deliver.

"Jack Tozer is a criminal."

Smith remained like a statue. Smoke curled from the bowl of his pipe.

Sebastian continued. "Jack Tozer has a case of money belonging to a gang of criminals in Newcastle."

Smith tried hard to keep his face expressionless, but he couldn't hide the gulp. "How do you know this?"

"I can't tell you."

Smith gave a thin smile and a sharp and disdainful snort, "Then your information is worthless."

"I can't tell you without assurances," said Sebastian.

Smith grimaced. "Are you asking me to make a deal of some kind? You know I can't do that."

Sebastian nodded. "Let me put it this way. Suppose I know a witness to Jack Tozer's dishonesty. A witness that is prepared to give evidence at the Assizes if necessary."

A glimmer flashed in the detective's eye.

"The downside is that the witness is a criminal himself. In fact, he's probably responsible for a whole host of minor crimes that, if cleared up, could earn someone a promotion."

Smith said wryly, "Too late for me, son, I retire at the end of the year."

"You can go out with a bang. Arresting a bent copper and clearing up the thick end of a hundred burglaries means that you would end your service with a couple of commendations and the reputation of a legend."

Smith imagined the mock-up headlines of the *Gazette* with a flattering photograph of himself. "OK," he said. "Let's talk business."

Saturday 27th April 1963

The dark blue Rover X sat in the car park overlooking Marsden Rock, its 3.8 litre engine ticking away the heat, the red leather interior comfortable and swish. It was the best Sebastian had experienced. He sat in the rear seat behind the driver, although the driver stood some twenty yards away smoking a cigarette and watching the cormorants soar into the sky. Shafiq sat in the front passenger seat, his body twisted so he could see both Sebastian and Jaden Hameed.

Hameed looked out of the window towards the Rock itself and then across to Souter lighthouse, the crumbling village of Marsden perching at its side on the cliff edge. He said, "Times are changing, Sebastian. This is a lovely place. Like all other lovely places, we hold it in awe, and wonder if there are times when we would move heaven and earth to behold it, to experience it, to value it. We come away with reluctance in our hearts and calculate the time until we can experience it again. That's what happened to me when I left here to go back to Yemen."

He paused a few seconds more.

"Lovely place? Ha!" His voice rose slightly. "We tell our friends about it, shower it with tributes, events and memories. We take photographs of it, capturing images that sell it. And slowly but surely the stories have an effect. Some friends come and agree with every word you've said. They tell their friends. And soon you can't get there because someone else is already there. The country track becomes a road, then a bigger, wider road. The moonlight is replaced with lamps, then streetlights and then the gaudy, garish monster that is neon. People come and bring their noise and leave their rubbish. Car parks like this appear. Barriers, white lines and signposts. Whole areas are cordoned off to protect the environment."

He waved his hands in the general direction of the sea and lowered his voice again.

"The reason why you went there in the first place becomes the same reason why you would never go there again, because magic cannot be shared. And on top of that, you have the guilty knowledge that it was you who helped destroy it."

Sebastian stared at him, saying nothing.

Hameed continued. "It's the same with friendships and relationships. Times change and relationships are put under pressure. Some endure but most break or become tarnished in some way.

Sebastian thought of Alice.

Hameed smiled warmly. His eyes fixed on Sebastian. "In June 1939 I was in love with a young girl from South Shields. She was a strange one in some ways, but she was fun. She was sixteen years old and, in some ways, she was forty." He paused briefly before saying "Today would have been your mother's fortieth birthday."

Sebastian nodded. It had been his first thought when he'd woke up that morning and prayed on his mind ever since. He'd gone through several celebratory scenarios of what would've happened if she'd still been alive.

Hameed continued, "Your mother was my first love. Her father came to me and asked me to leave her alone."

Sebastian said, "I know this. You left and went to Yemen and my mother took up with my father."

Hameed shook his head. "You don't know it all." He glanced out of the window for a few moments and watched the driver light another cigarette. His gaze returned to Sebastian. "Just after the war broke out in September, I received a letter from your mother saying that she was married to Reginald Crawley. She also said that he had gone away to fight. I later heard from a family friend that Reginald had been killed and that your mother had given birth to you. It must have been a terrible time for her. It was good that your grandfather was there to help her. I have a lot of respect for him."

Sebastian smiled. "He's a wonderful old man."

Hameed drew a deep breath and exhaled. "I knew Reginald Crawley. He was a fine young man, albeit a bit dim, who was besotted by your mother. When your mother married him, he would've been very, very happy. Even though she was already pregnant by her former boyfriend."

Sebastian's face contorted in shock. "What?"

"Your father was not Reginald Crawley." He paused again before quietly adding, "I'm your father, Sebastian."

Sebastian needed air. He grabbed the door handle and flung it open. He pushed himself out into the clean, fresh sea breeze and staggered away from the car gasping as he went. The driver threw away his cigarette and braced himself for a fight before a signal came from the car that everything was OK.

Sebastian blinked back tears. His whole life reeled by. His mother hadn't said. His grandad hadn't said, surely he must have had suspicions. And Blanche! For Christ's sake his mother must have said something to her.

Behind him, Hameed said, "I'm sorry to have to tell you like this, Sebastian. I know it's a shock. I never expected to have to tell you this story. I have a lot of proof that verifies what I am saying. You can have it if you want it. I even have analysis of blood samples. They do not lie."

"Why are you telling me this? You've destroyed everything I've ever believed in, at a stroke." He turned to face Hameed. "I don't even look like you. I'm not even the same bloody colour, for Christ's sake!"

"I'm not an expert in genetics," Hameed replied, "but I know someone who is. And he says that you are most definitely my son." He pulled his coat tighter to ward off the sea breeze. "Over the years I've watched you closely, from afar. I have been kept informed of your career and managed some situations on your behalf."

Sebastian turned towards him, curiosity written all over his face.

"On occasions, you have had trouble with suppliers. I saw that those problems were overcome. We recovered Alice's camera and coat when she was attacked and made sure that she was protected as our friend. These are little things to an organisation like ours."

"The Sand Dancers are a criminal organisation."

Hameed smiled wryly. "We are an organisation that is very much more established in the legitimate circle of business. I've seen to that. However, sometimes we bend the rules slightly." He touched Sebastian on the arm. "Come back to the car. We need to talk more about some of the rules we've bent recently."

38

Monday 29th April 1963

Jack Tozer was no mug. He'd heard a whisper that some detectives from Newcastle had been in to see the Super. Not unusual in itself, but a casual remark from a file clerk named Phoebe had him wondering why his personal record had been pulled from Admin. It could be straight forward. He had found the case of gems and logged them at the station. However, the Newcastle people would know by now that there was another case and would ask 'Why hadn't the officer who found the first case not found the other?" Jack would say that it was dark and that he had chased one of the thieves over the wall. The cases must've been separated at some time and the other one had fallen somewhere and disappeared. Someone else had found it and was living in the lap of luxury.

It was a feasible story, but another feasible story, as far as his bosses were concerned, was that Jack Tozer had taken the case and stashed it somewhere. Jack had been a policeman long enough to know that people had been arrested on less circumstantial evidence and convicted. But there was no hard evidence.

It was obvious that the sooner he put his plan for medical retirement in place the better. An appointment would be made to see the police surgeon this week to set the ball rolling. It would take a month or two and he would have to be on sick leave within the next twenty-four hours. The only downside to that was he wouldn't have access to any information as to what was going on. Officers on sick leave couldn't visit the station.

There had been an air of uncertainty, if not desolation, in Tommy Heath's house since Sebastian had divulged his conversation with Jaden Hameed. Tommy had refused to believe it until Blanche confirmed that Hameed and Billie had been 'active'. She'd tried to give the relationship an air of romance by saying that they were a couple very much in love. Tommy had stormed out to the pub down the road and come home later that night roaring drunk. Yesterday had found him with the mother of all hangovers and completely mute about the subject. This morning he was a bit tetchy.

"It doesn't matter who your father is. I'm still your grandfather and my daughter was your mother."

Sebastian nodded. "That's what I thought too, grandad. I never knew my father, at least the man I thought was my father. And now that I do know, I don't know what to feel. I've looked at all the stuff he gave me. I'm no expert but it looks genuine. I have no feelings for him beyond that he seems a good genuine man. I don't know how I should be feeling. The major change as far as I'm concerned is that I'm now in the same boat as Blanche."

Both Blanche and his grandfather turned to him.

Sebastian said, "I'm a half-caste."

Blanche quickly glanced at Tommy, who stood open mouthed.

"Half-caste," Tommy repeated. "Oh my Lord."

Blanche ordinarily would have smiled and said, 'Welcome to the club', but the look on Tommy's face prevented her from doing so.

"Bloody half-caste," said Tommy. "Oh sweet Jesus!"

Sebastian shrugged. "I don't feel any different because of it."

Tommy said, "As long as you don't go broadcasting it about then no-one needs to know."

Sebastian said, "My father is the head of The Sand Dancers. Christ only knows what that makes me."

"A Muslim for a start," said Blanche.

Tommy groaned again.

Sebastian shook his head. "I'm not religious. I'm quite happy to play at being a Protestant whenever it suits."

He couldn't stand the routines and dogma associated with organised religion. Its formality, posturing and false sense of occasion made him regard it as a frightening, judgemental hypocrisy. It was obviously designed to keep control of the masses and he couldn't understand how people didn't see through the veneer of pretension and blackmail that was part of any established faith. "Anyway, enough of all this rubbish. It's time to talk about the plans we have for Jack Tozer."

Tommy said, "We? Does that mean us here? Or does it include your dad now?"

Sebastian said, "There's no call for that, grandad. We needed the help from the Sand Dancers and we're getting it. It's a bit complicated and not entirely legal, but it'll bring Jack Tozer to book for sure. Jack needs to get his just reward and I for one am not bothered how he gets it. There are two plans. One is legal, with the help of the police. And one is illegal, which features the Sand Dancers. I have a foot in both camps. I need you both to help me."

"OK son," Tommy said, "Tell us what we need to do."

Tuesday 30*th* April 1963

Jack Tozer pulled out of his drive and turned to go down the street. A white van stopped to allow him to pass. He waved his thanks and drove to work with a plan to retire from duty early with severe pains. He had practiced his walk and pained expression, and he'd had plenty of that lately, without even having to try. He'd varied the tone of his groans until he was satisfied that they were sympathetic to the level of pain he was projecting.

He parked the car and walked up the stairs to the Sergeant's office and began wincing whenever someone passed the door. He pushed some paperwork around his desk and went through its drawers looking for personal items that he didn't want to leave behind. There were none; Jack Tozer wasn't the sentimental kind. He limped along the corridor with a mug in his hand and just as he passed an office full of typists and clerks, screamed in pain and threw himself to the ground. The mug shattered in the doorway. Staff poured out of offices to see what had happened. Jack wore a suitably pained expression and moaned loudly as he rubbed his hip and leg.

A typist knelt down and Jack smelled her luscious, flowery perfume and felt the brush of nylon against the back of his hand. He could feel himself getting aroused, but this wasn't the time or place. Although if he could accidently brush against her breast, it would be a bonus.

"Oooooh! My hip," said Jack. "It's been giving me gyp for weeks. It just gave way."

He tried sitting up and asked for support. Three typists tried to assist. He managed to touch all three without arousing suspicion.

"Get me back to my office," he said, "I'll be OK."

"You need to see a doctor," said one typist.

"Do you need an ambulance?"

Jack declined the ambulance. The casualty department would want to do tests and they may suspect he was spinning a yarn.

"I've had trouble for weeks," he said, "but I've just got on with it. The last few days have been agony. I can hardly walk."

A bespectacled Inspector appeared and said, "You need to go on the sick, Sergeant. You can't work like that."

Jack nodded. "I'm in a lot of pain, Sir. I'll rest a little in the office and see how I go on."

The Inspector said, "You heard what I said, Sergeant Tozer. You are unfit for duty. You will retire from duty and go and see a doctor. That's an order."

"Yes, Sir," said Jack.

This was better. A higher ranking officer had told him to retire from duty. Now he needed to go to the property store in the basement. He had a case to collect.

Reclaiming the case was easy and Jack limped back to his car. He cast his eyes back to the old red brick building and muttered, "Sorry, old girl, you won't see me again." He drove to High Shields railway station and parked the car next to Holy Trinity Church. He climbed the steps and boarded a train to Newcastle.

Detective Sergeant Smith sucked on his pipe and looked over his desk towards the sallow complexioned Detective Chief Inspector. His name was Walker.

Smith saw himself as a younger man in him. He recognised that he'd had plenty of opportunity early in his career, but like a damp firework it had spluttered and sparked and eventually, despite many attempts to reignite it, fizzled out. Walker's firework had turned into a Catherine Wheel and whirled around in bright colours, fizzing and flinging sparks all over the place.

Walker said, "Is Tozer on duty now?" The Chief Inspector didn't bother giving Jack his rank. As far as he was concerned Jack Tozer didn't deserve it anymore.

"He is."

"Right, then. Your informant has made a fine initial statement that Tozer has the case and the money. That's enough to arrest him on suspicion. Then we'll search his house and find whatever we find. Ring Tozer and ask him to meet you at the cell block. That won't raise any concerns. We'll take it from there."

Smith glanced over Walker's shoulder at the two detectives standing behind him. Smith picked up the phone and dialled Jack's number.

Seconds later Smith put the phone down and said, "Jack's gone sick. He left half an hour ago."

Walker slammed his hand down on the desk in frustration. He considered his options. To wait would hold back any investigation and depending on why Tozer had gone sick, the time frame became too elastic. The quiet approach he had hoped for was retreating further by the minute. "Right! We have no option but to go to his house and arrest him there."

Smith sucked his pipe. "Best of luck. Let me know if you need any help."

One of the detectives said, "We don't need any help, thanks." His expression was one of scorn, not gratitude.

Fifteen minutes later a large black rover pulled up outside of Jack Tozer's house. Walker and his two detectives approached the front door and knocked. There was no reply. They waited a few moments more, and then Walker nodded to the taller detective, who trooped off to the rear of the house. Walker turned to survey the street. Only one house overlooked the side of Tozer's house. A woman was cleaning the upstairs windows. He walked down the path into the street and crossed the road. The woman answered the door before he got there.

She said, "He's not in."

Walker gave her his biggest smile and said, "And you are?"

"My name's Gloria. This is Mrs. Wood's residence. I'm her cleaner. I've been cleaning here for nearly fifteen years."

Walker nodded, keeping the smile in full view. People like Gloria were a godsend. They knew everything that happened in the street and surrounding areas and weren't frightened to tell anyone prepared to listen.

Walker was prepared to listen.

"I'm trying to contact Jack Tozer. Do you know him?"

"He left for work about half eight."

"Oh I see," said Walker feigning ignorance. "And he hasn't come back?"

"Oh no. He won't be back until this evening. I saw him pull his car off the drive and go down the street. He waved at his friends and then left."

"His friends?"

"Yes. Four blokes in a white van."

Walker was confused.

"How do you know they were his friends? Have you seen them before?"

"Never clapped eyes on them in my life. But I saw Mister Tozer wave to them. The van pulled up outside his house and the four men got out and went in. I presumed they must have been friends because they had a key. They started unloading boxes and put the bigger ones in the garage. They were only here about ten minutes."

Walker's face had lost its smile and a pair of knitted eyebrows alerted Gloria that not all was well.

She said, "I haven't done anything wrong have I?"

Walker was quick to reassure her.

"No everything is OK, Gloria. Thank you for your help. I'm sorry I missed Jack. We're old friends, you see, and I was in the area so ... Anyway, I'll call in at the station. Thanks again. Goodbye."

Gloria closed the door and thirty seconds later resumed the window cleaning.

Walker summoned the detectives and gave them a brief resume of Gloria's observations. He detailed the taller detective to stay at the house and took the other one back to the car. They drove off steadily down the street.

Detective Sergeant Smith kept a stern expression on his face as Walker told him his story. Inwardly he was amused that the city detectives had failed with their basic enquiries. Policing was best done by local men with local knowledge and local responsibility. He acknowledged, however, that it wouldn't have made any difference on this occasion. Still, he was always pleased when flash harry detectives tried to show their suburban cousins how to do things properly and fell flat on their face.

Smith said, "He may have gone to see his doctor. He may have gone shopping. Knowing Jack, he may have gone to visit a lady friend."

Walker glowered at him.

Smith said, "You've left one of your men at his house. You can wait until he reports back or, seeing that you're going to arrest him anyway, ask the magistrates to issue a warrant to search his house."

Walker said, "I'll go and see Balfour," and exited the room.

Smith smiled, asking Superintendent Balfour to make a decision and get an answer back on the same day would be a miracle.

Shafiq made the phone call to Jaden Hameed.

"It is done. The goods were delivered without Sergeant Tozer's knowledge."

"Thank you."

"There is one other thing."

"What is it?"

"Sergeant Tozer has gone to Newcastle."

There was a brief silence then Hammed said, "He is being followed?"

"Yes."

"Then stay with him. Let me know if there are any changes. Please inform Sebastian."

Sebastian received the call. As he replaced the phone in its cradle he said to his grandfather and Blanche, "This looks like the last lap."

39

Jack Tozer jumped off the train and got back into his car. It had been just over two hours since he had parked there. He made his way through Laygate and up to Harton through Westoe. In some ways he felt emotional. He had taken the first steps to being retired. He would collect his pension, sell his house, and move up to Scotland. He'd take the case of money and invested it in various enterprises. No-one knew him in Scotland. He could stash wads of cash in a variety of banks and no-one would be any wiser. He laughed. Then laughed louder. There would be a lot of Scottish women glad that he'd made the move north.

Jack was still smiling when he entered his street. He saw a dark blue van parked in his drive. Some police officers were taking stuff out of his garage and putting it in the van. He pulled over and stopped the car. He watched for a few minutes trying to fathom what was going on. He didn't recognise anything. What the Hell was in those boxes?

Detective Sergeant Smith answered the phone.

"Come and see me. Now," said an authoritative voice. The line went dead.

Smith groaned. He trudged up the stairs to the Superintendent's office and knocked on the door.

"Sir?"

"Come in, Sergeant."

Walker was sitting there.

"I'll come straight to the point. Sergeant Tozer's house has been searched and a quantity of stolen goods recovered."

Smith's eyebrows almost hit the ceiling. "Bloody Hell!" Stolen property in Jack's house? That was incredible. He never had Jack down as a thief.

Balfour ignored the profanity. "It would appear that the Sergeant has been carrying out his own crime wave, or at the very least trading in stolen property."

Smith whistled. "To say I'm surprised is an understatement, sir."

"Quite," said Balfour. "But there is more."

Smith sat down without being invited. He was stunned.

"Tell him, Walker."

Walker said, "Do you remember a fire at a house in Broderick Street last week?"

Smith nodded. "The occupier was a woman called Fada. She's well known in the area."

Walker said, "It was an arson attack. Someone threw some paraffin into the house and set it alight."

"Yes, I read the report."

There was a silence as they waited for the penny to drop.

"Bloody Hell," said Smith, "Don't tell me Jack set fire to the house as well."

"We found his uniform jacket. There were traces of paraffin on the sleeve. We're sending it down to the forensic laboratory for tests, but we're pretty sure that it's the same stuff that was involved in the fire."

Smith sank into his seat running the information backwards and forwards through his brain. It didn't add up. Jack Tozer had a lot of service behind him. And although there had been many complaints against him during that time, none of them had stuck. He found it difficult to believe that even if he was a thief, he had started making simple mistakes like this. It didn't fit in with what he knew about Tozer. He had become very careless or was losing his marbles. "With all due respect, sir, are you absolutely sure of this?"

Walker's eyes narrowed. "Are you doubting my word, Sergeant?"

"No, sir, it's just that Jack's not that stupid."

"I've said it before. The closer you look, the more you find. The stolen property speaks for itself. The paraffin on his uniform, although waiting confirmation, is sufficient to identify him as our chief suspect."

Smith nodded. "I appreciate the points you've made, and Jack is no angel, but in my opinion, based on what I know about Jack and the evidence being put forward here, there's something fishy about the whole thing."

Balfour said, "We deal with facts and hard evidence. And the evidence here suggests Tozer is guilty of committing crime. Add these to the suspicious death of his fiancée a couple of months ago and you've got all the indications of a rogue policeman. We can't let the likes of him continue walking around besmirching our good name. He'll be behind bars by the end of the day."

Walker added, "Once we find him."

Sebastian sat in the front passenger seat of a blue and white Ford Cortina driven by Shafiq. When they reached the village of Harton, Shafiq parked up near St Peter's Church and waited. They wanted to see the arrest of Jack Tozer. A Sand Dancer minion had been following Jack all day. He would report back to an office somewhere and a message would be delivered to the car by another minion.

Both men idly watched customers to-ing and fro-ing from the garage over the road. Twenty minutes ago they had left Tommy Heath and Blanche Fada in Catherine Street with strict instructions not to open the door to anyone until they returned. They had protested. Sebastian had insisted. He didn't know what was going to happen next and he didn't want any worries about them to distract him.

According to Shafiq, the police were about to arrest Jack Tozer. Sammy's statement had been made and Jack was now a suspected thief. Shafiq had told him about the cleaner in the police station contaminating Jack's uniform with paraffin, so Jack was also a suspected arsonist.

Sebastian said, "I still can't get over the fact that you've had Jack set up for something he didn't do. Why is that?"

Shafiq selected a cigar and lit it before answering. He had the decency to open the window slightly to let the smoke out.

"It is a safety precaution, Mister Crawley. I have said before, we are professionals. When we decide to do something, we do it properly. The case of money may never be found. The owner of the money will never be traced, and your friend Samir is a criminal. Altogether, that does not provide a satisfactory conclusion. That means Sergeant Tozer may not be convicted. The paraffin is an insurance policy, and so is the stolen goods provided by your friend Samir. He had a lot of property. He is a very successful burglar. He will be helpful to us in the future."

Sebastian had pangs of guilt about involving Sammy, but Sammy wanted his help. There was no way that he would give up his line of business, so the protection offered by the Sand Dancers would benefit him in the long run. Sammy knew that it was only a matter of time before he was arrested.

"But how do we know that the paraffin used in the fire at Blanche's house is the same as the stuff on Jack's uniform?"

Shafiq glanced at Sebastian suspiciously, deciding what he should tell him.

"We are certain it is the same."

Sebastian considered the reply.

"But how can you be sure? The only way it could be the same is if the person who was at Blanche's house was also at the police station."

Shafiq said nothing. He blew a cloud of smoke out of the window.

Sebastian thought about what he had just said.

"The cleaner did it? Are you joking? The cleaner set fire to Blanche's house?"

Shafiq lazily shook his head. "It was not the cleaner. The cleaner works for us. We gave her the paraffin to smear on Sergeant Tozer's uniform."

Sebastian stared at Shafiq in astonishment.

He said, "The cleaner is a Sand Dancer. The Sand Dancers had the paraffin. Are you saying the Sand Dancers were responsible for setting fire to Blanche's house? Why on earth would you do that?"

"A decision was made, Mister Crawley. It had to look real. Steps were taken to ensure that Miss Fada came to no harm. She was never in any danger, but her distress had to appear genuine. We felt that you could not be informed because you would have advised us against it. Miss Fada was about to be relocated anyway. This way would only bring it forward and generate a lot of sympathy. She will be re-housed shortly, just off Ocean Road in a much better house than Broderick Street. She will be better off in the long run. However, she must not know this until she is settled. There is an expression, yes? The ends justify the means. I believe that is appropriate here. That is why it is better, sometimes, for you not to know the truth. If you are to be a Sand Dancer, you must know this."

Sebastian shook his head. "I'll never be a Sand Dancer."

Shafiq grinned. "Never is a long time, Mr Crawley."

Jack Tozer tried to stifle the growing sensation that his world was about to collapse. He didn't understand the activity around his house. There was nothing there to incriminate him. He decided to leave. He would spend the night in the Sea Hotel and consider his options. If necessary, he would attend the police station in the morning with a solicitor. He turned the car round and drove towards St Peter's Church.

Shafiq looked at his watch as a man approached his window. He wound the window down.

The man said, "You have to call the office. We have lost Sergeant Tozer."

Shafiq raised his eyes to the roof and managed to say OK through gritted teeth.

He turned to Sebastian. "I'll make a call from that telephone box over there. Hopefully we can locate Sergeant Tozer before he is arrested." He got out of the car and handed a few coins to the messenger, who walked away towards the village centre.

Sebastian settled back into his seat. He let out a deep sigh. So much for the Sand Dancers being a bunch of professionals. It just showed that even the best plans relied on human beings, and human beings were flawed.

He looked straight ahead of him and saw a familiar car driving towards him. It took him a few moments to realise that the car was Jack Tozer's, and that it was being driven by him away from his house. As it passed Shafiq's Cortina, Sebastian saw Jack's face contorted with anxiety. He never noticed Sebastian.

Sebastian had a decision to make. He slid into the driver's seat and fumbled with the keys. It had been a few years since he'd driven anything like this. His National Service stood him in good stead after all.

He started the car, turned 180 degrees and set off after Jack. As he passed the telephone box, he glimpsed Shafiq staring at him in astonishment.

Sebastian saw Jack's car heading towards Westoe. He followed at a shade over the speed limit to gain ground. By the time they reached Westoe Bridges, Sebastian was about one hundred yards behind. The journey down Fowler Street and right into Ocean Road brought them closer. If Jack noticed anything at all, it wasn't apparent. He followed him until he pulled into the car park of the Sea Hotel. Sebastian signalled left and parked in Pier Parade. He swiftly crossed the road as Jack entered the reception area of the hotel. There was nothing else to do but wait and see what happened.

He waited an hour before daring to go into the hotel. He walked past the ageing porter and approached the receptionist. He gave her his biggest smile.

"Could you tell me if my friend has checked in yet? I'm due to meet him shortly?"

She returned his smile. "Of course, sir, What's your friend's name?"

"Jack Tozer."

She checked the records. "I'm sorry, sir. No-one of that name has checked in today. Would you like me to have him paged in case he's in the bar or lounge area?"

Sebastian shook his head. "No thank you. Not at the moment. I'll come back later." He smiled another smile and walked towards the exit.

The porter approached him, "Are you Tommy Heath's boy?"

Sebastian ran his eyes over the man before answering. "Yes I am. I'm his grandson."

"Thought as much when you came in. Heard you asking the receptionist for Jack Tozer. He a friend of yours?"

"Actually, he's not. But I need to see him."

"Checked in under the name of Gordon Young."

Sebastian stared at him. "You know him?"

"Nicked me a few years back. Bent the rules a bit. Doesn't play square."

"Do you know what room he's in?"

The porter looked over both shoulders before replying.

"Wages are poor here. Man needs to earn a living. Family to support."

Sebastian took the hint. He dug out his wallet and extracted two one pound notes. He thrust them into the porter's hand and said. "Buy your missus a bunch of flowers and a box of *Milk Tray*."

The porter smiled briefly and said "23" before ambling off to stand in the corner.

Sebastian climbed the stairs to the second floor and counted off the rooms until he saw the small brass plate with 23 in black numbers.

He knocked.

40

Bob Jarvis was a porter at the Sea Hotel in South Shields. He'd been there for over ten years. He'd seen many people come and go, including the rich and famous and those that thought they were rich and famous. Mostly you got ordinary folk going about the business of enjoying the little bit of luxury that the Sea Hotel could offer. Occasionally, people stepped out of line and the police were called to sort things out. Sometimes, people brought back people who they shouldn't have been with. All Bob did was keep his eyes and ears open and tell his police contact.

Bob waited until Sebastian disappeared up the stairs before going into an office and picking up the phone. He dialled the local police number and asked for Detective Sergeant Smith. When the call was over, Bob dialled another number he had written down in his notebook. When that call was answered, Bob said, "Thought you'd like to know that your lad Sebastian's here asking for Jack Tozer."

The door opened.

When the shock had worn off, Jack Tozer shouted, "What do you want?"

"Aren't you going to invite me in, Jack?"

Jack grabbed his coat off the nearby chair and barged past Sebastian. "I'm going out."

Sebastian resisted the urge to punch him in the face. He knew that if it came to blows Jack would win hands down. He followed him down the corridor. "You can't go outside. Your mates in the CID are looking for you. You're going to get arrested. You're going to prison, Jack, for a long time. They hate blokes like you in prison. You won't last five minutes."

Jack stormed down the stairs with Sebastian in hot pursuit. As they reached the reception area, Bob Jarvis stood by the entrance in a show of authority, but he backed down once he spied the look on Jack Tozer's face.

Sebastian followed Jack outside. He ran over the road into the South Marine Park. He followed and shouted, "You're not going to get away with this, Jack. Not this time."

Jack turned. "Get away with what? I haven't done anything."

"Then why are your mates trying to lock you up?"

Jack had reached the lake, scaring a couple of swans and a few ducks. "I haven't done anything. I have no idea why they're looking for me. I just need time to think."

"You're a thief and an arsonist. You might even be a murderer, you bastard."

Jack froze. "What are you talking about?"

"You were seen with a bag full of money. You set fire to Blanche's house, and for all I know you threw my mother down the stairs and killed her."

Jack walked slowly towards Sebastian, who stood firm. "I never did any of that."

"Sebastian!" shouted a voice from behind.

Both men turned to see Tommy Heath and Blanche Fada standing twenty yards away.

Tommy Heath shouted again. "Sebastian, step away from him. Let the authorities deal with him. No point in getting involved with scum like that."

Jack sneered. "Do as your grandad tells you, little boy. Don't get yourself involved in men's games."

In an instant, twenty years of waiting and seeing life take its course, inactivity and taking a step back disappeared as Sebastian's frame unleashed a torrent of pent up anger and frustration in one punch. Blanche screamed as his fist connected with Jack's jaw. Tozer teetered and fell like a heavyweight boxer. His body thudded to the ground and twisted over the edge and into the lake. Sebastian held his broken hand as the intense pain cut through his anger.

Jack Tozer was out cold and in danger of drowning.

"Well, we can't let him drown now can we," said Detective Sergeant Smith who marched towards them accompanied by two uniformed officers. He nodded to the two constables, who got down onto their knees and reached into the lake. By the time Jack was dragged ashore he was conscious again and moaning and clutching his jaw.

"Looks like he won't be talking for a while," said Smith. He directed the constables to call an ambulance from the police box over the road. He turned to Sebastian. "With a punch like that, son, you could take on Henry Cooper. Luckily, I didn't see it, if you know what I mean, otherwise I might have to book you for assault. The way I saw it, Jack Tozer tripped and fell. Knocked himself out, didn't he." He pointed to Sebastian's hand, "Better get that hand seen to."

Tommy and Blanche hugged Sebastian. "That was a helluva right hook, son. His lights went out immediately."

Sebastian smiled, then laughed. Blanche joined in.

Later that day the three of them sat in the comfortable front room of the house in Catherine Street. Sebastian was nursing a cast for his two broken knuckles. Tablets issued by the hospital were blunting his pain. There was an air of gloom. A letter had been delivered telling Tommy that his house was to be demolished.

"It's been a funny kind of day," said Sebastian.

"I'm not laughing," said Tommy.

Blanche said, "Well, Mister Heath, that's two of us about to start a new life in a new house."

Tommy nodded. "I don't want to move. I'm told old for shit like this."

There was a knock on the front door. Blanche went to answer it. She returned a few moments later followed by Shafiq and Jaden Hameed. Tommy shuffled to his feet.

Hameed said, "I'm sorry to intrude, Mister Heath."

"What do you want?"

Hameed glanced around the room. "It's been many years since I stood here. It feels ... comforting." He turned to Sebastian. "I can feel your mother's presence here. It may be your grandfather's house, but she made it a home."

Sebastian nodded his thanks. "But it'll be gone shortly. By the end of the year there'll be nothing left. The whole area will be gone."

Hameed said, "Then we have to treasure those memories that we experienced." He stood by the door into the kitchen. I sent flowers to your mother's funeral. They were lilies. They were your mother's favourite flower. She wanted to have them for her wedding, to me. I promised her that I would give her lilies every time there was a special occasion. And I did. On her birthday, I would send her a lily,

without a message. She would acknowledge it by sending me a poem by an English poet called A.E. Houseman. It's only four lines long. I read it so many times I know it by heart.
He would not stay for me, and who can wonder?
He would not stay for me to stand and gaze.
I shook his hand, and tore my heart in sunder,
And went with half my life about my ways.
It is a moving piece and summed up our relationship. We wanted to spend our lives together but ..." his voice trailed off.

Tommy said, "I'm sorry for you, Mister Hameed. I didn't know how things would turn out."

Hameed smiled. "You have nothing to be sorry for. Tragedy is part of life. You do not need me to tell you that. However, we must try to prevent tragedies. What is more, we need to try and make our lives rich in memories. Today was one of those days. The police had plans for Jack Tozer. My organisation had plans for him also, and all of those plans were compromised by one punch." He grinned at Sebastian.

"Jack Tozer is in hospital. He will be arrested, and the justice system will take its course. It remains to be seen whether our noble organisation's efforts are needed to ensure Tozer goes to prison. We still don't know where the money is. It remains unaccounted for. I'm sure that those people who are owed the money will be recompensed at some time in the future. As for Sebastian, who knows? A modest little business bringing in a modest salary is fitting for a modest man with modest ambitions. However, there are openings in my organisation for a man who can strip back those modest ambitions and be different."

Sebastian said, "The Sand Dancers are criminals."

Shafiq winced in the corner of the room.

Hameed shook his head, "Criminals? Who are we to judge? Jack Tozer was a man employed to uphold the law. Yet he is a criminal. You are a man who has lived by the law, as most men do, yet, on occasions have broken it. Some people say they have only bent the rules. That isn't so. In the past few days you have been involved in conspiracies and perverting the course of justice. Today, you committed an offence of Grievous Bodily Harm. Is this rule bending or law breaking?"

Sebastian didn't reply,

"We are not criminals like the American gangsters. We like to think of ourselves as ... as ..."

"Robin Hoods?" said Shafiq.

"Not Robbing hoods?" Blanche burst out laughing. It broke the tension in the room. Everyone joined in.

"Perhaps not quite, Shafiq," said Hameed, "I'd prefer to say that our activity is noble-cause criminality."

Sebastian smiled. "Criminals with a conscience?"

"You could say that. I am in a position that allows me to use influence and persuade people to do things for me. Sometimes I send trusted colleagues like Shafiq to do some diplomatic work."

Shafiq's chest swelled.

"But when it comes to matters I care about. I do it myself." He glanced at his watch. "It is time."

Sebastian expected to see Hameed and Shafiq get ready to leave but instead there was another knock on the door.

Blanche said, "I'll get it."

When she returned, she said to Sebastian, "You've got a visitor." She stood aside to reveal a rather bemused Alice.

Sebastian bounded across the floor and swept her up into his arms.

Hameed said, "I could not let this happen again."

Sebastian lay in bed in the Sea Hotel under the name Gordon Young. Alice lay beside him asleep and smiling. She was pleased to see him she had said, but she'd also spent a couple of hours explaining that she wasn't at all happy to have had her future kidnapped by some political dealings between a Sand Dancer godfather and her own 'Uncle Jim'. She also said she had returned because she wasn't happy with the way she had left and felt their relationship deserved better.

"It doesn't mean I'm here to stay," she had said, "but I can't say it took much persuasion to bring me back."

As the Town Hall clock struck midnight, he turned to gaze at Alice. He raised his cast like a Roman Senator and his review of the month produced a firm thumbs up.

THE END

Printed in Great Britain
by Amazon